THE
Maiden's
Sword

THE SEEKERS

BY ETHEL HERR

The Dove and the Rose
The Maiden's Sword

ETHEL HERR

THE

Maiden's Sword

BETHANY HOUSE PUBLISHERS
MINNEAPOLIS, MINNESOTA 55438

Published by Bethany House Publishers
A Ministry of Bethany Fellowship, Inc.
11300 Hampshire Avenue South
Minneapolis, Minnesota 55438

Printed in the United States of America.

Library of Congress Cataloging-in-Publication Data

Herr, Ethel L.
    The maiden's sword / by Ethel Herr.
        p.   cm. — (The seekers ; 2)
    ISBN 1–55661–747–X (pbk.)
    1. William I, Prince of Orange, 1533–1584—Fiction. 2. Netherlands—History—Wars of Independence, 1556–1648—Fiction. 3. Netherlands—Kings and rulers—Biography—Fiction. I. Title. II. Series: Herr, Ethel L. Seekers ; #2.
PS3558.E713M3   1997
813'.54—dc21
                                               97–33839
                                                 CIP

To
Willeke Huijsing

Dear friend and sister in Christ from Delft, Netherlands.
Hartelijk bedankt
for years of loyal support, active assistance, manuscript reviews,
and the beauty of an honest heart for God.

Martha Doolittle

Dear firstborn daughter who grew up partly in Pieter-Lucas and
Aletta's country, always a bit under the influence of
Willem van Oranje.
Thank you, my dear,
for learning well the ways of Holland, literature, and prayer,
then for using your expertise in all three to help me
polish this book.

Ethel Herr is a writer/historian, writing instructor, women's speaker, and the founder/director of Literature Ministry Prayer Fellowship. She has seven published books, including *Chosen Women of the Bible* and *An Introduction to Christian Writing*. She and her husband, Walt, live in California.

CONTENTS

LETTER TO THE READER

John Motley, a noted late nineteenth-century historian, called the Dutch Revolt "one of the most complicated and imposing dramas ever enacted by man."

Pieter-Lucas and Aletta didn't have the benefit of his perspective when they were dragged irresistibly into the conflict. Nor did they need it to tell them that war was ugly. How it complicated their lives in spite of every effort to achieve simplicity and faith is the story of book two in THE SEEKERS series.

Once more, a few words are in order to help the reader sort out the history from the story. History books tell us much about William of Orange, his four successive wives, and his fine old family. His mother, Juliana von Stolberg, raised seventeen children (including Willem, Jan, Ludwig, Adolph, and Juliana) in the imposing old castle atop the hill of Dillenburg. We can find Dirck Coornhert, too, in the pages of those books, along with Ludwig's ragtag army of Beggars and their opponents, King Philip II of Spain and his infamous Duke of Alva. Counts Egmont, Hoorne, and Aremberg were colleagues of Willem and gave their lives in the conflict. Lucas van Leyden was a recognized artist whose paintings and engravings survive to this day. In the city archives of Breda, we find the names of Bailiff Van den Kessel, goldsmith Pieter van Keulen, and his housekeeper, Lysbet (Betteke) de Vriend. Jan van Leyden will long live in the recorded history of both political and religious infamy.

The rest of the characters did not step directly from the history books. The van den Gardes, Engelshofens, Laurenses, and de Smids were born in my imagination. So were Tante Lysbet, Yaap, Barthelemeus, Oma and her son Hans, the colorful street thief Mieke, and Alfonso the Spanish soldier. Add to this the host of named and unnamed servants, church members, boatmen, soldiers, and official personages.

I trust, though, that as you join me in taking up imaginative residence in the world of William of Orange, you will discover each character to be as real as your family, friends, and neighbors.

The thinking processes of these new friends may perplex and even annoy you at times. When they do, simply recall that European society was just beginning to shake itself awake from the long sleep of the Middle (Dark) Ages. The sixteenth century saw the first flowering of an artistic and scientific Renaissance, a massive religious Reformation, and an unprecedented series of political revolts.

Sixteenth-century residents knew little about time constraints and historical perspective. Glass windows and garbage collection were new innovations, and life was expected to be a perpetual painful struggle hovering on the edge of sudden unexpected death. Executions were tragedies only to the families and close friends of the condemned. To the rest, they provided entertaining spectacles and graphic warnings. Medicine was a mixture of primitive herbalism and cultic superstition. Life was both violent and religious, crude and mystical. Church leaders of all kinds were wrestling to unlock the secrets of biblical hermeneutics and still resorted to the old practices of casting horoscopes and pronouncing curses.

As you read, search between the lines and beneath the naive-sounding attitudes, the sometimes strangely worded phrases, and look expectantly for an amazing brotherhood of souls. You will not be disappointed. For the new friends you make here are all significant ancestors of our own struggles with life and freedom and faith in a constantly changing and unpredictably violent world.

HISTORICAL BACKGROUND

*I*n September 1531, Juliana von Stolberg and her new husband, Willem the Rich, rode through the heart of Germany's Westerwald countryside into the tiny village of Dillenburg, nestled at a bend in the River Dill. Willem, a quiet and unambitious lesser nobleman, who was not rich in anything but children,[1] never attained great fame. Nor was Dillenburg likely to be known beyond the borders of western Germany.

To Dillenburgers, the five-centuries-old Nassau castle that dominated the hill above the village stood as a massive artistic reminder of the ever present influence of the noble family that lived in its plain halls, tilled its gardens, and hunted in the neighboring forests. Here villagers received gainful employment, a place of worship, herbal healing, and protection from marauding warlords.

In neighboring districts, the Nassau family exerted considerable influence. Juliana ran a school for noblemen's children.[2] Her herbal cures often found their way to other regions. She gained a reputation for her pious Court Ordinances, which regulated everything from hours for meals to acceptable manners of speaking and dressing, to mandatory attendance at daily Bible readings and prayers.

In 1534, Willem became one of the first noblemen to openly proclaim his household Lutheran under the German Peace of Augsburg. This meant declaring all his subjects for Lutheranism. On the side of their hill, he

---

[1]Willem the Rich had fifteen children of his own from two marriages, in addition to four of Juliana's by her first marriage. All but one, who died in infancy, were raised to adulthood.
[2]Willem and Juliana were dedicated to improving education for both boys and girls. She ran the school up until the year before her death at the age of seventy-four.

built the first parsonage expressly designed for a Protestant minister.[3] Politically, Willem's wisdom was highly respected throughout western Germany. Rulers from surrounding areas came to him, and later to his son Jan, for counsel and help in settling disputes.

Still, no one ever dreamed of Dillenburg as a center of worldwide influence.

Then in 1544 an apparently insignificant event changed all that. Willem's nephew, Rene van Chalon, died childless on a French battlefield. In his will, he left his land holdings in the Low Lands[4] and those of his wife in the Orange district of France to eleven-year-old Willem, the oldest of Willem and Juliana's five sons.

In order to claim his inheritance, the young Willem had to remain under the tutelage of the Holy Roman Emperor, Charles V. Living as lord of his palace in Breda, Willem also spent much time in Brussels, where he was educated in all the fine points of becoming an influential Catholic prince.

A favorite of Charles V, the charismatic, fun-loving young nobleman from Dillenburg bore the title of Willem van Oranje. Not only was he governor of several cities and provinces of the Low Lands, but he was appointed to high positions in the military and political advisory councils of the government as well. Willem had every reason to expect to live the luxurious life of a pampered prince, dedicated to pleasure, military duties, and his family. Handsome, attractive to women, and a bit vain, he was prepared to enjoy a lifetime of power and accolades.

But his upbringing in Dillenburg would not allow him to see his dreams come true. Soon after the emperor abdicated his powers to his son, Philip, and to his brother Maximillian, Willem learned that King Henry of France and the newly crowned King Philip of Spain had agreed to completely wipe out all forms of religious heresy, using the Spanish military troops now quartered in the Low Lands.[5] Philip sent Willem back to his landholdings with instructions to promptly execute all dissenters.

Willem was horrified. From his mother he had learned that no person

---

[3]While the old castle no longer stands, there is a tower monument to the House of Nassau. The church and parsonage are still there for the visitor to see, though not open to public viewing.

[4]Land including modern Netherlands, Belgium, and Luxembourg.

[5]When, on a peace mission in the presence of both kings, Willem heard of these plans, he gave no outward sign of his inner outrage but went home and tried to find ways to prevent them from being enacted. This remarkable feat of self-control earned him the nickname Willem the Silent, by which he has been widely known ever since.

should be forced to pay for religious convictions with his life.[6] His early training left him totally incapable of approving, either as active participant or silent onlooker, any plan that condemned thousands of virtuous men and women to massacre. Instead, he warned the men whom he'd been instructed to execute to flee. From that day on, he incited Lowlanders to resist the intrusion of Spanish troops on their soil.

For years Willem labored to save the lives of his subjects while at the same time maintaining a semblance of loyalty to Philip, his sovereign. But both Philip and the Lowlanders were intractable. Gradually, across the countryside and in the halls of Willem's own castle at Breda, under the leadership of his brother Ludwig and a group of Lowland noblemen, a revolt took shape.

In 1567, the Duke of Alva was sent to the Low Lands to carry out an incredible death sentence pronounced by Philip. In the spirit of the infamous Inquisition that had ravaged Spain and Portugal, the document targeted the entire population (three million people) of the Low Lands, with the exception of a few persons named, as hopelessly tainted with heresy and deserving of extermination.

Seeing that his own life was at risk, Willem took his belongings and household and fled to Dillenburg. From the drafty rooms of the old family castle, he issued pamphlets, explaining the cause of the revolt and begging Lowlanders to support him in it. He commissioned Ludwig as commander of the revolt and traveled across Germany and France, selling his own personal belongings and imploring fellow noblemen to donate funds for the effort.[7]

Dillenburg became the gathering place for men of renown who sympathized with the revolt to plan their strategies.[8] Some became his spokesmen, carrying messages back and forth to leaders in the beleaguered provinces. Ludwig and others launched the first battles in the revolt but with little real success.

From Dillenburg, on August 31, 1568, Willem finally wrote an official declaration of war against Alva. Then he left the sanctuary of Dillenburg, mustered troops, and crossed the Maas River into the Low Lands to engage Alva in battle. When this attempt failed, he returned to Dillenburg,

---

[6]Juliana's father, Count Botho III von Stolberg, was unusually tolerant for his times. He had witnessed Martin Luther on trial at the Diet of Worms in 1521. While he never became Lutheran himself, all of his children did so, with his blessing.

[7]According to one estimate, sixty-five percent of all monies that kept the revolt going came from the Nassau family, thirty-four percent came from Protestant nobles and German Protestants, and one percent came from Netherlanders. *The Golden Age*, Bob Haak.

[8]A visitor to Dillenburg's hill can still look at a spreading linden tree, which tradition says was the site of at least one such strategizing session.

where he gained new strength for the fight ahead. For the next four years, Dillenburg remained the center of discussion and planning for the politics that would one day change the way Europeans ruled themselves.

In 1584, Willem was assassinated.[9] Not until forty years later did Willem's son Maurice fight the final battle in the revolt that robbed Philip of his sovereignty in the Low Lands. The emerging nation became a refuge for those who wanted to think and worship according to their conscience. The rest of Europe and the developing Americas followed suit.

Unnoticed and unheralded at that pivotal point in history, Dillenburg was silently exerting an undreamed-of influence on the western world. For the way Europeans looked upon the right to dissent in religious opinions would never be the same after the Nassau brothers dared to champion the cause that their mother, Juliana von Stolberg, taught them to hold precious.

---

[9]He was the fourth and last of the Nassau brothers to die in the cause. Adolph was killed in the Battle of Heiligerlee in 1568. Ludwig and Hendrik died in Mook-Heide in 1574. Only Jan survived and served as head of the Nassau household in Dillenburg until his natural death in 1606.

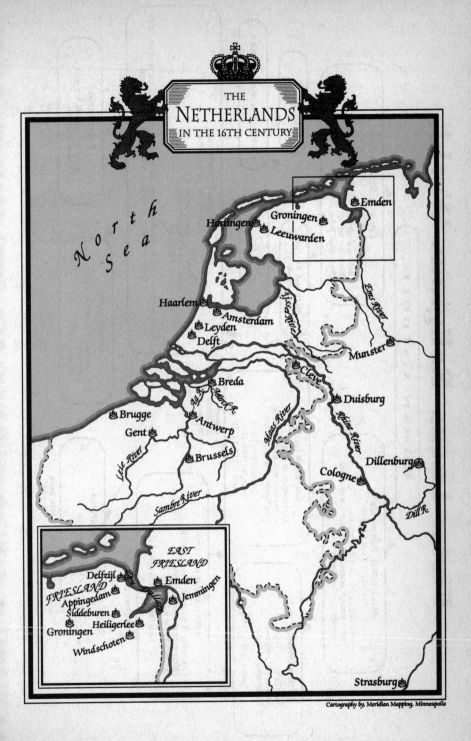

THE

NETHERLANDS

IN THE 16TH CENTURY

North Sea

Emden

Harlingen Groningen
Leeuwarden

Haarlem

Amsterdam
Leyden
Delft

Breda

Brugge

Gent Antwerp

Brussels

Ijssel River

Ems River

Munster

Cleve

Duisburg

Maas River

Rhine River

Dillenburg

Cologne

Leie River

Sambre River

Dill R.

EAST
FRIESLAND

Delfzijl

FRIESLAND Emden

Appingedam Jemmingen

Siddeburen

Heiligerlee

Groningen

Windschoten

Strasburg

Cartography by, Meridian Mapping, Minneapolis

Pieter-Lucas' Religious World

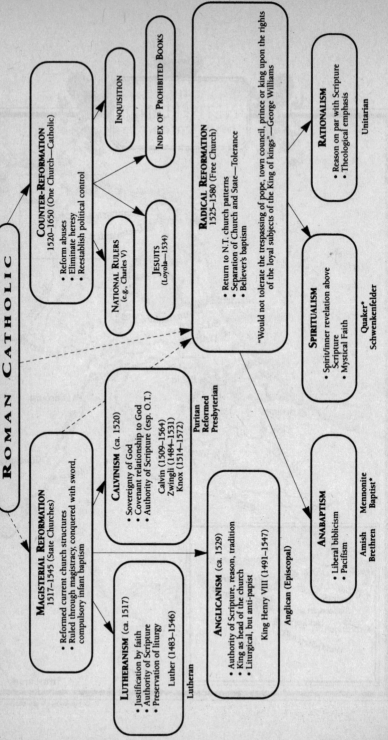

ROMAN CATHOLIC

COUNTER-REFORMATION
1520–1650 (One Church—Catholic)
• Reform abuses
• Eliminate heresy
• Reestablish political control

INQUISITION

INDEX OF PROHIBITED BOOKS

NATIONAL RULERS
(e.g., Charles V)

JESUITS
(Loyola—1534)

MAGISTERIAL REFORMATION
1517–1545 (State Churches)
• Reformed current church structures
• Ruled through magistracy, conquered with sword, compulsory infant baptism

CALVINISM (ca. 1520)
• Sovereignty of God
• Covenant relationship to God
• Authority of Scripture (esp. O.T.)

Calvin (1509–1564)
Zwingli (1484–1531)
Knox (1514–1572)

Puritan
Reformed
Presbyterian

LUTHERANISM (ca. 1517)
• Justification by faith
• Authority of Scripture
• Preservation of liturgy

Luther (1483–1546)

Lutheran

ANGLICANISM (ca. 1529)
• Authority of Scripture, reason, tradition
• King as head of the church
• Liturgical, but anti-papist

King Henry VIII (1491–1547)

Anglican (Episcopal)

RADICAL REFORMATION
1525–1580 (Free Church)
• Return to N.T. church patterns
• Separation of Church and State—Tolerance
• Believer's baptism

"Would not tolerate the trespassing of pope, town council, prince or king upon the rights of the loyal subjects of the King of kings"—George Williams

RATIONALISM
• Reason on par with Scripture
• Theological emphasis

Unitarian

SPIRITUALISM
• Spirit/inner revelation above Scripture
• Mystical Faith

Quaker*
Schwenkfelder

ANABAPTISM
• Liberal biblicism
• Pacifism

Amish   Mennonite
Brethren   Baptist*

• Organizationally broke off from Anglican Church but were influenced by Anabaptist ideas.

Abrams en Zonen: [Ah-brahms en Zo-nun] *Abrams and Sons.*

Anabaptists: Groups of Reformation churches, so called because of their insistence on believer's baptism as opposed to infant baptism. They did not themselves use the term *Anabaptists*, which literally means *rebaptists*, believing their adult baptism as a confession of faith was the only true baptism.

Apothecary: From Dutch word *apotheek* [ah-po-take], meaning *pharmacy.*

Beguinage: [Bay-guee-noj] French word for local site of Beguines, or lay order of charitable sisters in late medieval Catholic church. Mostly they were in the Low Lands and France. They shared their wealth but didn't take religious vows and were free to leave when they liked. They dispensed mercy, medicine, and physical goods to persons in need.

Beggars: Fanatical rebels who wanted to free the Netherlands from the control of Spain's King Philip II. They posed as Calvinists, and indeed many were. Their motives were a mixture of political ambition, personal discontent, and religious zeal.

Ban: Practice used in Anabaptist churches of excommunicating members whom the local assembly deemed were no longer practicing the required disciplines or adhering to the doctrines of their religious community.

Blood Council: Inquisitional tribunal set up by the Spanish government to examine all persons in the Low Lands suspected of heresy. King Philip II and his regent, the Duke of Alva, called it the Council of Troubles, but Lowlanders referred to it as the Blood Council, because it brought so many of them to confiscation of goods and execution.

Button leek: Literal translation of Dutch word *knoflook*, which means *garlic*.

Children of God: Name taken by many Anabaptist groups. They never referred to themselves as Anabaptists.

Engeland: Dutch for *England*.

Flux of wombe: Old English term for *hemorrhage* following childbirth.

Heatte: Old English term for *fever*.

Hidden Church: Any church assembly meeting without approval of existing government, forced to meet in secret, usually in homes, attics, or barns.

Ja: Dutch for *yes*.

Jongen: [Yong-un] Dutch for *boy* or *lad*.

Kasteel: [Kahs-tail] Dutch for *castle*.

Kasteelplein: [Kahs-tail-plane] Dutch for a large open square located in front of a castle. A *plein* is a *city square*, usually a market square of some sort.

Knights of the Order of the Golden Fleece: Advisory council of local noblemen called together at the discretion of the ruler of the Netherlands (e.g., King Philip II), who functioned as their president.

Low Lands: Area now encompassed in borders of Belgium, Luxembourg, and The Netherlands (Holland).

Man: [Mahn] Dutch for either *man* or *husband*.

Mieke: [Mee-ka] Dutch name applicable to a street girl or woman.

Moeder: [Mu-der] Dutch for *mother*.

Munster Rebellion: Radical group of Anabaptists who took over the city of Munster, Germany, and tried to set up the Kingdom of God there. Jan van Leyden, their leader, claimed to be King David and the Messiah.

They practiced polygamy, communal living, and violence. They were deposed by the city fathers but gave the whole Anabaptist movement a bad reputation that stayed with them all the way into the twentieth century. However, after their fall, Anabaptists became adamant pacifists and refused to carry a sword.

Oma & Opa: [Oh-ma, Oh-pa] Current Dutch terms for *grandma* and *grandpa*. Belonging to the twentieth century but giving the feeling intended by the sixteenth-century words *grootmoeder* and *grootvader*.

Oude Man: [ow-de mahn] Dutch for *old man*.

Physicke: Old English word found in herbal books. Refers to medicine—the profession or a person practicing medical or herbal arts.

Popish or Papist: Describing any person or practice that followed Roman Catholic ways.

Que no?: [Kay no?] Spanish for *right?* at the end of a sentence.

Robustious: Old English word for *robust*, used in seventeenth-century herbal book.

Splintery new: Literal translation of Dutch phrase for *brand new*.

Straat: [Straht] Dutch for *street*.

Stuiver: Dutch coin comparable to our penny.

Tante: [Tahn-tuh] Dutch for *aunt*.

Tot ziens: [Tote seens] *See you later!*

Vader: [Fah-der] Dutch for *father*.

Vaderland: [Fah-der-lahnd] Dutch for *fatherland*.

Verboden Boecken: [Fair-bo-den Bu-ken] *Forbidden books*. The Catholic Church compiled a list of books that they forbade parishioners to read. Transgressors could be treated as victims of the Inquisition and be imprisoned or executed. Books, when seized, were often burned.

De Vriend: [Duh Freent] *The Friend*.

Vrouw: [Frow] Dutch for either *woman* or *wife*.

Waterlanders: One of the main branches of Anabaptists. They held views that were a bit more tolerant and liberal than other groups.

Willem van Oranje: [Vil-um fahn O-rahn-yuh] *William of Orange*.

Wombe: Old English spelling for *womb*.

PROLOGUE

Breda

5th day of Wine Month (October), 1561

*T*he first rays of sunlight broke through the early morning mist on the horizon, and Roland, Breda's grand old bell, began to ring from the top of the Great Church's gothic tower. One ring, two, three, four, five, six . . . The jubilant vibrations hung in the air like children reluctant to leave.

While the strains lingered, two young people stepped out into the market square. They looked around at the festive colonnades hung with garlands, ribbons, and banners. Then hand in hand they darted across the cobblestones the full length of the market square until they stood before the bridge that led across the moat to the *kasteel*.

Pieter-Lucas, a lad of thirteen years, had mussed hair sticking out around the fringes of his worn felt cap, and his brownish nondescript breeches and doublet had obviously been hastily assembled. By contrast, Aletta, also thirteen, was picture perfect, her golden hair and pink-cheeked face securely framed in a starched white headdress. Every fold of her pale blue dress and gray woolen cloak hung in precise order.

"Pieter-Lucas," she began, "where is your opa?"

The boy chuckled. "You know Opa, always keeping us guessing what's next," he said, trying to sound convinced.

"But he said to meet him at the gallery when Roland peals six times, and he grows terribly disturbed with us if we keep him waiting. He's never late!"

"I know. I know." Pieter-Lucas had to admit there was something amiss. But he could not say that to Aletta. He was her protector.

"Where did he go this morning without us, anyway?" Aletta asked.

Pieter-Lucas shrugged. Every time Breda celebrated anything with a festival, Opa would take Pieter-Lucas and Aletta out into the streets before another soul stirred there. He'd show them all the decorations, explain how each cornice carving was done. He could talk for hours about the paintings that hung on the gallery by the *kasteel* gate.

"Breda couldn't possibly have a festival until we've inspected it and pronounced it ready, could it, Opa?" Pieter-Lucas asked the old man one day.

He would never forget that amused smile on Opa's face nor the confident tilt of his head when he replied, "*Nay*, never!"

Today's festival was probably the most special one ever. Prince Willem van Oranje, gracious lord of the local *kasteel*, was bringing Anna, his newly wedded "gracious second wife," from Germany. Even Opa said he'd only once before helped Breda welcome a new princess. This was one celebration he would not miss.

Aletta tugged at Pieter-Lucas' hand. "Did he tell you where he was going?"

"*Nay*. He just woke up early and couldn't wait. You know how excited he gets over all the decorations."

"Well, come on, let's find him," Aletta coaxed. "He might be in the church."

"*Ja*," he agreed, "that's one place we can look."

They retraced their steps back to the market square. At the door of the church, Pieter-Lucas was reaching for the heavy handle when he heard a shrill piping voice calling from behind them.

"Be ye lookin' fer yer opa?"

"God have mercy!" he gasped and wheeled around, instinctively putting his body between Aletta and the uninvited intruder. The creature who stood before them was no stranger in Breda. No one had any idea whether the small woman with twiglike limbs and a sharp pointed nose was a woman or still a girl. Nor did anyone know her real name. Because she was dressed so raggedly, they all called her Lompen (Ragged) Mieke.

Where she came from was the subject of many wild tales. Some said she was a hundred years old and lived in a magical cave in one of the many woods around Breda, where she roasted human babies in a huge black caldron. Others swore they'd seen her arise from the ground on misty nights when demons were prowling about and casting spells on the citizens.

No matter what else people might think about her, all agreed she was a thief. She could find a way to enter any building she set her evil eye upon and help herself to anything she wanted. Nobody trusted Lompen Mieke—not ever, for anything!

Pieter-Lucas stared at the intimidating creature. His heart pounded so hard inside his doublet he felt certain Mieke must be hearing it. He took a breath all the way from his toes, lifted his chin, placed his hands on his hips, and said, "What makes you think I'm looking for my opa?"

"B'cause it's a festival day, an' ye two always goes with him on these mornin's, an' this mornin' he comed out here all alone an' done falled into difficulties."

"What kind of difficulties?" Pieter-Lucas didn't know which was more terrifying, to believe Mieke's report or to wonder what sort of trap she was laying for him by telling him some beastly tale.

Mieke nodded her head toward an alleylike street that ran alongside the City Hall on the opposite side of the square. "He's done met with a sword an' lies a-groanin' on th' cobblestones, all by hisself."

Pieter-Lucas started and felt his body lurch in the direction Mieke had indicated. Aletta was holding his elbow with both hands, and he could hear little gasps coming from her with each new dubious revelation.

"Where is he?" he demanded.

"In th' alleyway b'hind that buildin', jus' by th' sluice works." Mieke was pointing now.

"Why should I believe you?" Pieter-Lucas demanded.

Mieke shrugged her spindly shoulders and spouted, "Go an' see fer yerself."

"Take me there and show me!" he said, almost wishing she wouldn't.

Without answering, she darted off in another direction, her dirty frayed skirts jostling barely above the ground.

"We have to go see!" Aletta urged.

"What if it's a trick?"

"What if it's not? Opa could bleed to death while we stand here fretting." Aletta was already shoving him toward the City Hall.

Without a word, he grabbed her by the hand and guided her across the square to the alley. "You wait here while I go look," he said, stopping at the spot where the road led away from the square. "Be ready to run or to come when I call, and don't go one step unless I say. If Mieke comes, or anybody you don't know, yell as loud as you can."

Pieter-Lucas released her hand and moved across the cobblestones on stealthy feet. Shadows from the old building, mixed with little wisps of mist, fell across his way in odd shapes. Ghouls, goblins, and demons lurked in this kind of place. He'd seen them in the paintings of Bosch and Brueghel. Besides, with Mieke involved, nothing evil was out of the question.

The farther he went from the market square, the louder his heart beat, and he began to feel something like iron fingers around his throat cutting off the breath. Then, just at the corner of the building where the alley made a sharp left turn and led to the Beguinage, Pieter-Lucas saw him. Lying on the ground with blood running away from his leg, Opa was moaning and crying out for help.

Pieter-Lucas knelt beside him. He laid one hand on his shoulder and another on a large lump protruding from his forehead. "Opa, it's me, Pieter-Lucas."

Opa opened bleary eyes and raised himself up on a wobbly elbow. "What happened? Where am I? *Ach!*" He slumped back to the ground.

"Just stay down, Opa," Pieter-Lucas said. He yanked off his own doublet, folded it into a cushion, and put it under the old man's head. "Here, this is softer than the street. You're in the alley behind the City Hall. Lie still while I call Aletta."

Pieter-Lucas stood to his feet, ran back around the corner, and called out, "Aletta, come quickly!"

He'd hardly returned to Opa when Aletta was kneeling beside him, tearing away the ripped leg of Opa's breeches and examining the wound. "The bleeding is slowing," she said, "but he needs some herbal salves, and I know not what more. Let me go get Tante Lysbet—she'll know. And while I'm gone, hold the wound together as tightly as you can. I saw Tante Lysbet do this to somebody once."

"How?" Pieter-Lucas wasn't sure he had the stomach for what she was telling him, but if it meant saving Opa's life . . . He swallowed hard and determined to try.

"Here, this way," she said. "Give me your hands."

She guided them till his fingers were pressing against the hair and the flesh. The blood was warm and sticky. She showed him how to wrap his fingers in the breeches' cloth and keep them from slipping.

"Just hold on till I return." She spread her gray cape over Opa for warmth and was gone.

"*Ach! Ach!*" Opa groaned. "Have to see the paintings, the paintings . . ." His last word faded like a slow dying hiss.

"Later, Opa," Pieter-Lucas said, "not till Tante Lysbet mends your leg."

He rallied and began talking again. "What hit me? So much to see . . . In such a hurry . . . Dashing down Katerstraat . . . *Ach!* Some castle guard I am!"

"Never mind, Opa. Tante Lysbet's coming and we'll get you home."

How simple he made it sound. But how could he be sure the assailant wouldn't return and attack him as well?

If only Opa hadn't insisted on coming out here so early when no one was about but thieves and wild swordsmen. What had anyone wanted from Opa anyway? He was no merchant with a bag full of gold. Only a poor castle guard, dressed in his faded uniform, ready for festival.

Opa loved a festival. It was the only time he seemed proud to carry a sword. "Not for guarding anything or threatening anybody, just for shining up and making a man feel like a nobleman when he marches on the street." He'd said it again for the hundredth time last evening. He was polishing his sword while Pieter-Lucas polished the bright buttons on his jacket. Opa's sword! It was missing from its sheath! So that was what the thief wanted! Was Opa's own sword used against him, slicing open his leg?

And what did Mieke have to do with all this? She was not wandering around the streets of Breda just for the purpose of telling Pieter-Lucas and Aletta where to find Opa. *Nay*, Mieke was always after something for Mieke. What was it this time?

After what felt like an hour, Pieter-Lucas heard steps. Not Aletta tripping lightly in her leather street shoes, but a solid clopping of clogs. He looked up to see Tante Lysbet coming toward him. The straight stern woman, who lived with Aletta's family and cared for her ailing moeder, carried the small black apothecary cabinet that held her herbal cures, but she came alone.

"Where is Aletta?" he asked.

"Gone to get your vader."

"Oh!" Pieter-Lucas trembled. It seemed that Vader Hendrick delighted in nothing more than ridiculing Opa, his own vader, whenever the man showed the slightest physical weakness. Strange how different the two men were. Both were *kasteel* guards by profession. But only Hendrick was one at heart. Opa had paint in his blood. He'd rather paint pictures any day than tote a sword, and Hendrick despised him for it.

"We will need his help to move Opa back home, you know," Tante Lysbet said.

Pieter-Lucas said nothing. Even if they'd managed without his help, once they got Opa home, Hendrick would be waiting with his mockery.

Pieter-Lucas watched Tante Lysbet kneel beside her patient and examine the lump on the forehead. Opa opened his eyes and smiled up at her. "The Healer Lady . . ."

"You had a nasty accident," she said. "We simply cannot let our neighbor lie in the street and bleed."

She fumbled in her bag, pulled out a folded wet cloth, and offered it to Pieter-Lucas. "Hold this to his head, *jongen*," she said, "and I shall work on the leg."

Pieter-Lucas took the compress in bloodied hands and put it on the lump. When Tante Lysbet put the salve on Opa's wound, he groaned again.

"It's all right, Opa," Pieter-Lucas consoled.

"I have seen much worse sword wounds in my day," Tante Lysbet said gently. "This one should heal quickly enough."

Opa tried again to raise himself on an elbow. This time he managed long enough to reply, "I may not be as young as I once was, but I'm still tough."

Once more, Pieter-Lucas heard footsteps approaching—heavy, clattering, but in a steady rhythm. It was Aletta with Vader Hendrick. Aletta knelt beside Tante Lysbet and the patient while Hendrick stood towering above them, hands planted firmly on his hips. His dark eyes smoldered and looked down over mustachio and pointed beard to the patient and attendants at his feet.

"So you let them fell you," he said, his words clipped and tinged with arrogance. "Took your sword, too, I see. The ancestral Van den Garde sword it was!" He ground the cobblestones beneath the toe of his heavy boot and swore a stream of ugly oaths.

Pieter-Lucas felt his blood churning and jumped to his feet. He stood looking up into Hendrick's angry face. "They laid an ambush for him, Vader. He never knew what happened."

Why did Pieter-Lucas always have to defend Opa against his own son? For sure, Opa wouldn't stand up to him. He always said, "Leave him alone. Your vader's anger makes him blind, and your words only feed that anger."

Hendrick was glaring at him. Pieter-Lucas looked away.

"I once had hopes for you," Hendrick said at last, a sneer of disdain coloring each word. "All these years I've showed you the ways of a Van den Garde worthy of the name—a man of courage. Still you run after this weak-hearted Opa of yours, who will always prefer the paintbrush to the sword. Look at him lying there on the cobblestones in his own blood, too wobbly to stand on his feet, not even able to crawl home. Is that your idea of a man?"

Pieter-Lucas' heart was trembling. Did he dare to say what he thought? Opa would never say it. But the boy was young and determined to learn not to fear Hendrick van den Garde. He must say it now while Aletta was present to hear him. He breathed deeply and spoke as loudly as his not-yet-changing voice would allow. "Opa never runs from danger nor puts another in danger's way. He pursues the paint that runs in his blood, he serves God, and he is a gentle vader. *Ja*, he's a man of the sort I want to be."

Hendrick looked as if someone had slapped him in the face. He took two steps backward, then screwed up his mouth and spat on the ground at Pieter-Lucas' feet. He formed both hands into tight-fisted balls and raised one in the boy's direction. "So you, too, have thrown away the sword of the Van den Gardes, the way of courage and bravery. Someday you will learn that he who holds to the paintbrush will never be anything but a coward."

He paused. Pieter-Lucas searched the leathery face for one tiny speck of compassion and found none.

"I should have known you'd be like him," the hard man said.

As Hendrick van den Garde leaned over Opa, the old man mumbled, "Son Hendrick, I once had hopes for you as well."

Without a reply, Hendrick lifted the man from the street. Tante Lysbet cradled his leg in her hands and followed alongside as the angry man carried his father down the alley to the Katerstraat, onto Annastraat, through the gate, and across the threshold into their little house.

Pieter-Lucas and Aletta came behind, saying nothing. Pieter-Lucas felt his innards globbing together into little hard knots, but something in him felt free at the same time. For once, Hendrick van den Garde did not frighten him into silence.

When they stopped before the gate that led into Pieter-Lucas' house, Aletta squeezed his hand and looked at him with adoring china blue eyes. "Pieter-Lucas," she whispered, "I think you are a very brave man! Just like your opa!"

He lowered his head, cleared his throat, and felt his heart soar. "I promise to try," he whispered back.

PART ONE

Victory

*The expectation of the righteous is
gladness,
but the hope of the godless comes to
naught.*

Proverbs 10:28 as quoted in Willem's
Warning (September 1, 1568)

*Our fortress is in Christ,
Our defense is patience,
Our sword is the Word of God,
And our victory is the sincere, firm,
Unfeigned faith in Jesus Christ.
Spears and swords of iron we leave to
those
Who, alas, consider human blood and
swine's blood
Well nigh of equal value.*

—Menno Simons
From John Horsch's "The Principle of Non-
Resistance as Held by the Mennonite
Church," 1927.

CHAPTER ONE

Breda

29th day of Spring Month (March), 1568

With the rising of a thinly veiled sun, the melting snow dripped faster and faster from the eaves of the ancient thatch of Maarten de Smid's apartment above his blacksmith shop. It had turned into an uninterrupted stream running toward the sloppy puddles on the mossy cobblestones two floors below before Tante Lysbet heard it.

Breda's *grand dame* of herbalism and midwifery walked toward the window, careful not to waken Maarten's wife and freshly birthed son resting in the cupboard bed on the back wall. She looked at the dozen streams of water, pulled aside the window curtain, and surveyed the cobbled street below. For no good reason she could possibly conjure up, the sight she saw there set her heart to beating in her throat. Three men walked toward the blacksmith shop. Two Spaniards in dress uniforms with gold braids and shiny buttons carried long curved swords at their sides. Beside them strode the local bailiff, a plume feather bobbing atop his hat with each approaching step.

Lysbet was not the sort of person to listen for sounds in the night or watch for suspicious goings on in the streets.

"Fear is nonsense!" she always said whenever she heard it in the voices of her neighbors. "Almighty God vindicates every man, woman, and child who holds a clear conscience." She'd learned the line from her moeder and, with only one exception, had found no good reason to suspect otherwise.

When her former employer, Dirck Engelshofen the bookseller, uprooted his family and fled the city, imagining his wife was under surveillance as a suspected witch, then she had wondered. But that was a year ago.

She couldn't deny that the entire country tottered near the brink of war. A growing number of Lowlanders were ready to rise up in revolt against the oppressive arrogance of their absentee foreign sovereign, King Philip of Spain. Son of the late Holy Roman Emperor, Charles V, he refused to honor the charter agreements issued by his ancestors to the cities of the Low Lands. Nor would he allow his subjects to worship God in any way other than that prescribed and administered by the Holy Catholic Religion. Tante Lysbet had no doubt that a just God would one day call King Philip to account.

And in the meantime? Many of her fellow Bredenaars crouched behind bolted doors, fearing the arrival of tramping boots, clashing halberds, and clanging chains. Ever since King Philip's henchman, the Duke of Alva, had arrived in the Low Lands, they'd all heard repeated tales of confiscations and executions from other cities.

"I shall squeeze those Dutchmen like soft butterballs," the arrogant Spaniard had reportedly boasted. Lysbet regarded the words as empty threats. Always she pictured the butter squeezed through iron fingers running out and forming itself into new butterballs.

Besides, in no city was fear as preposterous as in Breda. Lysbet could count on the fingers of one hand the people who had ever been executed here for heresy. And they were all foreign refugees, no doubt godless criminals at heart to begin with. In Breda, no righteous man or woman would ever die at the hands of the authorities. In her mind, that had always settled it.

Why, then, did those three men in the street below unsettle her so?

Begone, foolish fears. Since her conscience was clear, why did her hands feel so clammy? *Nay,* 'twas but an evil spirit tormenting her.

Resolutely she moved from the window and crept on tiptoe to the sleeping cubicle behind her. Something in the deep silent slumber of both mother and child mocked the stubborn pounding in her own heart. And in her ears rang an inexplicable warning: "Run for your life! RUN FOR YOUR LIFE!"

Then the voice changed and so did the words. Heavy footfalls and voices approached up through the worn stairwell. The words were unintelligible, in a language she'd grown accustomed to hearing in the streets ever since Alva's Spanish soldiers came to be boarded by the citizens of Breda.

When the three men she'd seen in the street below filled up the distance from floor to ceiling in the small apartment, Lysbet spread her arms eagle-wing fashion to protect her patients and protested, "Be still. The new mother sleeps."

Ignoring her, one of the soldiers spoke in accented words, "Thees eez the one?"

Without waiting for an answer, both soldiers unsheathed their swords and pointed them at the distraught midwife. "Be you Lysbet de Vriend?"

"*Nay.*" She held her voice firm, while every muscle in her body quivered. They were looking for Betteke, called de Vriend (friend) because of the many unselfish ways she befriended others. Hardly a criminal deserving of arrest.

The men gaped at her. "Aha! So you not want to cooperate?" They shook their heads with exaggerated mock outrage and looked toward the bailiff, who up to this point had remained silent. "What say you, señor . . . bailiff? This is the woman we seek, *que no?* Right?"

Nay, it could not be. Lysbet shook her head, blinked her eyes, swallowed hard. Why could she not awaken from this ludicrous nightmare? Surely the bailiff would set them straight. He knew her well.

Without looking at her, he muttered, "Ask her."

The soldiers came closer and their swords brushed against her apron. "Lysbet, housekeeper of Pieter van Keulen, the goldsmith? That is you, *que no?*"

Her heart cried out, *Great God, Nay. Let them not find her.* Tante Lysbet had known the servant girl since her days in the orphans' house, long before she became Van Keulen's housekeeper. A simple girl she was, but with an amazing winsomeness and a faith so deep and pure it shamed all who knew her. Lysbet knew the wild wooded spot where the girl lodged and had been watching out for her since she fled there after the goldsmith was arrested. Each day Lysbet took her food to eat and dry peat for a fire to warm herself.

The tightness in her muscles intensified. Must she lie to these men and tell them she was the woman they sought in order to protect Betteke? Or tell the truth so she might stay on here and care for the newborn child and its mother? Surely, the soldiers would never think to search for Betteke out in the wood.

She lifted her head and asked, "Do I look like an eighteen-year-old housemaid? If he wills to do so, the bailiff can direct your minds on the path of truth."

The choking cries of a newborn called from the cradle behind her. Lysbet moved toward the infant, but her would-be captors blocked her way.

"You go not so easily free, señorita," barked one soldier.

With a voice as smooth and cunning as sticky honey, the second asked, "If not Lysbet de Vriend, who, then, are you?"

What could she answer that they would not use against her? What did they want from her anyway? Money? She had none. Secrets? Also none. *If you tell the truth, your righteousness will vindicate you.* The memory of her mother's voice prodded her.

"I am simply Lysbet," she said with quiet dignity. She left her voice suspended in the air now filled with increasing howls from both infant and new mother. She turned to attend to the patient at her back, but a soldier grabbed her by the arm and yanked her across the room.

"Aha, but of course. This is Lysbet the *Physicke.*"

"Midwife and healer to Gretta Engelshofen, bewitched wife of the bookseller," added the second soldier. With a nod toward the bailiff, he added, "You should have kept the orders straight."

Lysbet froze to the spot.

"So . . . you are Lysbet, *physicke* to Mad Gretta?" She felt the tip of a sword press the question into her left ribs.

"*Nay,*" she answered quickly.

"*Nay?*" The second sword point jabbed her in the right ribs.

"*Physicke*, then, of the wife of Dirck Engelshofen?" The question came in honeyed tones again.

Like a fly entrapped, Lysbet lifted her head and strained against her captors' grip, crying, "Let me go. I've done nothing wrong! Unless it is a crime to dispense God's mercy to the suffering." She spat out the words with as much sarcasm as she could show.

By now the young moeder was screaming hysterically from her bed cupboard across the room. Lysbet called out to her, "Be calm, Petronella. Our God will care for you."

Surely He must do it. The woman was young, only a girl, and this her first child. Her moeder was newly dead, and she had no family living nearby. Lysbet felt a rush of tears and swallowed them back.

The soldiers laughed. "And who will take care of you, Lysbet, harborer of witches?"

Lysbet bristled. She opened her mouth to make a defense, then thought better of it. Instead, she pleaded with the foreigners. "Have you no mercy on this poor moeder?"

"Ah, we are very merciful to the innocent. But as you say, her God will care for her."

"And she has a husband. What could she need more?"

They laughed again. Lysbet protested vigorously, but the bailiff stepped forward and bound her hands with chains at the wrist. Then all three men hustled her with brusque movements down the stairwell, through the noise and flying dust of the blacksmith's shop, and out into the puddles of melting snow.

"Let me go," Lysbet screamed. "I am innocent."

A sword pricked the small of her back, and one of the Spaniards, garlic reeking from his breath, said, "Be still, or we shall fasten a screw to your tongue." Then throwing a length of nondescript cloth over her face, the bailiff tied it so tightly around her neck that she could no longer see even the light of day, and her wails of anguish produced nothing but muffled cries. With each thudding step, the sword pierced into her flesh till she felt rivulets of warm blood trickling down her back.

Nay, nay, nay! she screamed at her own heart. *I am righteous. I shall be vindicated.*

For what seemed like hours, Lysbet was jerked along, slipping over endless cobblestones, spattered with freezing mud, aching from a pace rendered inhumane by enforced blindness. Where were they taking her? The question drove her mad with a frenzy of fear until she heard Roland chiming out the hour from his clock tower. He sounded so near behind her that she felt the vibrations beneath her feet and knew they must be crossing the market square before the Great Church.

When at last the party slowed down and dragged her over a threshold, she knew they had entered *The Crane's Nest*, the bookshop of Dirck Engelshofen.

"Remove the blindfold," a soldier shouted to the bailiff, who followed the sharp orders almost before they were given.

Like a manipulated puppet in the grand procession of the Holy Cross on Pentecost Sunday, Lysbet thought. Had he no spine, no mind to think his own thoughts, to do what he knew was right?

As the restraint came off, the ruffled nursemaid breathed deeply and rearranged her flattened nose in an attempt to recapture her dignity. She blinked her eyes several times against the light.

One of the Spaniards stood smiling at her. She averted the gaze of his eyes. "So, does this place not make you feel more at home?" That annoying poisonous smile colored his voice, dripping deadly sweetness from each awkwardly accented syllable. She did not answer him.

"What a pity," he went on, "the dear bookseller was forced by his possessed wife to leave this lovely cozy spot."

"Even more's the pity he did not take all her devilish books along," the other soldier added, grinning like a naughty child. "You will show them to us, *que no?*"

Lysbet did not lift her head, nor did she speak. She ignored the men's intrusive stares and studied the patterns of grout between the dark floor tiles. Here in this very spot she had read the books that taught her to worship God in new ways. Here she'd seen love enacted in Dirck Engelshofen as he cared for his ailing wife. Many had called the woman mad. "Beloved of God and precious," her husband said again and again in the tone of voice he used when talking to her, in the tender look in his eyes when he looked at her, in the patience he exercised when she screamed at him in one of her demented rages.

"You will show the books to us?" The question came again, along with a sharp prod from the point of the sword.

Lysbet gasped at the pain, then said simply, "I know of no such books to show."

"Aha! The woman's memory not so good anymore, eh?"

"She needs a story to remind her. Tell her, Señor Bailiff, about Mad Gretta's last confession."

The bailiff cleared his throat in sharp staccato rhythm and spoke stiffly. "Ah, *ja*. When Vrouw Engelshofen stood before the examiners . . ." He cleared his throat again, and Lysbet, still staring at the floor, watched his feet shuffle nervously back and forth across the line between tiles. "She confessed," he said.

Lysbet knew in her bones that he lied. She looked up into the official's eyes and demanded, "What did she confess?" She noted his shifting eyes and marveled at the uncomfortable sense of delight it gave her.

"Ah, *ja*, but she confessed her guilt."

"What guilt?" Lysbet had an odd feeling of control.

Before the bailiff could answer, Lysbet felt the swords in her back once more. The soldiers laughed and one bellowed out, "As if you knew nothing. You stall for time."

"Tell her the rest," demanded the other.

The bailiff coughed again and went on. "Well . . . of course Mad Gretta confessed that she had hidden her books of magic in this house." He moved his hands nervously back and forth and did not look at Lysbet. "She said that you, Lysbet, would know where they are."

"I should know the whereabouts of books of magic that never did exist? What a venomous lie!" She felt the swords probe deeper yet into her sides.

"All goes much easier with you when you lead us to the books quickly, señorita." The tall soldier's voice sounded gruff.

"*Nay*," Lysbet cried out, taking care neither to move nor to breathe deeply lest the swords draw more blood. "There are no books. Gretta was no witch. She has not been executed."

"Tie her!" ordered the fat soldier. "We go to search the midwife's quarters above."

The bailiff took a long chain from his justice bag and shackled her feet together, just far enough so she could stand without losing her balance, but not far enough to allow her to walk freely. With a second chain, he tethered her hands, and with a third, he joined the two lengths together.

"*Nay, nay, nay!*" Lysbet screamed. "I am an innocent Bredenaar . . . you cannot treat me so. . . . God have mercy!"

Once more the bailiff threw the length of cloth over her face and anchored it around her neck, muffling her screams and nearly cutting off her breath. Finally, he grabbed her around the waist, pulled her down to a sitting position, and tied her to a three-legged stool.

"Almighty God," she cried, not at all certain He could hear her prayers any better than the bailiff could hear her smothered voice. "What have I done to deserve this? I am innocent. Gretta is innocent. There are no books of magic in *The Crane's Nest*! Almighty God, are you listening?"

Vaguely she heard the Spaniards' shouts of revelry and the thunderous tromping of heavy boots in the attic room above the bookshop. Her back and side stung with raw wounds. Her head ached. Her sack prison was intolerably hot. She gasped for air . . . her body was slumping . . . her mind floating. . . .

Lysbet awoke with shafts of sharp sunlight lying across her face. Where was she? What happened? Why was her head so dull, her body so racked with pain, her bed so hard and cold? She tried to stretch her arms, but they could not move. Gradually, a world of excited voices drifted toward her.

"We found it! Eureka!"

"This your box, señorita, *que no?*"

My box? Señorita? She felt strong hands tugging at her body, lifting her up from what she discovered to be a tile floor and pushing her into a standing position against the wall. What was she doing here? The widely grinning face of a fat Spanish soldier greeted her, and it all came back. She had swooned in the presence of these miserable godless tormentors? She tried to reach down and smooth out her rumpled dress, but the shackles held her fast. At least her head was no longer covered. Tears of angry shame smarted around the crinkly edges of her eyes. She fought them back.

"Señorita Lysbet, wonderful midwife of Breda"—the smooth-tongued words of the tall Spaniard brought her back to the reality of her nightmare—"tell us about this beautiful wooden box." He thrust a familiar small box at her. Its intricately carved birds and flowers made her gasp.

"Where did you find this?" she demanded.

"Aha!" both soldiers shouted with obvious glee.

"She knows it," said the fat one.

"Tell her, friend, how we uncovered it hidden in the far corner of her sleeping room, behind the piles of Señor Engelshofen's extra books."

It did indeed look like her box. Her vader had brought it to her from the market in Antwerp on her tenth birthday, the day she knew she wanted to become a Beguine sister. "Use it to preserve your most prized treasures," he had told her. And she had. Her first prayer book, a lock of hair from the first baby she had delivered, the wooden crucifix her dying mother had laid in her hand, the yellowed pamphlet from Tante Anastasia with the story and last words of her grandfather, who had been beheaded because he did not follow all the orders of the Church.

But she had left her box in her room in Maarten de Smid's apartment, and its key nestled right now in her bosom, hanging from a chain around her neck. She eyed her captors narrowly and waited, trembling.

"Your treasure box, *que no?*" The fat Spaniard's toothy smile sent shivers up her spine.

"I left no such box in this place," she insisted, fighting to preserve a calmness she did not possess.

"We shall see," suggested the tall one. He approached her seductively and reached his hand inside the neck of her dress. "She carry a key here somewhere," he said with glee.

Lysbet drew back, but without the use of her hands she was powerless against his rough advances. She leaned forward, trying to reach the intruding hand with her teeth, but he yanked her head back by the hair and commenced to search for the key. For what seemed an eternity, he allowed his hand to roam freely over her upper body, all the while muttering, "Has to be here . . . treasure box keys always hang close to heart. . . . Aha, Eureka!"

He grabbed the key and yanked it from her bosom, wrenching the chain off over her headdress. "Now we see how perfectly it fits." He rubbed his hands together, then with exaggerated ceremony inserted the key into the lock and turned it.

Lysbet sat rigid, pretending not to care or see. *Almighty God*, she prayed in silent desperation, *Your Son made blind eyes to see. Send him now to make scales of blindness to fall upon the seeing eyes of these wicked men. They must not see Tante Anastasia's pamphlet. Hear me, O God. . . .*

She watched the box lid spring open. Both Spaniards hovered over the little box, looking into its depths like pirates gloating over stolen gold pieces.

"Aha! What treasure you guard, señorita."

She heard the shout and felt an elbow jabbing her upper arm.

"Look! Look! Look at the treasure!"

Eager not to appear guilty by fear, Lysbet looked at the books the Spaniards were waving before her. Thanks be to God, Tante Anastasia's pamphlet was not among them. Was this the miracle she'd prayed for?

But her joy was short-lived. For her captors were waving four booklets in her face. Too small to be Bibles. Nay, worse!

The Magical Arts!" the fat soldier called out. "*Ways to Practice Witchcraft! How to Live Like a Witch and Not Be Detected!*"

The tall one shoved one final title under Lysbet's nose and grunted, "*Spells and Potions to Use Against the Clergy!* So these are your treasures? Tell us, what more you hide in your bosom?"

Lysbet shivered. How could God betray her so? "I know nothing of these books—or any books like them," she said. "Before Almighty God in heaven I swear that I have never seen them before. Nor did Gretta Engelshofen."

Both Spaniards laughed a loud howling laughter that sent visions of hellish monsters dancing in Lysbet's mind.

"The witch lies," they bellowed.

"Cover her head again," the fat one barked to the bailiff.

"And give her back her precious key," ordered the other, "that it may go with her to her new home and remind her of the awfulness of her deeds." With rough movements, the fat one slung the key on its long chain over her head. Then he lifted Lysbet's chin with his finger and spoke with mock affection. "Come, dear lady, we take you to a strong tower of delights."

Lysbet closed her eyes and choked on the tears that ran down her throat. Powerless to do aught but pray and wait, she yielded to her rough captors and sent strong words heavenward. *Almighty God, do you care any more what will happen to Vrouw de Smid and her newborn child, open to false accusation of being brought into the world by the aid of a witch? To Gretta Engelshofen? To Betteke behind that hedge of thorny roses? To Lysbet the Physicke?*

———

Emden
29th day of Spring Month (March), 1568

In the far north country of East Friesland, the days were tapering off into long twilights. Pieter-Lucas van den Garde walked to the house of Hans the weaver-preacher just after the evening meal and did not carry a lantern. His business would be swift.

Straight and tall, the nineteen-year-old pulled his cape close around his body in the icy wind. He made his way quickly through 'tFalder, the refugees' ghetto bordering the eastern side of the harbor of Emden. At the house with the steep thatched roof that sloped nearly to his shoulder, he knocked boisterously and waited.

The door opened and the preacher appeared. Not quite old enough to be Pieter-Lucas' vader, Hans was a gentle man. But tonight, his long bushy beard and heavy brows seemed to hold a foreboding air. And the low shaggy beams of the large single room, combined with the blended aroma of herbal brews, weaver's wool, and burning peat, made Pieter-Lucas feel hedged, trapped.

"Come in." Hans gestured toward the roughhewn table by the hearth.

Pieter-Lucas looked around the room. Hans' moeder, Oma, was busy at the hearth stirring a pot. His two daughters helped her.

"I must talk with you alone," Pieter-Lucas said.

Hans arched his eyebrows and sighed. He picked up a lighted lamp and Pieter-Lucas followed. Across the single room, past the large loom at one end, they slipped through the secret panel in the wall that led into the hidden church where Hans' flock met on Sundays to worship. Children of God, they called themselves, while the rest of the world mocked them with the name Anabaptists (Rebaptizers).

The room was cold, and the sight of the backless benches in the lamplight sent a shiver down Pieter-Lucas' spine. Hans was staring at him.

"What is it, *jongen?*"

Pieter-Lucas twisted the old felt cap in his hands and said, "Ever since Harvest Month (August), Aletta and I have met with you to learn to become members of your church. Every week we've come. Do you realize it's been seven long months? At Christmas you allowed us to become publicly betrothed and told us that as soon as the New Year had come, we could set a wedding date. Here it is Spring month and still we wait! How much longer?"

A tremor vibrated in Pieter-Lucas' chest, and he tapped a toe in the rushes beneath his feet. Last summer when he had agreed to join the little group of believers, it seemed so small a price to pay for the hand of the girl he had loved all his life and could not live without. But the process had stretched out through the gloomy winter months, and his young spirit grew increasingly restless.

Hans nodded his head and after a pause spoke evenly. "I am sorry you find it so difficult to wait."

Pieter-Lucas' mouth hung open and his arms waved an impatient gesture. "Is that all you have to say?"

Hans stood expressionless for what seemed to Pieter-Lucas like a long night when sleep refuses to come and every part of the body aches with the dead stop of time.

"Speak to me!" Pieter-Lucas demanded at last, his voice an exploding musket ball of urgency.

Hans raised a hand. "I cannot give you an answer," he protested.

"What do you mean? You're the leader of the group that meets in this place." Pieter-Lucas spread his hands out to the benches on all sides. "You can't give me an answer?"

"I can feel it with you, son. But I—"

"Nay," Pieter-Lucas interrupted, punching Hans' chest with his finger. "You have no idea what I feel. Did you ever have a childhood sweetheart? Somebody you did everything with all your life? Then, when she was finally old enough to become your vrouw, her family snatched her out from under your nose and carried her away to a far country so you had to spend months looking for her? When you found her, her vader promised you her hand, then turned you over to a group of elders who had long forgotten what it was to be young and could only think of ways to keep you waiting?"

Hans was shaking his head, but Pieter-Lucas ranted on, "The bafflement is more maddening than a man can endure. Last year, when I found Aletta and her family here in your house, I was ready to put her on my horse and ride off into the future of our dreams. Instead, I learned that her vader had joined what I had always heard was some strange sect, and if I wanted to claim my bride, I, too, had to become one of them."

"And you nearly have," Hans said.

"Nearly! Bah! Repeatedly I have told you that I am willing to live by your cherished beliefs. So why the delay? I feel like a Jacob who's worked already my fourteen years for Rachel, yet you refuse to tell me how much longer! At least Jacob could count the days."

Hans' brown eyes looked softer now. "Give us one more week for an answer!" he said.

"What sort of an answer?"

Hans scratched the back of his head, then stroked his beard and sighed. "I . . . I cannot say with certainty. All my elders must agree, you know."

"And if even one of them says I must wait longer, or I do not measure up?"

Hans shrugged, spreading one hand upward.

Pieter-Lucas glared at him. "I'll tell you what then. I shall not wait one day longer. I am ready for the baptism and the vows you ask. If your elders insist on demanding something more, something they cannot—or will not—explain to me, I will forget the baptism and find another way." He pulled his worn felt cap down over his ears and started toward the door.

Hans stood beside him and spoke in a sterner voice than Pieter-Lucas had heard from him before, "*Jongen*, I doubt not your words, and I do understand more of your bafflement than you have any idea."

"Then?" Pieter-Lucas stood with hands on his hips, waiting.

"I also know that if we allow you to have the thing you want before you are ready to obey the voice of God in all things, the day will come when some men in our fellowship will take it as their duty to ban you from the church and take your wife from your hearth. Far better to practice caution and preparedness today than risk facing the ban tomorrow."

Pieter-Lucas looked at Hans with smarting eyes. He opened the door and walked through without a final farewell. Before he'd stepped across the threshold, Hans took him by the shoulder.

"One more week," he said. "You have my word."

Pieter-Lucas hesitated, then tipped his head sidewise toward his teacher. "After that, I cannot promise to wait another day!"

In the lingering twilight, he hurried through the streets toward *Abrams en Zonen*, the clandestine printshop where he worked for Aletta's uncle Johannes. His feet crunched the crusting slush that slickened the maze of muddy ruts and street cobbles. His face stung with the pelting of an icy evening wind. And in his mind, he wrestled with the uncertainties of his tomorrows—and Aletta's.

If the elders put him off again, would he have to choose between Dirck Engelshofen's wishes and his Aletta? Life had stolen many precious things from Pieter-Lucas—moeder, vader, Opa, everything he'd grown up with. He had only two treasures left. The paint in his blood and the girl in his heart. Both burned in his bosom, and he would never—*could* never—let them go!

When he'd climbed the steep narrow stairway to *Abrams en Zonen*, he kicked the street shoes from his feet. He hugged himself in search of warmth, then blew on cupped hands and scurried up one more flight of stairs to the attic with its steeply sloping roof line. This was the cramped room where he designed dull title pages for the Children of God's *verboden boecken* and then curled up on his sleeping palette and slept at night.

When he'd warmed his hands on the chimney stones, he lighted the oil lamp and set it on the low windowsill.

Next to being with Aletta, this was the part of his day he looked forward to most. Every night before he lay his head down to sleep, he mixed paints and played with colors and formed images on a canvas—always pretending he was the Master Painter of Breda. Aletta had given him that title the day they spent with Opa in the Great Church of Breda, when a priest anointed Pieter-Lucas for the work of an artist. It was these nightly secret appointments and her happiness at receiving each new painting from his hand that gave him hope.

Tonight, though, a heavy sadness, almost a hopelessness, stiffened his fingers as he pulled a small leather bag from its hiding place behind the table where he did his daily work. He untied and loosened the drawstring on the bag. The items he pulled out and spread along the windowsill felt so sacred in his hands that he feared almost to touch them. Three old paintbrushes and a palette knife had been rescued from Opa's devastated studio. The four pots of paints he had created using his grandfather's secret recipes. The wooden palette he'd carved himself looked just like the one Opa had used all his life.

He reached for his three-legged stool, determined to paint. Instead, he seemed to see himself already seated on the stool as an old, solitary, white-headed man. Wrapped in a heavy moth-eaten cloak, he was painting dark and splotchy scenes beside a fireless chimney here in this lonely attic. And in his ears he seemed to hear Opa's voice reciting a puzzling warning he'd given the boy so many times he couldn't help but memorize it. "This passion to paint is a monster in your blood. Never satisfied, it will always demand more than you can give. Without the hand of God and a good wife to check and soothe and prod and guide, it will consume your heart and mind and leave you with nothing but ashes on your palette."

Until now, Opa's strange words had left him shaking his head, wondering. Tonight, they made terrifying sense and echoed around the walls of his brain, quickening the racing of his heart. Why had he not seen it before? Without Aletta at his side, all the painting dreams in the world would turn into choking nightmares.

"*Nay, jongen,*" he cried aloud. "It cannot be! I will not allow it!"

Possessed of a furious urge to redirect his own fate, he reached behind the table and pulled out a large cloth-wrapped package leaning against the wall. He tore off the covering, revealing the clean framed canvas he'd been saving for the wedding picture he would paint for his bride. Feverishly fearful lest he lose his nerve, he seated himself on the stool and with sweaty hands settled the canvas on his lap, propping it against the wall. One at a time, he wiped his palms on his breeches, then breathed deeply and let the air out in a fine noiseless trickle.

For a long moment he stared at the canvas. Then, all unexpectedly, like the sudden breakthrough of a powerful ray of sunlight on a dismal cloudy afternoon, a dazzling idea began lighting all the lamps in his head. The setting was Opa's studio in the woods outside of Breda, where he used to paint. In the center, beneath the rose-colored glass window, he and Aletta stood, hands joined, before a clergyman in a plain white robe.

In the shadows of the background to the left, a canvas rested on an easel with tools and paints spread out on a table beside it. In deeper shadows to the right, Hendrick van den Garde was slinking out a half-opened door, a rusty sword dangling from his belt.

"The hour has come, *jongen,*" he told himself. "The sooner you begin—and finish—the sooner you will be ready." Not Hans' idea of preparation for a wedding, but Hans didn't have it all under his control, and Pieter-Lucas could no longer sit and wait.

He grabbed a chunk of charcoal from the table and began sketching in the figures of a man and woman. His hands trembled. He would work—*nay*, play—as long as his eyelids did not droop shut. A deep laughter rumbled up from his belly and kept rolling off his lips until it filled the attic and echoed around the rafters.

CHAPTER TWO

Breda

29th night of Spring Month (March), 1568

*D*amp silence wrapped the grove of oak and linden trees in a shroud of nocturnal mists. It oozed through the untamed profusion of an ancient hedge of heather and wild rose vines and into the abandoned ruins of a wattle-and-thatch structure that drooped with its gaping vine-covered doorway, sagging roof, and broken windowpanes.

In a corner of the single room filled with weathered rubble, a tiny fire burned in an earthen pit surrounded by a circle of broken tiles. In its gasping light, Lysbet (Betteke) de Vriend sat coughing into the heavy woolen cape that wrapped her trembling frame. She bowed her head over a low table. The crude piece of furniture had only one leg intact and was propped up on the opposite side by a pile of unidentifiable debris and draped with a wrinkled square cloth obviously created for a much larger table.

"Holy Vader in the Heaven." The huddled young woman—barely more than a child, she was—spoke the words as earnestly as if the Vader she addressed could be seen and felt sitting beside her in the primitive shelter she called home.

"Even though you sent no angels today," she went on, her voice muffled, "yesterday they came bearin' enough peat for my fire and bread and broth for more'n two evenin' meals. Thanks be to you for daily bread."

For a long space she kept her head bowed, her rough hands folded. The fire leapt elusively upward, weaving a web of constantly shifting ribbons of light and shadow across Betteke and her dismal surroundings. Grasping one of the chunks of heavy black bread from the table, she dipped a ragged corner into the pot of broth, lifted it to her mouth, and tore off a bite-sized piece.

"Would to God I could see the angel He sends each day," she mumbled between bites.

An irrepressible feeling of scratchy fullness from deep in her throat overpowered her and sent her into a fit of furious coughing. She rubbed her chest, wincing as she cried out, "*Ach*, but it pains!"

When at last the cough subsided, and a spring of tears leaked out around her eyes, she set about once more to consume her evening meal. Slowly, deliberately, she savored each bite as if it were some delicacy from Prince Willem's table. Then lifting the small pottery dish to her lips, she drank the remaining broth, letting the warm salty liquid trickle into her mouth and down her hot irritated throat. Was that a scrap of meat, or did her imagination prod her tongue to feel what was not there?

"It's real." She chewed on it as long as it held enough form to be felt between her teeth.

At length, when the surprise morsel had disintegrated, she set her dish on the table, wiped her mouth on the edge of the cloth, and bowed her head. Once more she offered thanks.

Then reaching inside her bodice, she pulled out a folded piece of paper and smoothed its wrinkles and creases on her lap. She leaned closer to the fire and began to read aloud, forming each word with affectionate precision:

"The Lord props up all who fall,
He raises up all who are bowed down.
All eyes wait upon Thee,
And Thou givest to all their food in due time."

Betteke let the words flow down into the crannies of her soul. Though she'd never known the love of a flesh-and-blood vader, her moeder taught her 'twas their "Vader in the Heaven" who saw to it that they always had just enough food to quiet the daily pains of hunger. Never enough for a feast, but at least a daily crust of bread, either with or without the pot of broth.

She knew it was because of His care that she had found refuge in these ruins. Long ago she'd discovered this quiet spot by peering through a tiny hole in the thorny hedge that encased it well. In those days the old retired *kasteel* guard, Lucas van den Garde, who lived in the house next to *The Crane's Nest*, came here to paint. She knew that's what he did here because she'd heard him and his grandson, Pieter-Lucas, talk about it as they walked in the wood. She had watched with surprise as he opened the secret door through the hedge.

For a short while one of his pictures hung in the Great Church above the altar of the Chapel of the Holy Ghost. Betteke had never seen anything so beautiful. Then one day angry men broke into the church and sliced it with a big knife. She cried for the whole day.

One of his paintings nobody damaged. It hung above the altar of the Beguine sisters, who dispensed mercy and medicine to Breda's sick. It showed Jesus touching multitudes of sick people, making the lame to walk and the blind to see, and making the sad joyful with His loving words. As long as she lived in the city, Betteke went nearly every day to look at it.

With her rough hands now slightly warmed by the fire, and her heart warmed by the memory of beautiful paintings, she folded the page from Meester van Keulen's big Bible and put it back in its place next to her heart. She moved toward the pile of rags that formed her bed on the other side of her fire. She had barely reached the bed when she heard noises just beyond the wall.

The wind? *Nay!*

A wild boar prowling about? She lay stone still, trying not to breathe. *Vader in the Heaven*, she prayed silently, feeling the rawness of her throat begin to urge her to cough again. *You promised to prop me when I fall, and I'm very close to fallin' just now into great danger.*

With effort she suppressed the cough that threatened to betray her presence. The noises drew closer, more distinct. She raised herself to an elbow and tucked her hair behind an ear, straining to listen. Footsteps!

Vader, Vader, let no wild beast find the doorway, she prayed in stunned silence.

But the steps came closer, leaves and twigs crackling under their weight. Now there were voices, first whispering, then speaking in an unintelligible mumble, followed by the halting, unmistakable cries of a baby.

"A newborn!"

She buried her head in her blanket and swallowed hard, choking back an explosive cough. She could hear her unseen visitors moving along the wall toward the doorway.

Could she put out the fire and hide before they found her? *Nay*, she must not think of her own safety. There was a newborn out in the cold of this damp foggy night, needing warmth and shelter. What sort of people had captured the infant and brought it here to invade her refuge?

She hadn't long to ponder. Already the light of a lantern flickered at her door, and a man came through, wearing a dark cape and a beret with earflaps. He led the halting figure of a woman, her arms filled with the blanket bundle from which came the baby's cries.

No wild boar here—or soldiers or child snatchers—but parents. Betteke smiled. Her body ceased to tremble. Even her cough fell calm. What sort of threat to their lives had roused this moeder from her childbed—and in the darkness of such a nasty night?

Betteke shrank back into the shadows of her bed and peeked out from behind her blanket just enough to watch and plan. She must help, but if she moved too suddenly, her presence would surely frighten them.

"Look!" the woman whispered. "A fire!"

With rapid instinctive responses, the young man stepped between her and the fire, as if shielding her from some unknown danger. His eyes shone in the dim light, wide and wary. If only she could assure him that this was a safe haven!

"Oh, husband," the woman's words were a sigh, bathed in tears.

How cold and weak she must be! Without a further thought, Betteke clambered to her feet and moved toward them.

"Here, friend," she said. "Lie here." She gestured toward her own bed, then reached out to help guide the woman there.

Instantly the woman gasped. Her husband shone the lantern into Betteke's corner. "Who offers a bed?" he demanded.

"Forgive me. I had no mind to startle you," Betteke said. "I haven't nothin' of great comfort to offer, but 'tis a trifle better than the rocky ground. An' your vrouw must have rest."

The man made no move in her direction. "Who are you?" he asked again.

"A servant girl."

He moved the lantern closer, searching her face. "Whose servant girl?"

"I be an honest woman," she said. "Looks as if we shiver in the same straits—all in hidin' for our lives. An' if your vrouw don't rest soon, she not a-goin' to run much farther."

She watched his face soften. Then reaching out her arms to them, she repeated her invitation. "Lie here. I promise before the God in heaven that no harm will come to you or your newborn from these ministerin' hands."

Without waiting for further response, Betteke busied herself rearranging her pile of rags into as comfortable a bed as possible.

The man said nothing but watched her every move. Warily, he removed the baby from his vrouw's arms and let Betteke guide her onto the makeshift bed. Betteke adjusted the woman's cape, tucking it in around the edges of her body, and watched a ghost of a smile wash across the wan face.

"We be blessed that the angel brought that extra pot o' broth yesterday," Betteke said. "Besides, I've a small crust of bread left from my evenin' meal. Had I known you were arrivin', I should've eaten nothin' and left it all for you."

"*Nay*, but we brought bread along for our journey," the man said. He bent over his vrouw and laid the bundled infant next to her.

"Journey? This woman mustn't be on no journey. My Vader's feathered a nest for her here. You'll stay till her confinement be done."

Betteke grabbed a stick, poked her fire into new life, and set the extra pot of broth on to heat. "So long as you stay here, my Vader's angels will give you all you need," she said as she worked. "Now let me hush lest my chatter call your pursuers through the darkness o' this ugly night."

With fingers adept at her menial tasks, Betteke handed the warmed broth to the man. She reheated the water in the little water bottle wrapped up with the baby in his swaddled cloths. At length she gathered together an assortment of debris from around the studio and built a rickety wall of sorts to shelter the young family. Then she huddled by the door, pulled her blanket tightly around her, and leaned against the wall. It would be a long wakeful night.

Through chattering teeth she whispered, "Good an' gracious Vader, keep my cough silent. You've brought this little family into my care and set me to guardin' their lives. No way can I let my hackin' cough call their pursuers here and turn this safe haven into a trap."

The night was long indeed. A cold wind swirled around the doorway, making a sound like the whistling of a shepherd for his dog out in the pasturelands. It blew leaves and forest debris in dizzy little circles at her feet. An occasional shower of rain brought sharp drops pelting against her cheek. Betteke shivered and buried her face in her arms. But she did not cough!

As the hours wore on, she tried every way to find a comfortable position to sit out her guard duty. But no matter which way she turned, her legs ached. When she could endure it no longer, she stood up, unfolding stiff limbs and moving numbed feet with difficulty.

Gingerly she stepped past the doorway, out from under the cover of the roof, and breathed in the cool, misty, almost-morning air. What glorious smells! Damp tree bark and washed mold mixed with the sweet pungency of a nearby clump of wild trilliums with freshly burst blooms.

The wind had gone, along with the rain. A faint hint of coming dawn lightened the scene before her, and a full moon shone powerfully through a thin canopy of morning fog. She walked out across the soggy forest floor, her steps uncertain, trampling wet leaves and snapping twigs in the web of old and new life beneath her feet.

Danger nagged at the back of her mind. *Venture not too far.* She seemed to hear a soft voice of warning.

But the promise of the morning stilled the voice, and she walked on, her attention arrested by a huge clump of newly sprouted mushrooms just beyond the next tree. She had barely reached the plump edible plants and was stooping to examine them when from the building behind her came the sudden piercing sounds of the infant's cry.

"Oh!" Straightening, she turned back. "The child, my charge!"

All in the same instant, she felt the overpowering urge to cough and saw in the trees nearby a movement that did not belong to her secluded forest. Soldiers! *Nay, Vader, nay!* her heart cried out, while the cough took complete control of her. *Let them not find the newborn child in my shelter,* she prayed.

She must be still. All this noise simply called to the soldiers. What could she do? With supreme effort she tried to swallow the cough, to muffle it in her cape. It only grew worse. Her chest heaved and pained as if someone had plunged a dagger into it. In the background, she heard the baby's continued cries.

The soldiers were headed directly toward her now. In an eyeblink she knew what she must do. Her cough would distract them and save the child. Between coughs, she called out over her shoulder, "Go away! Go! The woods are filled with mad and angry spirits! Go!"

If only the child's parents would hear and heed the warning and the soldiers would hear and be superstitious enough to fear. Instead, the soldiers came closer.

She took off into the woods, running as fast as she could coax her legs to carry her. She ran on and coughed and coughed, the soldiers drawing closer with each step.

"They'll arrest me," she gasped, "and throw me into prison."

Prison? The memory seemed to give her new energy. If they put her there, she'd never again smell the forest bark and mold and trilliums or hear the wakening sparrows or refreshing breezes rustling through the branches of the giant spreading oaks, birches, and lindens.

Last year they'd taken her Meester van Keulen to the prison, and for no good reason. Something about taking part in the ugly image breaking in the Great Church. He didn't do it, that she knew. Much too gentle, he was, for that. Besides, he was in Gorcum that day.

At first they had let her visit him in the nasty prison. Each day she took him food and smuggled pages from his big Bible, folding and stuffing them inside the rolls of bread. Always she had smiled and tried to make him feel better, then had gone home and cried and vomited behind the garden wall.

When they no longer let her visit him, they came to take possession of his house and to cart her away to prison. But she'd seen them coming, and grabbing his big Bible and a few blankets, she had run out into the forest.

"*Halt!*" The soldiers were shouting at her now. Her chest ached, her legs felt as if they would buckle beneath her. Her head pounded and swam, and her cough never quit. How easy it would be to stop running. But *nay*, she must lead them so far away from that crying infant that they'd neither hear nor suspect his presence.

She ran on until she stumbled on a large tree root and fell into a heap on the edge of a thicket of brambles. She heard a voice shouting in heavy Spanish accent, "And who are you?" The words rang with disgusting glee.

From the background, another answered for her. "Lysbet de Vriend, *que no?*"

Laughter and shouts of triumph rang out through the forest.

"Betteke!"

"At last we found her!"

The whole pack swarmed over her. She felt hot breath on her forehead, rough hands ripping off her clothes, and pain, pain, pain! Then all went black, and she slipped from pain and fear and coughing into merciful oblivion.

30th day of Spring Month (March), 1568

Tante Lysbet passed her first night in the tower prison wrapped tightly in her long black cape and sitting huddled on a large low block of wood in a corner. The filthy straw-strewn floor beneath her feet sent cold shivers through her body. She hugged her knees, resting her head on her forearms and longing for warmth, the suspension of thought, and sweet soul-numbing sleep.

As if the heaven were deaf to her cry, her mind raced all night long, chasing after terrifying images—Spanish soldiers wrenching her from Vrouw de Smid's newborn infant, Gretta and Dirck Engelshofen laden with armloads of *verboden boecken.* . . .

"Moeder was wrong," she mumbled into her lap. "God does not vindicate every woman with a clear conscience. Either He is no longer watching—or He is no longer almighty!"

A strange tight feeling held her shoulders rigid, cramping her legs, and setting her teeth to chattering. The scenes in her mind turned bloody—an infant slain, Dirck and Gretta Engelshofen tied to a common stake, her own body paraded through the streets in disgrace toward a scaffold!

"God!" she shrieked out at last, "how can you stand by and let all this happen?"

From the opposite corner of the cell in a pile of straw came the voice of Lompen Mieke, Lysbet's single cell mate. "Hold yer mouth so's a body kin sleep!"

How could it be that she, the pious midwife, was forced to make her bed in a dungeon with this notorious thief? Could she not at least have been given some sort of likewise innocent companion so that they might console each other in their persecuted straits?

She fought to stay awake and watchful through the hours of the night and yearned for morning light. Off and on she heard Roland calling out the hour of the night. But the voice sounded muffled, as if strangling. Its mournful tone made the night drag more slowly and filled her with a soul-crushing heaviness.

The single torch burning from its holder on the wall sent ghostly shadows dancing through the rafters, around the walls, and into her face. When the torch had burned itself out and the first blush of new-sprung light shone through one of the two high windows in the cell, Lysbet heard a loud clanging of armor, a jingling of chains, and the sound of heavy voices approaching. Metal clanked on metal, and the door creaked open. She watched a pair of soldiers drag a woman into the cell and dump her like a bag of newly digged onions to the floor in the middle of the room. Without a backward glance, they marched out and bolted the door with a shuddering thud.

The crumpled woman lay so still that Lysbet rose from her place and knelt beside the silent form. "Great God," she prayed, "whoever she may be, don't let her be dead."

She lay her hand on a shoulder and felt warmth. Instantly, the woman began to cough. Deep, rattly, persistent, it set her whole body to trembling. Lysbet lifted her to her arms, brushed the matted hair back from a flushed young face, and gasped aloud.

"Betteke! Lysbet de Vriend!"

Under her breath, she mumbled, "I should have known she'd come to this state, alone out there in that shambled studio with no shelter, only damp and cold and nothing to sustain her but wild mushrooms and the pitiful rations I managed to send out to her every day. It was enough to give the dear poor child a deadly illness."

She sighed and shook her head as if to dislodge some persistent fogginess. "I thought she would at least be safe from her pursuers there. The place was so well hidden."

But God had deserted even this trusting, helpless soul. Angry at the enormity of the divine betrayal, Lysbet barked a command to Lompen Mieke in the midst of her straw pile. "Gather together all the clean straw you can find and make a bed for this poor sick woman."

"Why should I?" Mieke snapped.

"Because she's going to die if you don't. That's all the reason you need."

"But it's mine—all I got."

The pout in the shrill voice only increased Lysbet's anger. "Petulant thief," she stormed, "I don't care what you have and what you don't. If you can't find enough kindness in your heart to help save the life of an innocent woman who's being consumed by raw cold humors in her lungs, then you need a flogging, not a bed."

"But she never did nothin' fer me." Her tone had turned saucy.

Lysbet didn't say another word but breathed deeply, as if filling her entire body with all the strength that vengeance could provide. She got to her feet and walked to Mieke's side. Grabbing her by the arm, she lifted her off the straw and tried to remove her to the other side of the cell. But she could only go a pace or two, for the woman's leg was fastened with a wide iron band and secured to the wall by a heavy chain. She shoved her to one side and grabbed up all the straw she could by handfuls. She came back and pushed a now thrashing, shrieking Mieke out of her way again and again until she'd assembled a scanty bed for her suffering friend.

The guard flung open the door and shouted at Mieke, "Hold your abominable mouth, wretch!"

"She stole my bed," Mieke retorted, pointing an accusing finger at Lysbet.

A smirk spread over his face, and he spat in her direction. "So somebody stole something from you for a change. Hooray!" He pulled his sword from its sheath and brandished it under her nose. "Now, you either hold your mouth, or we'll have to help you do so, do you hear?"

Mieke retreated to her corner, sputtering and sniffling. An occasional obscene phrase punctuated her low grousing mumble after that, but she uttered no more screams.

Lysbet removed her own cape and spread it across the straw, then helped Betteke onto the makeshift bed and wrapped her the best she could. "Pay the insolent little thief no attention," she mumbled to her patient.

Then she called out to the retiring guard, "Heer gaoler, can you send a Beguine sister here to administer healing herbs to this sick prisoner?"

"Woman, I don't run no healin' place here. In case you forgot, this is a prison. Folks that need healin' should think about that before they do the unlawful deeds that send 'em here in the first place." Without pausing to hear her reply, he barged out of the cell.

"We've done nothing amiss," Lysbet protested. "At least a cup of water, given in the name of Jesus . . ."

She heard a titter from Mieke's corner and felt warmth rise in her cheeks and dignity well up in her throat. In the name of justice, they couldn't treat her like this.

She looked down into the distressed face of the orphan servant girl. She was red with an advanced *heatte* and racked with an incessant cough. Her eyes never opened but oozed tears. Lysbet cast a net into her mind for words of comfort and drew in nothing but anger. She held her tongue and simply smoothed the forehead and massaged the shoulders and hands. "I'm with you, child," she whispered, calmed herself by the gentle actions. "I'll do all I can."

In the meantime, her mind was doing what it did best—searching for a cure. A healing concoction of anise dried by fire and mingled with honey. Perfect for cleansing the heaviest breast of all phlegmatic super-fluities. If she could only get word to the Beguines, they would bring her the brew, poultices, blankets. . . .

Lysbet hovered over her patient, wishing, waiting, listening to the cough, wondering. . . . At regular intervals, now, she heard bells sounding from the Convent of the St. Catharina Sisters just outside the city wall beyond the tower. Was that where God had hidden himself?

When Lysbet had grown so hungry she felt certain she would soon collapse, a guard entered the cell bearing a hunk of black bread and a mug full of nondescript, lukewarm liquid for each prisoner. She put the liquid to Betteke's lips.

"Drink it, friend," she said. " 'Twill give you strength."

"Thank you," Betteke whispered, then drank it to the bottom of the mug. For a bit, her cough subsided just enough to allow her to drift into a fitful sleep.

No sooner had she fallen asleep, however, than two uniformed men with dark hair and thick mustachios burst into the cell. They carried long curved sabers at their belts. Heads held high, boots clicking, they stood over the sleeping woman and called out, "Lysbet de Vriend, in the name of His Majesty King Philip and his regent, the Duke of Alva, stand forth!"

Tante Lysbet gasped. "The woman is dreadfully ill," she said, "and sleeping soundly for the first time since they flung her to this floor at daybreak."

The soldiers laughed. "Too ill to answer questions that could save her life?" taunted one.

"Too ill for anything but sleep," she told him. "She has a dreadful case of oppressed lungs. If only you would send to the Beguines to bring some healing brews and poultices."

"We shall see how ill she is," the second man challenged, jabbing Betteke with the toe of his heavy boot.

Lysbet cringed and covered her mouth with both hands as she uttered a little distress cry. The soldier looked at her with stern steely eyes, then kicked the sleeping woman again.

"Wake up, young heretic!" he shouted.

Both men grabbed Betteke by the arms and pulled her to a sitting position. Lysbet watched the puffy eyes flutter.

"Tell us," the taller of the two soldiers demanded, "are you not Lysbet de Vriend, housekeeper of heretic, Pieter van Keulen?"

Her breath came heavy and shallow. She nodded and said in a voice so weak it was nearly inaudible, "Housekeeper to Pieter van Keulen."

The other soldier jabbed her in the ribs and ordered, "Speak up! We hear you not."

"*Ja, ja.* What did you say?" the other prodded with mock sweetness.

"I am," she began a bit louder, "housekeeper . . ." A spasm of coughing ripped through her.

"To the heretic, Pieter van Keulen?" the first soldier demanded.

"You stall, scullion," taunted the other.

"To Pieter van Keulen," she answered between coughs.

Jabbing her in the shoulder, the second soldier prodded her on. "And agree you that he is a heretic?"

"I know not what a heretic is," she protested, "but my meester is a man like God."

Both men laughed.

"Like God, was he, when he entered God's holy Great Church and took his axe to the statues and windows and destroyed all those priceless icons the men and women of Breda need to help them worship God?"

Tante Lysbet cringed as she watched Betteke labor to breathe. She reached out to her and laid a hand on the girl's forearm. "Easy, child."

A soldier shoved Tante Lysbet into the straw. "Hold your mouth, you witch," he growled.

Witch? The word resounded in her brain like an impossible nightmare. She righted herself and watched and listened, incredulous, as Lysbet de Vriend seemed at last to bring her cough under control.

"My meester never did the things you say," she said evenly.

"Was it not true that he refused to pray to the saints in the church?"

"He had no need of any of those things in order to worship God," she said with growing strength and coherence. "Jesus said, 'God is spirit and all who worship Him must worship in spirit and in truth.' He never mentioned icons."

"Where did you learn the words of Jesus?" the first soldier said with a jeer.

"Read them for myself."

"You read them?" He laughed, then turned to his companion. "You heard her? She read the words? A peasant orphan turned servant and she claims she can read."

The other soldier stooped down to her level, then balancing himself on bended knees and looking directly into her eyes, he challenged her. "Pray tell us, how did you learn to read? Your meester taught you, didn't he?"

"My Vader in the Heaven taught me," she answered simply.

Tante Lysbet listened with especial attention. She'd heard rumors of this story but had not quite believed what she heard.

"Come, tell us the truth," the kneeling soldier begged.

" 'Twas my moeder what first tried to teach me."

"Your moeder? She knew how to read?" the kneeling soldier asked.

Betteke smiled. "She was once a right fine moneyed woman, b'fore my vader died. Many times she tried to teach me. Said it was the most important thing in life for me to learn. But I was still so young an' couldn't seem to learn. Then one night she lay a-dyin'. . . ."

The standing soldier waved his hands before her and interrupted, "*Nay*. We want to hear how your meester taught you to read from the big Bible he kept hidden in a chest."

"But he didn't do that," Betteke insisted, her voice even, her eyes looking straight at him.

"Then we want to hear no more," he said.

Trying to gather evidence to silence van Keulen, Lysbet decided. Surely she was hearing sounds of evil spirits flitting about, cackling in her ear every time they passed her way.

The kneeling soldier raised a hand to silence the other. "*Nay*," he said, "but I very much want to hear the rest of this story." Then, turning toward Betteke, he said, "Go on, child."

Betteke smiled. "I was a sittin' by my moeder's bedside a-holdin' her hand and fearin' with all my innards. She'd been silent an' ever so still for a long, long while. Then, just before she closed them beautiful moeder eyes fer the last time, she looked hard at me an' said, 'Your Vader in the Heaven has written a treasured book. I saw one once in the hands of a travelin' preacher. I heard him read from its pages, and the words were more wonderful than anything I ever heard from another man's lips.'

"Then she grabbed me by the wrist an' said in her most beggin' tone, 'Ever' day you live, ask our Vader to give the Book to you.'

"I asked her how I'd know it when I saw it. 'He'll tell you, child,' she said.

"I asked her how I'd know to read it without her to teach me. I can't ever forget her answer. 'If'n He loves you enough to give it to you an' tell you what it is, think you He won't also teach you to read it?' "

"So," taunted the standing soldier, "when you going to tell us how Pieter van Keulen taught you to read his big Bible?"

Lysbet bristled. How dare he persist in trying to trap Betteke? She opened her mouth to come to her friend's defense. But Betteke was already speaking. "I can't never tell you that because it'll never be the truth."

"The truth!" He spit out the words. "What do you know about the truth? Anybody in their right mind knows God is not going to come down from heaven and teach anybody how to read. So whatever story you have to tell us is surely something your simple imagination has given you so you can defend your wicked meester."

Betteke hesitated for only an instant, then said, "The truth is, when one day I did find a copy of God's Book, I did what my moeder had told me to do. I begged my Vader, if the words in the big book were so important that He wanted me to know them, would He please show me what they said."

She paused and Tante Lysbet watched the man on bended knee before Betteke. A strange look—half disbelief, half wonder—spread across the dark face.

"And?" he prodded her. His companion still stood, shifting his weight back and forth from one leg to the other, tapping his fingers nervously on the sheath of his sword.

"The marks on the page stood straight an' tall like uniformed men," she went on. "In the beginnin', I remembered some of them what Moeder had showed me. Then all of the sudden, in my wonderin' mind, I fancied

I heard them sayin' a string of words more marvelous than anythin' I'd ever heard."

The standing soldier threw back his head and laughed a loud hollow laugh. A smile of derision curled his lips. "And what might those marvelous words be?"

Betteke lifted her head and met the smirky challenge in his eyes with a peaceful calm such as Lysbet had scarcely seen in anyone's face. "'The Lord is my Shepherd. I want for nothin',' " she recited. She raised a forefinger, pointed it in his direction, and added, "An' I can tell you it's true. I never want fer nothin'. Never!"

The man opened his mouth as if to taunt the girl. But no words came out and the smirk dissolved from his face. The prison cell fell utterly silent except for the faint sound of sniffles from Lompen Mieke's corner. The soldiers reminded Tante Lysbet of giant pig bladders once filled with air, now pricked by the point of their own sword and deflated. The kneeling man pushed himself to his feet with an air of almost reverence. Together, they slipped out the door, the one speechless, the other mumbling, "All we need for now . . . we'll be back. . . ."

Tante Lysbet gathered her young charge in her arms and whispered, "Betteke, Betteke." Then not knowing what more to say, she wept, pouring out heavy tears into the girl's long matted hair.

———————

Nighttime returned to the cell. Mieke crept as far into her corner as her leg-irons and chains would allow. Without a word about straw, she curled up on her cape and was soon snoring rhythmically.

"Pathetic creature!" Tante Lysbet whispered. Surely there must be something she could do for her. Then she remembered back to her early days in the Beguinage, how she and the other Beguines had tried teaching the girl to care for herself and others. But she only robbed their stores and misused the sisters until they despaired of helping her. *Nay,* Lysbet had done all she could.

She turned to help Betteke settle in for the night.

"Sorry it couldn't have been softer and warmer," Tante Lysbet muttered.

"Most comfortable I've had since I left Meester van Keulen's," Betteke whispered. "You've treated me most kindly this day, and I shall give thanks to my Vader in the Heaven."

Even after the servant girl's breathing grew more steady and sleeplike, she coughed sporadically.

If only I had the herbs to make her well! Lysbet mused. Maybe God will have mercy yet. *Nay*, she told herself, *God does not visit this tower.*

In her mind, she heard a soft reprimand. *Ah, but He has visited you here this day.*

"How?" Lysbet challenged the voice aloud.

The answer came back, *In His strange and beautiful little Betteke!*

Lysbet knew it was true. Still, she trusted no one and determined to keep awake to be sure all stayed in order. She stationed herself on the block of wood where she'd spent her previous night and prepared to sit this one out as well.

Somewhere in the middle of deep thoughts about the amazing power in Betteke's simple, uneducated trust in the Vader in the Heaven, Lysbet slipped into a dream world. Peopled with Spanish soldiers, Beguine sisters, and laughing children, it didn't make a lot of sense, but old Lucas van den Garde hobbled around through all the scenes, smiling and using his paintbrush to put a dot of color on everyone's nose. He had just touched the end of her nose with the bristles of his brush when she heard a rustling in the straw beside her and shook herself quickly awake.

Straining her eyes in the faint torchlight, she made out a figure in long full cape crouching beside Betteke. She heard voices whispering and cocked her ears to catch it all.

"A gift from the Beguines," she heard the incredible words. "Your friend will know how to use it?"

"Praise be to my Vader," Betteke replied.

Lysbet strained to see the visitor's face. Which Beguine might it be, and how did she know to bring the herbs? A shiver tripped down her back.

"Can you tell me again those words from God's book? I never heard anything so beautiful. Must learn them for myself."

Tante Lysbet felt the hairs stand erect on the back of her neck. Deep down inside, her mind screamed out, *Betteke, Betteke, hush. It's an inquisitor come to trap you!*

Almost as if she'd heard, the girl didn't respond to the question. Instead she made some shuffling noises Lysbet could not identify. Then she heard the visitor whisper, "Nay, you cannot give me your precious pages."

Nay, indeed! What was Betteke doing?

"Take them if you'll read and learn them. I've already carved them into my heart."

"How kind of you! Rest well."

The mock gentleness sent terror to Lysbet's soul. In a sort of benumbed silence, she watched the figure slip out the door. Betteke lay back down and began once more to cough.

Tante Lysbet rose and went to her patient. "Your gift from the Beguines—let me see and apply it. Your body needs it badly."

"You heard?" Betteke asked between coughs.

"I did," Tante Lysbet said. She trembled as she examined the row of bottles lying in the straw beside her. She uncorked each one and sniffed at its contents to satisfy herself that they were genuine. Anise seed, honey, and the poultice of horseradish. Everything she would have ordered. Whatever his devious plan might be, the visitor had indeed been to the Beguinage. She lifted the large jug filled with brew and smelled its contents. "Black mullein boiled in wine," she said. "Perfect for loosening raw humors and bringing an end to the *heatte* and the cough and spittings of corrupt rotten matter that so torment you."

She set to work mixing and administering all the familiar herbs, excitement rippling through her body, visions of a healed Betteke bursting in her mind.

"How did it happen that he brought these things to you?" she asked.

"My Vader sent him," Betteke said simply.

"And what did you give him in return?"

"The page from the Holy Book where it says, 'The Lord is my Shepherd.'"

Tante Lysbet shivered. "I hope he does not use it as evidence against you."

"Why should he?"

Tante Lysbet marveled at the trusting, loving soul that flowered with such beauty and fragrance in this plain orphan girl. How could she tell her that this man's job was to catch in traps all who did not hold faithfully to the doctrines and traditions of the Papist church, especially those who read and cherished pages from God's Book?

"Beware, my child," she said simply. "Such soldiers are trained in the deceptive arts."

Betteke grabbed her by both hands, looked full into her eyes, her own face the picture of a contentment such as Tante Lysbet had never experienced in all her struggling life. "You've kindly warned me, friend, an' I thank you. But methinks you mustn't know how powerful are the words I gave that man tonight. God himself says His words are like a sword that pierces men's hearts and makes them want to repent and be rescued from their sinful ways."

"I only hope you're right." Tante Lysbet sighed. "They must let you go free. You have so much love to give to this warring world."

"God an' I know I've done nothin' deservin' of the stake, but if these wicked men choose not to listen to His voice, He'll give me the strength to die like a brave soldier for His cross."

"Here," Lysbet said, removing her hands from the girl's grip. "We must finish with the herbs. Lie down now and let me spread the poultice on your rattly chest."

As Tante Lysbet worked, Betteke spoke again. "One thing more. Don't you forget it. Whatever that man may do with the paper I gave him, I shall go to my death prayin' my Vader in the Heaven will not leave him alone till he cries out to Him to be his Shepherd too."

All through the night, Betteke slept without a cough. From Mieke's corner Lysbet detected a never ceasing succession of gentle weeping sounds.

CHAPTER THREE

Emden

6th day of Flower Month (May), 1568

*P*ieter-Lucas knocked on the door of Hans' house and struggled with an uncomfortable combination of excitement and dread. Inside he would find Aletta preparing herbal cures with Oma Roza and her granddaughters. But he had not come to see Aletta!

Oma ushered him in. The big room was filled with steam and the aroma of brewing herbal potions. He shuffled across the floor to the far end. All the way, he gazed at Aletta and she at him with the sort of intensity they might expect if they knew they were not to see each other again for a long, long while.

With one final glance at his betrothed, Pieter-Lucas shoved open the secret door behind Hans' weaving loom and entered the bare-walled meeting room of the Children of God. His heart beat an apprehensive pattern in his chest as he walked toward the row of elders seated on benches facing the table below the high bare windows.

The abrupt silencing of their low-pitched conversation sent him a familiar disquieting message. Over a month ago now, Pieter-Lucas had given Hans one more week to arrange permission to set his wedding date. They'd chosen, instead, to bring him back here to this place every week and question him until they were satisfied that he was ready.

Always the sessions ended the same way. Hans would say, "You are learning well. Come back in one more week."

They had repeated this now for five weeks. Each week, Pieter-Lucas determined not to submit to the maddening examination any longer. Then he went home and ate dinner at Dirck Engelshofen's table and simply could not find it in himself to threaten to take this kindly man's daughter away by stealth. So each week he returned and answered more questions.

Pieter-Lucas seated himself and surveyed the group of men. Next to Hans sat the chief elder, tall, grayed, stern. His questions always made Pieter-Lucas feel small and ignorant. Beside him was Johannes, the printer, married to Aletta's moeder's sister, a fiery man with a sharp nose and firm ideas. Being a part of Aletta's family, he was not allowed to help them decide the matter, but he could ask as many questions as he liked, and he seemed to delight in making the young man uncomfortable.

Then came the weaver who lived behind Hans. Next to him sat the fisherman who had lost an arm in a boating accident. He always smiled and tried to soften the hard words from some of the others. Finally, on a bench by himself and leaning on a cane, sat the gnarled little old man everybody called *Oude Man*. He didn't hear well and always asked to have everything repeated. Then he'd look serious while he stroked his white beard. Almost without exception, he'd end up nodding his approval to whatever the others decided. "Wise decision," he would say with an air of irrefutable authority.

What questions would Pieter-Lucas be asked this day?

"Who was Jesus?"

"How can one have salvation?"

"What is the meaning of baptism? The taking of a civic oath?"

"I've already given you all the answers," he wanted to shout. "Just let me have my bride." He sat quietly waiting, but his toe tapped insistently on the straw.

Hans broke the silence by clearing his throat. Rubbing his hands together, he looked at Pieter-Lucas. "Almost we have made the decision you are waiting for. First, two more questions." He gestured toward the fisherman.

The man straightened his body on the bench, laid his single arm on his knee, and asked, "I want to know, in the years ahead, when God blesses your union with a son, what will you teach him about our doctrine of nonresistance?"

Pieter-Lucas said without hesitation, "No son of mine will ever carry a sword—only a paintbrush!"

"Nor will you carry one?" Hans added.

"Never have I. Never shall I!"

The elders nodded their heads slightly, and *Oude Man* mumbled, "Wise words, young man, wise words indeed."

Then the chief elder spoke. "I, too, have one final question." He stared at Pieter-Lucas with an unsettling expression. "When you have married one of our young women, you will become a part not only of her family but also of the larger family of the Children of God. Are you prepared to become one of us, in heart and mind and purpose, to live with us and die with us?"

Pieter-Lucas felt his heart stop and perspiration run down his neck. The question was filled with blind alleys and branch-covered traps. He must begin on safe terrain.

"As I learned from you, I trust the blood of Jesus Christ as the only work acceptable by God to earn my salvation."

The elder nodded. "That means, then, that you trust not in the sacraments or in confessing your sins to a priest to save your soul from eternal damnation?"

"*Ja,*" Pieter-Lucas agreed.

"But what of living with us here? I hear it rumored that you cherish plans of pursuing a life work that will take you and your wife away from our community, perhaps cause you to live where there are no others of our like faith."

Pieter-Lucas looked at each face and considered his words carefully. "Before my opa died, I was anointed in the Great Church of Breda for a special job in God's world," he began. "Opa told me I was to use the gift of painting to bring about healing in a world ruled by the sword. If I am to pursue this calling, I must do my apprenticeship. I know not where that will take me. But wherever I go, I am prepared to live by the faith you and Hans have taught me, to live as one of the Children of God."

"And to encourage and instruct your wife and children to do the same?"

"That is my intent."

"But are you ready to face death for the crime of being a baptized Child of God?" Johannes pressed the point, his whole being astir.

Pieter-Lucas felt six pairs of eyes fastened on him. He must speak his heart. "From the safety of this place I could easily say, *ja,* I am ready," he confessed, "and mean it with all my heart."

"You will say it then?" Johannes prodded him.

Pieter-Lucas stared at his circle of interrogators. Aware that his answer to this one heart-wrenching question could finally cost him the thing he'd waited so long to gain, he phrased his answer with especial care. "I've heard that many of the Children of God, especially in the early years when persecution was a daily occurrence, welcomed the martyr's sword—some even sought it. If that is what is required of me, then I fear I shall never be ready. I think I would be willing to die if need be, but until I stand before a Papist who is pointing a sword at me, waiting for my brave words to incriminate me, I can never know for sure."

The men sat stunned, then broke into a buzz of conversation. Finally, above the hubbub of the discussion, *Oude Man's* cane pounded on the floor, and his authoritative voice spoke. "Truer words have never been heard in this place." He raised his cane and pointed it at each man in turn. "Is there a man among us," he challenged, "who could truthfully answer such a question before he reaches the moment when that answer will determine whether he lives or dies?"

Only the mad beating of Pieter-Lucas' heart broke the silence that held the room in its grip for a long space. Then *Oude Man* spoke again. "I am ready to welcome this honest young man into our company."

"I, as well," added the fisherman, nodding with his whole body.

One by one the men agreed with the *Oude Man* except for the chief elder, who stared at him again and asked, "So you know what it means to become one of us in every part of your life, and you are ready to do so?"

Pieter-Lucas bristled inside. "As far as a man can know." He held his breath and waited. What more could there be?

The tall straight man nodded toward Hans, who spoke for the group. "Pieter-Lucas, on the basis of your confession of faith in Jesus Christ and your commitment to the doctrines found in His Holy Scriptures, we are ready to give you both baptism and marriage."

"How soon?" Pieter-Lucas asked.

"Before Flower Month has ended," Hans said, a smile lifting the corners of his patriarchal beard and a sparkle coming from his warm brown eyes.

"This month?" Pieter-Lucas exclaimed.

"We entrust you and your soon-to-be bride to God's protective care," Hans said, a hearty smile rounding off the corners of his bearded mouth.

In an eyeblink Pieter-Lucas' whole world came to life with light and bird songs and new hope. With great effort he restrained himself from giving vent to the full enthusiasm filling him. He smiled on them all and said with as much reserve as he could muster, "To you all, a hearty thanks!"

Hans smiled. "You may go now, *jongen*. I think you bear some good news that your betrothed will be eager to hear."

———

Once Pieter-Lucas had passed through the room, Aletta continued to work at Oma Roza's roughhewn table, spread with bunches of dried herbs and an assortment of jars and mixing paddles. But her heart refused to be tethered to the task.

Two terrifying questions consumed her attention and determined the pace at which her heart beat. If the elders finally decided that Pieter-Lucas' faith was not good enough to qualify him as a member of their church, would Vader Dirck let her marry him anyway? If not, what would she do?

Once before her vader had separated them. She would never forget the anguish in her soul when Vader Dirck, fearing reprisals by association with Hendrick van den Garde, the image-breaker, had refused to let her see Pieter-Lucas. Then he'd taken the whole family far away, and she and Pieter-Lucas spent months wondering whether they would ever find each other.

She could not let him do it again! But to disobey her vader and leave her family in order to marry Pieter-Lucas. . . ?

Great God in the Heaven, let me never face such impossible choices, she cried out in her soul as she went on crushing herbs, stirring brews, mixing potions, and speaking to no one.

By the time the secret door opened, Aletta was faint with apprehension. But one look at Pieter-Lucas' face, lightened as if by some inner flame, and a new strength surged through her. She abandoned her place at the table and rushed across the room to him. "They said *ja?*" she shouted.

He grabbed both her hands in his. "The questions are over. You are to be mine!"

"But when?"

"Before this month is ended!" His words sounded like the ringing of a golden bell.

She clapped a hand over her mouth and squealed. "Oh, Pieter-Lucas!" Then turning toward Oma, she began, "Oma . . ."

The older lady was smiling, waving a hand, shaking her head, and speaking. "Now, go to home. The girls and I will finish the work."

Aletta gasped. "Thank you, Oma," she said, reaching for her cape and slipping her feet into the street shoes beside the door.

Hand in hand, the almost-bride-and-bridegroom stepped out into the street where a spring shower had newly passed. It left the cobblestones shiny and turned the sky into a blue field dotted with billowy white clouds. Above the bright red tile rooftops, a pale swath of rainbow colors spread, as if from a celestial paintbrush.

"A promise in the heaven!" Aletta exclaimed.

"Remember the day you first promised to wait with me for this day?" Pieter-Lucas asked. He wrapped an arm around her waist.

Aletta laughed. "Out in that old deserted animal shed, and you dressed in a monk's disguise. You were going out to find Hendrick for your moeder, and I was frightened half to death."

Pieter-Lucas gave her a squeeze, and she snuggled up close till she felt the vibrations of his chest as he talked.

"And I thought I would be home within a few days. *Ach!* How much we both had to learn about life and promises." He sighed. "The darkness of those months was like a long winter night—cold, starless, desolate. . . ."

Aletta pulled back from his embrace to smile at him. "That's all past now! It's only a bad dream, fading quickly into the shadows of night." The gorgeous and cozy "now" wrapped her up and bound her to her smiling soon-to-become bridegroom.

"*Ja, ja,*" he said. "It's so near I can hear it whispering delights in my ear. Then I'll be through with title pages forever, and we'll ride off to Dillenburg and the Julianas' herb garden." His voice sounded as if it were floating toward the soaring clouds above.

"You'll never be content to spend the rest of your days drawing and painting little pictures of herbs for the prince's sister!" Aletta knew he would always chafe until set free with a full palette of paints and huge canvases.

"Only till the war is over," he reminded her. "Then off to Leyden to study with the great painters who learned from Lucas van Leyden. Opa promised it, and so has Juliana. *Ah!* But our wedding brings us one step closer!"

"Always I dreamed of our wedding day," she said, "even when we were children and you were carving all those marvelous little wooden animals and drawing all those creatures with my initials intertwined among the horns and whiskers, tails and noses."

"Whatever did you dream about weddings back then?"

"Oh," she said, her mind whirling with pleasant memories. "Fragrant candles, glowing jewel-like windows, rich paintings, soul-stirring strains from the big old organ, an elegant black gown, and a wreath of summer flowers plucked fresh from your moeder's garden. I planned it all a hundred times!"

"Not quite the way it's going to be, I fear," Pieter-Lucas said, kicking a stone ahead of them in the cobbled street.

She sighed. "I know it can never be so grand and splendrous as I'd planned. Such dreams are childhood fancies."

He shrugged. "Dreams don't make a wedding, my love. A clergyman and two hearts ready to become one—what more can we ask?" The sound of his voice and the adoration sparkling in his eyes made her heart skip nearly out of control.

One more house lay between them and their destination. Under the gigantic spread of a budding oak tree, Pieter-Lucas stopped and whirled her around to face him. He lifted her chin with his forefinger and said, "I only wish it were today!"

He had a fanciful lilt in his voice, a dreamy look in his eyes. Breathless, trembling, torn between desire and fear, she stood dumb before him. For an instant, nothing seemed as important as being close to Pieter-Lucas. Then she heard the sound of not-too-far-distant footsteps and pulled free from his grasp.

"We've only a little while," she said softly.

In whispered tones, he added, "Then we shall be forever free from delayed promises and prying eyes."

While her heart beat wildly, she reached out her hand to him and urged, "Come, let's go home before some elder finds us lingering too long beneath this tree and changes his mind."

Breda
15th day of Flower Month (May), 1568

Tante Lysbet lay on her back on a bed of stale straw, both hands pillowing her head. She stared out the high barred window at a sky turning pale blue in the light of dawn. The silence of the dingy cell was broken only by the song of birds in the trees below and the raspy breathing of Betteke at her side.

"How many weeks has it been since we've seen a tree or a bird?" she mused.

If she were alone in this unjust suffering, stoicism might come easier. After all, she was an old woman with a life that had been filled with opportunities to lend her hands to the assistance and healing of others.

But Betteke here—young, pious, compassionate—was forced to spend her dwindling energies in an undeserved confinement, struggling just to take a breath. Where was justice for her? Lysbet looked across the cell at the spot where Lompen Mieke had been chained earlier. Impudent, greedy, caring only to hurt others. After one short week in this place, the guards had set her free to go pick pockets once more. Lysbet choked back the emotions that shattered her stoicism. Betteke was coughing again.

The cell door opened and a pompous procession of official personages swaggered through. They came every day. Heartless in their persistence, they plied both Lysbets with questions designed to intimidate them into a confession that would make them appear worthy of death.

"Bloodlusting tormentors!" Lysbet fumed inaudibly.

This morning the procession was led by a jurist in billowing black robes, hung with a floor-length cowled sash of crimson velvet. He came to a stop directly above Betteke and ordered, "Stand forth, woman, and hear the judgment of the courts."

Still not fully awake, her whole body convulsing with deep coughing, Betteke struggled to raise herself to her elbows. The judge was not satisfied.

"On your feet, woman," he barked.

"Have you no mercy?" Lysbet pleaded.

The soldiers flanking the judge on both sides stepped forward, their halberds gleaming in the ray of sun that filtered through the dust and grime of the windowpane. They lowered their weapons and pointed them in her direction.

The judge sneered. "If you're so concerned about mercy, show a little yourself. Drag her to her feet."

Lysbet hesitated, breathing deeply, trying to calm the anger that burned in her bosom. *God*, her heart cried, *if you're anywhere in this cell, please help.*

The judge kicked at Lysbet and shouted, "Make haste, you dallying hag."

At his signal the soldiers moved closer, till their halberd blades hovered so near she fancied she felt them indenting the sides of her head-dress. Deliberately, she ignored them and bent over Betteke. Slipping the girl's arms around her neck and grasping her with her own arms, she struggled to her feet. When Betteke could no longer hold on to her neck, Lysbet maneuvered herself around to support her from the back, lifting her up by the armpits. With enormous effort, she bit her tongue and refrained from shouting at the judge to make his own haste before they both fainted fast away.

"That's more like it," he gloated.

Then he pulled from his pocket a scroll, untied its cord with a flourish, and cleared his throat with disgusting affectedness.

Lysbet buried her face in Betteke's headdress and prayed, *Great God, if you have a drop of mercy left for this poor innocent woman, then allow her not to hear the awful words about to be poured out upon her ears.*

Already the judge was reading as if his document were a declaration of triumph over his last great enemy. But Betteke's cough did not slacken, and her body sagged in Lysbet's arms.

"Whereas the examiners have investigated Lysbet de Vriend in great detail," the dull voice began, "and whereas she freely offered to one of the inquisitors a page of the *verboden boeck*, the Holy Bible, in her moeder tongue."

Lysbet cringed, remembering that awful night, wishing she'd found a way to stop her unsuspecting friend from making that one fatal error, yet knowing it would not have been enough to save her life.

"And whereas her master, Pieter van Keulen, condemned to heresy for participation in the image-breaking of Harvest Month, 1566, has confessed to having heard of her participation in same image-breaking proceedings; and whereas the city magistrates have reviewed the facts and witnesses to this case, and the Council of Troubles has pronounced said Lysbet de Vriend guilty of desecrating the sanctuary of the Great Church of Breda by trampling the sacred host of the Eucharist under foot on the day of the image-breaking riots; His Highness, the Duke of Alva, has determined that Lysbet Jacobsdochter de Vriend of Breda is condemned to death by burning at the stake."

All through the reading, Betteke coughed without a break, then stopped short. Lysbet felt a tear trickle across her cheek. *God*, she prayed, *you finally visited this unholy place and answered one prayer.*

"Woman," the judge roared one more time at Betteke, "have you heard the words my lips have read to you?"

"As my Heavenly Vader has willed," Betteke said, "so be it unto this His handmaiden."

"You shall learn the depths of the mercy of both His Majesty King Philip, and the Duke of Alva," the judge offered, his smile too broad and his voice too honeyed to be trusted. "Every day between now and your execution, a priest shall come to you and offer you the opportunity to repent and be reinstated into the Holy Catholic Religion. If you are wise, you will heed his words so that you may save your soul from eternal damnation after your body has been reduced to ashes."

As pompously as Betteke's cruel tormentors had come, they paraded out of the cell without a backward glance.

Lysbet laid her patient out on the straw with all the gentleness her strength would allow. Betteke smiled up at her. "My Vader knows I didn't do it, and He'll help me die with peace an' joy. An' the man I gave the promises to can never forget them—never, never, never."

Lysbet grabbed a cracked dirty mug and offered it to her patient. She cringed as she put it to the girl's lips and prayed, "God have mercy once again."

Almost she believed He would do it.

CHAPTER FOUR

Emden

21st day of Flower Month (May), 1568

*I*n the midst of the 'tFalder section of Emden's rutted streets stood the house of Johannes, the printer, and his brother-in-law, Dirck Engelshofen, the bookseller. On the back side of the building, a steep narrow stairway led up the alley wall to the unmarked upper-story rooms where the two men ran *Abrams en Zonen*.

The roughly glazed windowpanes in the topmost story let in but little of the cloudy daylight and even less of the perpetual breezes. Pieter-Lucas bent low over the drawing table in his attic cubicle. He wiped sweat from beneath the straw-colored curls that hung over his forehead and struggled to keep his eyes from drooping shut.

"Come on, *jongen*," he snapped. "Just a few more strokes and you'll have this irksome title page done."

He jabbed his pen into the inkwell before him. If only it were a brush and a full palette of paints—rich ochres, brilliant vermilions, blues and greens. . . . It was paint that ran in his blood, not printer's ink.

"*Abrams en Zonen*," he scrawled across the bottom of the page. Not that it was operated by Abrams and his sons. The name was a disguise designed to give no clue either to the names of the owners or to the nature of their religious persuasion. The Children of God were masters at this kind of survival deception. With one more dip of the pen, he finished it off with the date, "MDLXVIII." The action was as mechanical as climbing the stairs to this daily meeting with discontent.

Last fall he'd been hired to draw cartoons for the books printed here. At least that was what Dirck Engelshofen had told him. To his disappointment, he soon learned that the books in this printshop seldom required a cartoon but always a title page. So title pages were his domain.

What dull projects they were! Like the books themselves, mostly small booklets or polemical pamphlets created to spread the doctrine of the new faith. Nothing like the ones he used to admire in *The Crane's Nest* back in Breda, with their elaborate designs and letters scrolled into exquisite pictures. Whenever Pieter-Lucas tried to insert even a small design or add a flourish to a letter, Johannes would send him back to his cubicle to "do it right." That meant taking all the joy and beauty out of it.

"Only the message counts." The short little man with pointed nose and piercing voice repeated this phrase to settle every dispute. It was enough to drive an artist into a shrieking fit.

"Six more days!" Pieter-Lucas laid down his pen with a sigh, uncoiled his torso, and extended his arms in a muscle-bulging stretch. "Aletta Engelshofen will soon be mine, and I'll take her and my paintbrushes and be gone from this dreary printshop forever!"

Pieter-Lucas blew on the page before him. Satisfied that the ink was dry, he got to his feet and straightened slowly. Ever since he'd been attacked while trying to defend Opa's painting in the Great Church in Breda, he'd had to struggle with a lame leg. Not as bad as Opa's leg after his encounter with the madman in the alley, yet it did cause an occasional discomfort and a perpetual limp.

"I'm too young to hobble," he sputtered.

With strong fingers, he massaged the leg until it consented to carry him with the freshly completed title page down a flight of stairs to the big room. Here, half a dozen men worked at their jobs—engraving plates, proofing text, operating the printing press, assembling and wrapping books. In the far corner by the bookshelves sat Gillis, Johannes' orphan servant, teaching six-year-old Robbin Engelshofen to read.

Pieter-Lucas approached his future father-in-law. Seated on a bench in the proofreaders' nook, Dirck Engelshofen was a straight tallish man with a clean-shaven chin, precisely trimmed mustachio, and pearly gray eyes.

He'd barely laid the title page on the table when there came a muffled knock on the door that led into the bookshop. The entire room fell into a lightning-strike silence. No one ever knocked on that door. Friends and family walked through it. Customers rang a little bell on the counter in the bookshop. Strangers did not know about the hidden stairway that led up to it from the alley.

To Pieter-Lucas, the secrecy of the bookmaking and bookselling business seemed strange in Emden. This was a city of refuge, where religious groups of every kind lived side by side in relative peace. Yet all were refugees who had been chased from somewhere else and feared to trust each other. He'd heard it said that Emden was known as the nest where Anabaptist eggs were hatched and given wings to fly all over the world.

Dirck Engelshofen moved quickly across the room and opened the door a crack. From the other side a deep voice simply asked, *"Abrams en Zonen?"*

Pieter-Lucas started. The inquirer knew the name! What about the purpose?

"And who would you be, if you please?" Dirck Engelshofen asked in reply.

"My name is Dirck. . . ." The voice trailed off as if the man had debated whether to say more and decided against it.

That voice! Where had Pieter-Lucas heard it before? He moved forward to get a closer look. Neither tall nor short, the man carried himself in his dark suit and cloak like a gentleman. He had a well-creased face with a broad sculpted nose and a mouth that resembled two short straight lines pinched together in the middle. Slipped into the frame of a perfectly trimmed white beard, it gave the impression of hiding beneath the wide floppy brim of his dark square-topped hat. Though his eyes were a soft brown color, they revealed a soul that was neither soft nor settled. Pieter-Lucas had seen them before somewhere. But where?

"Dirck. . . ?" Dirck Engelshofen left an obvious blank space for the visitor to fill in.

"*Ja*, that it is." The man paused. "I've been told you have a book-producing enterprise here, and I have brought something which I trust you will be willing to help me distribute. 'Tis a document of great importance to all who champion the cause of freedom in the Low Lands."

The man reached into a black bag hanging from his waist and shortly produced a pamphlet. Before he could put it into the hands of Dirck Engelshofen, Johannes shoved his way between the men and pulled the door open a trifle wider.

He reached for the pamphlet and read aloud with a studiedly officious tone, *"The Justification of the Prince van Oranje"*—Johannes glanced up at his caller, then went on—*"against the false lies, by means of which their perpetrators seek to accuse him of injustice."*

"Our Prince Willem van Oranje?" Pieter-Lucas asked, his body edging toward the door. "How did you come by this document?" He heard the words tumbling from his mouth and looked into the stranger's penetrating eyes.

Before the startled man could answer, Pieter-Lucas pointed a finger toward him and blurted out, "We've met before in the dungeon of Batestein castle. You persuaded Brederode to free my friend Yaap and me."

The man's mouth softened into a faint smile, and he made as if he would speak. But Johannes had a firm hand on Pieter-Lucas' shoulder, shoving him back into the room. "*Nay*," he interrupted, "we do not find your document of any importance in this place."

He began to shut the big door, but Pieter-Lucas grabbed and held it forcibly open. "Listen to the man, Johannes," he pleaded.

"At the least, we might let him tell us the purpose for this," Dirck Engelshofen interjected, his tone conciliatory.

Johannes stood with feet apart, hands planted on his hips, and glared at them both. "What think you two?" he demanded. "We are not in the business of entertaining strangers who come unbidden onto our premises, armed with pretty-looking pamphlets that bear the trusted name of some popular exiled prince."

"But I told you, this man is no stranger," Pieter-Lucas insisted.

"What know you about him?"

"He saved my life. If he hadn't pleaded my cause before Count Brederode, I'd have been left to rot in that old Beggar's dungeon."

"So?" Without another word, Johannes shoved the door shut and leaned his short rotund body squarely against it.

Johannes was usually a mild-mannered man. When once riled, though, he reminded Pieter-Lucas of a wild animal resisting capture.

"Let him in," Pieter-Lucas pleaded.

"Like a fox into a hen house? What sort of fool do you take me for, *jongen*?"

"He is no fox. He's a good man." Pieter-Lucas towered over him, glaring. His whole body trembled. "Either let him in or let me out!"

Pieter-Lucas watched the sweat beads pour over Johannes' balding head and dribble down from under his flat tam cap. The man stood resolute and for a time said nothing, only muttered unintelligible words under his mustache. Then, with a manner as markedly calm as he had been agitated minutes earlier, he stepped back from the door and said, "Go then, if you must. Just remember, under the thatched roof of this shop, I am the master and not accustomed to allowing my employees to come and go at will."

Pieter-Lucas hesitated only long enough to breathe in deeply and look back over his shoulder. Dirck Engelshofen had returned to his worktable but gazed intently at him. In the expression in his eyes and the quick flash of a smile, the young man saw concern and approval, covered with a gauzy mask of warning.

"I'll be back soon," he said, then went through the door and limped down the stairs into the drizzly alley below. He looked first to one side, then to another, mumbling, "Which way did he take?"

Hesitating only an eyeblink, he dashed off over slippery cobblestones toward the lowering sun. At the far end of the alley, he searched in all directions. No sight of the dark cloak, the full white beard, or that distinctive broad-brimmed hat. As he stood, the heavens opened and dumped a heavy cloudburst that sent him backing into the shelter of an overhanging doorway.

"*Jongen.*" A voice at once deeply resonant and greatly restrained startled him.

Pieter-Lucas felt the protective pressure of a hand on his left shoulder. He glanced sharply back and straight into the bearded face he had been so furiously seeking.

"*Heer* Dirck?" he gasped.

"Be still," the man warned, unsmiling. "Follow me. Not on my heels, but at the distance and speed of a large lumbering coach."

His cryptic message delivered, the man crept out into the continuing rain. Pieter-Lucas followed as he'd been instructed. Up one street and down another he sloshed through the deepening puddles, careful to keep the outline of the dark cloak and flat-topped hat in sight. All went well until the cloak tails disappeared to the right. When Pieter-Lucas drew near the spot where he calculated that the man had turned off, he found no street. And not one of the identical shop fronts stood ajar or gave other indication that the man intended him to follow that way.

Pieter-Lucas wiped at the raindrops running over the narrow band on his hat and washing his face. Why did he feel so compelled to go on with this secretive following of a man he'd only once met in a drafty pest-ridden dungeon? Renewed thoughts of Aletta and their wedding challenged his logic. For all his protestations to Johannes, he had to admit that the shadowy figure of the man he'd been following through the now diminishing rain was far more a stranger than an acquaintance.

He halted in the middle of a puddle and pondered the course of reason. "You don't have to go on, *jongen*," he said in a voice so low he scarcely heard it himself. "No one is pursuing you at knife point." Involuntarily, he looked back over his shoulder to make sure his statement was true.

Perhaps Johannes had been right. He knew not where he was going nor who he was following nor where the pathway would lead him. And what would Aletta say when he didn't return? Once before he'd left her to pursue an errand of mercy. Misfortune had befallen him, and he didn't see her face again for months. He couldn't do that again.

At that instant he noticed a narrow space between the buildings. It was one of those mysterious, nearly hidden alleyways of the sort that used to both fascinate and terrorize him when he was a child. Many were the evil plots he imagined to be directed against him at such spots. Almost like a crack in the wall, it opened up, barely wide enough for a body to slip through sidewise. Did he dare to try it? Was it a trap?

Before he could make up his mind, he felt a strong hand on his arm tugging him into the alley and heard a hoarse whisper in his ear. "This way, *jongen*, this way."

Without thinking, he jerked free and prepared to run. The man who had stopped him held him firmly. "Fear not," he said. "No danger here."

Pieter-Lucas prodded himself toward composure. A Van den Garde may never wield a sword. But one thing he would never be was a coward—it mattered not what Hendrick had said about it.

To his surprise, Pieter-Lucas found that the way down the tight little alley still held a trace of the charm of his childish forays. He had to remind himself he was a man now, following the lead of a man. This was a real adventure—no imaginary escapade. Together he and Dirck made their way between tall brick walls until they came at last to a dead end. The man in front rapped gently on a small door on the left wall. Pieter-Lucas shivered with excitement in the cool dampness of impending twilight.

Then, all in a flurry, the door opened and the shadowy man pulled Pieter-Lucas up a tightly curved flight of worn stairs. A buxom matron led the way, carrying a lighted lamp and babbling continuously, grousing about her bothersome visitor and his irresponsible ways that were unbefitting a gentleman of his station. The air smelled of stale pipe tobacco, musty books, and sour cabbage. At the top of the stairs, the woman handed the man her lamp and left them. They climbed on up into an attic room with neither doors nor windows. It was heated by the chimney passing through from the lower floors.

The man gestured for Pieter-Lucas to sit on the three-legged stool at one side of a small table, where he set the lamp. Then he removed the pack from his shoulder beneath his cloak and sat on the other stool. He rested his elbows on the table and looked intently at Pieter-Lucas.

"The day we first met in Old Brederode's dungeon seems like an eon ago." *Heer* Dirck smiled weakly and never moved his gaze from Pieter-Lucas' face.

"You remember me?" The possibility left him unsure whether to admire the man or fear him. The smile may be disarming and the eyes gentle, but they held a restlessness that pierced clear through their object.

"Stepson of the Beggar Hendrick van den Garde," he answered evenly.

Pieter-Lucas gasped in reply and shifted his hands abruptly to his lap.

"I never forget a mistreated prisoner," the man continued, "having been one myself. Falsely accused, you were, even as I."

"You said this afternoon that your name is Dirck. I should remember more."

"For now that's quite enough. As for me, I've no need to ask you either your name or the nature of the journey that brought you to this place . . ." Dropping his voice to a whisper, he added, "From Breda and Dillenburg."

"You're telling me you came not to *Abrams en Zonen* on a whim, then."

He shook his head slowly while the flickering light flashed rays of silver through the white wool of his beard. "*Nay*, I rarely go anywhere on a whim."

"How did you know to search for me here—and why?" Pieter-Lucas felt his heart racing. As he had always imagined it, unbelievable things happened to those who slipped through these magical cramped alleyways.

"Prince Willem told me I would find you in the printer's nest of the Anabaptists. Awaiting a wedding day. Is that not correct?"

"How comes Prince Willem to know all that?"

Dirck chuckled. "You know not his ways as well as I anticipated. But then, perhaps you have been away too long." He reached across the table and laid a reassuring hand on the young man's arm. "He awaits your return."

"The prince wants me to return to Dillenburg? *Nay*, that cannot be."

"*Ja*, but he does."

"Why?"

"Your loyal services are of great value to his cause."

"Willem van Oranje said such things?"

"I swear to it."

How could it be? For the few months he lived in Dillenburg, he had run some messages for the prince. But as he ran, he'd been mostly preoccupied with a relentless search for his lost love. He was not at all like Yaap, who had neither a woman at home nor paint in the blood to divide his loyalties. From this special friend, Pieter-Lucas had learned what it meant to be a messenger for his prince—a total sacrifice of time and life and passion.

"Not the sort of life for me," he'd said every time they returned from a trip.

Pieter-Lucas cleared his throat and tapped nervously on the table with the forefinger of his right hand. "If he knows so much about my plans and where I lodge, how is it that he sends you here to tear me away from my soon-to-be bride?"

"His mission is urgent."

"How urgent? In only six days, my bride and I will be wed, and I take her back to Dillenburg."

"First he needs you here in Friesland."

"To deliver the pamphlets?" Pieter-Lucas asked, not taking his eyes from the wrinkled face.

The man reached into his black bag and took out the same pamphlet he'd produced earlier at the printery. "Here." He placed it on the table before him with a gesture so reverent Pieter-Lucas almost feared to touch it.

Pieter-Lucas read the words on the cover in a subdued voice. *"Justification of the Prince van Oranje against the false lies by means of which their perpetrators seek to accuse him of injustice."* Gently he lifted the cover, then leafed through the handful of pages, not reading, mostly wondering. Why had the prince written this? How came Heer Dirck to be peddling it?

"Every Lowlander needs to read it," Dirck said. He leaned forward and added an emphatic, "Now!"

"But why? Since the prince fled to Dillenburg, he's in no imminent danger."

Heer Dirck went on, his manner agitated, his voice lowered. "So you have not heard King Philip's most recent proclamations through Alva?"

"I only pick up snippets of gossip from the Beggars in our streets. Most recently they have gathered outside Emden, planning for a battle confrontation with the Duke's troops somewhere nearby. But I know not more than a little of that matter."

The man stood to his feet, picked up his stool, and brought it closer to Pieter-Lucas' side. Seating himself again, he spoke in a hushed voice, muffled by his bushy beard. "In Dry-Stick Month (February), Alva issued a summons to Willem van Oranje and his brother Ludwig van Nassau, along with four other noblemen, to appear before his infamous Blood Council within thrice fourteen days from the date of the proclamation. The penalty for disobedience was perpetual banishment from the country and confiscation of all estates and goods."

"Surely Alva did not expect them to walk into such a trap!"

"Perhaps not," the man replied, "but Alva will never leave a trap unset."

"I suppose you're right." Pieter-Lucas nodded while his mind spun in dizzy circles.

"Most recently," Dirck said, his voice heavy with sorrow, "Willem's son, Philip Willem, was abducted from his classes at the University in Leuven and carried hostage into Spain."

"Unthinkable!"

"Indeed!" The older man nodded. "The prince has decided that his time to act has come. He is planning a many-pronged military invasion under the command of Ludwig. But if his strategies are to succeed, he must have the support of all the Lowlanders—not just Beggars and other Calvinists, but Papists, Lutherans, and Anabaptists, as well."

"Anabaptists?" The thought startled Pieter-Lucas. "The whole world knows they will never carry a sword, under any circumstance—not even in self-defense."

Dirck nodded. "Willem knows that very well, and he asks not for their swords."

"What, then, does he expect from them?"

"Prince Willem also knows the Anabaptists believe in doing acts of kindness to the oppressed and injured—bestowing gifts of food, performing acts of healing, opening homes in hospitality, perhaps even giving a few gold coins." He paused, then spread out his hands toward Pieter-Lucas. "Can you not see how important this is?"

"I . . . perhaps," he stammered. "But surely my part can wait just one more week, till the wedding is past."

Dirck shook his head. "Time we do not have! Ludwig's forces are already gathering in the fields near Groningen, and Alva's troops approach from the south. Six days from now a major battle may be over, and the prince's cause either be saved or lost!"

Pieter-Lucas punched a fist into his hand and ground it hard. "There must be another way."

Dirck lowered his head, folded his hands on the table before him, and hesitated briefly before looking up and speaking again.

"King Philip has placed *all* Lowlanders—three million men, women, children, including you and me and your bride—under sentence of death for heresy! In the whole land only a handful of persons, especially named, are exempted."

"Impossible!" Pieter-Lucas shouted.

Dirck raised a hand and, with a shrug, sighed.

"But it cannot be!"

"We're all condemned to die! Once the revolt fails in the Low Lands, even the leaders of Emden may no longer be able to give us refuge."

"*Nay.* Emden must always be safe. Alva has no power in Germany!"

"*Jongen*, war has many ways of altering the boundaries of power. Mark my word, if the prince's cause goes down to defeat, all Anabaptists everywhere will hang or drown or burn."

"Not in Emden!"

"*Ja!* In Emden!"

A steady rhythm of shocked silence beat against Pieter-Lucas' ribs.

Heer Dirck rearranged his collar and sat erect, and without looking directly at Pieter-Lucas, he said, "You have experience with courier runs for *Abrams en Zonen, ja?*"

"I have," the young man said simply. He knew the circuit well—Appingedam, Winschoten, Harlingen, Groningen. . . . He'd run it many times. Dangerous job it was, especially with Beggar troops and Alva's men prowling about everywhere. Yet deep down in the pit of his stomach, he knew he had to do it—for Willem and for Aletta. The rhythm in his heart turned from shock to terror, arising from a sense of duty he simply could not shake.

If he left in the morning, he could take the pamphlets to a certain vegetable merchant at the market in Siddeburen. This tradesman often carried books to the others for him. He could slip out at dawn and be home by nightfall.

"Well, *jongen?*" The deep voice at his side interrupted his plans.

"I go!" He stood and headed for the door.

"At daybreak?"

"At daybreak!"

Dirck handed him a sturdy leather bag, and Pieter-Lucas stepped out into the sunset. An image of the kindly old face framed with a snowy white beard engraved a pattern of comfort into the unsettled grooves of his mind—the place where he wondered how he'd tell Aletta.

———

An uneasy near-silence hung over the workroom of *Abrams en Zonen* following the departure of Pieter-Lucas and the stranger. Johannes puffed and mumbled to himself like a low rumble of receding thunder. The workers had stopped their customary chatter, while Gillis and Robbin took to whispering their reading lesson in the corner.

Dirck Engelshofen stared unseeing at the sheets of manuscript on the proofing table before him. What was there about that stranger who carried his name and spoke like a nobleman that aroused his own curiosity, yet made Johannes so angry?

"I should worry about Pieter-Lucas out there running after him," he told himself. "Who knows where he'll lead him and to what purpose? Yet I cannot fret."

Why, then, were his fingers drumming a succession of rapid little patter beats on the table? And why did his whole being so restlessly resist the call of the pages awaiting his attention?

He slapped his knee and straightened himself on the bench, then barked a sharp silent command to his reluctant spirit. *Back to your task, old man.*

Running a hand through his hair and smoothing his mustache down along his upper lip, he forced his mind to read. "Baptism is the betrothal of the soul to the heavenly Bridegroom. The Supper is . . ." They were nothing but wooden words marching across the page!

Dirck leaned his elbows on the table, and resting his chin in his hands, he dreamed of the old days back in Breda, when his friends Barthelemeus and Meester Laurens used to come by *The Crane's Nest* to talk about the day's events, the dangers, and to exchange ideas. If only he could call his academic circle together. They might know something about this other Dirck who refused to identify himself by any other name. Barthelemeus, the traveling cloth merchant, went everywhere and knew everybody. Meester Laurens, the schoolmaster, could explain where they came from and what this meant and whether they should be trusted or not—and why.

But this was Emden, not Breda. His academic circle had been splintered. Reluctantly, he forced himself back to the work at hand. "Baptism is the betrothal . . ."

This time he was interrupted by the door bursting open. He looked up and into a familiar smiling face.

"Barthelemeus!"

"Dirck!"

Dirck jumped to his feet and ran to embrace his friend. "How could you know I was sitting here longing for a meeting of the old circle at *The Crane's Nest*?"

"I've come fresh from Breda, friend."

"*Ja?* Tell me all about it." Dirck gestured toward the bench opposite his own, and the two men sat. Barthelemeus' face grew sober as he shook his head.

"I have not much good news, I fear."

"Alva's troops have taken the city over, I suppose."

Barthelemeus nodded. "They swarm the streets and board in the homes—"

"Some lodge in *The Crane's Nest*?"

"Just as we anticipated. 'Tis sad, Dirck, sad indeed."

"And Laurens?" Memories of the man ten years his senior called forth a heart full of respect and apprehension.

Barthelemeus sighed. "He who was so eager for us to flee Breda to safety will adamantly refuse to do the same to the day he dies. And I fear his determination may hasten that day."

"They've imprisoned him, haven't they, because he refused to sign that oath of allegiance to papism and the king?" Dirck drew his shoulders up, not wanting to hear the answer.

Barthelemeus nodded. "They did."

"Did you see him?"

Barthelemeus shook his head. "I talked with his wife. They still allow her to bring him food each day. But it breaks her heart to see that he and Pieter van Keulen the goldsmith are forced to sleep on thin mats, along with a vicious murderer from Flanders and a host of unseen vermin that crawl through the straw."

Dirck swallowed hard. "We knew it would come, Barthelemeus. Why, then, does it pierce me like an arrow shot from some unexpected ambush?"

"I know," he said, still shaking his head. "It brings me much sorrow as well."

Their eyes met across the table. Barthelemeus stirred uneasily, tapping his fingers on the table. He did not look up for a long moment.

"You have more news?" Dirck asked.

"They also imprisoned Tante Lysbet in the end of Spring Month."

"Whatever for?"

"For possessing evil books."

Dirck started. "What sort of evil books?"

"They claimed they found her little wooden treasure chest in the attic room of *The Crane's Nest* filled with pamphlets about witchcraft."

Not knowing whether to laugh or cry, Dirck stared at his friend, his mouth hanging open, his arms spread flat across the table. "You've been having nightmares."

"Living nightmares," Barthelemeus said, raising his eyebrows. "When the Spaniards moved into *The Crane's Nest*, they said they found a pile of the evil books on the shelves as well. Then they spread word about the entire city that your vrouw was a witch who used your bookshop for a coven where she and Lysbet trained young women in the diabolical arts."

Dirck sat stunned. "The magistrates of Breda believed that?"

"Humph!" Barthelemeus grunted. "The whole city is under the thumb of Alva and his oppressive representatives. Nobody dares to act by what they believe to be true. They must do as they are told or prepare for banishment."

Dirck felt disbelief grow into a rage so foreign to his nature that it frightened him. "What will they do to Tante Lysbet? To Meester Laurens? To Van Keulen?"

Barthelemeus shrugged. "God only knows. But, Dirck, there's still time for you to flee danger."

"Me?" Dirck asked, pointing to his own chest. "I've already fled. They'll not pursue me here."

Barthelemeus leaned forward and looked Dirck squarely in the eye. "You know nothing of the long and cruel arm of Alva. He will find you. Believe me, he will."

"But this is Emden," Dirck protested.

"You said the same about Breda once. The road is well traveled between there and here. Please take heed to my words, friend. You must flee again!"

"Not now," Dirck objected. "My daughter is to marry next week. Besides, where else could we go?"

"I take my family to Engeland. At the moment, Queen Elizabeth seems not disposed to root out and prosecute Lowland dissenters. She even entertains ambassadors from Prince Willem, who beg her for military assistance. Come with us along."

Dirck sighed. "I must stay here, at least until this long-anticipated wedding has passed." The firmness of his voice belied the trembling of his whole being inside.

Barthelemeus leaned back on his bench and folded his hands on the table before him. "Consider well what I have warned you, brother Dirck."

"I thank you," Dirck said, still trying to calm the quavering in his innards.

"Our ship does not leave for a day or two. I shall be back. Perhaps you will change your mind and join me yet."

CHAPTER FIVE

Emden

21st afternoon of Flower Month (May), 1568

*A*letta Engelshofen scurried in out of a heavy downpour just as the sun began to break through the clouds about halfway to the horizon. She set down the covered basket that served as her apothecary cabinet, then slipped off her platform street shoes and removed her soggy hooded cape, hanging it on a hook near the ceramic stove in the corner. She shook her head as if to free the long blond tresses from their severe confinement in the simple white headdress worn by all women of the Children of God.

"God has smiled upon my afternoon," she said to her moeder. The short little lady sat on a low stool before the open hearth stirring the evening meal in a black iron pot. "Smells like one of your tasty fish and cabbage stews."

Moeder Gretta laughed. She had a finely sculpted nose, snappy dark eyes, and a narrow mouth and chin. Aletta always found her smile contagious and her words few. "Whatever our faithful Lord provides, Oma's herbs improve," Moeder said.

"That's not all her herbs do." The young woman removed a long loaf of bread from her bag and set it on the table. "Today I visited seven patients. Vrouw Bakker's cough is over. Little Hennie's inflamed eyes are clean—"

Aletta stopped short when the door flew open and ten-year-old Maartje burst into the room, her plain brown dress and cape spattered with mud, her miniature headdress windblown. "Tante 'Letta, come quickly," she called. "Emilia needs you!"

"Emilia?" Aletta looked at the girl, puzzled.

"Her baby comes not out."

Aletta spread her hands. "Where is the midwife?"

"Gone to call the surgeon."

"The surgeon?" Aletta felt a shudder run through her body. "Birthing is a woman's business, not a man's."

Maartje narrowed her eyes and said softly, "I heard the midwife say she thought the child is already dead."

Moeder Gretta uttered a sharp cry. "Butchers, those surgeons are. *Ach! Ach!*"

"Why did you not call your oma?" Aletta asked the girl who had come for her. "I am only her student."

"She's out in the countryside with some farmer's vrouw. Just come. Vader insists."

"But I know not what to do. I've never done it before. How. . . ?" Aletta grabbed her moeder by the arm and looked at her with imploring helplessness. "What if I make a mistake and the baby dies—or the moeder?"

Moeder Gretta patted her hand and said, "Fear not, my child."

"Come with me along, Moeder."

"*Nay,*" the woman protested, pulling back. "I'm not even an herbalist. Just keep the woman warm and calm, and follow the instructions in Tante Lysbet's herbal."

"Tante Lysbet's herbal?" Of course. Aletta patted her bodice where she kept the book and used it every day. Tante Lysbet had used it for all the years she cared for Moeder Gretta in her long illness. She said it was her moeder's before her. When Aletta left Breda, Tante Lysbet had given it to her. But Aletta had never even read the birthing pages!

"May I be your assistant?" Maartje tugged at Aletta's hand.

"I won't go without you," Aletta said, offering a faint smile. This granddaughter of Oma Roza, the Herbal Healer Lady of East Friesland, had followed Aletta into many an untried situation. How often the girl's warm enthusiasm, concern, and insatiable curiosity buoyed her up through a stormy duty.

Still hesitant inside, she slipped into her shoes, pulled her cape from its peg, and picked up the basket. As she reached for the door handle, Moeder gripped her other arm.

"Give this to your patient," she said, handing her a steaming pot. "Broth from tonight's soup. I pray you Godspeed!"

Aletta stepped out into the freshly cleansed air. Maartje led her by the hand around the corner and past a row of high houses to the squat little home of Karel and Emilia, who were a part of Hans' and Oma's hidden church. Before the house, Karel paced the cobbled street, puffing on his long-stemmed pipe, staring hard at the ground. A strange sound—half moan and half mumble—accompanied each step.

In front of the dark green door, Maartje's vader, Hans, awaited them. "Thank God you've come," he said, reaching for the door handle.

"I know not what I must do," Aletta said. "I only know it's a God-loved little life, and I cannot believe He wills it to be lost."

"I have prayed for you," Hans added, "that you will hear God's voice and administer His grace in your gentle touch."

Something in the bearded widower's calm easy manner gave the trembling young herbalist a new sense of assurance.

Hans opened the door and ushered Aletta and Maartje into a world of subdued light, stuffy odors, and loud wailing. She found a handful of neighbor women clustered around one side of the curtained bed in the far corner. That must be the spot where they had confined Emilia to the birthing stool. Aletta had seen these uncomfortable-looking contrivances on several occasions but never witnessed one in use. It was a semicircular wooden chair of sorts, with arms and nothing but a narrow ledge around the inside edges for a seat. The birthing woman sat perched on this ledge while the midwife stationed herself in front to guide, tug, and catch the baby when it came.

Aletta hurried to the far side of the room, hardly giving her eyes time to grow accustomed to the dim light. She noticed a plume of steam issuing from a kettle hanging over the open fireplace and an oblong wicker-basket crib, draped with curtains of its own and sitting by itself just outside the circle of hovering women.

"An empty basket," Aletta whispered and clutched Maartje's hand. Something in the sight before her brought back the fears she had dismissed just moments ago.

"Your moeder prays for Godspeed," the girl whispered, "and my vader too. Our God will help you."

If only it could be so simple. Maartje was still a child with so much of life yet untasted. Yet something in her simple faith stroked Aletta's troubled soul. She squeezed the girl's hand. The fears did not go away, but she now knew she could go on, one halting step after another.

A woman had risen from her place in the group and was moving toward them. Probably as old as Aletta's moeder, she was built like her too—short and slight. Her hair was so well ensconced in her headdress that Aletta could only guess its color to be gray. She did not smile as she approached.

"I live across the alley," the woman said, barely above a whisper. "I've helped bring three babies to birth in my many years." She stretched out a pair of rough dirty hands. "I know not the arts of a midwife, but these hands are at your service, whatever you need."

"I'm sure we'll find something important for them to do," Aletta said, her head awhirl with questions.

At this instant, the women ceased their wailing, and the abrupt silence was pierced only by a low steady whistle from the water kettle above the fire. Aletta found Emilia sitting in her miserable birthing stool, leaning her head and shoulders against a woman at her back. Her pale face was wreathed in distressed wrinkles and sweat, her eyes were closed, her lips cracked. With her hands she gripped the arms of the stool in an attempt to keep from falling to the floor. Aletta laid a hand on her shoulder. How dreadfully she trembled!

"Fear not, Emilia, my sister," she said, suddenly knowing no more fear for herself, only a compassionate terror for her patient. "Our God who loves your child will carry you through."

Emilia's eyes opened a crack and she breathed a labored, "God bless you, angel."

Aletta knelt beside the woman, stroking her arm. In her mind she heard her moeder's parting words, "Keep her warm and calm." Little wonder that the pains had stopped while the woman remained in such excruciating confinement.

"How long has she sat in this torturous stool?" Aletta asked the neighbors.

"Since the first pains began."

"When was that?"

A mumbling of voices filled the room. At last she heard a solid answer. "Yesterday."

Standing to her feet, Aletta began giving orders. "First, we put her back into her bed with a warming brick and a soothing hot drink."

She heard an outburst of gasps from all around her.

"*Nay!* That can't be done!"

"Why not?" Aletta stared at them, unperturbed.

"No child is ever birthed outside a birthing stool."

"Obviously this child is not ready to be birthed in one. You will help me move her into the bed."

She turned toward the eager child at her side and said, "Maartje, fetch what bricks you can find from the fire."

"Forget not your moeder's broth," the girl said.

"As soon as we have her bedded down, you may bring it."

Aletta nodded toward several of the women and added, "In the meantime, we move the patient." Hesitantly, each woman found a spot. Together, they lifted the pregnant-heavy woman and laid her into her bed, with Emilia crying out in pain and Aletta offering her soothing words of comfort. Maartje was already there with the first cloth-wrapped brick, and the woman who had held Emilia's head was tucking blankets and propping cushions.

Aletta opened her apothecary bag and handed a small bottle of dried herbs to the old woman who had offered her hands. "Take this wild thyme, boil it in a small pot of wine, and give it to her to drink after she has finished the nourishing broth. 'Twill warm and relax her while I prepare my potions."

She pulled Tante Lysbet's tattered leather-bound book from her bodice. Seating herself on a low stool by the light of the fire, she opened its familiar pages. The original printed entries contained much useful information, but in the margins and on every unprinted page, scrawled in uneven handwriting, she found the most marvelous cures of all. She never knew which ones came from Lysbet and which from her moeder, but she'd learned to consult the marginal scribblings first.

The pages on birthing were all scrawled by two different hands. Eagerly she read, moving her lips but uttering no sound.

When Birthing Comes With Difficulty
First, send out all the neighbors and make the house quiet.

If the noise begins again, that shall I do. For now, I welcome their presence and assistance.

Second, put the patient in a warmed bed and give her a hot soothing drink—a nourishing broth, followed by one of these herbs boiled in wine—wild thyme, giant fennel (with a little myrrh), or horehound.

She lies in bed and sips the broth. The thyme boils on the fire.

Leave the patient in her bed until her pains are coming too close to give her a quiet repose in between. If pains should stop and need to be restarted, try one of these mixtures. Babies seem, even in the wombe, to have strong wills—or to be prevailed upon by demons—I know not which. But I have never known a living child that would not come forth with one of these remedies or the other.
A. Darnell in poultice form, mixed with barley meale, myrrh, saffron, and frankincense, applied to the belly . . .

I have neither barley meale nor saffron.

B. Horse-tongue—give half an ounce of powder of the root in a draught of sweet wine.

Oma has a jar of horse-tongue powder. But I have none.

C. Decoction of madder root is so great an opener that being only once applied, it brings down the birth and afterbirth.

Madder root? Decoction? I carry such with me at all times. Excellent in stanching blood and mitigating inflammations. Perhaps. What else?

D. Bellflower (columbine) seeds very finely beaten to powder. Give in wine—a singular medicine to hasten and facilitate a woman's labor, and if the first taking is not sufficiently effectual, repeat it again.

Perfect! With this one I shall begin. Aletta hurriedly pulled from her basket a tiny bottle of the precious powdered seeds and a flask of wine. She mixed the potion and sent it in a cup by the hand of her old lady assistant.

"Give it to her for a gentle sipping," Aletta instructed.

The woman reached for the cup and hurried to administer it while Aletta proceeded to read the instructions.

When once the pains have resumed, take a small root of the sow-bread, hang it around the patient's neck, and it will help to ease the discomfort while still bringing the child speedily out.

Sowbread root? Ja, ja. That I do have. I hope we will need it soon. She pulled it from the basket and set Maartje to finding a ribbon or thread for hanging it.

With no warning, a low moan came from the bed, followed by a piercing howl. Aletta rushed to Emilia's side. She rested one hand on the patient's shoulder and held the herbal book in the other. Between mumbled assurances of "Calm now. Thanks be to God, it has begun," she read on.

When the pains resume, feel the patient's belly, pressing downward, encouraging the movement of the child toward the opening.

Timidly, Aletta lifted the cover, placed her hands on the round belly, and pushed on the taut hard ball of a baby. Then the spasm subsided and the belly relaxed. Aletta continued to push. But nothing more happened.

"Is there more potion in the cup?" she asked of the old lady.

"Here." She put it in Aletta's hand and said softly, "After so long a time with no pains, the first ones to begin again can be slow between. Methinks it best to keep giving her the potion and pressing the baby."

Aletta gave the weary moeder the rest of the liquid, continuing to offer her words of comfort. Then she went back to pressing on the soft belly for what seemed an hour. Suddenly she felt it tighten again. Once more, Emilia's whole body contorted with the spasm and she cried out.

"Push the baby harder!" came the cry from one of the neighbors.

"Put her on the birthing stool!" shouted another.

"Keep her skirts down. Don't look at the baby as it comes" came the instructions from close at Aletta's elbow.

The room had turned into a beehive of women's voices, each trying to outshout the others for a hearing. As the second spasm waned, Aletta stopped long enough to command loudly, "Leave the room, all of you!"

A buzz of gasps and *nays* followed, and Aletta felt the bodies closing in around her as she continued to press on Emilia's belly.

Suddenly, the little old lady began shouting at the rest, "Go, go, go! All your noise will frighten this child so much that he will never show his face in the world."

"Who made you the midwife?" cried one angry woman.

"Go, go, NOW!" The little old woman waved her spindly arms at them. They acted as if she were not even there.

When all had grown quiet with Emilia again, Aletta stood to her feet and addressed the women still clustered about the bed. "You must leave us alone, or this child will never be born."

The women fell to a low mumbling. "Young thing, she is," one sputtered. "What does she know about it?"

Aletta spoke calmly with an authority in her voice that surprised her. "The midwife was not able, with all her experience and arts, to bring this child safely." She held up the herbal book above her head and went on. "I have in this book the advice of a mother and daughter who delivered more babies into this world than you and I have ever seen. Their first instruction was to send you all out in the beginning. Disregarding that advice was my greatest error."

More gasps and clucking murmurings hummed about the room. Aletta continued, raising her voice a bit. "Now, I implore you, if you have a drop of compassion for this woman and her child, leave me this instant and let me get back to the work before me." Aletta stuffed the herbal into her bodice, then wiped her hands briskly together and concluded, "Good day, honorable women, good day."

She reached out to the old woman. Laying a hand on her arm, she said, "But you must not leave me. We need you here."

"Me?"

"I cannot do it without you."

The old woman sidled up to Aletta, threw her shoulders back, smoothed out her apron, and sighed. Slowly, still mumbling between themselves, the rest of the women looked at one another, then began slinking away out the door. One stopped at the threshold and called back over her shoulder, "If the child is dead, don't lay that to our charge."

Aletta's heart beat rapidly and she swallowed the tears that welled in her throat. She lay one hand on the now still belly and the other on Emilia's forehead, wiping off fat beads of perspiration. "My moeder prays us Godspeed," she whispered, "and so does Hans." Emilia opened her eyes and smiled up at her.

Suddenly Aletta felt a sharp kicking movement in Emilia's belly. Emilia started, her eyes alight.

"It lives!" she said. "My baby lives!"

Aletta felt Emilia's body tightening into another spasm. She called to Maartje, "Bring the sowbread root."

Aletta pressed harder than ever on the baby. "It moves!" she cried. "Come, help me."

Maartje was at the bedside now, struggling to place the ribbon around Emilia's neck. The old lady was there too. Another spasm came, then another.

Emilia was screaming, her face red, her hands tearing at the bed, her whole body contorted. "It comes!" she shouted.

The old lady yanked off the bed covers and ordered, "Pull up her skirts and look."

Just then Emilia's body went into one more spasm, and the baby's head and shoulders came into view.

"Take it by the shoulders and tug," said the woman. "Easy, easy."

As if in a fog, Aletta did all she was told. Before she knew what was happening, the baby was freed and the old lady was cutting the navel cord and attending to the moeder. Aletta stood beside the bed, a slippery baby squirming in her hands.

"It's a girl!" Maartje exclaimed.

Stunned, Aletta hesitated just a moment, then suddenly realized that a pair of outstretched arms was reaching for the baby.

"Give her to me," Oma the Healer Lady said, smiling at her.

"Oma! I thought you were with the farmer's vrouw." Aletta felt her strength drain clear to her toes.

"I arrived in time to see you at your finest."

"You watched me?"

"I watched and prayed God to guide your hands. I am so proud of you, my herbal daughter."

"Oh, Oma, I hardly know what I did."

Oma assumed her typically efficient manner. "Now," she said, "the child needs cleaning up and wrapping. The moeder needs rest, and you need to step outside where your young man waits a bit impatiently for you."

"Pieter-Lucas! Oh!" She looked at her bloodied hands and skirts, then back at Emilia and the baby. "But, Oma, you still need my help."

"*Nay*," Oma said. "I have Maartje and this old lady who assisted you so well. There's a basin with a jug of water in the corner. Go, my child, now."

Oma carried the baby toward the table, and Aletta stumbled off toward the basin. Still in a daze, she washed the blood from her hands, then started for the door.

"First," Oma stopped her. "I need to know what herbs you gave to our patient."

Aletta blinked. "Bellflower seeds, beaten to a fine powder and mixed with a little wine," she said. "And Maartje hung a piece of sowbread root about her neck."

"That is all?" Oma asked.

"That and the little pot of Moeder Gretta's fish and cabbage soup broth."

"Well done. I could have done nothing better."

The cries of a newborn filled the air as Aletta hurried across the room. "Oh, *ja*," she called back over her shoulder, "and on the fire a pot of wild thyme is boiling in wine."

Before she could reach the door, it opened, and in burst a tall straight woman and a severe brusque man carrying a large black bag. They brushed past Aletta, not looking at her, and strode into the room with an air of authority, tinged with irritation. "The surgeon and the midwife," Aletta mumbled.

Trailing behind the official personages, the long line of ousted neighbors clambered through the door and hurried to take their places once more around the bed.

"What goes on here?" the surgeon thundered.

Oma approached him, holding the infant in her arms, and said with an ironic sweetness, "A lovely girl child has just been birthed."

"By what sort of trickery came she forth?" he demanded.

"Trickery?"

"God sent His angel," Emilia whispered.

Ignoring the moeder's words, the midwife turned to Oma. "You, mixer of strange potions, tell us how came you with your magician's art to bring forth a living child from death in her moeder's wombe?"

"I know not how you determined that the infant was dead," Oma said. "'Tis obvious that she waited only for her moeder's warmth and quiet peace of mind to make her entrance into our world."

Quietly, the little old lady assistant shuffled over to where Aletta stood looking on. "If he'd come before you, we would have had to call the mourners."

"What do you mean?"

The old woman whispered into her ear, "He would've dismembered the baby and removed her from Emilia's wombe, piece by piece."

"*Nay!* He couldn't do it."

"See that black bag he carries?"

"*Ja*".

"Full of tools for cutting up and pulling out."

So that was why Moeder Gretta called him a butcher! Aletta shuddered. The woman grabbed her by the arm and tugged her toward the door. "Now, take my advice and hurry home before the surgeon learns that you were the one who delivered this baby."

"What would he do to me?"

"Make you answer too many questions."

"What will he do to Oma?"

"They'll do her no harm. She's the revered Healer Lady of Emden."

"But . . . I cannot understand," Aletta whispered, holding back.

"Go!" She threw Aletta's cloak over her shoulders, then opened the door and shoved her out. Aletta wrapped her cloak tightly around her stained clothes and stepped out into the hazy almost-twilight.

Three men stood brooding over the door and gave her their full attention—Karel, Hans, and Pieter-Lucas.

"My vrouw and child?" the first man asked.

Aletta, still dazed from the words of the old woman, forced a smile. "Your vrouw rests. Your new daughter is a perfect little creature," she said.

"Mock me not, young lady," the man retorted.

"I guided her into birthing myself and held her little body in my own hands."

"And the surgeon?" Hans asked. "What does he in there now?"

Aletta stared at Hans without speaking. A lump too large to swallow filled her throat and threatened to block off the air.

"What does he do?" Hans repeated.

"He . . . he storms about," she began at last, "accusing your moeder of using a magician's trickery to bring a dead baby back to life."

"He dare not touch my child!" the vader said.

"*Nay,*" Hans assured him. "My moeder is a strong woman. No one snatches a newborn from her protective arms."

"I go in," the new vader announced and barged through the door with Hans at his heels, reaching out to pull him back.

Pieter-Lucas stepped to Aletta's side.

"You were a brave woman," he said, taking her by the elbow and guiding her away toward home.

"Oh, Pieter-Lucas, I was so frightened. In fact, now that I know what horrible things the surgeon had planned, I am more frightened than ever."

"What things?"

Aletta shook her head. "He would have killed the child."

"Killed her? But how?"

"Make me not say it," she pleaded. She felt Pieter-Lucas' arm encircling her, and she half snuggled into its soft warmth.

"Aletta, my dear Healer Lady," he said, "I am so proud of you. You saved Emilia and her baby. I would not like to think what her husband would have done if you had not come."

She looked up into his wonderful blue eyes. Filled with that worshipful look he always gave her, they almost lifted her spirits, but not quite. Just for the moment she yearned to run home, bury her head in a feather bag, and sob—all alone.

"As always, my love, your words are kind," she managed.

She sighed and they walked on through the streets without another word. An early risen moon was beginning to dart in and out between the scudding clouds of a twilight sky. It shed a faint light on the rain-slickened cobblestones and began to lighten the load of sorrow she carried. When they'd reached the corner nearest Aletta's home, they stopped again as they'd done so often before beneath the protective spread of the oak tree, now filled with tender young leaves.

Pieter-Lucas cleared his throat and took both her hands in his. "One thing I must tell you before we go in for your moeder's evening meal."

If only she could search his eyes! But he stared at her hands and massaged them with strong fingers. "What is it, Pieter-Lucas?" she asked, tilting her head close.

Raising his head slightly, he stumbled on, "I . . . I must go out on courier duty tomorrow."

"What?" she gasped. "How can Oom Johannes send you out now, of all times?"

Tugging at her hands, he spoke much too quickly and with an air of mock cheerfulness. "I have not to go far this time. I shall leave as the sun shows its face, and you have my word that I return before it disappears." He was looking at her now, his eyes probing hers as if begging her to trust him.

It should work just the way he said. Why, then, did her mind persist in dredging up old frightening memories? Two other times when he'd left on some quick errand, promising to return soon, terrible things had happened. The first time he nearly lost his life in the image-breaking in the Great Church. The other time he was trapped in a dungeon, and before he could free himself and get home, her own vader had taken her away. That time they'd been lost to each other for nearly a year.

"What could be so important that you must go now, so near to our wedding day?" she pleaded.

He sighed, looked intently into her eyes, and lowered his voice. "Prince Willem has an urgent need that only a runner with Children of God connections can fill. 'Tis for his cause—and the Low Lands—that I go." He lifted her chin with the tip of his forefinger and, smiling reassuringly, added, "And for you and me."

"How can that be?" Confusion was causing her heart to pound.

"We live in a world at war," he explained. "Until Prince Willem and his forces wrest our *vaderland* back from the Spaniards, you and I will remain exiles, with no way to go to Leyden or for me to become the Master Painter of Breda."

"Can no one else run this errand?"

He shook his head. "You act as if it were some great dangerous duty. It's really one of the simplest runs I've ever done—across Den Dullart to Siddeburen and back. Just trust me, Little One. Can you not do that much?"

All arguments stuck in her throat. She had to give him the answer he wanted. No matter that fear pounded at the door of her heart more than on any of his other trips from Emden. Nor must he ever suspect that she sensed something terrible lying out there on his pathway, waiting to change his plans and keep them apart once again.

Aletta lifted her gaze to the dearest face on earth and studied each line and shading of color, fixing it indelibly so that she would not forget one detail while he was away. "I will trust," she said, holding each word reluctantly before she let it go, "and pray you Godspeed!"

He must never know how hard that promise came nor how profusely her confused heart bled.

CHAPTER SIX

Emden

21st night of Flower Month (May), 1568

*P*ieter-Lucas climbed the last of the stairs that led from the Engel-shofen's family rooms up through the printery and on to his sleeping quarters in the attic of *Abrams en Zonen*. He set his lamp on the low windowsill and rubbed his hands together slowly, firmly, massaging down the excitement. "One more thing before I run off for a day," he told himself.

From their hiding place behind the table, he pulled the wedding canvas and Opa's tools. He spread the tools on the window ledge and propped the canvas close to the lamp, then seated himself on the three-legged stool and scrutinized his work.

"Almost finished!" He whistled. "Just a few more lines of shading and a title!"

The scene he had begun those many weeks ago was filled in now. Background, actions, and faces glowed with redolent colors and transported him into his dreams—his and Aletta's.

Almost too eager to control his hands, Pieter-Lucas dipped into the paintpots with his knife and mixed them on his palette until he had produced several swatches of varying shades of bluish gray. Gently, as if handling a fragile piece of blue pottery, he took down the painting and laid it in his lap. "A line here and a dab there, a little shading under this cheek," he mumbled, adding the finishing touches.

"Can it be ready?" Could it ever be ready—good enough—to give to his bride?

He propped his chin with its day's-end stubble in his hands and leaned his elbows on his knees, staring hard at the painting. He could not move his eyes from the figure of Aletta standing by his side before the altar. The longer he stared, the more erratically his heart raced. How pleased she will be! Only six more days!

"Time for titling," he announced to his world of title pages.

With a tender delight such as he'd never before given to creating a title page, he swirled his brush in the dab of shading paint he'd just mixed. Then he scrolled a line of gorgeous letters across the top of the canvas:

THE MASTER PAINTER AND HIS HEALER LADY

"One thing more it needs," he decided. In a frenzy, he mixed paints again until a pearly white color emerged. Carefully, so as not to smudge the fresh lines with his hand, he created a simple dove, wings outspread, hovering over the heads of bride and groom. He smiled, tilted his head to one side, and said aloud, "A dove is for anointing!"

He set the masterpiece up to dry, then stowed away his tools and paints. Thoughts of the less-than-pleasant duty awaiting him at sunrise knocked at the door of his consciousness. "Go away!" he ordered them. "Tomorrow waits until tomorrow. Tonight I am Aletta's anointed Master Artist."

Like a man engulfed in a golden fantasy, he wrapped up in his blankets, lay on his sleeping mat, and drifted off into an expectant bridegroom's dreams.

22nd day of Flower Month (May), 1568

Daylight had scarcely brushed the line of rooftops when Pieter-Lucas rose from his sleeping mat. Over the shirt that served him night and day, he pulled on the tight-fitting hosiery-breeches and short doublet of a Frisian country peasant, then draped them with a long dark cape to shield against the wind that blew with a perpetual chill. A furry cap and platform clogs completed his costume. He grabbed Dirk's bag of books and his own knapsack, into which he'd stuffed the street clothes he pulled off last night, and headed for the stairs.

He lingered by the titling table long enough to survey the painting and, for one choice parting moment, give his heart to the excitement it spawned.

"No one must find this treasure," he mused, slipping it down behind his worktable, taking care that the damp surface did not touch the wall.

At the bottom of the two flights of stairs just inside the back door, he packed Dirk's bag of books into the generous-sized market basket that completed his farmer disguise. Then he stepped out into the moist morning air and gathered enough straw to protect the books and enough cabbages, carrots, and onions from Moeder Gretta's garden to fill up the basket and hide the intent of his trip.

He'd not yet reached the street when his lame leg began to hurt. Only rarely did it cause him real pain, and then it came without warning or reason. Why this morning, of all mornings? "God, did you not remember I have to be home before sunset?" he sputtered under his breath as he limped toward the harbor.

At the edge of Den Dullart, he joined a group of local farmers boarding the boat that took them every Saturday across the waterway to sell their produce in the markets of a handful of Frisian villages. Once at the market, he would seek out the stall of a man whose name he did not know, but who both bought and sold garden vegetables. He would exchange his basket with all its contents for an empty one and whatever messages the man might wish to send with him. The man, in turn, had his own ways of distributing the books to the Children of God scattered over all of Friesland.

The sun was nearing its zenith in the sky before Pieter-Lucas lugged his heavy basket through the single street of the village of Siddeburen.

"Should have been here long before this hour," he groused. "Good thing I don't have to go farther today."

He stood in the market square beneath the shadow of the church clock tower and surveyed the little clusters of tables, stools, and stalls. Nearby a woman sat on a stool cooking pancakes over an open fire. Everything in his bone-weary body yearned to sample her offering, to sit and rub his leg in the near warmth of the midday.

"*Nay*," he chided himself. "Work first, then eat and rest and head straight home."

Reluctantly he moved off, the aroma of the freshly baking pancakes following him. He passed a potter, the knife sharpener with his giant whetstone wheel, the butcher, the fishmonger, the baker. And today he even saw a lace maker. A dentist had a victim ensconced in his chair, and next to him a noisy merchant boasted of the miraculous cures in the tiny bottles of bloodred liquid he held up for inspection. He found only one produce farmer, but he was not the one with Anabaptist connections.

He limped on by, aware that the man stared at his load of vegetables. When he'd gone the circle around and was again approaching the pancake lady, he knew the man he sought was not here.

What now? Once or twice before this had happened. He'd had to run all the way to the farm in Winschoten or to the weaver's shop on the outskirts of Appingedam. But both points lay several hours' journey from here. In neither case could he possibly make it home by sunset, even if his leg were not troubling him.

Beckoned again by the smells of baking pancakes, he stopped before the enticing wares. "A hungry man has but straw for a brain," he told himself. "Eat first, then I'll have a mind to decide what to do."

He rummaged in the drawstring pouch hanging on his belt and produced a coin. He held it out to the squarish woman with leathery skin and dingy white headdress.

"An extra *stuiver* for a dollop of bee's honey." She did not look in his face but scraped the cake from the pan as she spoke.

"If you please." He reached back into his bag and offered her a second coin.

As he sat on the edge of the market square munching the pancake and a carrot from his bag, the answers began to come clear to his weary mind. He must go to the house of the weaver in Appingedam. It was a trifle closer than Winschoten. True, he could not go there as a farmer. He would have to stop at his hideout along the way and replace his disguise with his own clothes, and that would take precious daylight time.

"Great God," he sighed. "I'm too weary to go on." He stood to his feet, swaying slightly. Pain shot through his leg. Had Aletta known this was going to happen last night when she urged him not to go away? If only she were here—or he there—his dear healer lady's smelly poultices, tender touch, and warm smile would put this leg back in order.

"No time to waste wishing for what cannot be," he cajoled himself. "Willem's pamphlets must go through, no matter how far the journey or how painful."

He hoisted the flexible-sided basket with difficulty to his shoulder, slung it over his back, and held it by the handles. Hobbling out of the market square, he left the town by a different way than he had entered.

The road ran from Winschoten in the south to Appingedam in the north. Known as the Would-Weg (Wood Way), it ran mostly through a wide soggy peat bog where Frieslanders dug fuel to heat their homes. A scrubby forest grew over the bog. Here and there the afternoon sun sent a shaft of brightness through the openings in the deep layer of brushwood and trailing willows, creating an illusion of spirit presences darting about.

Pieter-Lucas knew that one misstep could plunge him into an irrecoverable disaster. All through the afternoon, he struggled to keep to the pathway, at times, simply to keep moving. About halfway to Appingedam, he turned down a little side lane, largely obscured by the low thicketlike woods on both sides. The way through the morass here was narrower than the main road, but he had not far to go.

With eyes keenly focused in the dimming light of the dense woods, he spotted the shelter he often used on longer courier trips for changing disguises or for resting through the night. On the back side of a hillock of solid ground stood the dilapidated remains of a house sagging into the side of the hill. Originally built of blocks of peat on a frame of fir tree trunks, all that remained was one trunk and a small section of peat walls and roof that ended in a pile of moss-grown peat.

With painful effort Pieter-Lucas stooped to enter the low doorway. A large ring of toadstools greeted him in the damp musty air, and tiny pricks of light came through from holes in the boggy thatch.

"At least it's not raining," he mused, seating himself awkwardly on a log stool he'd once set up with a block of wood for a table. On his breeches, he scraped the mud off a carrot, tore the skin off an onion with his fingers, then took a bite of each. Cool, sweet, pungent, they teased his mouth deliciously.

"Had no idea I was so hungry again!" He chuckled at the thought.

"And sleepy," he added when he'd finished his meal. But had he time to sleep and still reach Appingedam before nightfall so he could arrive home by sunrise tomorrow?

"Just a short hare's nap," he promised himself. "Won't take much, and perhaps my leg will complain less if I let it rest."

He dumped his load of vegetables onto the makeshift table, then flattened out the large soft basket on the floor with its thick carpet of moss. He lay down, propped his feet on the log, and spreading the cape over his body, he drifted into a deep slumber.

The next thing he knew, he opened his eyes and felt the rough surface of the basket beneath his back. The darkness of the room was no longer pierced by pricks of light from outside.

"It's night!" he said, clambering to his feet and poking his head out through the doorway. A soft mist filled the night air, but through the trees he saw a faint glow as the moon tried to break through. A chorus of swamp frogs croaked in rhythm. Overhead an owl screeched.

"Not only did I not make it home by nightfall," he moaned. "I didn't even reach Appingedam!" A vision of Aletta sitting by the window watching for him pricked his conscience. "And all because of a farmer that didn't go to market and a wretched leg!"

Shivering in the damp cold, he yanked at the farmer's hosiery-breeches and doublet and scolded himself. "You've wasted enough time, *jongen*. Now, make haste!"

He had barely started to pull on his breeches when he heard a sharp cry arising from the pathway about at the point where he'd left it to climb the hillock to his shelter.

"Ouch!" The voice echoed through the woods.

"What is it?" A second followed.

"A farmer's cabbage!"

Pieter-Lucas suppressed an enormous guffaw and pushed the hair back from his ears. He strained his eyes, hoping to see something on the pathway below. The voices continued.

"Impossible!"

"It's a miracle!"

"A miracle?"

"*Ja!* Cabbage for starving soldiers—in a swamp?"

"I told you we should've deserted Ludwig long ago," one said.

"Ha! Like I said, never should've joined him in the first place," snarled the other.

"Confounded rich noblemen!"

"Living like kings, driving us like slaves!"

"Starving us half to death!"

Deserters from Ludwig's army! Insolent traitors! Pieter-Lucas' heart drummed its anxious rhythms. He should go grab his cabbage away and tell these grumbling dissenters how Willem and his brothers had sold and pawned their family's treasures in order to raise funds. And for what? To feed and pay the likes of these scoundrels!

"If we can ever get out of this accursed swamp and find Aremberg, we might have a chance to be real soldiers," one voice was saying.

"With gold in our bags," the other finished. "At least Alva's captains pay their troops!"

On impulse, Pieter-Lucas turned back into the room and grabbed as many of the onions and cabbages as he could carry. Outside the door, he threw an onion directly toward the spot from whence the voices came. It landed with a solid thud followed by two loud cries.

"What was that?"

Quickly he threw another, which hit one of the men, invoking a shriek of pain. Next he heaved a cabbage, then another onion and one more cabbage. Suddenly all the creatures of the night fell silent except for a lone owl that began to shriek. One mournful call followed another, until the whole bog echoed with its eerie voice.

"Demons!" screamed one of the men.

"Let's get out of here!"

Pieter-Lucas struggled to keep from laughing outright. He heard a scrambling of feet and the voices moving deeper into the bog. Next he heard a gigantic crackling sound, followed by groans and a muffled splash. A soldier had fallen into the bog.

"Help! Pull me out!" The cries filled the swamp with a muted soggy echo in competition with the owl.

"I come!" shouted his companion. Then came another crashing splash and still more cries, and Pieter-Lucas could restrain himself no longer. He covered his mouth with his cape and laughed.

"That should keep them busy for a while," he told himself. "By the time they extricate themselves from that mess, this onion-throwing demon will be far from here, and the wretches will never come back. He continued chuckling as he pulled on his waist-length doublet and old felt hat. Quickly he packed Dirck's pamphlets into the knapsack, along with a few carrots and onions for munching down hunger growls. Then stuffing his farmer's disguise into the basket, he hid it away in the darkest corner of the shelter and started down the little hill, feeling his way along the trail. His eyes adjusted to the dim rays of light shed by the watery moon till he could faintly see the trees.

The rest had been good for his leg. He was able to move with a minimum of hobbling. In no time he reached the main road and was on his way once more to Appingedam. He'd gone only a few steps on the road when he noticed that the loud chorus of swamp noises was giving way to something very unlike a swamp. A steady swishing-thudding sound like the tromping of a million feet and horses' hooves was coming down the road to greet him. Through the trees he saw an occasional flicker of light.

"An army," he whispered. "God, make it Ludwig van Nassau, not Aremberg."

He took refuge behind a grove of tall willow trees and set himself to observe the procession.

At the head of the line marched several foot soldiers carrying lighted torches. Their faces, long and sober, looked ghastly in the lurid light they carried. Their uniforms could be either Spanish or Lowland. One looked like another to Pieter-Lucas in the dark. Directly behind the first troop came two men mounted on horses, looking neither to the right nor to the left, speaking not a word. Pieter-Lucas peered cautiously at their faces. He had to know whether these captains were friends or foes.

In the unsteady light of the torches, he recognized the sharp-featured face and pointed beard of Ludwig that protruded beneath the heavy metal battle helmet. And the man by his side? He, too, looked like a Nassau— Adolph, perhaps, from the royal court of Denmark. Adolph was the one brother Pieter-Lucas had never met, but he'd seen his portrait hanging in Dillenburg's great hall. He felt relief drain strength from his legs and shoulders and leaned into the mossy tree trunks to wait out the passage of the troops.

Apart from the incessant massive footfalls and the subdued cloppings of horses' hooves on the soggy roadway, the slow but steady advance was accompanied by a mist-shrouded silence. It sent shivers down Pieter-Lucas' spine. Good thing Hendrick van den Garde couldn't see him crouching now behind these trees.

"Go back to your paintbrushes!" Pieter-Lucas could hear Hendrick's raspy voice and feel its venomous sharpness as clearly as if he were really speaking.

But Hendrick was not out here. Or was he? After all, he was one of the militant Beggars that made up a large part of Ludwig's patriot army. For all Pieter-Lucas knew, Hendrick might be marching past him at this very instant. He found himself staring into every face illuminated by a lighted torch, searching for that strange and violent man, hoping never to see him yet unable to stop looking.

For what felt like hours, the troops filed on and on. Foot soldiers, musketeers, pikemen, cavalry—the parade grew endless. When the last mounted soldier had passed, Pieter-Lucas ventured out onto the road. The air, laden with smells left behind by the large cavalry, seemed swarming with strange spirits as well. Here and there through the trees that lined the causeway, he saw a glimpse of sky, already lightening. Daylight would make the way easier to see—and a lone merchant lad easier to spot.

A growing swell of disabling fears tumbling through his brain fed his footsteps with new energy. Oh, to be through with this whole business and to arrive safely back home with his Aletta! Never again would he leave her side. Why, oh why, had Willem chosen him for this mission?

He trudged on, apprehension accompanying each step. His eyes looked about, searching for stray soldiers. If he met some, how could he persuade them that he was no Alva sympathizer nor a spy? These were, after all, days when no one believed the words or explanations of anyone he met along the road.

And if any soldier—Spaniard or Lowlander—should discover he was headed for an Anabaptist weaver's cottage, even God himself could not help him! If he could believe all the things Dirck had told him, then it might be true that Willem would allow him the right to live like a Child of God in a land of exile.

But Ludwig's soldiers? That was another color of a horse. Many of these men were Beggars—wild Calvinist rebels who boasted about fighting for freedom to worship God as they pleased. That's all it was—freedom only for themselves and their ways. They had no more patience with a Child of God who wanted the same freedom than with a Papist set on taking their freedom from them.

By the time Pieter-Lucas could see ahead to the break in the woods, a diffused light invaded the blanket of fog creeping into the edges of the woods. In the ghostly stillness shrouding the predawn world, a sudden chill crept over his body, and he wrapped his arms snugly in his cloak.

Long ago he used to beg his friend Yaap to tell him stories about his life as a messenger. It all sounded so exciting, so noble, chasing through dangerous places, knowing you were helping the prince's just and righteous cause. But at the dawning of this new and dreadful day, the adventures and dangers of a messenger no longer held any excitement for him, only a tormenting disgust and dread. Perhaps Hendrick was right, and he was a coward after all.

His melancholy reverie was interrupted when he looked up and saw through the fog the figures of two men, one obviously fleeing from the other. At the edge of the wood, he could barely see the pursuer raise his arm and point it toward the other. Pieter-Lucas heard a loud crackling shot ring out and echo through the woods, the disastrous news spreading from tree to tree. The victim staggered on a few more paces, then crumpled into the roadside bramble bushes with a moan. Pieter-Lucas darted once more behind a clump of trees, where he stood motionless and tried not to breathe.

Stunned, he watched the pursuer hurry to the body and turn it over. He appeared to meet with no resistance as he rummaged through his victim's garments. With increasing frenzy, the man ripped at the clothes. Finally he stood, kicked the body, and let out a storm of curses. Empty-handed, he turned and marched off into the fog, his boots tromping a loud battle cry down the pathway.

Pieter-Lucas clung to the tree. Appingedam lay just beyond him, almost within reach. Yet what if he should encounter the man with the firearm before he reached the town? He pictured it all too clearly. Once the soldier had shot him, he'd confiscate the contents of his knapsack. What better evidence could he ask to incriminate his victim than a stash of Willem's campaign pamphlets?

He'd carry him and the books off to Alva's captain. Together they'd make a bonfire of the books in some city square. Then with great glee they'd hang Pieter-Lucas' body from a tree by the roadside, where all passersby could see and shudder and be warned never to give aid to the cause of Willem van Oranje. In fact, that may be what he was planning to return and do to the man he'd already killed and kicked into the bushes.

One thing was certain. Pieter-Lucas could not stay here.

Dangers or no dangers, Willem's pamphlets had to go through, and he had to get back to Aletta. "Great God in the Heaven"—he found himself praying without uttering a sound—"how can I fulfill my mission to Willem and keep my word to Aletta?"

Only the soft oozing and plopping of thickening fog broke the silence. Pieter-Lucas stood motionless. Instead of any great wisdom, he sensed what he thought were the eyes of the Anabaptist God boring into his soul. No voice spoke audibly through the mist. Yet a clear train of accusing thoughts moved through his brain.

Good and pious Child of God, are you? Of course, when it'll get you a vrouw! God isn't fooled, especially when He watches you out carrying messages urging men to carry arms. Now that you are in grave trouble, what makes you think you can call on God and He will answer you—you charlatan?

He covered his ears and growled out into the swamp, "Nay! 'Tis not so. 'Tis not so!" Then softly he whimpered, "Great God of my opa, you know how hard I have struggled to believe all Hans has taught me, and how I did not want to come on this trip but did it anyway because I thought it was what you demanded." As he stood shivering behind the willow, he sensed one more strong thought possessing him, this time bringing peace. *Go forward, Pieter-Lucas, for the cause you pursue is mine. Just never forget that I once died to purchase your soul as well as your mind and will not rest content until you give it all to me.*

So clearly did the message come that he began to think it was audible. He shook his head and cast darting glances in all directions.

"What does this mean?"

No answers came—neither through the jabs of his conscience nor through a nearly audible voice. Instead, there flowed over him one clear conviction. He had to take the road to Appingedam.

Through the fog he crept out into the causeway, his whole body shaking. When he reached the spot where the man had fallen, he heard moaning.

"Help! Help!"

Pieter-Lucas started, his feet literally springing from the ground. A trap! He should have known. He prepared to run back the way he'd come. *Nay*, there was still life in the body gunned down, and he could not leave that man in trouble. He must give aid to any human being in need.

How often he'd heard Hans say, "If you suffer for kindness offered, then in some special way you are walking in the steps of your Savior, and He will care for you in the end." He never expected to find use for these words on this trip.

Was this God's way of answering his desperate prayer? How it would ever help bring him back to Aletta, he couldn't imagine. Yet he knew he had to do it, perhaps only to prove himself worthy to take a Child of God for a vrouw. It was their way, after all.

He stepped off the path, grateful that at least here the ground beneath the plants did not sink into the morass but felt solid. Just enough dawning light came to his aid through the fog so that he could see the man stretch a hand out toward him. He stooped down and took it in his own.

"Thank God, you're here," the man groaned.

That weak halting voice—he knew it! Pieter-Lucas drew closer and looked into the face splattered with blood and wincing with pain. *Nay!* He gasped.

"Yaap? Tell me it's not you!"

The young man's eyes opened wide, and he reached out. "Pieter-Lucas . . . friend."

Pieter-Lucas swallowed down the tears that rose up in his throat. On their last ride together they had come to this north country, Yaap bearing a message from Willem, and he, Pieter-Lucas, in search of Aletta. They'd seen Count Ludwig in Leeuwarden, and he'd suggested they go to Emden to find the Healer Lady of Friesland. It was a long and complicated scheme for finding Aletta, which worked much easier than Pieter-Lucas had dared to dream.

"Last I saw of you, you had a broken leg," Pieter-Lucas said. "I didn't want to go on to Emden alone and you insisted. So I left you in the dubious care of some Beggars in Groningen. But, Yaap, this is worse than a broken leg. Here, let me hoist you to my back. Have to get you to Aletta. She's a healer lady now. She'll know what to do."

"*Nay*," Yaap protested, moving his head ever so slightly from side to side. "No time. Go to Ludwig . . . give him my cap . . . tell him I've seen Count Aremberg on the march."

"But you need help, Yaap. I can't leave you here . . . to . . ." He couldn't finish.

"Messages have to get through . . . not the messengers."

"*Nay*, Yaap!"

"Aremberg's coming! Hurry!" the dying man whispered.

Yaap's hand patted him on the arm, then slid away. With what little light the dawning day afforded, Pieter-Lucas could see the head roll to one side, the mouth gaping. "Yaap," he pleaded, "Yaap, come back."

The only answer that came was the call of a long-horned owl returning from its night of hunting.

CHAPTER SEVEN

Emden

22nd day of Flower Month (May), 1568

*A*letta could not sleep the night before Pieter-Lucas was to once again run a mission for William. Her nightlong vigil with apprehension came to an abrupt end when Pieter-Lucas stirred in the attic room above. She lay dead still, head propped up against the wall of her bed cupboard and listened.

"Ouch! His leg is bad!" The message shouted itself through her weary brain.

She knew it the instant he began his cumbersome descent down the long stairway. If only she could keep him here and be his nurse today!

"We're not children anymore," she reminded herself. "No longer do we talk about dangerous adventures with the safety of distance and imagination to protect us. We are full grown now, and danger is our everyday companion."

The deep rhythmic thumping of her heart against the wall of her chest told her that what Pieter-Lucas would face today was no ordinary danger. Just what it was, she didn't know, but the fear of it brooded over her, building like the clouds and winds of a slow-moving thunderstorm. Where, when, or how would the lightning strike?

She rose from bed at the regular hour and tried to go about her day as any other. But her body craved sleep, her mind clung to the single image of her beloved's long blond curls and adoring blue eyes. In mid-morning, when she and Oma set off to visit their round of patients, she went like a dumb sheep following its shepherd.

They had hardly begun when an out-of-the-ordinary duty overtook them. They turned a corner and discovered two uniformed soldiers under an oak tree. One lay on the ground moaning. The other hovered over him and looked up as they approached.

The hovering man stared at Oma's apothecary cabinet and called out, "Vrouw, be you *physicke?*"

With an unusual air of caution, Oma eyed the two men before giving her answer.

"I dispense herbs," she said.

"Then you will help us?"

"I can try. Only God makes well. What is it?"

"My friend here was injured in an altercation with a fellow soldier. Surly old viper, he's always practicing his sword-wielding on the rest of us."

Oma knelt beside them and Aletta followed. The victim had large cuts in one leg and one arm. His wounds oozed blood in the center, but around the edges, they had dried somewhat, sticking his clothes to the skin.

The man prattled on. "Can't imagine why they ever let that madman join the army, and—"

"Bring me some water from the canal," Oma interrupted, nodding toward the soldier. A bit startled at first, he obeyed, still grousing as he went. "Soldiers aren't what they used to be. . . ."

"Shall I mix the Paré salve?" Aletta offered, a feeling of wariness making her uncertain.

"If you please."

She felt a faint dampness in her palms as she set to mixing the salve. A *digestive* of the yolk of an egg, oil of roses, and turpentine, the recipe was as amazing as it was simple. "Accidentally discovered by Paré, a French battle *physicke,*" Oma had told her. She never went anywhere without the ingredients, for it helped so many different wounds.

The talkative soldier returned with his helmet filled with water, and they ignored his incessant prattle. Oma poured water onto the dried spots on the soldier's leg and arm, loosened up the clothes and lifted, then tore them away. Next, she spread on the salve, dressed the wounds with a clean rag, and gave the patient a few kind words when he cried out in pain. Her work completed, she said to the uninjured man, "Find him a bed in a warm place and give him a pot of hot broth. He should walk no more than necessary until the wounds begin to mend."

Then directly to the patient, she added, "And may God be your healer."

Aletta and Oma hurried on to their intended visits for the rest of the day. Both women remained uncharacteristically quiet. Oma never mentioned the strange morning encounter, and Aletta did not ask the questions that perplexed her. When in late afternoon they returned to Oma's house and Aletta carried the apothecary chest to its place in the herbal pantry, she sensed a melancholy chill enshrouding the household.

At the door, Oma laid a hand on her shoulder. "Compassion is always God's way," she said, her voice tinged with pain, "though sometimes costly."

"You've always taught me that no matter what we believe about non-violence, we must never refuse aid to a suffering human being, whether he be a soldier or not. Is that not so?" Aletta asked.

The older woman cleared her throat. "'Tis very true. Yet dispensers of God's compassion do not always enjoy the understanding of all His people." She reached for the door as if to close it, and Aletta knew her time had come to move on.

A damp breeze wrapped itself around Aletta as she rushed home. She shoved Oma's troublesome words out of mind by telling herself that Pieter-Lucas may be home. When she did not find him there, she felt no surprise, only a sad apprehensive ache.

He did not come in time for the evening meal. She ate little, said little, and had ears only for a knock on the door. Even when her brother, Robbin, tried to coax her with his words, "Smile, sissy, smile," she all but ignored him. Methodically, she cleared the dishes from the table, leaving one plate with a cup and spoon in Pieter-Lucas' place.

"Think you that he comes yet tonight?" Moeder Gretta asked.

"He promised," she answered.

"Remember," Moeder said, busying herself with the washing of the dishes, "some promises lie beyond our power to keep."

Aletta sighed. "How well I know, Moeder." It was the knowing of this very thing that tormented her so deeply. Surely he had done all in his means to get home by nightfall. So what had prevented him? His leg? Or something worse? She fought to keep her imagination from suggesting answers.

Moeder Gretta extended an open palm, facing upward, before her. "Tomorrow lies in the palm of Almighty God," she said, "along with today. He protects as well one day as the other."

What if He had decided not to protect? An old vision from Aletta's childhood crept into her mind. Back in the Great Church in Breda, an enormous eye was painted on the ceiling just above the place where the people sat for services. "The Eye of God," her vader told her, "staring down at us." He never said more, yet Aletta felt God must be watching for her to misbehave so He could punish her.

While she no longer felt the Eye glaring at her since her vader had helped her pray for God's forgiveness, still there were moments—like right now—when she was tempted to wonder what she'd done to make

God angry again. Or was it Pieter-Lucas who had erred this time?

Yet how? Together they had both submitted to everything Hans and his elders asked of them. No one would ever know how many times they'd resisted a temptation to defy the impossible waiting rules, to run away and find a priest to marry them.

"What more, God? What more?" Her heart ached with the desperate words.

Just then a knock came on the door. Not the three short taps Pieter-Lucas always used, but one gentle insistent rap. Yet perhaps just this once . . . Aletta stood fixed to the floor as Vader Dirck answered the summons. Robbin followed hard on his vader's heels and stood by his side.

Vader pulled the door open. Standing in the framed darkness, Aletta saw Hans with her vader's old friend Barthelemeus and a stranger with a long white beard.

"*Nay, nay!*" Aletta murmured, clasping her hands over her mouth and staring at the visitors. If only willing could make it so, they would be transformed into her blond, blue-eyed bridegroom in an eyeblink!

The stranger spoke in tones so low she had to strain to hear.

"Forgive us that we disturb your evening," he said with the smoothness of a nobleman. "We must meet with you and your partner in the printshop immediately."

Who was this strange intruder? Did he have a secret word about Pieter-Lucas? Was it so bad that she, Aletta, could not be told? Her vader was a wise man and she should be able to trust him. But as she watched him step into the night, she trembled.

Robbin tugged at her hand, pulling her down to his level. He put his mouth close to her ear and said, "That stranger who just came to our door, you know, the man with the long white beard?"

"What about him?" Aletta asked.

He lowered his voice to a whisper, and his lower lip trembled. "He came to the printshop with a bag of books."

"When?"

"Yesterday." He pinched her cheeks with miniature fingers and pushed them around till she was looking him squarely in the eye, then spoke, emphasizing each word as if his life depended on it. "Oom Johannes chased him away and banged the door!"

"What sort of books did he carry?" Aletta asked.

He shrugged. "I don't know, but Oom Johannes was really angry when Pieter-Lucas chased after the man!"

Aletta watched the boy's eyes open wide and felt a bit of his alarm. As much to calm herself as to console the frightened child, she encircled him with her arms and said, "It'll be all right, Robbin. With Vader to take care of us, you know we are always safe."

For an eyeblink, the six-year-old snuggled into her embrace. Then he pushed back, smiled at her, and fingered the ends of the laces that held her bodice together. From the other side of the room, Moeder Gretta's voice called, "Come, *jongen*, let's get to bed."

Aletta sent him padding across the floor to his moeder. Then she walked to the window and sat beside it, staring into the blackness of the night with its faint patches of fuzzy golden lamplight coming from windows up and down the street.

She remembered what it was like to be six years old and have no bigger weights to carry than the pain of a wounded knee or the nagging fear that she'd never learn to read well enough to sample those beautiful big books on Vader's shelves. Vader always seemed to love to take her in his lap and teach her to read a few more lines.

She'd never forget how safe she felt in his lap. She was a woman now, and Vader couldn't help her anymore with the things that made life difficult. Things like delivering babies and mixing Paré salve for strange wayside soldiers and wondering where her bridegroom was, whether he'd be home in time for their wedding next week . . .

She daubed at dampening eyes and listened to the ominous noises coming from the printshop above. Footfalls crossed the floor and the voices, subdued at first, grew quickly excited. At times she recognized Oom Johannes' loud stormy shouts. What sort of urgency fed the flames between those men up there? With each succeeding outburst, Aletta found more dampness to daub.

As from some faraway place, Aletta heard Moeder Gretta calling, "Aletta, my child, sit no longer waiting. Your bridegroom comes not before another day."

She looked up but found no words to answer. In the flickering light of the table lamp, she watched her moeder remove her headdress and loosen her hair from its plaited bun, letting it flow down in sparkling silver ripples around her narrow shoulders.

"If you would be awake when he comes, you must sleep while it is night. Come now." Moeder's voice went on as she continued removing the layers of her daytime clothes. When she had nothing left but her long underdress, which at night became a sleeping gown, she crossed to where Aletta did not move from her chair beside the window.

Aletta reached out, taking her moeder's hand in her own, and said, "I wait until Vader comes back down."

Gretta frowned. "You may wait a long time. For myself, I go to bed, and if you are wise, you will do the same. Good night and rest well."

"Rest well, Moeder."

Aletta watched the woman who had once given her birth. The whole idea carried far more meaning than it had even a week ago, before she'd helped Emilia through her nightmare of a birthing. How tiny Moeder looked, swallowed up by that billowing nightdress, defenseless against whatever storm was raging above them. How could she treat this like any other night? What did she know that Aletta had not been told? Was she privy to some plot being formed, both under Aletta's nose and behind her back?

Moeder had scarcely climbed into bed when Aletta heard the footsteps from above descending the back stairs. Closer and closer they drew until the door at the rear of the room opened and Vader entered with the white-haired man close behind him. Each of them lugged a bulging bag, which they set down on the table.

Books? Aletta sat motionless in her dark spot beside the window, scarcely breathing. If this smooth-appearing stranger was indeed the one who had come to the printshop with the prince's pamphlets as Robbin insisted, then no doubt he had sent Pieter-Lucas away on his urgent errand. If so, how genuine was that errand? After all, Pieter-Lucas had not returned when he promised. She stared hard at the man. He must eventually do something to betray his true character, and if only she could remain undetected long enough, she would catch him.

Without missing a move, Aletta watched both men. They crept to Vader's cabinet, where they pulled out more books—among them, his big old Bible. He wrapped it in his cape, then stuffed it, too, into his bag. What danger awaited them so grave that he must part with this most precious of all his books? He had learned to read from that one. And where were they going to hide them? Aletta clasped her clammy hands around each other, twisting the fingers until they pained.

Now Vader and the visitor were removing clothes from their pegs on the walls and stuffing them into the bags of books, pulling pictures from the walls and laying them among the linens in Moeder's linen chest. One by one, Aletta watched all the things that made this house their home disappear from their places and leave emptiness behind.

The stranger reached for a picture just beyond the window where Aletta sat and tripped over her feet. He drew back, hands raised, nearly falling backward in his haste.

"You," she said, glaring at the man. "You thief. How is it that you fooled my vader into emptying all our belongings into bags so you can carry them away?"

Stunned surprise turned to amusement on the face before her. "Why, no one has ever accused me of being a thief before. Perhaps your vader can best explain."

She moved quickly to where her vader stood over Moeder's chest, a picture in hand, his mouth hanging open. Pointing at the stranger, Aletta demanded, "Who is this imposter, and how have you let him beguile you so?"

Vader laid down the picture and smiled. "I should have known you were awake here somewhere watching." He paused, then went on, stopping at each word as if hesitant to go further. "This man is God's voice of warning."

"How can you believe the warning of a stranger, especially in Emden, where we all know we are in no danger?"

"He's a close friend of Barthelemeus, who has also brought us troubling news from home this day. We must leave at once!"

"Moving again? *Nay*, Vader. At least not before morning," she pleaded. Her legs tottered and her head swam lightly.

"We must do all possible under cover of darkness, child."

"B-but where can we go that's more safe than Emden?"

"We board a small boat. . . ." He paused.

Aletta stared at him, not believing. "Board a boat?" The words felt so strange stumbling from her mouth that she couldn't even be sure she recognized them.

Vader continued, his voice heavy with hesitant compassion. "Barthelemeus takes us to Engeland with him."

"Engeland?"

"There is no other way." He gestured toward her. "And it's only for a time."

She shook her head vigorously. "Vader, you know I cannot leave this place while Pieter-Lucas wanders about delivering pamphlets for this stranger you have invited into our house. And next week is our wedding day. How could you forget?"

Startled, he responded, "Forget? Never! In fact, I've spent the last hour begging for more time simply so that we might complete the wedding first."

"What, then, could make it so urgent that we cannot wait one more day? I know he'll be home tomorrow."

Vader drew a deep breath and let it out slowly. "We must go now while there is yet time, for those who pursue us will not wait for a wedding or anything other."

"Who would pursue us and why? Are we not with friends in this place?"

Vader laid a hand on her shoulder. " 'Tis more complicated than you can know, my child."

Reaching up, she grabbed the flaps of his doublet, looked straight into his eyes, and pleaded, "Vader, please be plain with me. I am no longer a child to be protected by ignorance. I am a woman about to be married!"

Vader Dirck smoothed the hair back from her face. He held it in both big hands, gazed deep into her soul, then cleared his throat. "I shall try. It appears that trouble follows us from Breda."

"From Breda? After all this time? How?"

"Barthelemeus tells me that Alva's men have spread rumors about me, claiming that they uncovered a pile of books about witchcraft in the shelves of *The Crane's Nest*."

"Witchcraft? You never owned such books!"

"I know. The rumors are untrue, of course, but the inquisitors are searching for us all the same, and our word will avail not at all when once we are apprehended and called before Alva and the inquisition of his Blood Council."

Stunned, she leaned against her vader and let him hold her in his arms for a long quiet moment. Everything within her trembled, so she could hardly get out the words. "Vader," she began, "can one more day make so much difference? Are Alva's men outside Den Dullart awaiting morning's light to spring upon you?"

He remained silent, stroking her hair with his warm firm hand. Just when he seemed ready to answer, the white-bearded man came closer and spoke at last. "Forgive me if I intrude. This young lady needs to know that I brought you the latest intelligence that makes your immediate flight necessary."

Aletta looked at him sidewise and, still clinging to her vader, challenged, "We've never met you before tonight. How, then, could you know such things?"

A faint smile lifted the corners of his mouth, and his beard nodded slowly in the flickering lamplight. "I, too, am a hunted man. 'Twas one of my watchmen reported to me this night that a group of Alva's inquisitors, in disguise of traveling merchants, lies dangerously close by. I, too, must flee."

She hung her head and answered simply, "I see."

Then, lifting her eyes to his face again, she said, "Still, I cannot leave without Pieter-Lucas. How would we find each other? Even if he came first and we all moved on together, how many more months must we study with yet another group of elders before we can be married? Oh, Vader, we have both waited so long and so patiently, and—"

"I know, child, I know. I have arranged it all," he began, then cleared his throat before proceeding. "Not in the way I wanted to, but in the only way open to me." He paused. In the lamplight, she saw tenderness and pain glistening in his eyes.

"How so, Vader?"

"You will stay here with Hans and Oma. Hans has instructions to complete the wedding immediately upon Pieter-Lucas' return."

She looked up at him and tried to smile. Never had she loved him more. But his words filled her with confusion and a sort of unsettling presentiment of disaster.

"How can I have a wedding without you, Vader, without Moeder and Robbin?" She fought to keep her voice even and her cheeks dry. "Wait with me, please."

"If there were some other way, believe me, I should take it." He gathered her into his arms, and she wept on his shoulder. Her sobs were dredged from a spot far deeper than she had any idea existed, and she felt his body tremble against hers.

With unspeakable anguish crushing her soul, she gathered up her own belongings and stuffed them in the bag she had twice before used for this purpose—when they fled from Breda, then later from Antwerp. All the while her heart cried out, *Great God in the Heaven, keep us safe and bring us back under the same thatch once more, and watch over my Pieter-Lucas. . . . Please, God, please!*

She heard no answers. But in her mind, she pictured the Eye of God again. All the anger was gone. It filled up to the brim with tears that spilled over onto her searing soul and eased her anguish.

———

Later that night Hans the Weaver stood at the window of his low-ceilinged house on 'tFalder harbor, strumming his fingers on the sill and watching the encroaching blackness of the night. This midnight darkness in the month of Flowers did strange things to him. Not gray and hovering for days as the long nights of winter. Rather, like the passing of a scudding thundercloud, it cast a heavy mantle over everything in its pathway, then lifted quickly. For reasons that he could never quite define, he always seemed eager to hang on to these short nights. But never more so than tonight.

"Great and merciful God," he murmured, his nose lightly grazing the leaded windowpane, "let the darkness hold until Dirck Engelshofen has finished bringing his family to safety in the ship anchored out on Den Dullart."

Hans ran his fingers through tangled hair and stroked his beard. From her apothecary pantry in the far corner of the room, he heard his moeder clear her throat. Turning from the window and walking across the room, he found her rummaging through bottles and boxes and sprays of herbs, packing them into her portable apothecary chest.

He put his arm across her shoulder and felt the bones through her layers of clothing. Dear, dedicated healer lady that she was, she never seemed to tire of these fragrant herbs and of the mixing of concoctions to alleviate the sufferings of others.

"Moeder," he said, "you pack as if you planned a long journey."

"You find that strange?" She spoke without looking up, continuing with her work. "Dirck Engelshofen's enemies sent him into flight this night. What is to hinder your enemies from sending you on your way the next?"

"What enemies?"

"Must I tell you who your enemies are?"

"Jan and Leonard, the rabble-rousers?" These two men had joined the group last winter when the big Waterlander group of Anabaptists had an explosive meeting and banned them. "They are noisy and bothersome," he admitted, "of the sort that get pushed around from group to group. I don't think of them as enemies—just a bit arrogant."

"Arrogance can be deadly, son, believe me."

"But they're still young. We mustn't be too hasty in judging them. You taught me that yourself. Besides, at our last meeting the elders decided that if the men cause one more altercation, we will ban them."

Oma Roza stopped her work at last and looked squarely at him, her hands forming a protective shell around a box of herbal seeds or powders. "Arrogant young men often do irreparable harm of the kind no ban on earth could ever cure. Have you forgotten the dreadful story of your own vader?"

"How could I forget it?"

Although it had happened before he was born, Hans knew the story only too well. Fiery ambition and unbridled arrogance had turned his vader, Jan van Leyden, into a mad, polygamous, self-proclaimed Messiah. Unfortunately, the men who set him up as King David in the city of Munster practiced believer's baptism, as did the nonviolent Children of God groups. Calvinists, Lutherans, and Papists failed to recognize the differences between the groups, calling them all Anabaptists. They used the outrageous arrogant acts of those few demented men as an excuse to treat all who rejected infant baptism as mad and violent Munsterites.

"Sometimes, Moeder, I wonder if Vader had not been martyred for his rabid cause, what quietness might have possessed him in his later years."

She shook her head and shuddered. "*Nay*, son, he was one of the men who grow never wiser with years—only wilder!"

Hans patted his moeder's shoulder and spoke reassuringly. "Surely the men in our little flock here are not of that demented sort."

"How can you be sure of that?" The authoritative air in her calm voice told him that she knew whereof she spoke.

"I'm just . . . well, they can't be that bad," he stuttered.

"You may turn a deaf ear to your moeder's wisdom if you choose," she said, returning to her work. "I only pray God will open your eyes before you—or we—have been mortally wounded by these influential young men."

Far down deep in the place where he could make no excuses or retreats, Hans knew she spoke truth. "You are right, Moeder," he said at last. "I shall prepare myself. Long ago, after my Lucia Elise died, I remember how you always said we should never let flight take us unexpectedly. I fear too many years of relative safety in this haven of refuge have made me complacent."

He kissed her on the cheek, then moved out into the room. Where should he begin? Halfway to the old wooden chest where he kept his Bible and a few precious books and papers, he was stopped by a soft persistent knocking on the door. Moving slowly, he paused with hand on the latch and prayed, "Gracious God, be our strong tower and sure refuge."

He opened the door and found Aletta there, clutching a large dark bag. Beside her stood the white-bearded stranger he'd met earlier this evening. A quiet dignified man with noble bearing and thoughtful manner, he, like all the rest in Emden, was a refugee. Also like the rest, no one dared to ask from what he fled. Dirck Engelshofen seemed confident he could be trusted. While Hans had no idea what the man's theology was, neither could he bring himself to mistrust him.

"Come in quickly." He gestured them through the door.

Oma moved to Aletta's side and relieved her of her bag before leading her to a comfortable chair beside the tall ceramic stove next to the herbal pantry.

They had scarcely entered when Hans heard a scuffling of feet approaching from the street. He squinted through the dark frame of the doorway into the anxious face of a faithful member of his congregation.

"Aelbrecht," Hans exclaimed, pulling him inside and bolting the door. "What brings you here?" The man had only one eye and no family and lived off the charity of various members of the flock. Nothing could ever hinder him from helping a brother in need, and Hans counted him amongst the truest of his friends.

"*Ach!* Brother Hans, they're scheming to catch you." He spun around in frantic little circles, scooping up the air with his hands as if he would gather all their belongings. "I told you they were up to no good," he chattered on. "I knew it, but I didn't know what I knew. It's time to go, Hans, time to go—"

"Calm down," Hans interrupted. "Who is scheming what and why and where?"

"No time to explain. Just move."

Hans grabbed the man by the arm and subdued him into one spot. "We go nowhere until you have told us what we flee and why."

The man winced, pulling to free himself from his pastor's grip. Hans saw a wild and fearful pleading in the agonized face that looked up at him through his seeing eye.

"The troublemakers, Jan and Leonard, have spread lying rumors to all the flock, and they plan to accuse you and ban you before the congregation."

Hans gasped. "When?"

"Tomorrow morning. There's no time to dally!"

"What lies do they tell?" Hans asked.

"That your vader was the notorious Jan van Leyden, Messiah of Munster, and that Oma uses herbal magic to entrap and drug the flock so you can set yourself up as Messiah of Emden!" Perspiration stood in beads on Aelbrecht's forehead.

Hans braced himself against the onslaught of the impossible words. How had news of his family made its way to this place? Never had he or Oma breathed a word of it to another living soul. Even his daughters knew it not—nor must they learn it from these men who intended him such harm.

"And how do they plan to remove me from the church? It is my home." Hans spread his hands in a gesture of surprised confusion.

Aelbrecht's shoulders trembled and he shook his head in long strong movements. "It's too awful. Just get out of here tonight, before it's too late."

Hans laid a hand on the man's arm, as much to steady himself as his friend. "Nothing could be more awful than what you have already divulged. I must know my danger before I decide whether to stand and fight it or flee."

For a long while, the man appeared to be struggling for control of overpowering emotions. Then wincing, he said, "I still can't believe it my-self, Brother Hans, but they are going to turn you over to the city au-thorities."

"City authorities?"

Dirck, the stranger, spoke up now. "What better way to remove you from your place? No city magistrate wants to let a son of Jan van Leyden run loose in his streets, especially if he has been told the man has mes-sianic ambitions of his own."

In the penetrating sober gaze of this outsider, Hans saw a look he feared to interpret. He heard the unspoken question, *How much of the rumors are true?* He must not admit to anything, either to the stranger or to his own friend Aelbrecht. He bore no guilt, nor did his moeder—only scars inflicted by the madman of Munster.

"For all these years, I've lived here as a law-abiding weaver, plying my trade, shepherding the flock God brought under my thatch," he said. "If I had such mad intentions as they allege, why would I wait so long to attempt them? Have I ever given anyone reason to believe I was possessed of messianic delusions?"

Aelbrecht shook his head. "Never! Those men are jealous and arrogant over their favor with men in high places. Wolves in sheep's clothing set on destroying this flock."

Hans stared at the floor and felt his hands grow clammy. "How came you by this information, my friend?" he asked.

More composed now, Aelbrecht replied, "I've never trusted those men. From the beginning I knew they intended to send you to the stake. So I played friendly with them and waited for them to let the truth be known. Little by little I've been putting some of their strange conversations to-gether, and then tonight I happened upon them when they didn't know I was nearby. Their tongues were loosed with wine and they babbled all I needed to know." He grabbed Hans by the arms and begged, "Believe my words and flee—now!"

"I believe your words," Hans replied, "but how can I flee and make it look to the whole world as if I'm guilty of all they say? The least I can do is to stand and defend myself. God's true sheep will know the voice of truth when they hear it, and they will not follow these impostors."

The white-bearded stranger spoke again. "If I may be so bold, I who have had much experience with both your rabble-rouser traitor sort and with city magistrates, I beg of you, Hans, listen to the warnings of this brother. Think not that you can do better by your courage. If the mag-istrates have already been warned, there is nothing you could possibly say or do to waylay their understandable fears."

"I fear not imprisonment for myself," Hans said. "But what of my flock? Who will tell them the truth?"

"Have you no elders who will plead your cause before the rest?" Dirck asked.

"I should hope they would all stand with me."

"They will, Brother Hans, and you know I shall always stand, though they strap me to the stake with you," Aelbrecht boasted.

"Then the answer is quite simple," the stranger said, taking charge of the situation.

"How?"

"You must flee from here now. Your elders will plead your cause before the rest. If they are wise and credible men, they will soon settle the difficulty, ban the troublemakers, and open the way for you to return."

"But where shall we flee?" Hans wanted to believe it could work so easily.

"I myself am a man in flight," the stranger told them. "I go before daybreak and you may go with me."

"Where?" Hans asked.

"A couple of my longtime friends, themselves refugees from many years back, have a farm out in the remote peat bog country just east of the Em River. Their house is dedicated to the harboring of refugees."

Hans eyed the man thoughtfully. If only he knew more about him. "That is more than kind of you, friend," he began slowly, unsure which word to put before another. "Are these people allied with the Children of God?"

Dirck cleared his throat. "They are indeed children of the living God. Are we not all? In a way that seems strange to both sectarians and Papists, they ask not for a declaration of a man's theology before they lend him aid. Which sort of bigotry he flees matters not. Their doors stand open." He said no more, just stared at Hans with eyes that would not let him go and waited.

Except for an occasional shuffle of feet, the whole room had fallen silent. Hans surveyed it all around. Oma's apothecary closet and the hearth where she created her healing brews, his weaving loom and piles of wool in the corner, the door that led into his hidden church—how could he leave it behind? He looked into each of the faces ringing him in the golden-hued lamplight. Aelbrecht, who incarnated pathos and a plea for protection; the stranger with his indisputable wisdom and offer of escape; Aletta, who'd been entrusted to his care; his moeder with her apothecary bags packed for flight; his own young daughters sleeping in the attic room above; they all looked to him, the king of this miniature besieged castle. He must decide for them all!

The expectant hush unnerved him. How could he run now? *Coward!* He could hear his flock shrieking at him and see the name engraved on his tombstone, if indeed anyone would consider his burial place worthy of a marker at all.

And if he stayed and fought it out—and lost? What, then, would happen to his moeder and her herbal ministrations? To his daughters, left orphans when he was carted off to prison? To Aletta, whom he was committed to deliver safely into the arms of her betrothed?

Why must this be so difficult?

For a long and heavy moment, no one moved. Hans' heart seemed to stop beating its rhythm in his chest. Then he heard the faintest sound of weeping and looked up to see Aletta leaning her head on Oma Roza's shoulder. His moeder held the young woman securely in the circle of her arm and murmured soft words to her.

"Moeder," Hans said at last, "you who have weathered far more storms of threat and flight than I can dream, tell me what course of action your wisdom declares."

The woman looked up at him, her eyes glinting in the lamplight, her hand stroking the head of her trembling assistant. "Son, the wisdom God has bestowed on this old woman says that we must all depart now! You serve not your flock well by allowing the wolves to ravage their leader, nor would I see my granddaughters thrown into their den."

"But, Moeder, what of the words of Jesus that say, 'the good shepherd puts his life at stake for his sheep'?"

"He also says that if they 'shall strike the shepherd, then the sheep of the flock shall be scattered.' I have prepared for this flight, as you have already observed, and I have no doubt the time has come."

Aletta lifted her head from Oma's shoulder and looked imploringly up at Hans. "Leave me not here alone," she cried out.

"If we go, you go along," Hans tried to reassure her.

"I cannot leave without Pieter-Lucas!"

"But . . ." Hans began.

"I will not be parted from him again, Hans, until you have joined us in marriage. My vader promised."

Hopelessly, Hans ran trembling fingers through his hair. He had indeed promised her vader not only to protect her but to marry her as well. Yet if they all stayed here, he could be arrested by morning and imprisoned, with no more chances to save himself or anyone—certainly not to perform a wedding.

"When will he return?" Hans' question felt lame even to his own ears.

Between sobs, Aletta replied, "Surely by morning. He said he had not far to go. He expected to be here by nightfall of this day. I know his leg was in pain when he left. But I must be here when he returns—for he will come."

"I am the one who sent the young man on his errand," the stranger said calmly. "I shall take full responsibility to reunite the two of you."

Hans watched the frightened young woman still cradled in his moeder's arms. Staring at the stranger, she challenged him, "Do you know where my Pieter-Lucas is?"

"I've no way of knowing that for certain," he replied.

"Then what can you possibly do to bring him to me?"

"I know the boatman who must return him to these shores," he said with authority in his voice. "I shall arrange with him to deliver your young man to you."

Hans watched fright melt gently into rest in Aletta's face. Then quickly, lest he lose his nerve, he breathed deeply and announced, "We go."

"Great God," he prayed as he removed his books from the chest and cast a longing, uncertain glance at the loom in the corner, "protect us— shepherd and flock and all—that your enemies may know that you are the one and only true God with might and majesty and great compassion."

CHAPTER EIGHT

Heiligerlee

23rd day of Flower Month (May), 1568

*P*ieter-Lucas stood still for a long while in the growing light of dawn, the fog dripping around his ears. He stared down at Yaap's body, and his fingers fumbled with the black felt cap his friend had given him. A ray of sunlight lay across the quiet bloodied face. "I am so sorry, Yaap," he mumbled. "So sorry!"

A sound of crackling twigs nearby brought him suddenly out of his reverie.

"Think, *jongen*," he scolded himself. "You cannot leave him here. Remember what designs the Spanish soldier will have when he returns."

Hastily he dragged the body back away from the road, deeper into the wood, and gave him a burial of sorts in the boggy mud. He covered it all with willow branches and undergrowth. When he tucked the cap under his arm and walked away, he felt slimy inside. How could he abandon his friend?

In his mind he heard the final raspy whispered warning once more. "Aremberg's coming! Hurry!"

"All right," he retorted, "I go! I go!"

He cast a hesitant glance down the way he'd just been walking. Appingedam and the pamphlets would have to wait! Turning left instead of right, he hurried back over the causeway that traversed so many leagues of crinkled peat fields and glowering willow forests. He trod the way alone in the early morning solitude and fought an overpowering wave of sadness all the way.

"*Ach!* Yaap," he moaned, "you were my friend, more than I ever knew! Until I saw your still face with the gaping mouth and staring eyes, I only thought of you as a talkative traveling companion—and Willem's trusted messenger. *Ach!* If only you'd come back. We need you, Yaap. What will happen now to the revolt? How can Ludwig do without you? And what of our vaderland—and Opa's promises—of Leyden and Aletta's Master Painter, and . . ."

When he reached the pathway that led off the main road to his secret shelter where he'd left his farmer's disguise, he stopped. "I'm dressed to visit a merchant—in my own street clothes," he said. "Once I've delivered my message to Ludwig, I must go on to the farmer's house in Winschoten. I'll need the farmer's disguise. No time to go for it now!"

His mind grappled with the dilemma and his hands reached down to smooth out his clothes. In horror, he discovered what the grayness of predawn had hidden from view. His hands and clothes were splotched with blood!

"I must take the time!"

Without another thought, he turned into the pathway and rushed to the shelter. Here he wiped his hands on the damp leaves and piles of moss-grown peat and changed into the farmer's costume. His bloody clothes he rolled into a ball and stuffed securely into a corner of the room. He packed his knapsack into the produce basket, covered it all with what was left of the cabbages and carrots, and hurried on his way.

About midday, not long after passing the road that would have led him directly to Emden, he began hearing voices in the wood alongside the road. Just ahead, off to the left, a wooded eminence of ground held a cluster of white buildings. Pieter-Lucas had never been inside, but he had espied it through the trees a time or two. Known as Heiligerlee—Holy Lion—it housed a cloister of monks.

Why all the voices? As he drew closer, he saw through the sparse willow wood the prince's orange-white-and-blue flags fluttering in the breeze.

Ludwig's troops? He gasped. In this idyllic spot? He turned down the little lane that led to the cloister and moved around to the back entrance, where a lush green vegetable garden spread out before him, and beyond, cattle grazed. Suddenly thankful for his farmer's disguise, he maneuvered around the little knots of horses, weapons, and soldiers and slipped in through the kitchen unchallenged. He followed the sound of voices and the inviting aromas of meat soup and sour bread into the great dining hall. Here he found Ludwig, Adolph, and their officers eating and drinking and telling loud stories.

Behind them, a noon sun streamed through the single long narrow window located up beneath the roughhewn rafters supported by plain white plastered walls. Pieter-Lucas felt small and obscure as he approached the great military men and touched Ludwig lightly on the arm.

"Your Excellency, Count Ludwig," he said and watched the man turn his pointed chin and snappy dark eyes in his direction. Without waiting for an invitation, Pieter-Lucas hurried on. "Your messenger, Yaap, sends news that Count Aremberg follows in your train—two hours, maybe three, behind you."

Count Ludwig's face sprang to life and he thundered, "Aremberg? Two hours behind us?"

The room turned into a buzzing hive of words and questions. Sitting beside Ludwig, Count Adolph looked at Pieter-Lucas with a skeptical frown. "Why did Yaap not come himself?"

"He lies buried in a bog on the edge of the wood, within a long bow-shot of Appingedam," Pieter-Lucas said, each word an exercise in defying pain.

"What?" Ludwig roared.

"I watched a Spanish soldier gun him down. Just before he died, he gave me the message. They were his last words. I buried him with my own hands beneath the swamp willows." He felt an unbidden lump rise in his throat, almost too large to be swallowed.

"How knew you he was Yaap?" Ludwig demanded.

Pieter-Lucas pulled the bloody cap from his bag and handed it to him. "Here," he offered. "He sent this to you."

Ludwig took the cap and turned it over slowly in his hands. "Ach! Gracious and merciful God, let it not be so," he mumbled, shaking his head in disbelief.

"He was my friend," Pieter-Lucas stammered, feeling his voice go limp.

Ludwig stared at him sharply. "How?"

"I tended his horse at the kasteel stables in Breda and went with him to Dillenburg."

"I knew you, too, then?"

Pieter-Lucas felt the count's eyes probing him. "We last met when Yaap and I delivered a message to you in Groningen. I was in search of a healer lady, and you sent me to Emden."

"Ah! Young Van den Garde!" Ludwig lay a hand on his arm. "Wait here while I put my troops in readiness. Then I have orders for you as well."

"But," Pieter-Lucas began to protest. Already two missions lay before him—the pamphlets and Aletta. Neither of them could wait for yet another.

Count Ludwig raised his right hand. "Just wait," he said. The firmness in his voice made further protest impossible.

Pieter-Lucas backed away and leaned against the doorframe. One more day was passing! What sort of supernatural force was tugging at all the threads of his life, trying to unravel him and his Aletta? He sighed and folded his arms across his chest, tapping a foot nervously.

Already Count Ludwig's voice bounced off the thick walls. "Time to array ourselves for battle."

From the group, one soldier spoke up with agitated manner. "This is hardly a place to fight a battle."

"*Nay*, but it is," Ludwig retorted and motioned with a wide sweep of his arm.

"The monks who live here are peaceful men," another soldier interrupted.

"Without our swords we scarcely could have persuaded them even to feed us a meal. How think you that they will allow us to invade their serenity with a battle?" shouted yet another.

"All popish monks, they are." Again from the first dissenter.

Ludwig raised a hand high and stamped his foot. "Silence! Aremberg lies not more than two or three hours behind us, with who knows how many Spanish troops. We've only time to put ourselves in order. No spot could be more favorable to our cause. The firm high ground is ours to hold, leaving our enemies to flounder in the bogs, in which no Spaniard is equipped to fight. Now, here is my plan. . . ."

For the next few minutes, Ludwig gave each commander his instructions. Some were to line up along the roadway where Aremberg would pass and engage his men in battle. Others would remain hidden behind one of the hills. None were to leave the high ground that cordoned off the bogs, and they were to accomplish a victory by forcing the landlubber Spaniards into the unfamiliar boggy terrain, where they would be entrapped by the sticky muck and drawn to their suffocating deaths.

Pieter-Lucas listened aghast at the impetuous enthusiasm of Ludwig and watched the men yield quickly to the influence of his fiery manner. In the pit of his belly, he felt pummeled by the awfulness of men planning to destroy other men and rejoicing at the prospects of a victory where blood would run in rivers at their feet.

"I'm more of a Child of God at heart than I realized," he mumbled to himself.

When the last of Ludwig's commanders had filed out the door, the nobleman turned to Pieter-Lucas. "When I sent you to Emden in search of the Healer Lady of East Friesland, did you find her?" he asked.

"I did."

"Know you how to find her once more?"

Pieter-Lucas swallowed hard. "*Ja*, Your Excellency, that I can do."

"Then for the cause of Willem and the Low Lands, go and bring her to us here. I can ill afford to lose my wounded men."

Pieter-Lucas looked at him long and hard. "I cannot promise that she will be persuaded," he said lamely. "She belongs to a sect that refuses to bear arms."

"Do your best, but do return—with or without her."

Ludwig moved to go through the doorway. Pieter-Lucas stopped him. "Your Excellency."

"*Ja?* Can it not wait?"

"*Nay!* I only encountered Yaap in the course of a mission for Prince Willem, which I interrupted to bring you the message."

"What mission?"

"Two days ago, a white-haired gentleman, a friend of Count Brederode—he calls himself Dirck—entered our bookshop in Emden with a parcel of your brother's pamphlets."

"So Willem's got Dirck Coornhert passing out his *Justification?*"

Pieter-Lucas nodded. "He sent me to deliver them to . . . certain contacts of the printery where I draw title pages and cartoons." He took care not to reveal his Anabaptist connections to this Lutheran commander of the Calvinist troops.

Ludwig shook his head. "My brother and his bloodless campaigns! While he's still passing out pamphlets, Alva will swoop down and cut us all to pieces."

With arms extended, he chopped at the air. "Get the Healer Lady now! The deliveries can wait."

"I go then," Pieter-Lucas said. At least it would bring him to Aletta sooner.

"And, *jongen*," Ludwig said, pulling the blood-stained cap from his pocket and handing it to Pieter-Lucas, "it's yours—and his job, as well, as soon as you return with the Healer Lady."

"But I'm not a messenger!" Pieter-Lucas gulped and felt his eyes widen.

"You are now!" Ludwig frowned at him. Without waiting for an answer, he was gone through the door.

Pieter-Lucas left by the way he had come in, through the back door and around the old buildings. Where before soldiers, horses, and weapons had been scattered in chaotic state about the grounds, now groups were forming, some marching into place, others hiding, all seeking dry ground, solid footings, strategic positions. Muskets rode in silence on the shoulders of their sharpshooters; horses pranced and paraded; brightly colored flags and banners waved across the pasture and over the gently rolling hills that surrounded the monastery.

It looked like a grand festival spread out over the countryside. From the corner of the cloister, Pieter-Lucas took one last look at the scene. Just beyond him moved a pair of banners carried by mounted cavalrymen. "Now or Never," read a blue one. "Win or Die," said the other on a brilliant orange sash.

"This is no festival," he said to himself. "If Prince Willem's House of Oranje doesn't win this battle or those that follow, the revolt will die— and I will never get to Leyden. . . ."

Pieter-Lucas tossed his knapsack over his shoulder and hurried down the road. Eager visions of his soon-to-be bride urged him ever forward. An occasional wash of unhindered sunlight warmed his back, and the forests all around him swelled with bird songs. The gentle protests of his clumsy leg he was able almost to ignore. One nagging question, though, followed him all the way.

How could he tell Ludwig that he could not fill Yaap's cap? The idea of trying to fill Yaap's bloody cap was as preposterous as it was frightening. He had a limp, he had no stomach for war, and he was about to take a vrouw. Besides, Ludwig's sister, Juliana, had a job for him painting pictures for the herbal she was creating, Willem used his frequent help in the stables, and they'd both promised to send him to Leyden.

Most of all, he was a painter. Carrying messages from battlefield to battlefield, dodging Spanish soldiers' bullets, was not for him. He shuddered. Someone else must do it.

No matter how loudly he repeated the logic to himself, one tormenting voice kept sounding in his ears. *This is wartime. Think you that Willem's going to let you sit around painting pictures with Yaap gone and Ludwig begging you to wear his cap?*

"Then I'll have to take my bride far away where no one can find us," he argued.

Ha! the voice laughed back. *Where are you going to find such a place? And if you do, how will you still your conscience?*

His mind staggered around in never ending circles. His heart pounded, and his feet moved faster and faster.

On the shores of Den Dullart, he approached a boat tied to the landing. A bearded older man with black jacket and tam sat nearby. He puffed on his long-stemmed pipe, blowing a cloud of tobacco smoke into the air and looking toward Pieter-Lucas.

"Boat for hire," the man offered, a tone of eagerness edging his voice.

"To Emden?"

"To Emden," the man replied, stepping into the boat that rocked gently with the slapping of the water against its bow. He guided his passenger in with him, then loosed the moorings immediately and began rowing across the water.

"In a hurry, I see," the man observed.

"Me?" Pieter-Lucas nearly laughed. Never had he seen a boatman move so fast and strain so intently at the oars.

"Ja. I saw you racing down to the water like as if you had the devil on your heels. Who you fleeing?"

Pieter-Lucas gripped his knapsack and pulled himself as far into the corner of the boat as possible. The man went on. "You're luckier than some of the men I've carried out here. A lot of soldiers going off to the war smoldering out in these bogs. But then, you probably know more about that than I do." He paused, his expectations of an answer hanging heavy in the air between them.

"So I've heard," Pieter-Lucas said, careful to maintain a wary tone.

The old man chuckled. "Funny thing about men. Think they're brave and strong and war is some exciting adventure. But let 'em see a battle— and not enough gold—and they can run home faster'n a scared hare across a heath."

He paused only long enough to catch his breath, then prattled on. "Y' know, people run away from many things. I've seen thieves running from their accusers, women running from their vrouw-beating husbands, children thinking any place must be better than home . . ."

Pieter-Lucas tried to close his ears. That was one thing a secret messenger must never do. Had to have his ears always scrubbed for those little markers that might lead him on a trail going somewhere he had to go. Not that he was a messenger, and yet, just for now he had to be one till he'd gotten Aletta back to Ludwig's camp, and . . . Maybe it was safer to listen than to let his mind carry him any farther down that terrifying path.

"One time a man jumped into my boat 'cause the bailiff was after him," the boatmen continued. "Something to do with his religion. Probably he was a Rebaptizer. They're always on the run, you know. I carried him across Den Dullart with the bailiff and his men chasing us in another hired boat. Once on the other side, they finally caught my passenger, and if they hadn't been so busy with him, I'm dead certain they would've arrested me as well. Dangerous even to give aid to a heretic, you know. Ach, me! Such gloomy times, these."

How much longer was this trip going to last? They should have reached Emden by now. Pieter-Lucas peered ahead in search of Emden's harbor. Instead, he discovered they were headed straight into the Ems River, south of Emden.

"Where are you taking me?" he demanded.

"To your destination." The boatman rowed harder.

"You agreed to take me to Emden, but we're on the way to Jemmingen."

"I take you to your destination." The man's even calmness was exasperating.

"Not unless you change your course." Pieter-Lucas grabbed at the man's arms and tried to wrest the oars from him.

"Easy, there," the boatman warned, "or we'll both end up treading water in the reeds, and that's not where either one of us ever thought of going."

"What sort of trick is this?" Pieter-Lucas shouted.

"Before the day is over, you'll thank me for saving your life, *jongen*," he replied.

"Saving my life? From whom or what?"

"You'll learn that all in good time, *jongen*, all in good time," the voice went on with maddening steadiness.

"Who are you?" Pieter-Lucas shouted.

"All you need to know is that I'm pretty skillful at using oars for a weapon. Now, just sit still for another eyeblink or two. We're almost there."

"Where?" Pieter-Lucas exploded. "The only *there* I'm interested in is Emden, and you're taking me down the Ems River!"

The boatman rowed on, silent at last. Straight ahead, on the eastern bank of the river, Pieter-Lucas saw the form of a lone mounted horseman. Waiting for him?

Almost instantly they were drawing up alongside the horse and beaching the boat. Wary of the stranger, yet eager to be free from his troublesome boatman, Pieter-Lucas dropped his coins in the man's outstretched hand and disembarked. At least he had reached Emden's side of the water. He prepared to bolt toward the north. But the horse and rider blocked his way.

The rider was completely cloaked in a black cape. Even his eyes remained half hidden by the wrappings.

"Mount with me quickly," he urged.

Pieter-Lucas examined the stranger. "How can I trust you when I've no idea who you are or where you plan to take me?"

"I am no stranger to you, Pieter-Lucas van den Garde."

"Dirck!" In a flash he knew the voice, then the eyes. Hesitantly, he mounted.

They were already moving—away from Emden. "Where are you taking me?" Pieter-Lucas challenged his abductor.

"To your friends," Dirck answered.

"But I have no friends out here, and I have orders to find the Healer Lady in Emden and return with her to Heiligerlee before sunset."

"Heiligerlee! Is that where you passed on my pamphlets?"

"*Nay*, it's where I found Ludwig preparing for the imminent arrival of Aremberg's troops. He sent me back to Emden to bring the Healer Lady. By now he already needs them."

"I take you directly to the woman you seek."

"Out here? Halfway to Jemmingen?" It made no sense.

"The Healer Lady is nearby, along with a few others."

"My bride?"

"Both of the women are safely hidden away in a spot so remote not even Alva could sniff out their whereabouts."

"Hans and his people haven't fled from Emden, have they?" The thought seemed spectral, even as he put it into words.

"I fear many of them have."

"Since I left?"

"Just last night they came this way."

"Who would want to do them harm?"

"I see you have yet to learn one important lesson, *jongen*. Every man has enemies in this world, and none has more than an Anabaptist preacher and his printer."

"But why?"

"Every flock has its troublemakers, and sometimes they are strong enough to arouse suspicions. Every printer has a past that he can never be certain will not follow closely on his heels."

"I knew Hans' group had troublemakers." Pieter-Lucas remembered the quarrelsome newcomers. "But the rest of the flock would never turn against him. And in Emden?"

"Even Emden may turn into a trap." Dirck's words sent a chill through Pieter-Lucas' body.

"Where can they go?" he asked. "I thought it was the last house of refuge for people who don't agree with the authorities—or with each other."

"Engeland, Silesia, even a few spots in Germany. God will always preserve some havens of refuge in little obscure places."

"Must they forever be on the run like hunted hawks of prey?"

As clearly as if he still sat facing the circle of elders in Hans' hidden church, Pieter-Lucas heard Johannes' piercing voice interrogating him, "You are ready to face death for the crime of being a baptized Child of God?" The question came suddenly alive.

Dirck sighed. "The likes of Hans and Dirck Engelshofen will only be able to stop running when Prince Willem wins this war and brings some order to the Low Lands."

"Until then?" Pieter-Lucas asked.

"No doubt you've heard the song these people are so fond of singing when their way seems filled with ferryless rivers and overturned coaches.

"Those who in God do trust,"

Pieter-Lucas joined him on the second line.

"And never in shame do stand,
Both young and old, men and women,
God strengthens with His hand."

"For these people," Dirck said, "survival is not a matter of military campaigns against a foreign tyrant, but of faith in a God strong enough to go with them, even through a hawk-hunting ordeal or a furnace of fire."

"I know," Pieter-Lucas said, then fell silent.

He spent the rest of the ride out over the boggy countryside and through another grove of brushwood and swamp willows wrestling again with the questions that had followed him all the way from Heiligerlee. If he refused to fill Yaap's cap and shoes, would Dillenburg close its doors to him and his bride? If so, where could he take her? And if he didn't do his part in driving Philip and Alva from the Low Lands, how could he and Aletta ever find a way to go to Leyden?

The circle had only one end. He must take Yaap's place!

Nay! That I cannot do!

He could not think about it anymore. Instead, he closed his eyes, surrendered the canvas of his imagination to the master skill of his mind, and dreamed of Aletta. His memory took him back to that day—it seemed like a lifetime ago now—when he'd had to leave Breda on an errand for his dying moeder.

"Promise you'll wait for me to return," he had begged of his childhood sweetheart, "and you'll never give your heart to another."

With that soft kind voice, the likes of which there could be no other on earth, she had said, "My heart is yours—always has been—always will be."

"Always!" How often since had that magical word revived flagging hope!

Everything in the memory of this girl with the golden ringlets, deep blue dancing eyes, and tender touch set a wonderful fire in his heart. All unanswered questions about courier duties and wars slipped momentarily into oblivion.

His dream jolted to an abrupt end at the entrance of a squat farmhouse on the edge of a forested bog. Dirck was nudging him to dismount.

Reluctantly Pieter-Lucas climbed off the horse and stepped lightly over the soggy ground, taking care to avoid the unpredictable flock of clucking hens swarming in every direction. Dirck knocked on the door, and a bent old farmer opened to them. He smiled and, taking the horse's reins from Dirck's hand, motioned them across his foot-worn threshold. They entered a smallish room heavy with the mingled smells of peat smoke, vegetable stew, and barnyard animals.

Pieter-Lucas blinked in the dim light as he held his breath and followed Dirck through a door beside the hearth into a large room. The roof and ceiling sloped sharply down to a long row of oiled paper windows nearly at floor level. Around a long table near the inside wall, a group of men sat on benches, their faces lightened as much by a pair of lamps as by the windows.

An uncomfortable silence hovered over the room. Pieter-Lucas looked around the table. Hans was there, the weaver, the one-armed fisherman, the chief elder, and three other faithful members of the flock. Where was Dirck Engelshofen?

Pieter-Lucas was searching the group a second time when Hans spoke. "Good afternoon, Heer Dirck and Pieter-Lucas." He gestured toward empty seats at the end of the benches.

"*Ja*, thank-you, Brother Hans," Pieter-Lucas stammered. "We've not come to sit. I bring an urgent message for our Healer Lady. I must see her at once."

All eyes were staring at him now.

"She is here, is she not?" He looked from Hans to Coornhert and back, all the while feeling the warmth and color rise to his cheeks.

"She is indeed here," Hans said. "But tell us first what is the nature of your message. You found one of our families in dire straits?"

"*Nay*. Not one of our families. Rather, Count Ludwig and the troops of Willem van Oranje are being pummeled, even as I speak to you, by Alva's men. His wounded need the herbs and healing touch of our Oma. Please let me go to her."

The chief elder glared at him. "How can you ask such a thing? You know we are lovers of peace, not supporters of war."

Pieter-Lucas felt his breath come rapidly and his stomach form into a hard knot. Ignoring the elder, he turned to Hans. "Tell me, Brother Hans, does your moeder offer her healing services to all suffering human beings as you taught me in our disciples' lessons? Or must she confine them to those who refuse to carry arms?"

Hans shifted on his stool. "My *moeder* has been gifted by God with so large a heart of compassion," he began, "that she would never let anyone, no matter what his mission, go unattended—not even if he intended her the greatest of personal harm."

The elder stroked his long beard and cleared his throat importantly. "However, we must keep her safely guarded in this refuge."

"Men are dying to wrest our vaderland from the Papists, and you insist on keeping the Healer Lady here?" Pieter-Lucas' anger surprised even himself.

The elder stood to his feet and pointed at Pieter-Lucas. "Today you show us your true nature. No Child of God will ever beg us to support any war, in any way."

"No man hates war more than I," Pieter-Lucas retorted. "Just this morning I watched a good friend gunned down by a Spanish warrior, not because he fought, but only because he carried a life-saving message to Count Ludwig. I am well ready to take vows of nonviolence for myself."

He paused to swallow down the anguish that rose into an unwieldy lump in his throat. "But the men who fight to win us access to our vaderland must have help if they would live to complete the job. If there is not in this flock any more of what Hans calls a 'neutral compassion,' then I must reserve my vows for the ears of God alone."

Pieter-Lucas felt a hand on his shoulder. "Brothers," Dirck began, his deep voice vibrating with the authority of wisdom. "Am I given to understand that this one man speaks as the sole voice of your fellowship? Or is it customary to engage in questioning and calling upon Almighty God for guidance?"

All eyes turned to Hans. With obvious discomfort, he began. "We have already arrived, through much questioning and prayer, at the decision that no baptized member of the group assembled here is to venture out of this place on any mission that could possibly be used against us. Under other circumstances we might reconsider."

"Your compassion is not unconditional, then?" Dirck asked.

Hans stirred uneasily. "In all but crises such as this, it is. At times wisdom dictates a temporary withholding of some sorts of charity."

"Oh?"

Hans sighed, then said with the air of a man before the Chief Inquisitor, "We are already in enough difficulty because of my moeder's kindness shown just yesterday to a wounded soldier in Emden."

The chief elder interrupted. "That soldier was arranged by our enemies as a test, that they might have evidence of her unfaithfulness to present against us."

Hans picked up his speech. "If we are to regain our flock in Emden, we must show an unusual sort of caution just now, one that involves rejecting your proposal as practical folly, no matter how much we might approve of it in principle."

"Your decision, then, is final?" Dirck asked.

"In our present plight it must be."

Openmouthed, Pieter-Lucas glared at Hans, whose face was a portrait artist's study in anguish. He must take his case directly to the Healer Lady and be on his way. He barged through a doorway he had spotted and into a smaller room, where he found Oma, her two granddaughters, Aletta, and a handful of other women sitting on low stools in a corner near the window.

"Pieter-Lucas!" Aletta cried. She sprang to her feet and came to him.

"Thank God you're safe!" he said, reaching out with one arm and holding her. For a long moment they gazed into each other's eyes, and he had to fight to restrain himself from giving her a full embrace.

He turned to Oma. "Count Ludwig and his army are embroiled in a bloody struggle with Alva's men. He's sent me to bring you with your herbs to help his wounded. Your elders will not let you go. I beg of you, for the love of God and our fellowmen, at least to give me a supply of your healing salves, that I might take them to the soldiers myself."

Aletta grasped both his arms in her hands. "I go with you, Pieter-Lucas."

"*Nay*, I could not take you there, Little One. 'Tis mine to protect you, not lead you into harm's way."

"But I will go. Oma and I decided it already."

"How did you know?"

"We heard it all through the wall. You cannot go alone. You know nothing of this healing business. Further, I will not let you leave my sight again."

Pieter-Lucas looked at the young woman and encircled her once more in his arm. A war of urges stormed through his being—urges to protect, to possess, to keep her next to his heart every moment, to be done with the whole war business, to ignore both Hans and Ludwig and carry off his bride into some faraway land of perpetual bliss.

When he looked up, he saw Oma staring at him, nodding her head. "Hans is right," she said. "I dare not to leave the flock just now. But Aletta is also right. She will be a valuable helper to you. I've taught her all I know, and she can teach you all you want to learn. Her apothecary chest is well stocked with herbs and salves for treating wounds."

"B-but . . ." Pieter-Lucas began his protest.

Oma lifted a hand and shook her head, then said, "You are well able to protect this woman. Here," she added, handing him a large lumpy bag. "It's filled with old rags enough to bind up a hundred battle wounds. And remember, our God goes with you."

Pieter-Lucas stared at Oma. "You mean it, don't you?"

"I do." She nodded.

Still a trifle dazed, he half smiled at the young woman still by his side. "I must ask your vader's permission to take you off alone before our wedding."

Aletta shook her head. "My *vader* has fled to Engeland."

"What?" Surely he must soon awaken to discover this was a bad dream.

"*Ach,* Pieter-Lucas! It was dreadful! He packed our belongings by lamplight, and before dawn the next day, he and Moeder and Robbin had all boarded a boat, leaving me with Hans and Oma."

"Why now, just when we were ready to marry?" He held her by both arms and searched her face and eyes for some clue that he could use to extricate them from this impossible situation.

"The Blood Council seeks my vader," she whispered.

"Why?" he gasped.

"Later, Pieter-Lucas, later." She patted his arm with her hand.

"Then we must go without your vader's permission." His heart pounded.

"Go where?" Hans' voice sounded from behind him.

Pieter-Lucas felt his body stiffen. "Surely you'll not forbid it!"

"Dirck Engelshofen left her in my charge," Hans cautioned. "How can I let you two run off together, unaccompanied and unmarried, to some battlefield?"

"But the need is urgent. We'll return in a day or two, in time for our wedding."

"Who knows where you may find us in two more days?" Hans said. "When you leave us here, it may be forever, or at least for a very long time."

Pieter-Lucas stood for a heart-stopping moment, staring at Hans. He could take the apothecary chest and go back to Ludwig alone. After all, he had warned Ludwig that the Healer Lady might not come. *Nay!* If he should return to find Aletta gone . . . There was no way to finish the thought!

"I cannot go without her," he said, holding tightly to her.

Lost in the torment of his dilemma, he realized Aletta was shoving the curls from around his ear with a cupped hand. "There is a way!" she whispered.

"How?" he muttered.

"Marry now!"

Like a shooting star the thought burst through his brain and exploded from his lips. "Of course! Hans, you could marry us now! For what do we wait?"

The weaver-preacher stared at them, an expression of puzzlement holding the features of his face rigid. Slowly he asked, "Are you ready to submit to our baptism?" The words, tinged with a haunting sadness, echoed around the room and bombarded Pieter-Lucas from every corner.

"For how many months have I been telling you that I was ready?" Pieter-Lucas asked in a low voice, hoping not to be heard in the next room. "Now your elders tell me that my promises not to go to war must include all things related to the war. If that is so, I must say no. I know not where the path of duty may lead me before Prince Willem has pried open the doors to our vaderland."

Hans shook his head slowly. "In a world where men and women are burned at the stake or drowned for nothing more than the sin of adult baptism," he said thoughtfully, "it is important that a man be truly ready before we baptize him."

"In the meantime," Pieter-Lucas said, impatience growing, "daylight grows shorter, Ludwig lies yonder in desperate need of the Healer Lady, and we waste time discussing religion." He moved closer to Hans until they looked directly into each other's eyes. "Can you not just marry us now and leave religious questions for later, when men's lives don't depend on us?"

Hans hesitated shortly, then whispered, "My elders would say it cannot be done. I think the question is, 'What would Dirck Engelshofen say?' "

Pieter-Lucas held his breath and felt Aletta's body quivering beside him as she spoke. "My vader left you instructions to marry us as soon as Pieter-Lucas returned. If he were here, he would beg you to do it now and send us on this mission of mercy."

"And if I don't?" Hans asked.

She hesitated, looked up at Pieter-Lucas, then back to Hans. "We have a healing mission to perform and a marriage promise long overdue to be kept."

Pieter-Lucas added, "We must go, either with your blessing or without. If you force us to it, we will find a clergyman of some other sort who will bless us on the way."

Pieter-Lucas looked for shock on the weaver's face. Instead he saw compassion. Hans stood silent for a space, then asked, "After the battle, where will you take your bride? How will you provide for her?"

Pieter-Lucas swallowed down the apprehension. "We go back to Dillenburg, where a door stands always open for us with the Nassau family."

God, may it be so, he breathed without a sound. He grasped Aletta by the arm and watched Oma move through the floor rushes to stand beside Hans. Moeder and son looked briefly at each other, then up at them. Oma was smiling.

"Come, follow me," Hans said, the tightness drained from his voice. "We have a wedding to make!"

"Aletta, he said a wedding!" Pieter-Lucas grabbed her by both hands.

"A wedding?" she gasped. Her eyes bubbled over with laughter and adoration!

Through the haze of a moment that could not be but was, Pieter-Lucas took his bride by the hand and led her across the threshold into a room both smaller and darker than the others. Hans already stood beside a table where Oma was spreading a white cloth and laying out an open Bible. One of Hans' daughters thrust a bunch of bright flowers into Aletta's hands, and the women formed a half circle around them in the hastily assembled sanctuary.

Aletta turned her face toward Pieter-Lucas. *A more beautiful face God never made,* he thought. And from somewhere in a distant fog, he heard the words he had all but despaired of hearing. "Marriage is an honorable ordinance of God, instituted in the beginning when He blessed the two human beings first created in His image and joined them together." The voice that just moments ago had occasioned such despair now flowed with wonder. Deeply drinking in the marvels of the moment, Pieter-Lucas heard only snatches of the preacher's recitation of all the things he had explained to them long ago, when logical understanding was stronger than ecstasy.

But when Hans looked directly at Pieter-Lucas and said, "Love her as your own body—as Jesus Christ loved the Church and gave himself for her," he heard every word.

In that instant he knew that marriage was more than keeping Aletta by his side forever. It meant binding himself to ensure her safety, her happiness, no matter what life might bring their way. Was he ready? Was he the man she deserved?

At last Hans asked him the eagerly awaited question. "Do you, Pieter-Lucas van den Garde, promise before God and your friends and family, both present and absent, to love, cherish, and protect this woman till death wrench you asunder?"

Pieter-Lucas looked into Aletta's soul and smiled, sending a quick prayer to God for help before he said, "That shall I do." His voice trembled and his heart swelled to the point of bursting. This was the woman who would always be by his side, giving relief to his halting leg, bearing his children, believing in the paint that ran in his blood!

"Do you, Aletta Engelshofen, promise before God and your friends and family, both present and absent, to love, obey, and care for this man till death wrench you asunder?"

"That shall I do!" Her whole being radiated with a glow he'd never dreamed.

With as much measured fervency as if he had all the rest of the day, Hans prayed over them. At the last "Amen," the groom and his new vrouw stood for a long moment, lost in the wonders only they could see in each other's eyes.

Then Pieter-Lucas gave the preacher his thanks and helped Aletta gather up the apothecary and her bags. They said their farewells and crept through a low door leading out at the back side of the house. There they found Dirck waiting for them with two horses. One he mounted himself, the other he offered to them.

"Blesje!" Pieter-Lucas exclaimed. "How did you come here?"

"We brought him from Emden when we fled," Dirck explained.

Pieter-Lucas mounted the horse who had carried him the length and breadth of the Low Lands and waited while Hans helped Aletta up behind him. Then he grabbed the reins and followed Dirck's lead back through the maze of roads.

The warmth of Aletta's body pressing up against his back and the reassuring pressure of her arms encircling his waist sent him into a frenzy of indescribable joy. She was no longer his betrothed. She was his vrouw! How soon could they travel alone, free to give the spurs to Blesje and speed onward toward the fulfillment of Willem's mission and their own resplendent visions?

When they reached the narrow pathway that would take them on alone, Dirck motioned them to stop. "You know your way from here?" he asked.

"That I do," Pieter-Lucas shouted in the wind.

Dirck sidled up and said, "About your marriage, back there in the farmer's home."

"You know?"

The man chuckled. "That surprises you?"

Pieter-Lucas stared at him. "You always know everything, don't you?"

Dirck held up his hand. "And you need to know one more thing before I let you go. An Anabaptist marriage ceremony is recognized as valid only in Anabaptist circles. All other people will consider this woman to be your mistress."

"So what are we to do?" Pieter-Lucas' heart seemed to stop still in his shirt.

"Do not leave Heiligerlee till you have enlisted the services of a priest to carry you through one more ceremony."

"A priest? What would Dirck Engelshofen say?"

"In matters of life and death such as this, I suspect he would urge prudence."

"*Ja*," Pieter-Lucas said, "that's just what he'd do."

"Only make certain the priest records it in his books. Then wherever you go, whoever may ask, you can always satisfy them that you are indeed man and vrouw." He looked at them both for a long silent space.

Restless eyes of a friend, Pieter-Lucas decided. "I hope we meet again soon."

"In good time, *jongen*, in good time." With a wave of the black-cloaked arm, their white-bearded friend set off to the north, and the newly marrieds rode south into the prevailing winds that never ceased whipping at the far north provinces.

"Was he a true flesh-and-blood man?" Aletta asked, barely audible, her voice vibrating warm breath into the hollow of Pieter-Lucas' back.

"What do you mean?" he shouted back over his shoulder.

"Was he maybe God's angel sent to care for us?"

He lifted his head to let the wind blow through his curls and laughed. "There is only one angel here, my love. The one who holds me in the circle of her arms."

CHAPTER NINE

Heiligerlee

23rd aftertoon of Flower Month (May), 1568

*A*ll the way to Heiligerlee, Aletta clung to Pieter-Lucas and wrapped herself tightly in the glow of the wondrous thing that had just happened to them.

"Aletta van den Garde!" She rolled the delicious combination of names off her tongue and shivered with excitement. "You belong to Pieter-Lucas, now and forever," she told herself over and over. Each time she said it, she hugged him as if it were the first time and the last.

Their journey led through wild green countryside with no houses or farms, to the accompaniment of sighing winds, rushing water, and singing birds. Clouds billowed and sailed through the skies above, and the air smelled of sea water, trilliums, moldy toadstools, and decaying peat.

But the way proved to be long, and the wind soon penetrated Aletta's clothes with an inescapable chill. Not accustomed to riding horseback, she grew weary of her precarious position. Even her arms, which for long had ached to hold her new husband, now ached from so long a holding.

Once they'd passed through the village of Winschoten, she thought she saw a streak or two of silver and red flashing through the dense trees. She heard Pieter-Lucas mumble something about soldiers and felt his body tighten in her arms. Shortly thereafter, a pair of men in tattered uniforms staggered across a field off to their left, headed toward a barnlike shelter in the field. One man fell, and the other limped on a few more paces, then fell himself.

Pieter-Lucas turned his head and shouted at her against the wind, "Spaniards!"

"How do you know?"

"Red sashes, dark mustaches, silver helmets. Perhaps the battle is over."

He urged Blesje on faster. It soon became clear that the fighting had indeed spent itself. The sights and sounds and smells on every side were worse than anything she could ever have imagined. The scene unfolded gradually before her, a mass of weapons and horses and broken bodies. Some were entangled in low tree branches, others sprawled across road-ways, and many floated in swampy bog lands. Her ears vibrated to the moans, both human and animal, to the occasional distant clashes of metal against metal. The stench of gunpowder, churned-up peat, blood, and horse manure was almost suffocating. Shuddering, Aletta closed her eyes, shutting out the horrific sight, and buried her face in Pieter-Lucas' back. *Great and merciful God,* she prayed silently, *help me. . . .* Her words trailed off as ghastly images flew through her head, imprinting themselves deep in her mind, choking her with fear and dread of what lay ahead.

When at last they'd reached the old monastery, Pieter-Lucas helped her dismount. She leaned against him and gasped, "I didn't know it could be so awful!"

"It's war," he mumbled, holding her tight in his arms, trembling him-self.

No wonder the Children of God preached nonviolence. Surely God was not pleased with all these cruelties done by men to men. Yet however much one might hate war or pledge to avoid it, what could one do when targeted by Alva's canons and chased into the peat bogs? But Aletta hadn't come here to moan about the awfulness of the sight while seeking comfort and protection in her husband's arms. She pulled away and spoke, at-tempting bravery. "Where do we begin?"

Before he could answer, she heard a muffled cry from behind her. "Help! Help!" The pleading word echoed over the desolate chaos. Turning, she spotted a Spanish soldier, half submerged in the muck of the bog.

Without another thought, she started toward him, only to feel Pieter-Lucas' arms pulling her back.

"He needs help," she protested.

"He is also mired in the muck," Pieter-Lucas retorted. "He's far stronger than you, and if you grasp his hand, you shall not save him. Rather, he will drag you under."

Stunned, she stared at Pieter-Lucas for a hard moment. He looked down, then away. "Besides," he mumbled, "we're not here to help Span-iards. Part of the plan in this place is to force the enemy into the bog and not to let him free himself."

"Oh, Pieter-Lucas," she cried out. "We must choose, then, only to let Ludwig's men live?" How much easier life would be if she could have committed herself to stay away from battlefields. That way, she would never have to look the enemy in the eye and try to forget he was a human being with the sort of wounds she had been trained to heal, or wonder if he had a woman at home awaiting his return.

But Aletta had seen the battle's bloody aftermath. Could she ever forget it?

Pieter-Lucas handed Blesje's reins to a stableboy. "Can you secure my horse and give him victuals?"

The boy, not much older than Robbin, answered roughly, "First show me coins."

Pieter-Lucas dug into the bag at his waist, producing a coin. The boy snatched it up, then took the reins and walked toward the stable, eyeing them both with scorn. "No place for a woman," he snapped.

He could not have spoken truer words, Aletta decided. She stayed close to Pieter-Lucas, who was toting her bags and guiding her toward the door of the monastery building. "Got to get you some shelter," he whispered.

At the door, Pieter-Lucas knocked vigorously. The split door opened at the top and a monk glared at them.

"I must find Count Ludwig. I've brought him a healer lady as he requested. Where is your dispensary, where we can receive the men?"

The monk looked down over his nose and said icily, "We have no dispensary."

"Any room will do—the kitchen or the chapel, or an empty cell."

"We did not invite the battle to these sacred grounds. If you must wage a war here, you must keep it all outside." He began to close the door. Pieter-Lucas held it back with a strong hand.

"This healer lady comes to enhance, not to pollute the holiness of your sanctuary. Surely you can respect her need for protection from a misguided bullet or the pike of some madman," he pleaded.

"Go, young man!" The monk slammed the door.

Pieter-Lucas' eyes held fire and he began pounding again.

Grasping his arm, Aletta prodded gently, "Can we not find another way? Maybe even an animal shelter of some sort. Men are dying, and we came here not to argue with uncooperative monks. They can hardly be expected to have sympathies for the cause of the Calvinist rebels."

He yielded to her tugging.

"We could go to the stable," she suggested.

"To make up beds for dying men in the dunged and vermin-ridden straw? And pay that impudent young lad another coin for each patient we bring in?"

A ponderous question mark hung between them, only partially removed when Aletta spoke. "I could treat them where they lie in the fields. Better than not treating them at all. We have no more time to stand here in doubt. Come, Pieter-Lucas."

At that moment another monk approached, pulling his hood about his head. He motioned and they followed, moving past a line of plastered cells, stopping at the last apartment. He shoved open the door and ushered them into a small barren room with a crude table and chair and a mat on the floor. A single window with heavy bars and sills the thickness of a man's hand shed scant light across the room.

"At your service," the monk said. "You need mats? Blankets? Water?"

"Please," Aletta responded. "And if possible, some way to heat water and wine and brew some potions."

"If you have an errand boy, send him to notify Ludwig that we are here," Pieter-Lucas added.

"I shall do all that you require," he said, slipping out the door.

Aletta's hands trembled as she set her apothecary chest on the windowsill. She arranged bottles of wound salve and herbal infusions and set the bag of rags in readiness. "We shall soon need a light," she said. "Night comes shortly upon us."

"Here's a short candle," Pieter-Lucas said, pointing to a thick candle in its wrought-iron holder on the table. "Good thing we are so near to summer solstice. Otherwise, we might be working in pitch blackness already."

She felt the admiration in his eyes fixed on her, watching her every move. "Oh, Pieter-Lucas," she said, "I'm so afraid. . . ." The words didn't begin to describe what she felt at the thought of helping soldiers—wounded, disfigured, with limbs blown off, faces bloodied, entrails gaping. . . .

"War is wrong," she said, shuddering. "I never knew it the way I know it now."

He laid an arm across her shoulder. "I shouldn't have brought you to this awful place."

"You didn't force me to come. I insisted, remember? Besides . . ." She paused and breathed deeply before going on. "Oma assured me 'twas God sent me here, and He would make me strong. I only hope I can remember that throughout the long and mournful night ahead."

"Perhaps, since Ludwig is the victor of the day, there will not be so many in need," Pieter-Lucas suggested.

"But we saw hundreds of bodies out there, Pieter-Lucas—enough to keep us busy for days."

He shook his head. "Mostly Spaniards, Little One, and mostly already dead."

She leaned against him and shivered. There were no words for that dreadful soul-piercing, suffocating fear she felt inside. She could only repeat again and again, "It's wrong, all wrong. . . ."

Suddenly the light from the doorway was blocked by a pair of soldiers, one half carrying, half dragging the other across the threshold. Both men were bloody, their uniforms torn. The odor of smoldering gunpowder filled the room.

"There's a *physicke* here?" the walking man blurted out.

Pieter-Lucas helped him lay his friend on the mat on the earthen floor near the window. Aletta knelt beside him and winced. One leg was a mass of raw bloody flesh. The man's eyes fluttered, and blood ran from a gash on the front of his unhelmeted head.

The stronger soldier looked at her with terror in his face. "He's my closest friend, his moeder's only son. I promised her I'd bring him home sound and strong. For the love of God, tell me he'll be well."

"I shall treat his wounds with the herbal salves God has provided," she said gently, swallowing hard, not looking at the man. " 'Tis only God can cure. Here, tear his trousers from the wounded leg."

She went for the salve and the rags. The monk stood at her elbow. "Here is water and a basin," he said. "You can send your assistant for more from the well behind the kitchen when you need it. A fire burns in the courtyard. What can I boil for the infusion you mentioned?"

She handed him a bottle of dried leaves of *boelkens* herb. "Remarkable for healing inward wounds," Oma always said.

"Use it all in a large kettle, and when it has bubbled and begins to send forth an aroma, bring it to me by the cupfuls," Aletta instructed.

She knelt once more by the suffering soldier, where his friend and Pieter-Lucas had removed the clothing from the injured leg. She and Pieter-Lucas applied the salve and bound the leg and the head with long strips of cloth. Finally, she wrapped him in a blanket and said, "Take your rest. As soon as it is ready, your friend here will bring you a refreshing herbal infusion to warm and strengthen you."

Even as she spoke, his eyes opened and looked straight at her with the hint of an attempted smile. To his friend, she said, "Now, let's give that nasty gash on your arm some attention."

"My arm?" he stammered.

"I see blood coming through the hole in your jacket. You'll not be of any help to your friend if you die of your own battle wound."

She had scarcely begun dressing the second man's laceration when another bloody soldier entered the room with a large ragged hole in his jacket directly over his chest. Close behind him another pair of limping men dragged each other through the doorway. She opened her mouth to call out to Pieter-Lucas for help, but he was already busy spreading out the mats the monk had brought and was beginning to attend to the latest victims. When the monk returned with a cup of steaming liquid, she sniffed it.

"Well done," she said. "Please bring more and help where needed in giving sips to the men as we dress their wounds. We shall soon need another cell for the ones who cannot walk and lamps to enable us to see in this growing darkness."

"I do what I can, Vrouw *Physicke*," he said and shoved his way out between patients crowding through the doorway.

Like a stampede of cattle, the soldiers filled the room with bloody, sweaty, broken bodies. Next, the courtyard filled and then another cell, offered by one more monk. Aletta and Pieter-Lucas moved about among the wounded scattered all over the monastery grounds. With growing expertise, they tore off clothes, dressed injuries, even removed gunshot and bound up broken limbs. A few healthy soldiers now joined several monks, weaving their way in and out, brewing and carrying cups of *boelkens* herb infusion, dispensing blankets, mats, lighted lamps, and buckets of well water.

Through half the night they worked, until at last no more men came to them. No more loud shouts resounded in the damp night air that hovered over the steamy morass. Pieter-Lucas put his arm around Aletta's waist, and she felt her whole body collapse against him. "It's too dark to search any longer," he said.

"We still have lights," she reminded him, too weary to go on, yet knowing that as long as men lived out in the bogs, the healer lady must push on to find and cure them.

"You, my love, are the finest and kindest of all women on earth. Yet I cannot let you search further. The terrain around us is more treacherous than you know."

Too weary to think anymore, certainly too weary to resist, she agreed and let Pieter-Lucas lead her by the light of a candle to a secluded spot behind one of the buildings. "I discovered this place earlier as we worked," he told her. "Stole a minute to beg an armload of hay from the stableboy and pile it here for you."

"My dear husband." She reached up and caressed his prickly cheek.

He was spreading a large cloth over the straw when a rough voice came through the darkness, "So you've found your way to the battlefield at last."

Aletta started! Hendrick van den Garde! There was no mistaking the voice. He had the most unnerving way of showing up always at the right time and place to torment her Pieter-Lucas. Last time it was in Emden when Pieter-Lucas had just found her. For days she and Pieter-Lucas had nursed his wounds, and never once did he give any indication that he even knew who they were. Now this! What was it all about?

Pieter-Lucas stood quickly, the cloth still in his hand. Aletta raised the candle to illuminate the man's face.

"That surprises you?" Pieter-Lucas asked.

Hendrick laughed and his face gleamed with cynical mockery. "Not at all. I see you brought no sword, just herbs and a healer lady."

Pieter-Lucas took a step toward the man. Aletta grabbed his arm and tried to hold him back. "Careful," she cautioned.

With a voice so clear and strong that it had to be hiding a deep-down terror, Pieter-Lucas asked, "You still think I'm a coward, don't you?"

The old Beggar soldier was moving toward him, his bushy brows, trailing mustachio, and pointed beard framing a pair of wild eyes in the lurid candlelight. "Painter, healer, coward! They will always go together!" he said with a sneer.

Pieter-Lucas' muscles tightened beneath Aletta's fingers. She tugged hard on his arm with both hands and whispered, "Calm, Pieter-Lucas, calm."

"Somewhere in the Gospel records," Pieter-Lucas said, "I seem to recall that Jesus came to give life, not to take it. You, who claim to be His follower, should be happy to learn that I am determined to imitate His life-saving example."

"You spineless Anabaptist!" Hendrick spat the words. "Hiding behind Jesus! You're all cowards, the whole bunch!"

Aletta pushed herself forward. "You seem to have forgotten that not so long ago this brave young man made the choice to save your life. If that was an act of cowardice in your eyes, then you have to live with the meanness of heart that afflicts you. But you will no longer call my husband a coward. Saving lives is his calling, not taking them. It is the bravest work in all the world!"

Aletta watched, amazed, as a look of horror crept over the dark face, and he turned and slinked off into the night, muttering, "Cowards, cowards, cowards . . ."

Pieter-Lucas took her in his arms and held her till the trembling in her breast grew quiet. " 'Twas better when he did not know who we were," he whispered. He rubbed his nose and lips into her hair and added, "My courageous vrouw."

Then reaching down once more, he spread the cloth over the straw and eased her onto the makeshift bed. He laid his cloak over her, planted a kiss on her lips, and whispered, "Rest well, my love. For what is left of tonight, I shall guard you."

She took his hand in hers and smiled a warm contented smile. Her eyelids closed, and as if in a distant fog, she heard his voice saying, "To-morrow, when our names are written in the priest's book, we shall have a real wedding night. . . ."

Exhausted, she drifted into a dreamless sleep.

———

Pieter-Lucas sat beside his new bride with his back leaning up against the outside wall of the monastery chapel. Little did it matter that he had not slept since this time last night, neither could he sleep now if he so desired.

The swampy night buzzed with a soft murmuring chorus of cries and moans, mixed with the melancholy sighing of the wind through swamp willows and pines, and punctuated with the occasional mournful shriek-ing of a swooping long-eared owl. His mind pulsated with images of bloodied bodies—grasping and gasping, maimed and dismembered, dy-ing and glazy-eyed.

One beautiful ray of light darted through each ugly picture. Aletta, his healer lady—gentle, selfless, tireless—moving through the stench and desolation of each battlefield memory like an angel of compassion, dis-pensing life and hope and wholeness. He reached out and caressed her head with his hand.

"Disturb not her slumber, *jongen*," he whispered. Withdrawing his hand, he pushed himself to his feet and paced the length of the wall. Beneath a wide section of windows at shoulder level, he paused and peered through the colored glass panes. Shimmering through the glass, a cluster of blurred, flickering candlelights created a wonderful golden il-lusion.

His imagination carried him quickly inside. There would be paintings on the walls, images in their niches, all the altar furnishings he'd grown up with in the Great Church of Breda. They'd been destroyed on that fateful morning of the image-breakings in Breda, and he'd missed them ever since. In the little church in Dillenburg, there were only a few carved icons, and in Hans' hidden church in Emden, no works of art had ever decorated the walls, nor would any ever be allowed.

"God, did you forget I am an artist?" he pleaded. "If only I could creep inside and let my soul soak up the beauty of the colors, the forms, and spirits fleshed out in paint."

Perhaps when daylight came he could take his bride in with him. They would enlist the services of a priest, and this tiny haven in a sea of misery would become their final bridge to an official marriage. Once she'd finished attending to the needs of the wounded, they'd go back to Emden to retrieve the painting and Opa's brushes from the attic room where he'd left them before they moved on to Dillenburg, and . . .

Pieter-Lucas pressed his nose against the colored windowpane and gazed with renewed longing into the chapel. When would he ever be free to give his life both to the glorious multicolored paints that surged through his blood and to that sleeping woman who impassioned his every breath? First, he must tell Ludwig that he could not fill Yaap's cap. Would it be enough reason for this unmarried military man that Pieter-Lucas had just married a vrouw and that Countess Juliana awaited their arrival in Dillenburg?

Turning his back on the chapel, he leaned against the glass window and looked up into the sky. Already it was brushed with a thin wash of pearly light. Rising up out of the hush around him, he heard the sound of a loud heavy sob so near that it startled him into renewed wakefulness. Coming from the chapel! He wheeled around and pressed his nose once more against the window glasses, trying first one color then another. He could make out no movement. "But it comes from inside," he told himself.

Who among the dead could have been so important as to bring mourners into this place? Count Ludwig? The darting thought grabbed him by the throat. He recalled that all through the night, the commander had not shown his face in the room where the healer lady he had requested worked. Now that he thought about it, Ludwig's soldiers had been remarkably somber for having just won a battle against Alva.

Before he realized he was moving, Pieter-Lucas had crept around the corners and stood before the chapel doors. He gripped them at the spot where time and hands had worn a smooth handle. Gently, fearing his own breath, he pulled the door back a crack.

Colors and fragrances rushed to greet him, and he yearned to surrender to the allure of the glowing sanctuary. But his eyes sought out the weepers until he spotted a single bare-headed mourner on the front kneeling rail, just behind two bodies lying on battle litters before the altar. Cautiously he crept inside and let his stockinged feet carry him quietly toward the litters. The weeping had stopped now, and except for an occasional sniffle from the mourner and a snapping crackle from a candle flame, the musty-fragrant chapel had grown silent.

About halfway between door and altar, Pieter-Lucas stopped. He watched from the back as the man on the kneeling rail pulled a piece of paper from his helmet. Unfolding it, he began to read aloud, punctuating it with more sniffles and occasional wails.

"Highborn, heartily beloved son, Ludwig."

A letter to Ludwig from his moeder, Juliana? The voice did sound like Ludwig's. Then Ludwig was the mourner, not the mourned. Feeling like a boorish intruder into the private sanctuary of another's agony, Pieter-Lucas retraced his steps. The continuing reading followed him down the aisle,

"With heavy heart I have heard how great is the danger and how heavy the business that confronts you there. May the Holy Trinity protect and shelter you. . . . I beg of you, my heartily amiable son, that you might live in the fear of the Lord, so that the enemy in these violent and dangerous times will not creep up on you. What I can do for you through prayer, I shall not spare any diligence to do."

When Ludwig finished reading, he folded the letter up and stuffed it again into his helmet. Then, resting his arms and head on one of the litters, he sobbed out, "Great and merciful God, why Adolph? So young, with so much to give to the revolt! Why did you take him now, God? Why?"

Adolph! Pieter-Lucas gasped. He'd reached the door again and was pushing it with his shoulder when one of its hinges uttered a shuddery creaking sound.

"Who goes there?" the voice of Ludwig shouted after him.

Pieter-Lucas did not turn back, but even as he shoved his feet into his shoes waiting outside, the door swung wide, and Ludwig was looking at him with a dazed expression glazing his eyes.

"Ach, jongen," he said.

"I beg your forgiveness, Excellency," he stammered. "I meant not to disturb your holy moment. If only my healer lady and I could have helped your brother!"

"No one could save him. The bullet and sword made quick work of his young life. He suffered not. 'Twas God, our Vader's time." Ludwig dropped his head to his chest and fought to regain a nobleman's control.

"I am truly sorry," Pieter-Lucas said. Then not knowing how more to console the man, he asked, "And who lies on the other litter?"

"Count Aremberg, Alva's commander."

"Thank God 'tis not another of your leaders," Pieter-Lucas exclaimed.

"We lost very few men in this battle," Ludwig said. "If only all our battles might be like this one, the Low Lands will be back in our hands in no time."

Pieter-Lucas started to walk toward the corner. "I shall awaken the *physicke* so we can return to our ministrations," he said.

"Very well. Only, for you, I have a more pressing job this day."

"More pressing than attending to your wounded men?"

Pieter-Lucas watched a small half smile tug at the man's mouth. "That's the healer lady's job. I send you to Dillenburg to bear the news of our victory"—the smile melted away and he sighed—"along with the sad tale of Adolph's decease." Ludwig shook his head slowly. "The first of my moeder's sons to die. May he also be the last to give his life for our cause."

Pieter-Lucas' heart raced and he felt dampness amidst the hairs on his hands and forehead. He shifted his feet, then stammered, "Your Excellency, I cannot go today."

"Why not?"

Pieter-Lucas opened his mouth, intending to tell this commander of all Willem's forces that he could not take Yaap's place, that he must go back to Emden and retrieve his paints and wedding picture and be on his way to Dillenburg. Instead, he heard himself stammer, "I . . . I cannot leave the healer lady. I must stay and escort her safely from here when her work is finished."

Ludwig waved a hand in the damp cool breeze. "I shall protect her. I know how soldiers are, but even they will respect an elderly woman."

Pieter-Lucas gulped. "You do not understand, Your Excellency. The healer lady you requested did not come. She sent her attractive young assistant."

Ludwig stared openmouthed. Before he could speak, Pieter-Lucas went on. "And she is my vrouw!"

"Your vrouw?" Ludwig exploded. "You didn't tell me you had a vrouw!"

"When last we talked, I didn't."

"But that was only yesterday."

"I know. Yesterday she was still my betrothed. We were to wed later this week. When she had to come with me, our clergyman married us and sent us on our way."

Ludwig scratched his head and looked Pieter-Lucas up and down, saying nothing. Then he stroked the point of his beard and let a long soft whistle escape through his lips. "God have mercy! As if the war itself didn't load me with enough concerns."

"Forgive me, Your Excellency. Prince Willem and your sister, Countess Juliana, knew of our intention to marry. When I left Dillenburg last year in search of my bride, the countess invited me to take her back to live in the *kasteel*."

Ludwig did not answer.

"Perhaps another messenger could go this time," Pieter-Lucas suggested.

The count shook his head. "Without Yaap, only you can go to Dillenburg." He paused. "Can your bride travel in haste with you?"

"She is strong of body and agreeable in spirit," he admitted with his lips, while his heart and mind protested. "But what of her unfinished herbal ministrations?" he asked.

"*Ja!*" Ludwig sighed. "Alva's revenge will be swift and bloody, and I shall need every man whole as soon as possible."

Both men stared speechless at the ground while a meadowlark filled the air above their heads with his plaintive song. Ludwig looked up at last and threw him a questioning glance. "Did anyone give you assistance last night as you worked?"

"Indeed, by the time we had stopped, a considerable force of monks and soldiers was helping with our task."

"Can they be trusted?"

"All those who worked at our side seemed to be men of compassion."

Ludwig sighed. "Know you where to find them?"

"That I shall do." Pieter-Lucas paused. "But first, I have one more difficulty."

Ludwig looked at him tentatively. "About Willem's pamphlets?"

"*Nay!* Although, I think I must take time to leave them in Winschoten."

Ludwig nodded. "I am of a mind to believe you should. We will need all the local support we can muster in these days to follow. What is it, then?"

Pieter-Lucas cleared his throat. How much did he dare divulge? Simply, he told him of the Children of God connections of Aletta's people and of Dirck Coornhert's warning about an official marriage.

Ludwig stood silent for a forever moment. "Tell me, have you and your new bride been rebaptized by this preacher?"

"*Nay.*"

Ludwig puffed a sigh of relief and ran his fingers through the hair on the back of his head. "Take care that you tell no one else what you have just told me. Among these Beggars, it could go ill with both of your lives—and mine—if you spread such word."

"I understand, Your Excellency. I say nothing."

"There is a clergyman in our camp who will do this thing for you if I ask him to, but it must be swift so you can be on your way."

Ludwig paused, then thumped Pieter-Lucas in the chest with his forefinger. "Just remember, as long as you serve this revolt, you must keep yourself from rebaptism and all other radical rituals."

"That I shall do," he promised. There was no way he could tell Ludwig that this would be his first, last, and only trip in service of the revolt. Not now.

"Then go, rouse your bride and instruct the monks. I shall bring the clergyman and meet you here as soon as possible." He paused. "One thing more. You are the only man who could ever take Yaap's place! Don't forget it."

Pieter-Lucas managed a faint painted-on smile and a dazed nod.

————

Aletta awoke to the sound of whispering winds, cawing vultures, and nearby voices. A damp mist lay on her hair and the cape that covered her body. Her legs ached and she shivered slightly, giving way to a shallow cough.

"If I were in a real bed, I think I should be perfectly content to stay here for the rest of my day," she told herself.

The rising sun was coloring the sky with the promise of a new day. She sat up and stretched her arms above her head, yawning deeply. The voices stopped and Pieter-Lucas appeared around the corner. He knelt beside her, smiling and kissing her forehead. With a finger laid against his lips, he urged, "Come, my love."

He reached out a hand and lifted her to her feet.

"I hope we find our patients improved this morning," she said, still chasing the sleep from her eyes. "And not too many new ones that we missed with the fall of darkness."

Pieter-Lucas took her by the shoulders and said, "Count Ludwig has other plans for us today."

"Other plans?" She sensed a cloud hovering over the adoration in his eyes.

He pushed her hair back from her face and stroked her long free-hanging tresses. "I've a long story to tell you as we travel."

"We travel? Back to Hans and Oma?"

"We go to a place you've never been before, a place I've longed to take you."

"Where? What? You hide all the keys under your hat," she teased.

He held her face in his hands again and laughed. "Ludwig is sending us to Dillenburg," he began, and without withdrawing his hands, he grew sober and finished, "to bear news of the victory of Heiligerlee and the death of Count Adolph."

Gasping, she grabbed his forearms. "Oh, Pieter-Lucas, was he one of the wounded we treated last night?"

He shook his head. "Nay. He died on his horse in the field."

In the long silence that followed, she nursed a weeping in her soul. At last she asked, "And what of the wounded men we came here to help?"

"The monks who assisted us last night will carry on."

She shook her head and tried to clear away the cobwebs of confusion. Would life's plans always change so drastically? She watched concern spread across Pieter-Lucas' face.

"We must travel at a much faster speed than either of us would wish. I told Ludwig you were strong and agreeable."

She tried to imagine what it would be like to sit atop a horse on such a long trip. "How many days?"

"Only three or four," Pieter-Lucas said carefully, "if we stop at night to rest briefly. But first, before we can leave, we have one more matter to settle."

"Ja?" She braced herself for yet another disturbing revelation.

Pieter-Lucas held her in the circle of his arm. "Ludwig has gone to summon his army preacher to do one more wedding."

"A Calvinist marriage this time?" In spite of herself, she felt a chuckle in her soul.

"Probably Lutheran. Ludwig's family is German, you know."

Excitement mingled with fear. Clearly, this ceremony would be no more like her dreamed-of wedding than the first. Aletta pulled up her hair and fastened her headdress, then arranged the ringlet curls around her face.

When they met Ludwig and his clergyman at the chapel door, the plans were laid with haste. They dared not use the chapel for the ceremony. Already the monks were angered that these wild troops had defiled their sanctuary with the body of a Protestant nobleman.

"We must take our ceremony out of doors," Ludwig said.

"We've just the spot," Pieter-Lucas announced. "The place where we spent the night outside the colored glass windows behind the altar. We can even see the candlelight."

In no time, the wedding party stood in order. The clergyman turned his back to the window, with Pieter-Lucas and Aletta facing him and Ludwig a bit to the side.

The clergyman held a book and went through a ceremony quite different from that which had accompanied the process the previous day. "Beloved young ones," he began, reading from the book, "you come here to me this day, seeking holy matrimony. . . ."

When Aletta heard the eagerly awaited words, "What God has joined together let no one sever in two pieces," she offered her most deeply felt smile to her bridegroom and he returned the offer. Never had he looked more handsome. At Pieter-Lucas' insistence, the battlefield clergyman recorded the date and place and names in his book. Their marriage was now official in the eyes of the whole world.

"We must leave at once," Pieter-Lucas said.

"First your instructions and messages," Ludwig retorted.

Aletta held tightly to the hand of her husband-indeed. Treading softly across the cold smooth tiles, they followed the bustling count into the chapel. Above the altar she noticed a simple crucifixion with flat figures painted in screaming colors. The room felt candle warm and smelled of musty woodwork, pungent incense, and dead bodies.

Ludwig was beckoning them toward a litter before the altar. "Come, children, you must see clearly for yourselves, that you might bear first-hand witness that Adolph is indeed among the fallen."

They stepped forward. Aletta forced herself to look at the still features, the pale rigid hands. If only she could have washed his wounds and spread on the salve his own sister would have applied had she been here! But it was not to be.

Walking to the second body, Ludwig motioned them once more to follow. "You must tell them also that you have seen the body of Count Aremberg."

Aletta shivered. Why must this be so important?

Ludwig answered her unspoken question. "For many years we were friends. He and Willem served together on the ancient council of ruling noblemen—the Knights of the Order of the Golden Fleece."

Ludwig reached out to the body and picked up a long chain with a golden image of a fleecy sheep hanging limp from a ring around its belly. "Take this to Willem. Tell him we took it from Aremberg's neck. We will give him a nobleman's burial."

He placed the ornament in Pieter-Lucas' open palm. For a long moment Ludwig stared at the dead count, then murmured, "How religion and war have divided us!"

After a pause he pulled himself erect, facing Pieter-Lucas and Aletta. "Now, make haste. I give you two letters—one for Willem, the other for my moeder. I only wish I could deliver them in person. Rather, I must remain here to nourish the fruits of our victory lest they be trampled under the foot of Alva's steed."

Pieter-Lucas and Aletta mounted two horses brought by Ludwig's stable men—Blesje and one other. Side by side they rode along the causeway that cut its way southward through the silent smoldering battlefield. An unhindered sun glinted on a thousand pieces of deserted armor strewn across the fields and shimmered on the wings of a thousand swooping vultures.

"It grieves me, my love," Pieter-Lucas said, "that we could not have begun our long-dreamed-of life together in a place far removed from this stench of war . . . and that my gift for you lies in Emden!"

Aletta smiled and spread an arm to the blue sky above, where mounds of fluffy clouds appeared white and glistening as if around the edges of the world. "Let us thank God we have each other, and we are at last alone." In her heart she nurtured dreams of a spot of solitude in some beautifully wooded meadow along the way, a place where birds would sing and she and her beloved would dance for a glorious hour among the grasses and bright spring blossoms.

PART TWO

Revenge

*The way of the Lord is a shelter for
the upright,
but calamity to the doers
(perpetrators) of iniquity.*

Proverbs 10:29 as quoted in Willem's
Warning (September 1, 1568)

*One salmon was worth
ten thousand frogs.*

—Alva to French Queen Mother

*The greater the sensation, the greater
will be the benefit to be derived from it.*

—Alva to King Philip

CHAPTER TEN

Breda

28th day of Flower Month (May), 1568

*B*etteke de Vriend lay on the pile of straw, freshly rearranged for her by Tante Lysbet. Too weak to raise her head, she pried open her eyes and looked upward at the smeary barred window on the far wall.

"Vader in the Heaven," she prayed, "I'd be so filled with joy to see just one ray of sunlight streamin' into this gloomy place—if it might please you to send it to me."

For more days than she could imagine, her only view into the world outside had been gray, often assaulted with drizzly pellets of rain. She hadn't seen so much as a patch of blue sky, a white fluffy cloud, or a soaring gull.

With Tante Lysbet for her cell mate and nursemaid, she never lacked for sunshine for the heart. All day long the older woman sat beside her, helped her eat and drink, made her bed as comfortable as possible, and combed her hair. Best of all, she read to her from the sacred sheets Betteke pulled from their hiding place in her bodice.

Yet Tante Lysbet seemed always to carry a heaviness of spirit. Often in the middle of the night, Betteke overheard her weeping and sometimes fuming in agitated whispers. Was she angry with the heavenly Vader? Betteke had never heard His name fall from the former Beguine's lips, except when she read the pages of God's Book.

Once more Betteke felt her heart rising to her Vader. *If you might be pleased so to do, won't you lay your warm hand on Tante Lysbet's shoulder an' tell her just how much you care for her?*

She had scarcely finished the prayer she offered many times each day and sunk down into the deep longing it always brought, when she heard the cell door creak open. Which one of their daily visitors would this be? The servant from the galley had already brought their daily rations. Was it the interrogators come to question Lysbet again?

Every day they asked the same questions about some books they'd found in her treasure box. Tante Lysbet's answer was also the same. "I never saw any books about witchcraft until you pulled them from the box where you planted them."

They would grow angry then and threaten to take her to the torture chamber and try her as a witch. But after each visit, Betteke asked her Vader to keep them from doing anything so awful, and so far they'd not done more than threaten.

Betteke opened one eye and squinted out into the dimness. This time it was her daily visit from a priest. The judge had promised it would be so. "Opportunities to repent and be reinstated into the Holy Catholic Religion," he had offered in a smooth and enticing voice.

Today's priest was the gentle one who seemed to have a true care for her soul. He seated himself on a block of wood near the spot where Betteke lay.

"Lysbet de Vriend, child, awaken."

She heard his soft voice, felt his hand shaking her shoulder. Silently she prayed as she did every day. *Vader in the Heaven, let me say what you want this priest-man to hear.* Then slowly she opened her eyes and watched him lift his arm above her and let the long loose sleeve of his robe hang nearly to her head.

"In the name of the Vader, Son, and Holy Spirit," he began, "I adjure you to reconsider your ways. You need only confess to me your sin of trampling the host in the Great Church. Gladly will I absolve and reconcile you to the Holy Catholic Religion."

She did not answer. How could she confess to the lie he insisted was truth?

"Child," he began again, "the mercies of God do not last a lifetime when we stubbornly reject them, as you have done. Your time comes quickly to a close."

He paused. Still she did not speak.

"Have you nothing to confess this day?"

Betteke finally looked directly at him and said between coughs, " 'The Lord is my Shepherd, I want for nothing.' That is all."

"Poor disillusioned child," he said. "That is no confession."

"They are the very words from God's Holy Book," she protested.

Shaking his head, he asked, "How many times must we remind you that the reading of that *verboden boeck* by anyone other than God's holy priests is a dangerous snare? It has drawn you from the safety of the Church and now plunges you into eternal damnation!"

"Why, then, did the Vader give it to us?" she asked.

" 'Twas given only to those men trained in special schools for the priesthood. Only they can read it without seeing wild distortions in its pages."

"How strange," Betteke began, halting at each cough. "I find God's words so clear on every page. It pours like oil of healin' and joy over the souls of all who read an' learn to love the Lord our God with all our heart an' strength an' soul an' mind."

Uneasiness clouded the priest's face. Abruptly he stood to his feet and paced across the cell, wringing his hands and crying out, "Save yourself from heresy, child!"

When she did not respond, he returned to the block beside her. With imploring eyes, he pleaded, "This is your final opportunity."

She heard a tinge of terror mingling with the compassion in his voice. "Your intentions are right kind," she assured him, "but you need not fret over me. My Vader cares for me now an' always will, even when this body lies cold in the grave. I only hope an' pray for you the same joy an' peace an' daily protection as He gives to me!"

"Benighted child!" He shook his head from side to side, then added in a heavy mournful tone, "I had so hoped that I could rescue you from damnation. I wanted not to believe you were filled with devils!"

From the other side of the cell, Betteke heard a gasp from Tante Lysbet and a desperate plea.

"Speak not so rashly to the suffering girl!"

The priest lifted a hand in her direction and ordered, "Protect her not in her heresy, lest you share her fate." Then kneeling beside Betteke, he gestured with open hands. "Tomorrow you meet your maker. If the God you have been deceived into blaspheming sees fit yet to show mercy, you will prepare for that meeting. So great is that mercy that one of His sacred priests will be here at daybreak to take your confession and absolve you of your sins before you be led away to execution."

He paused, as if waiting for a penitent's pleas to rise to him from the straw. Instead, Betteke wiped a tear from her eye and said softly, "If tomorrow is the day determined by my Vader, then I go. I weep only because He gives me no more time to beg of you to let Him be your shepherd too."

Without another word, the priest turned from her and shuffled out of the cell, his shoulders drooping.

Betteke let her body go limp as a spasm of coughing seized her. The more she fought to be still, the more furiously it overpowered her. *Lovin' Vader*, her heart cried out, *give me strength*.

At that instant the coughing monster sent a knife piercing through her chest. It wrenched up a dark bloody phlegm and expelled it from her mouth in huge hot clots. She reached out with wild hands and felt the eager grasp of her nursing friend and the gentle pressure of her other hand caressing her forehead, smoothing back her damp matted hair. Somewhere through the fog, the pain, and the hacking of the cough, she heard Lysbet's golden voice.

"Rest, my child, rest." The calming words were followed by a nearly inaudible angry complaint. "If only they'd bring me more black mullein or a broth of garden cummin!"

Betteke grabbed at Lysbet's hand and whispered a pair of lines from the sacred pages. " 'With the increase of my innermost anxious thoughts, my Vader's consolations make my soul unshakable.' "

With the last drop of energy oozing from her body, Betteke pried her eyes open. The face hovering over her was blurred, but from across Tante Lysbet's shoulder, she saw a long broad band of sunlight coming toward her from somewhere up and beyond the window. It spread steadily until it bathed her face. "Hearty thanks, Vader."

She offered Tante Lysbet a weak smile.

"Fear not," she managed to whisper, then closed her eyes again.

Her coughing ceased; the *heatte* and the pain vanished. Softly, effortlessly, she felt herself slipping away into a deep trancelike sleep. A joy such as she'd never known possessed her. . . .

———

Tante Lysbet watched the tension drain from the weary body, listened to the breathing grow rattled, watched its rhythm ebb.

She took both of the girl's limp hands in her own and whispered, "Merciful God, let your angels rejoice in releasing her from all the suffering—now!"

Instantly there came from Betteke a long shuddery sigh and the parched lips moved slightly. Lysbet leaned close enough to hear the words, and in her fancy, she heard strains of music with them. "My Vader, my Shepherd . . ."

Then the music stopped and the lips and the rattly breathing fell silent. Lysbet held fast to the hands and strained to hear one more cough, one more sigh, to see the faintest flutter of an eyelid, to feel a whisper of a breath.

Nothing came.

When she heard Roland call out twenty-four bells, she reached into the girl's bodice and lifted out the sacred pages nestled against a still warm chest.

"The way that simple unlettered child could read these words and understand them put even a priest to shame! What a wonder!"

With trembling fingers, Lysbet closed the lifeless eyelids. She'd never seen that face so peaceful. "Thank God, at last Betteke is free of pain and coughing spasms," she said.

After a long vigil with wonder, she wiped a tear from her cheek, then pulled the cloak up over her friend's head. Retreating to her own corner, she held the handful of pages and sobbed the rest of the night through.

———

Dillenburg
29th morning of Flower Month (May), 1568

The blackness of a long night was succumbing to the promise of dawn as Pieter-Lucas and Aletta rode into Dillenburg. In Aletta's mind, the past four days ran together into one blurred picture of horizons jogging to the rhythm of a horse's gait or undulating with the bilious pitching of a ripple-slapped boat. Day ran into night like a painter's palette stirred with a pointed stick. Faces and village streets, forests and bogs, all accompanied by savory stews, hunks of dried bread, wild berries, and handfuls of cool well water—she could no longer sort them out in her bone-weary mind.

The exhausted travelers found the little village slumbering at the foot of its *kasteel*-crowned hill. Turning from the trek path on the banks of the Dill River, they started up a steep and winding roadway.

"In daylight the old fortress is more beautiful than you can imagine," Pieter-Lucas said.

Aletta scrutinized the looming outline above them and tried to imagine the colors of the walls, the trees, the clouds, the sky overhead. A single brilliant star hovered over the silhouette of a large tower and twinkled as if to celebrate their arrival.

"I believe you," she sighed.

As if in the fog of a deep dream, she rode up the hill beside her husband, tired, apprehensive, eager. About halfway to the top, without warning, a loud chorus of hunting dogs from inside the walls broke both the silence and her dreamy ponderings. "Do they greet all guests so?" she asked.

"All guests—friend or foe," Pieter-Lucas assured her. "I cannot imagine anyone sneaking onto these grounds unnoticed."

Now roosters were crowing as well, and the landscape before them brightened quickly. A fresh breath of life shook Aletta awake, and she sat straighter on her mount. Just as they came to the stone tower gate and guardhouse, the first rays of sunlight lit up the whole sky. The tower where the stars had so recently sparkled was no longer a shadowy outline. She saw clearly its matching tower of similar size and shape, along with an array of lesser towers and walls and parapets.

"A place for creating fantasies!" she whispered.

Everything moved quickly after this. They passed through a series of imposing stone arches, across a moat, and entered the walled fortress, now glowing golden in the rising sunlight.

"The Julianas' famed herb garden," Pieter-Lucas said, pointing to the left and down at the foot of the hill inside the wall.

"Where you draw those wonderful pictures of the herbs?"

"The very place," he said.

Aletta gazed at the large area ringed by lindens, oaks, birches, and a low stone fence. In the dawning light, she reveled in the beauty of the neatly ordered garden and its muted tones of indistinct colors. "Oh, Pieter-Lucas," she exclaimed, "I should be happy if they would simply give me a bed in that garden."

Pieter-Lucas laughed. "Until it rains—or snows. Then I think you would be clambering at a doorway into the *kasteel*."

Shortly the roadway led underground, a gigantic tunnel climbing steeply until it opened into a spacious courtyard. A large and colorful flag, displaying the coat of arms of the House of Nassau with its crowned lion, sword, and darts, fluttered in the breeze from atop the main building. Nothing else stirred in the early morning air.

Pieter-Lucas dismounted and helped Aletta do the same. She watched him tether the horses to a post near the imposing old carved doors at the base of a tower-crowned building.

"First we find Prince Willem and his moeder," Pieter-Lucas said, slapping Blesje's flank. "Then I'll settle you in your stable."

Just then a small side door opened and a portly man stepped out. He had a dark pointed beard and a mustache and carried a large ring of keys. He blinked briefly in the light of day, then looked at them. A quick recognition lit his face. "Good morning, *jongen*," he offered. "You have come back at last. But so early in the morning?"

"Aha!" Pieter-Lucas said, moving to join him. "So good to find someone awake. I have two urgent messages from Count Ludwig—one for Prince Willem, the other for his moeder, the Countess Juliana."

"Come, enter the hall, and I shall bring them word of your arrival."

The man ushered them into a large room. It was dark and chilled with the sort of dampness held fast by ancient stones rarely touched with the warmth of a roaring fire. They sat on a long low bench beneath a row of high narrow windows that opened onto clouds scudding across a pale blue sky.

Aletta snuggled up close to Pieter-Lucas, grabbing his arm in hers and leaning her head on his shoulder. He gripped her with his other arm and leaned his head against hers. She felt his curls brush her forehead and whispered, "I love you, dear man."

"And I you, beautiful vrouw."

He squeezed her arm, and for a long moment they held each other. Aletta was nearly drifting off to sleep when a quick shuffling of feet on the other side of the room brought both young people to a hasty start. They sat erect.

Prince Willem! Aletta blinked. She'd seen this man many times in Breda, but always at a distance as he rode his horse through the streets or walked in his garden across the River Marck from the wood where she and Pieter-Lucas played. Never had she been in the same room with him.

He's fully dressed, she noted. The black cap that hugged his head, the white starched ruff, the black jacket with chains of gold brocade—all were in the precise order one would expect of a man freshly come from his dressing chamber. Yet the anxious expression on his face and the heavy droop of his shoulders told her he'd probably been awake all night long.

Along with Pieter-Lucas, she rose instantly to her feet and greeted her prince with a curtsy.

"Welcome to Dillenburg," Willem said, his voice tight. "I see you brought along . . . your new bride?" The faintest hint of a smile spread across his face.

"*Ja*, Your Excellency." With eyes sparkling, Pieter-Lucas presented her. "Aletta, daughter of Dirck Engelshofen, the bookseller, is now my vrouw."

Willem gave her a half bow and a smile. "Welcome, Aletta, vrouw of my trusted servant." Then, his face turning sober, he looked directly at Pieter-Lucas. "I expected Yaap with news from Friesland. You come in his place?"

Pieter-Lucas moved uneasily from foot to foot. "That I do."

"He is occupied with other errands for my brother, then?"

Aletta sensed her husband's anguish. Hesitantly, as if trying at one time both to swallow and expel his words, he gave a simple answer. "I wish that were true."

"What, then?" Willem's response came quickly.

"He lies buried in a Frisian bog."

"*Nay!*"

"Felled by the bullet of a Spanish soldier. I witnessed it myself, felt his dying breath upon my face as he gave me the message that he carried to Count Ludwig."

Willem hung his head. Aletta sensed in his silence the struggle of his own heart. At length he looked up. "Ludwig and Adolph have faced Aremberg in battle, then?"

Pieter-Lucas paused. "Five days ago at Heiligerlee."

"Heiligerlee?" the prince asked. "I should have expected Winschoten or perhaps Groningen. But a battle in a cloister?"

"Count Ludwig did not intend to stage it there," Pieter-Lucas answered. "Aremberg came more quickly than he anticipated."

As he talked, he pulled two packets of post from his knapsack and held one out to the prince. "I am learning that battles go not always as their commanders plan."

Sharp darts of alarm registered in the prince's brown eyes, and he came closer, grasping the document offered to him. "The news is not good, then."

"Our God smiled upon Ludwig in battle, Your Excellency. Heiligerlee was, after all, the ideal field—deadly for an enemy unfamiliar with the treachery of a peat bog. But you must read Count Ludwig's words for yourself. Not all give cause to rejoice."

Willem tore away the wax seal and ripped the paper open. Intent, somber, he appeared to devour the words in much the same way Aletta imagined a hungry beggar would attack a hunk of dry bread, tearing it with his teeth, chewing and swallowing as if nothing else in life mattered. She watched the drooping of his shoulders, the sad lines in his face. What herbs did she carry in her apothecary that might help to take away the heaviness?

Nay, foolish one, she reprimanded herself, *remember you not where you are?* This was the household of the two Julianas. Besides Oma, no greater herbal healer ladies lived anywhere. With them to attend to this man, their own flesh and blood, what need would he ever have for Aletta's services?

The prince had finished the letter and stood staring at it. His silence and bowed head bespoke numbness and shock. At last he asked, "Saw you the body of my brother Adolph after the battle with your own eyes?"

"*Ja*, Your Excellency, I did," Pieter-Lucas answered.

"On the battlefield, with the blood still on him?"

"*Nay*, rather laid out in state at the altar of the chapel in the monastery."

"And what of Count Aremberg?"

"I saw his body as well. I watched Count Ludwig take this trophy from his neck. He asked me to bring it to you." Pieter-Lucas had pulled the heavy gold chain from his satchel and laid it in Willem's open trembling palm.

Willem held it straight before him, the chain draping over his fingers, and the golden lamb swinging lightly from the hanger that girdled its middle. "We—Aremberg and I—were once brothers of a sort," he mumbled. "Knights of the Order of the Golden Fleece, committed to protecting the rights and the peace of our countrymen—together!"

Slowly, he lifted the chain and put it around his own neck, letting it come to rest atop the identical chain already hanging there.

"If only Adolph and Aremberg could serve the cause as sacrificial lambs, sufficient to end this war and stop the bloodshed!"

He fingered the two chains, then murmured, "But Alva will never stop until King Philip's death sentence has been fulfilled."

Willem looked up at his messenger and reached out a hand. "Give to me my moeder's letter. I take it to her." Then under his breath, he muttered with a huge sigh, "She told us Adolph would not return. She knew. *Ach*, why Adolph?"

In the dim light Aletta thought she saw a pair of tears sparkling, one on each of the prince's cheeks. She felt a wash of tears sliding down her own face as well.

"I'll instruct the steward to show you the room where you may rest from your journey and refresh yourself for the next," Willem said flatly without looking at them. "Later, when I have consulted with my moeder and my brother Jan, I shall call for you."

Aletta watched her prince trudge out through a high archway in the wall and felt the weight of each step penetrate like an arrow into her soul. She grabbed Pieter-Lucas by the arm and squeezed. "What next journey?" she whispered. "You are no messenger."

Pieter-Lucas encircled her waist and drew her close. "Yaap is no longer here to do it." His voice sounded tight, distant.

A dart pierced her heart. "You didn't promise to take his place, Pieter-Lucas?" She looked up into his eyes and waited for him to reassure her it was not so.

"N-nay."

"Why will the prince call you, then?"

Still holding her in his arm, he shifted restlessly and did not look at her as he answered, "We are living in his household, and it is a time of war. There may be times when . . . when he has no one else to send."

A great shuddering loneliness swept over her. Her family had fled to Engeland so she could be with this man. How could he bring her to this strange place, then leave her here? Her body began to shiver.

She felt his forefinger stroke her cheek and looked up into the warm wonders of his smile. "We have not to think about it now, my love. These hours belong to us alone."

The two stood in silence, eyes probing eyes beyond the smiles and words to the deep places of each other's souls. She watched pain and admiration wrestle for supremacy. Did his pain make his admiration more intense? Or was it admiration that gave sharpness to the pain? Either way, she knew that as long as he breathed, he would always make her feel protected, treasured, cherished.

CHAPTER ELEVEN

Breda

29th day of Flower Month (May), 1568

When the gray light of dawn crept in around the fringes of the darkness, Tante Lysbet rose to her feet and walked to the window. The sky yielded gradually to the strokes of a multihued paintbrush, and a hint of the rising sun tipped the wings of a pair of flying gulls with gold.

"God, for days Betteke longed to see just such a sky," she cried out, "and you withheld it day after day, no matter how she begged. Now you send it, after she has passed on. . . ."

Passed on to where? The thought stopped her mouth and stirred her mind.

Where, indeed, was Betteke's soul? Yesterday's priest had offered her one more opportunity to escape eternal hellfire—if she would repent. But his accusations were lies, and she had nothing to repent of. So what then? Lysbet shook her head as if to dislodge the tangle of religious cobwebs. Did any priest have the power, after all, to decide such things?

While Betteke still breathed, she had often told her of the page in God's Book that promised "to let go of this body is to make our entrance into the presence of the Lord."

Lysbet returned to the window and stared, transfixed. How brilliant the colors in the heavens had grown! "If what Betteke said is true," she said aloud, eager to convince herself beyond question, "then she has truly arrived in the heaven. Could it be that her Vader-Shepherd has decorated His skies that we might celebrate with Him?"

Lysbet lingered at the window until the colors faded into the pale blue of an early morning sky. She reached into her own bodice and reverently slid Betteke's sacred pages into their new place, close to her heart.

"Vader in the Heaven," she began. Never had she expected to address God so. Creator, Protector, Savior—all these she knew and spoke readily.

But Vader? A new fire had been lit in her heart.

"On this sun-robed morning," she prayed, "you have delivered your child from the indignities of an unjust execution. Now I know you are indeed in this place. Can you forgive me that I so long doubted? Can you teach me to trust as Betteke trusted?"

The cell came instantly alive with a wondrous, awesome something that Lysbet didn't have a name for. In her soul, she felt an overwhelming joy in the forgiveness of her newfound Vader. All the ugly fears that had plagued her ever since the day the Spanish soldiers and Breda's bailiff had dragged her here seemed to melt away into an unimaginable peace. Drowsiness tugged at her. Rearranging the fetid straw into a semblance of a bed, she lay down and closed her eyes.

"Thank God," she prayed as she drifted toward sleep, "Betteke's suffering is past, and her enemies have been cheated of their coveted revenge for an action never done but only imagined in their darkened minds."

The next thing she knew, men's voices were buzzing above her and a boot was kicking her in the side.

"Wake up, you lazy heretic!" The shout grated on her ears and jabbed at the peace of mind that had so recently lulled her to sleep.

She opened her eyes and felt dizzy. The cell swarmed with soldiers, the bailiff, and a priest. Not the gentle priest of the last visit with Betteke, this was the one that always accompanied the inquisitors and men of the law. She shivered, hearing already in her mind his mocking words and proud indignities. The men waved their lances and halberds over her, their faces fiery with a menacing sort of delight.

"So, you took pity on your little friend here," the priest derided her. Didn't she always take pity on her?

The priest's voice dripped with sarcasm. "You could not bear to see her endure her deserved shame at the stake, so you put her out of her misery as she slept."

Incredulous, Lysbet pulled herself to a sitting position and gaped at the man. "What?" she asked.

"Cunning idea, Tante Lysbet, former Beguine, midwife, healer lady." He chuckled. "Thought we'd never suspect you, eh?"

"I know not what you are saying," Lysbet retorted. "My dear Betteke was relieved of her suffering by the disease that ravaged her body."

The whole retinue laughed raucously.

"Good story!"

"Shrewd scheme!"

Lysbet's heart was racing. She looked up into the faces of a pack of wolves, ravenous for human blood, and once more she knew fear.

A soldier grabbed her by the arm and yanked her to her feet. "All your pretty trickery will not save your life, fair and bewitched healer lady."

"The pain of the stake that you spared your friend will be yours instead," said another with beguiling sweetness.

"You cannot mean it!" she protested, trying to pull her arm free.

"Murderers always die the death."

"Even Beguines and healer ladies."

"Especially when they lie!"

"You know full well that I did not murder my friend."

"You squander your words, woman," a soldier shouted at her.

The priest stepped forward, holding a small rosary with a crucifix attached. "Even so, our God is merciful, though I will never understand how He could extend mercy to a murderess. Nevertheless, I am under obligation to offer you one last opportunity to confess your guilt and make your peace with God." He held the crucifix before her face, ready to carry on with his intended ritual.

"I have already concluded my peace with God," Lysbet said.

"What other priest has been here this morning?" he challenged.

Lysbet looked at him for a long while. Her heart beat wildly and her palms dripped sweat. What could she say that would not infuriate them further? With deliberate calmness, she did not answer.

A soldier approached and slapped her face, his wide fingers stinging into her flesh, extracting tears from her eyes. "You answer not, impudent witch?" he asked.

"Jesus Christ, God's great High Priest, has forgiven my sins," she said simply, a newly born joy welling up at the thought of it.

"Blasphemy!" shouted a voice from the back of the others.

"Why do we dally? The stake awaits us!" came another.

Two men tied her hands behind her back. Another pair pulled her hair loose from its coif atop her head and ripped her outer garments from her body, leaving her in her nightgown. Betteke's sacred pages fluttered to the ground.

"*Hei! Ha!* What is this?"

Lysbet cringed. *Great God*, she prayed in silent agony, *protect your words. Let them not fall victim to such sacrilege.*

"*Verboden boecken!*" shouted a soldier with unbridled glee.

"What more evidence need we to send this pagan woman to her death?" asked the priest. He made a pantomime of washing his hands and added, "I am innocent of her blood."

"He is innocent indeed!" shouted the rest in chorus.

The man who had retrieved the pages threw them to the floor, and they all pounced upon them, grinding them into the straw. Then he snatched them up once more and, stuffing them roughly back into Lysbet's gown, announced, "They, too, must be burned, lest their evil spirits infect this prison more than it has been already infected by the demons of heresy."

Demons in God's book? Lysbet could bear no more. She burst into an audible prayer. "Vader in the Heaven, forgive these wild men. They know not what they do."

Instantly, two of them grabbed her around the torso. One held her head fast while another pried open her mouth and manacled her tongue with some sort of metal screw. Pain seared her tongue and shot through her entire body.

"That will teach you to talk," the man that held her taunted, then shoved her forcibly to the floor. Another grabbed her up and dragged her through the door out into the morning air. In quiet desperation, she struggled to rise above the pain, to take her last opportunity to listen to the singing birds, to look on the colorful flowers and feel the golden sunshine. Still celebrating Betteke's entrance into her Vader's presence? And her own entrance as well!

Unexpectedly, she didn't chill at the thought. Instead, a warm and beautiful calm settled over her. The feeling was neither a numb resignation nor an exhilarated joy, but a sort of celestial anticipation, an eagerness to go see the God she now called Vader.

The priest sidled up to her and said with mock intimacy, "Just to prove how merciful our God is, Tante Lysbet will have not to bear her own shame on this day. All Breda will be told that in the *kasteelplein* of Breda, Betteke de Vriend was executed at the stake, along with her master, Pieter van Keulen, the goldsmith."

"And it will be so recorded in the annals for posterity to read," added the bailiff.

"*Ja, ja*. It shall be so recorded," the soldiers chanted in chorus, then burst into raucous laughter.

From behind her, Lysbet felt hot breath on her neck and smelled the odor of yesterday's garlic. Then a heavy dark cloth was thrown over her head.

"Today, all Breda must believe that Lysbet de Vriend burns at the stake," the bailiff explained.

God, you are truly merciful! Lysbet heard her heart declaring the thing she had so often questioned. But the pain had finally grown so intense and the air so heavy beneath the blanket that her mind refused to give her anything but blank pages, shredded and tossed to the wind and plucked from the air by vultures. The mercy came through when she slipped into oblivion, feeling nothing, thinking nothing, hearing nothing.

She came awake enough to realize that rough hands were tying her to a splintery surface at her back. Her head was still covered, her screw-pierced tongue swollen to the size of many tongues, and her bare feet were being punctured by sharp dried straws.

The stake! Unthinkable! Her moeder had been wrong. Innocent women must sometimes pay for imagined crimes. But suddenly it didn't matter anymore. She felt the pain and anguish drain from her tormented soul.

"Great Vader," she managed, "let me die in peace like Betteke!"

A hedge of thorns seemed to seal her off from the din of the crowd around her, and she felt warm, protected. Breaking through into her memory, she heard the cough-wracked voice of Betteke repeating again and again, "Fear not, Lysbet. Our Vader's consolations will keep your soul unshakable."

Tante Lysbet bowed her head and waited for the liberating flames.

Meester Laurens had never seen an execution. He'd heard about them all his life. When he was still a boy in Germany, the whole flock of the Children of God where his vader was an elder had to flee from the threat of execution. Later, living in Antwerp, he remembered seeing colorful banners fly above the streets when there was to be an execution of heretics. More than once he had watched from the safety of a basement window to see people rushing off toward the city *plein*, carrying basket lunches to eat while they enjoyed the spectacle of heretics burning at the stakes.

For years after that, he had nightmares about soldiers chasing him with a sword. Once he'd moved to Breda, though, the nightmares ceased. Everybody knew that in this city a citizen could worship as he pleased as long as he did it quietly. A handful of foreigners fleeing here seeking refuge for their contentious ways had met the stake on the *kasteelplein*. But citizens? Never!

On the morning that Laurens was escorted out of the prison and through the streets, he knew he was about to see an execution. But there were neither banners nor basket lunches. Instead, people milled about and mumbled, each man pulling his cloak closer to his body and shuddering with the dread of whatever might come next.

Laurens suspected that no one said the words, but they all knew this was not Breda's idea. Alva had insisted. They must either sacrifice a few of their innocent victims, or he would come with his Royal Army and purge their streets and houses of the slightest trace of anything he decided was heresy. To Alva and King Philip, there was no such thing as an honorable, quiet, nonpapist worshiper!

How else would Laurens ever have been brought to this place? All of his adult life, he had taught schoolboys and enjoyed the respect of everyone he knew. He'd taken his family to services in the Great Church and read his Bible behind closed doors. No one ever questioned Meester Laurens' loyalties—until Alva came.

Then one day last summer, Alva-trained magistrates put a paper before him and a pen in his hand and ordered him to sign an oath of loyalty. "I hereby swear allegiance to His Majesty, King Philip, and the Holy Catholic Religion," it read. It went on to promise that he would never "use heretical books or spread false doctrines" in his classroom.

He refused to sign the oath. So they barred him from his classroom and threw him into prison. Still, he could not believe that a burning stake lay ahead! Now chained to a Spanish soldier, he shuffled along the cobblestones between the gloomy crowds of onlookers and prayed in silence. *Great God, why have you betrayed me? When my friends fled to safer places, my vrouw, Adriana, and I stayed on for your sake. Breda was our parish, the place where we served you. Did you not find us faithful enough?*

He looked down at the cobblestones of St. Jansstraat beneath his feet. Here and there he heard a gasp as he passed by.

"Not Meester Laurens!"

"Poor old man!"

Weep for my beloved Adriana, he wanted to say to them. For all the months he'd been in the tower, she had come daily to bring him cheese and butter and cabbages and clean blankets. The last time she came, two nights ago, he'd told her to run away and hide. "Lest they bring some harm to you," he warned.

Oh, God, he prayed, *who will care for my Adriana when my body has been burnt to ashes? Even our sons have fled to Engeland, and she cannot go to them alone.*

No thunderbolt came from the heavens, no verse from the Holy Book, no still small voice in his soul. His feet stumbled onward.

Adriana! My Adriana. The deep wrenching pain of a broken heart set up an overpowering wailing inside. *Will I ever see you again?*

It should be enough for him that the God of justice walked with him in the way, would go with him through the fire, would care for his vrouw. He'd always thought it would be so. Yet now that he must walk with wrists in chains and a stake at the end of his way, suddenly, it was not enough.

"God in the Heaven!" he cried out. "God! Do you not care?"

A soldier's elbow prodded him from each side, and two voices spoke at once, "Hold your mouth, madman!"

He looked up and saw that the mournful procession of condemned criminals had come to a stop before three single stakes that formed a half circle in the center of the square. Each stake arose from a pile of wood and hay. From a metal brazier in the center, the acrid smell of burning coals wafted across the scene and aroused terror in his soul.

Laurens was one of five prisoners, each guarded by a pair of soldiers bearing swords and spears. "Five prisoners . . . three stakes. Who will die, and who go free?" Laurens held his breath.

Pieter van Keulen, the innocent goldsmith, had already heard his sentence read to him in the prison cell. "Death by fire!" Next to him stood Balten de Backere, well known by all Breda as a violent murderer. If one shred of justice lived on, one of the stakes had his name already inscribed on it. Then came Reynier Vincent van Eecklo, a mysterious stranger from some undisclosed city. The charges? Also a mystery.

Between the stranger and himself stood a lone and silent woman with her head covered. Lysbet de Vriend, van Keulen's housekeeper? *Great God, don't let it be that poor child.* Nay, it couldn't be Betteke. This woman was too tall. Besides, she did not cough. All who had been prisoners for the past weeks knew about her cough. It bombarded every wall and had caused her former master no end of anxiety.

Who, then? Tante Lysbet the Midwife? Laurens' vrouw told him she was also in the prison, but she didn't know the charges. Whoever the unknown woman was, he found it strange indeed that they covered her head—and that she remained silent.

Van den Kessel, the rotund bailiff, stood forth to address the crowd, strutting like a peacock in full feather display. With a gigantic flourish, he unrolled a scrolled paper, eyed his audience, and cleared his throat officiously before he began to read.

"Whereas Pieter van Keulen, goldsmith, heretic, image-breaker, possessor of *verboden boecken*, has savagely attacked the sacred icons in the Great Church on the twenty-third of Harvest Month of 1566 and led his housekeeper into similar acts of sacrilege; and whereas he has steadfastly resisted all efforts to bring him to godly penitence over said acts; on the authority of His Majesty, King Philip, and His Lordship, the Duke of Alva, and the official appointed Council of Troubles, I hereby pronounce judgment on this man. He shall be fastened to the stake and his body burned to ashes. Furthermore, all properties of said heretic are declared to be confiscated for the benefit of King Philip and for the furtherance of the

Church to which his rash acts were designed to bring discredit. It shall be done and executed as above in the presence of these many witnesses on this twenty-ninth day of Flower Month, 1568, that all Breda may be purged of the curse brought upon us by his insurrection against the king and the Holy Catholic Religion."

The accused held his head high and let them lead him to the first stake. As they fastened Van Keulen with chains, binding his hands securely to his sides, Laurens hung his head and closed his eyes but found no words to pray. The accusations and the sentence were more awful than he remembered.

Next, Van den Kessel read Balten de Backere's judgment, sentencing him likewise to the stake. The criminal writhed in his chains, shouting ugly obscenities. With difficulty, his guards chained him to the stake at the other end of the line. Then they fastened a screw to his tongue, unleashing a tirade of angry painful groans.

The crowd grew restless as the agonizing process dragged on. The bailiff stood stoically in his arrogance. With the mannerism of a showman in the marketplace, he turned to the woman, puffed out his chest, and flashed a smirk of especial satisfaction. Once more he cleared his throat noisily and began to read: "Whereas the examiners of Lysbet Jacobsdochter de Vriend have examined said woman in great detail . . ."

Lauren gasped. *Nay*, God, *nay*! Not Betteke! He found his own arms straining at his manacles.

". . . and whereas she freely offered to one of the examiners a page of a *verboden boeck*, the Holy Bible in her moeder tongue . . ."

How like this trusting girl to offer a page from her master's Bible to some sly soldier! Laurens shook his head and let it fall to his chest. How many pleasant hours he recalled in the early weeks before they began forbidding her to visit, when she had brought some of those very pages to her master! How often the messages they held had brought new courage to his own soul.

The bailiff's raspy voice droned on, but Laurens refused to listen until the judgment was pronounced. "Condemned to death by burning at the stake. . . ."

He could restrain himself no longer. "Chain me to the stake in her place," he cried out. "For God's sake, let the girl go free!"

Instantly his guards pulled him back. Van den Kessel cast a mocking glance in his direction and laughed. "What a noble martyr spirit you show, old man! Your turn comes, and you have enough misdeeds of your own to atone for."

Laurens crumpled inside.

As if in a fog, he heard the bailiff read on, sentencing Van Eecklo to be held in prison for life. Then, curiously, he heard a sentence for Tante Lysbet the Midwife. She had been banished, the document said, for insubordination in not signing the oath of allegiance demanded of all midwives and schoolmasters, and for possession and promulgation of books of witchcraft, as discovered in her treasure box in *The Crane's Nest*. Said books were to be burned, along with de Vriend's body.

More false accusations! He knew for a fact that she had signed the oath. He had scolded her for it at the time. She insisted she had no choice. Midwifery and herbalism were her life, and she must do whatever was required of her to protect herself. He also knew she had never possessed books of witchcraft. And in *The Crane's Nest*? A more preposterous notion could not be!

But where was Lysbet now, that she might hear her judgment? Had she already been banished? Or was the woman to be executed Tante Lysbet after all? He was still staring at the bailiff when a clanking and foot-shuffling sound came from the direction of the Great Church. The crowd parted to let through a pair of soldiers, who escorted one more prisoner to the ring of execution.

"Adriana!" Laurens gasped. How dare they shackle her to these boorish soldiers?

She held her head high and looked only at her husband. Her eyes told him that she was at peace, and somehow he could hear her thoughts, *Take courage, husband.*

Laurens felt his teeth chattering. In spite of the warmth of the sun, he shivered, and a nagging apprehension overpowered him. He refused to look at the bailiff, whose face, he knew, would be shining with that same smirky delight it had worn with each of the other pronouncements.

"We come now," Van den Kessel said, "to this final judgment for Meester Laurens, dismissed schoolmeester, longtime secret pagan."

Secret pagan? Laurens cringed and hung his head. He could not bring himself to watch Adriana's agony as Van den Kessel read one more listing of false accusations.

"Inasmuch as he has for so many years planted deception and false doctrine in the hearts and minds of our young men and has steadfastly refused any instruction to the intent of reforming his ways; and inasmuch as his guilt is more reprehensible than any judgment could ever recompense; and inasmuch as he is indeed worthy of death by fire to purge away such monstrous sins; but inasmuch as God and his Church are both merciful to the innocent, which said Laurens' vrouw has proven herself to be; and inasmuch as she has interceded for him with great importunity; His

Majesty's Council of Troubles and the Duke of Alva have concurred on a sentence, far milder than his crimes deserve, consisting of the confiscation of all earthly goods and the perpetual banishment of his person from the Low Lands. Before the setting of this day's sun, said Meester Laurens and his vrouw are to be escorted beyond our borders by a retinue of armed guards, never to be allowed to return. So shall it be done under authority of His Majesty, King Philip, and His Lordship, the Duke of Alva."

Confiscation? Banishment? But no stake! *Great God, you have been gracious to return me to my vrouw! But our home and the books! Nay, let them not take my precious, precious books!*

He looked at his vrouw and tried with his eyes to express the groan he dared not utter with his mouth. *Oh, Adriana, Adriana, did you hear? Our home, our books . . .*

Her lips were moving and he understood. *But we go together!*

One quick glance at the bailiff revealed the smile of a gloating champion. "Although for this time you have escaped the stake," he said, "think not that your life will ever again be your own, Meester Laurens. You are banished with a solid warning, to be heeded judiciously, that if you should ever attempt to violate said exile, the above mentioned mercies will no longer be extended, though your vrouw should offer her own body in sacrifice on your behalf."

He reached out toward his victim, placed a forefinger under his chin, grinned, and said with a thump of finality, "A stake shall always be reserved in readiness should you grow arrogant or careless. Forget it not, meester."

Laurens stared, undaunted, into the man's eyes and watched a flash of terror flicker there. The bailiff turned quickly away. Addressing the executioner nearby, he commanded, "Light the fires," then, crossing himself, he added, "in the name of the Vader, Son, and Holy Ghost. Amen."

Meester Laurens gave one last look at Pieter van Keulen. Their eyes met and the victim called out in a clear, triumphant voice. "Fear not for me, brother." Then, across the circle to his former housekeeper, "Fear not, Betteke. 'The Lord is King forever! Hallelujah!' "

The flames were licking at van Keulen's feet. He lifted his eyes heavenward and a grimace contorted his face. Laurens could watch no more. He closed his eyes and tried to stop his ears, then waited for it to be over.

The execution in Breda's *kasteelplein* dragged on all through the day. Once the victims had died, only a few of the onlookers lingered. But Meester Laurens and the other prisoners were forced to stay until the executioner's fires lay lifeless on the cobbles. The air was filled with the stench of burnt flesh and hair. With the coming of the afternoon, a soft mist drizzled over the scene, mingling steam with smoke.

The captors who held the prisoners passed the time by tormenting them with a barrage of taunts. One soldier thrust his face up close to Laurens' and derided, "If you took half as much care to protect your vrouw as you do to defend your stubborn heretical ideas, you'd have begged for one more opportunity to sign the oath and be set free."

"Might even have gotten your schoolboys back," suggested the other, his voice heavy with mock wistfulness.

The first man shook his head and pretended pity. "What a shame! What a shame! Our merciful magistrates would have grasped your penitent request with both hands, you know, so eager are they to clear a citizen."

His sneering grin revealed a mouth full of snags and his breath reeked of rancid food. Determined not to break under the twisting of their tormentors' screws, Laurens did not say a word but felt sweat coursing down the back of his neck and his arms.

How he yearned to go to his vrouw, to put an arm around her and lead her away from all the filth and stench and ugly words. At one point, when she looked so weary he feared she would swoon across the cobblestones, he could hold his mouth no longer. "Can you allow her, at least, to sit on a bale of straw? She is innocent, by your own confession—and a woman!"

The soldier that guarded her stormed at him, eyes snapping, "You tell us what to do? You scummy prisoner!"

He stepped toward Laurens and slapped him with a broad rough hand. Laurens gasped for air, then pleaded, "Handle her gently!"

The soldier slapped him once more. "Would you rather we had burned her before your eyes? Ungrateful, defiant wretch."

" 'Tis not too late to erect another stake and create one more spectacle here, you know," jeered the soldier fastened to his arm. The whole retinue of soldiers laughed. It was the large hollow laughter of the sort of violent men who snatch at other men's foibles—real or imagined—to give them courage to hold their own heads high.

Pain seared Laurens' face and he felt his legs go weak beneath him. For Adriana, he must be strong. Forcing himself to ignore the pain, he looked at her, trying to offer some sort of comfort. She showed a weak but brave smile, then hung her head against her chest. He could see it was trembling.

Great God, where are you? Laurens cried out in his heart. Then, ignoring the continuing taunts of the soldiers, the smarting pains that ran in streaks down his cheeks, the rain that fell in chilling drops, he stood dumb and waited.

God, please! he prayed again. *Speak to me.*

In that instant, a quiet insistent memory nudged its way into his consciousness. *The Lord is King forever! Hallelujah!*

Every day in the prison, he and Pieter van Keulen had consoled each other with those words from one of the psalms Betteke had brought to them. Was van Keulen seeing the King with his eyes now? And Betteke? Tante Lysbet? He looked at the piles of ashes that had this morning been his friends, and knew they were.

But what of himself and Adriana? Still in chains, waiting for banishment! At least they lived. For some strange reason, God must have willed it to be so.

The Lord is King! Hallelujah! The words ran on and on, unflinching before his doubts, drowning out all the noise and confusion and pain. They wrapped themselves around every part of his being, and little by little, he let them warm his aching heart. Forgetting that there were ears to hear, he whispered, "The Lord is King! Hallelujah!"

His guard jabbed him in the ribs. Not caring, he next spoke it aloud. "The Lord is King! Hallelujah!"

A whole ring of guards guffawed. "What lord is king?" one jeered. "Surely not his!"

Midst the thunder of laughter that they set up, Meester Laurens raised his eyes heavenward and whispered once more, "The Lord, my Lord, is King forever! Hallelujah! Hallelujah!"

One soldier shouted, "Enough nonsense and dawdling. The pagans have been reduced to ashes. We've a long march to the river and a longer trek to the frontier."

"Let us be on our way!"

"Prisoners, before we move," shouted another, "take a last look at what remains of your brothers and sister in crime. Let the image burn into your brain and never forget it."

"One misstep," hissed the soldier to whom Laurens' arm was chained, "and this will be you!"

Hurriedly, the soldiers dragged the prisoners from the square. They hustled Reynier off to the tower. Laurens and Adriana were shoved into a waiting coach. Laurens reached out to his vrouw with his free hand, but the soldier yanked him back. He searched her eyes, and she gave him a smile of relief and hope.

God, my King, he prayed silently, *show your power and bring to naught the evil plans of our godless enemies. Keep me calm that my vrouw may not see me overwrought nor be consumed of anguish at not being able to console me.*

When the coach began to move to the rhythm of the horses' steady gait, Laurens felt God's everlasting arms holding him up. He offered to his Adriana all the undying devotion he could pack into his fervent gaze. Her eyes sent back a message of confidence and peace. Like soothing oil, it bathed his wounds, both visible and unseen.

Chapter Twelve

Dillenburg

1st day of Summer Month (June), 1568

*P*ieter-Lucas came awake to the sound of a loud repetitive banging. Startled, he tightened his grip on Aletta, lying curled up in his arms. He buried his face in the locks of silken honey-colored hair and muttered, "*Nay*, a thousand times *nay*."

For the moment, he had no idea where they were, how long they'd been here, nor what time of day or night it might be. Nor had he any intention of leaving his bed. But the knocking persisted until he pried open his eyes and glowered at the door. A slender ray of sunlight filtering through a single high windowpane shone directly on the keyhole.

Ach! This was the big old castle sprawled over Dillenburg's hill. When they'd entered here, he'd closed the wooden door and fancied that was enough to lock the whole world outside. No catastrophe could be sufficiently urgent to pull him from his bridal chamber before he was ready.

Pressing Aletta closer, he kissed her neck and mumbled at the unseen intruder beyond the door, "Go away—far, far away!"

But the knocking went on, accompanied now by a young man's voice. "Gerard, chamber servant to Count Willem, with a summons from His Excellency."

For a long moment Pieter-Lucas did not move. Then reluctantly he slid his hand along his vrouw's arm and let her go. She grasped his hand and whispered, "Leave me not."

"Willem summons," he said. "I must go." He wrapped her up in one more lingering hug, then dragged himself out of the bed and across the room, where he pressed his mouth against the rough timber door. Fearful that his voice would defile the Aletta-hallowedness of the room, he spoke barely above a whisper.

"*Ja?*"

"Count Willem requests your immediate presence," came an urgent reply.

Pieter-Lucas scratched his head and combed his unkempt curls with his fingers. He pulled his breeches on over his nightshirt, then opened the door a crack.

"Tell him I come," he said to the courier, a young boy who stood barely as high as Pieter-Lucas' shoulders.

"I am to bring you with me along."

"Then give me an eyeblink more," the still-drowsy young man begged.

He turned back to Aletta sitting on the edge of the bed. Since their second wedding ceremony behind the chapel at Heiligerlee, he'd not once left her side, and it felt as if he were tearing his very self asunder. He went to her, bent over, and planted a kiss on her forehead.

Holding both his hands in hers, she begged, "He cannot take you away so soon!"

"I shall do my best."

It should be so simple. He'd already more than fulfilled his obligations to Yaap and Ludwig, and he'd never promised Willem a thing. Yet . . . he lived in this place, at the prince's mercy—and there was a war. . . .

He watched his bride open her mouth, say nothing, close it again. Her struggle to be cheerful spread a thin veil over her disappointment and wrenched at his heart. How could he leave her?

Not allowing himself to look into her eyes again, he disentangled his arms from her grip. "I'll return before I go anywhere," he assured her, "just as quickly as possible!"

"*Tot ziens,*" she whispered.

He felt her anxious smile follow him to the door. Slipping into his shoes and pulling on his jacket, the reluctant bridegroom followed Willem's courtier out into the chilly air.

In the reception hall where Pieter-Lucas had given Willem Ludwig's messages, he found the prince pacing the length of the room, hands clasped behind his back, eyes staring straight at the floor ahead of him.

"Alva's revenge has struck!" Willem lamented.

The words sent a shudder down Pieter-Lucas' backbone. He stood in shocked silence, afraid yet curious to hear more.

"I knew Ludwig's victory in Heiligerlee would enrage the old cat," he muttered. "In one day, he passed sentence on my brothers and me, banning us forever from the Low Lands, confiscating the last bit of our goods. Then with a flourish of the same pen that signed our banishment, he ordered the execution of our imprisoned noble friends. Finally, he razed and torched the stately old House of Culemborg, where Brederode held the first banquet of Beggars two years ago. And he promises more!"

"More, Your Excellency?" Pieter-Lucas swallowed down the revulsion rising from a troubled stomach.

"The indignity of Aremberg's defeat simply lit a torch to a pile of brushwood set in place and awaiting a spark. Nothing will stop the conflagration. Not a corner of the Low Lands shall escape."

"What must I do?" Pieter-Lucas asked, urging his heart to stop racing so.

"My brother Jan and I are preparing an urgent reply to some fresh intelligence just received from Dirck Coornhert."

"Where is he?" Pieter-Lucas' mind whirled.

"In Duisburg, near Cleve, on the Rhine. If you depart after the morning meal, by riding hard you should yet reach him by sundown and be back tomorrow." Willem pulled a scrap of paper from his doublet. "Here. Study these directions well. Inscribe them on your mind, then destroy them before you leave."

Yaap had once told Pieter-Lucas that a secret messenger never carried written directions. He swallowed hard.

"From now on, Alva will ensure that none of us has a moment of leisure to enjoy our exile." Willem was through the doorway and nearly out of sight before he'd finished.

Pieter-Lucas stood numb in the middle of the floor. He tried to convince himself that the prince's words were but the empty delusion of a man burdened with the weight of a troubled world and a petty drunken vrouw. But he knew they were true, and he dare not disappoint his prince, who clearly thought of him as Yaap's replacement. And so, for the moment, must he be.

Back in their room, he found Aletta barely dressed and with an unconvincing smile painted across her face. He, too, must feign lightheartedness. He swept her up in his arms. "Come quickly, Little One," he invited. "The morning meal is served, and it is the rule of the house that all must eat—at seven and ten in the morning, two and five in the afternoon, and eight in the evening."

She frowned. "What happens if you don't?"

"They'll call you the Hanged Maiden and make you pay a fine to a large stone statue of a maiden with an iron ring out in the garden."

Together they laughed a brittle laugh. Nervously, he took her by the hand and led her to the door. Here she grew sober, pulled him to a stop, and asked, "Willem thinks you are his Yaap messenger, doesn't he?"

He patted her arm and struggled with his words. "I fear wartime makes us all into things we are not. I go not far this time."

"Not back to Friesland, then?"

"*Nay*," he assured her. "Willem says I shall be home tomorrow."

She hooked her arm into his and gave him a half smile. "May Willem be right."

He looked long into her wistful eyes and said something he could never believe to be true. "Perhaps the war will soon be over."

———————

A billowy wind gusted around the hilltop in Dillenburg. With one hand, Aletta tightened the wrap of her dark cape across her shoulders. With the other, she clung to Pieter-Lucas as they plodded down the road that was taking him away from the *kasteel*. At the gate he took her in his arms. "Pray me Godspeed," he begged.

"And a safe passage," she added.

"At least I go not to a battlefield wearing a soldier's uniform and toting a sword."

Neither did Yaap! Remembering, Aletta forced a smile and said, "I am most grateful."

He hovered over her with adoration in his eyes. "You are a brave woman, my love," he whispered.

His parting kiss was so long and so deep that she nearly forgot it had to come to an end. When at last he pulled his lips away, his arms still lingered about her. Her heart vibrated like the strings of a fiercely plucked lute.

She watched him mount his old friend, Blesje, and ride off over the bridge, down the hillside, and out of reach, waving as he went. The wind brushed the dampness from her cheeks and wafted the kisses she blew toward him on the path below.

"Great God in the Heaven," she whispered into both hands cupped over her mouth, "Prince Willem may think he's another Yaap, but we all know better. He has paint in his blood, a limp in his leg, and a vrouw who yearns to hold him close."

When the last glimpse of her new husband had vanished behind the roofs of the village, Aletta turned sad steps toward the herb garden. At the morning sup, when Pieter-Lucas had presented her to Juliana the Younger, the noble lady had invited her to meet her there.

Aletta found the weed-fringed pathway that led her down the hillside and through an opening in the fence. Flower Month had filled the trees with bright new greenery, singing meadowlarks, and cuckoo birds. She stopped at the entrance and let her eyes roam freely over the plot of growing things.

Stepping into the enclosure, she breathed deeply. Delicious aromas of rosemary, sage, savory, thyme, and lavender blended with other unknown fragrances. Plucking a sprig of rosemary, she crushed the needles between her fingers and, holding them to her nostrils, inhaled slowly and smiled. "Did my Pieter-Lucas draw your aging branches and needles for the Countess Juliana? Or," she added, examining a clump of bright new calendulas, "your sunny blossoms of last season?"

With the discovery of each new plant, she imagined she felt her artist husband's presence at her side, heard his voice, watched his fingers sketching. "Someday," she mused, "when he returns . . ."

"In the meantime," she went on, her skirts brushing against a spreading bush of lavender, "I shall follow the countesses up and down these rows and learn new ways to transform these lovely leaves and flowers, stems and roots, into life-giving potions."

When she was stooping down to look at a patch of unknown shoots, she heard a sound of weeping coming from beyond the large clump of berry bushes to her right. "You should have waited for the countess," she chided herself.

Standing quickly, she fled through the maze of plants and out into the pathway. She had reached halfway to the *kasteel* when Countess Juliana met her. She wore a large white apron over her plain dark dress and carried a basket on her arm.

"So you have already been there," she said.

"I fear I did wrong," Aletta confessed.

"But I invited you."

"I should have waited until you came."

"Why? It has no gate with locks."

"I . . . well, I was enjoying the plants so much, I did not realize until I neared the patch of berry bushes that I was not alone. Then I heard weeping beyond the berries, and my heart smote me greatly for rushing in to disturb someone's vigil with sorrow."

" 'Tis my moeder, Juliana the Elder." The noblewoman smiled and laid a hand on Aletta's arm. "She has a bench in that corner where she often repairs to think and pray, and just now her heart is sore grieved over Adolph."

"After this I shall take care to avoid her grieving spot," Aletta finished.

"She expects us all to come and go," Countess Juliana assured her. "Come now. I can only show you a few of the plants today. One of my patients in the miller's house on the edge of the village needs a call. I should like to have you accompany me."

"Nothing would make me happier. I spent my whole time in Emden doing just that with Oma. Everyone called her Healer Lady of East Friesland."

"You learned much from her?"

"Very much! And I am eager to learn from you as well."

Together they walked through the rows. The noble healer lady talked in a subdued voice and avoided her moeder's praying corner as she introduced Aletta to a handful of her plants: bearclaw for digestive difficulties, liver floweret for wounds both internal and external, coltsfoot for coughs, and herb-grace to take away crudity, rawness of humors, windiness, and old pains of the stomach. The more Aletta heard, the more she yearned to know.

Often as Juliana introduced a plant, she would begin with the comment, "This one your Pieter-Lucas drew for me." Then she would launch into a fascinating story of its unusual origins or properties or uses.

All too soon she announced, "No more for today. I take a snippet of fresh borage to bring cheer to my patient, and we go. The woman we visit fled with her husband and newborn infant from their home the end of Spring Month. She had endured terribly long and hard birth pains and much ripping and seems never to have recovered from the weakness brought on by prolonged flux of the wombe."

"Is there a cure?"

"I've tried many potions and read all the books in search of a remedy. My moeder and I have concocted a new recipe, which I've brought today and pray it works."

"Did they come from far?" Aletta asked.

"I know only that it was a long journey of many weeks."

"How tragic! It's amazing that the moeder did not die en route."

"Young moederhood defies impossible threats," Juliana said.

"And the baby?"

"He does much better than his moeder. Like a miracle child."

Aletta remembered Emilia and sensed a growing eagerness to help this patient. All unintentionally, her feet quickened their pace. Yet why the urgency? She was not the healer lady here. She must be calm inside.

————

The aging mill lay beside the river at the spot where the water rushed around a bend in rippling rapids. Unlike the wind-driven mills of the Low Lands that Aletta was accustomed to, it had a large wheel that dipped into the water and powered the stones that ground the grain, setting up a dreadful shuddering clatter.

An elderly stoop-shouldered woman met the two herbalists at the door of the house. "Oma Maryka," Juliana had explained. "Her husband owned and ran this mill until he died. Now his son keeps it going still. They mill all the grain we consume at the *kasteel*. They also crush herbs for us. When my patient and her husband arrived with their baby, this family offered to give them lodging. In exchange, Maarten helps with the millwork whenever he is not busy at the blacksmith shop at the *kasteel*."

The older lady escorted them up two flights of creaking stairs. They were worn smooth and sagged in the middle. The whole building trembled and hummed with the sound of the gears and millstones and crushing grain below.

They found their patient asleep in her cupboard bed on the wall. The baby slept in his basket near the hearth in the large single-room apartment. Aletta gazed in wonder at the child with his chest rising and falling in perfect rhythm and his breath making soft airy noises. How either he or his moeder could sleep with all the noise and rattling, she could not imagine.

Oma Maryka stood beside the young woman, wiping her hands on her apron. "She's slept nearly the whole day. Could hardly even coax her to nurse the infant."

"You gave her the decoction I left with you when I came last?" Juliana asked.

"*Ach*, surely so!" she said. "I give her just a little four times a day as you instructed. But when she stands to her feet, she grows faint and complains that her head pains and swims miserably." She shook her head and added, "I know not what will happen to her—and that baby. Dear me, dear me . . ."

Juliana parted the bed curtains and looked in. She motioned Aletta to come closer.

Softly, hardly above a whisper, she said, "You see how pale she is."

Aletta clapped a hand over her mouth and gasped. "Petronella! How thin she's grown!"

"You know her?"

"We played together in the streets of Breda when we were girls. We've shopped together for fish in the market. We've sat together in *The Crane's Nest*, reading some of my vader's big books. Not long before my vader took our family from Breda, her moeder died, and she went to live with an older sister in Geertruidenberg. I had no idea she had married. Maarten, son of Nicholaas de Smid, is her husband?"

"His name is Maarten, and *ja*, he is a smith. That is all I know."

"His vader was the blacksmith who shoed Prince Willem's horses in his shop," Aletta explained. An odd mix of pleasure and dread bubbled up inside of her.

Juliana nodded. "Aha! That's why he brought Nell here."

Instinctively, Aletta sat beside her friend on the bed and took her hand in one of her own. She lay the other on her forehead. "Petronella, you cannot slip away from us. Not now, with this splintery-new son with the perfect nose, smooth skin, and pudgy little fingers. He needs you."

Aletta let all she'd ever learned about herbs slip out of mind. For now she was no herbalist, only a friend who must find help. Turning to Juliana, she pleaded, "You must have something in your apothecary that can restore her. You must!"

"We hope and pray this latest recipe will do it," Juliana said. Then gently she jostled the patient's shoulder and called, "Nell, oh, Nell, time to awaken."

Petronella stirred slightly and her eyelids fluttered open.

"I've brought you a friend, Nell," Juliana said, smiling.

Aletta stroked Nell's arm and smiled at her. "My Petronella!"

Never taking her gaze from the now wide-opened eyes, Aletta watched a look of puzzlement give way to the light of recognition.

A smile spread over the tired face, and Petronella spoke in labored, breathy tones. "Aletta! How can this be?"

"The story is too long for now. In the days ahead, as you mend, we will talk."

CHAPTER THIRTEEN

Cleveland Countryside

1st day of Summer Month (June), 1568

The banishment trek to the German frontier region of Cleveland spread over two grueling days. Sometimes by coach, sometimes by boat, Meester Laurens and his vrouw remained chained to their captors. Never free from the soldiers' loud coarse language and rough mannerisms, Meester Laurens yearned for a solitary spot to hold his Adriana in his arms, to weep with her over their losses, and to ponder their pathway ahead.

At the point where the Waal River merged with its parent, the mighty Rhine, the soldiers ordered their trekkers to pull the boat to shore and lash it to a willow trunk. Here they freed the couple from their chains and sent them on their way with two instructions.

"Walk straight ahead toward the city in the distance."

"And remember, the moment you cross back over this frontier into the Low Lands, the stake awaits you both."

The soldiers left their ominous warning hanging in the soggy midday air and returned the way they had come.

Dazed, Laurens pointed to the church spire on the far rim of the world and mumbled, "Somewhere out there lies our new home."

Where that somewhere might be, he had no idea. Thoughts and plans had been tumbling through his mind ever since he'd heard the shocking word, "Banishment." He supposed he should find some comfort in re-membering that this was the area where he had been born and where he had lived until he was nearly twelve years old. Yet when his family fled here, so did their friends. Secret religious dissenters, they'd fled to Antwerp and learned to read the Bible and be rebaptized.

Today, almost fifty years after that flight, he must forget the dreams of childhood and search out a safe place for his vrouw. Perhaps in Cleve, principal city, home of the fabled Swan Castle sitting atop a row of high cliffs that overlooked the Rhine. The Duke of Cleve had a reputation for being kind to nonpapists, and perhaps they'd find a community of like-minded believers there.

Laurens lifted the woolen bag his wife had brought along and slung it over one shoulder. "We go to Cleve," he announced, amazed at the as-surance in his voice.

With his other hand cupped around her elbow, he directed her steps along the muddy pathway that cut across the wide flat pasture before them. Though the sun was somewhere above their heads, the clouds kept it from warming their way. The damp cold penetrated his clothes and he struggled against the stiffness of too long sitting with knees up under his chin.

"What an abominable way to treat a good wife!" Laurens said. "No roof over your head, no bread for your belly, no money in my purse . . ." He shook his head from side to side in quick little movements, as if to dislodge from his mind the glowering thunderclouds of the past three days, and the uncertainties of the weeks before them. Then he put his free arm around his wife's waist and pulled her toward him.

Adriana patted his arm goodnaturedly. "We are alive and alone, and Alva's men let me gather this one bag of necessities before they dragged me from our house."

"What sort of necessities?" He thought about the few precious trea-sures they had gathered over a long full lifetime—now gone. *Nay*, worse—confiscated, stuffed into the already bulging coffers of unworthy men, or burned to ashes.

"A few pieces of clothing to keep us warm, a cooking pot or two, my moeder's old damask cloth, what was left of bread and cheese from the pantry," Adriana was saying.

"My books?" he asked tentatively, afraid to hear the answer.

"*Ach!* How I wish it could have been," she said with a sigh. "I begged the soldiers to let me bring just one or two, but they did not allow me to touch a one."

"I knew it would be so," he said. Visions of his books illuminated by the flames consuming them caused him to tighten his embrace. He leaned his cheek against her capped head and tried not to think about it.

Adriana snuggled into Laurens' embrace and they exchanged the sort of smiles that bespoke the quiet contentment of long years together. Slowly, trying as much to reassure himself as his vrouw, Laurens said, "I know that the God whose honor I was protecting when I refused to sign Alva's oath will not desert us now."

Adriana pushed suddenly back from his grip and said in a bright jubilant voice, "Look! We draw near to a wooded grove, and just around the bend in the road, methinks there lies a sleepy village."

"So it does appear." Laurens smiled and let her coax him forward by the hand. Still, an unsettledness goaded him. A village meant strange people encased in the tight cocoon of their own long-honored traditions and familiar faces. He and Adriana were outsiders—to be stared at, laughed at, examined with suspicion.

"Could it be a good place to rest awhile? There may even be a wayside inn." Adriana's voice combined weariness with anticipation.

"The day is yet young," Laurens answered, having no heart to remind her that they had no coins to pay for an inn. Where they would spend this first night, he had no idea. Silently, he prayed, *Great God, King forever, show us the way.*

As they came opposite the dense shrubs, a rustling among the branches gave him a start. "*Hei!* Who goes there?" he blurted.

" 'Tis only the wind or a hare," Adriana suggested.

"Shh!" Laurens was not convinced.

Instinctively, he crept forward, spreading his arms wide as if to shield his vrouw from whatever danger might be intent on pouncing upon them. Except for the slight movement of a few leaves in the breeze, all grew quiet in the wake of his challenge. But he led Adriana on in silence, never taking his eyes or ears off the menacing willow bushes that continued to threaten from the roadside.

The noises did not come again, and by the time they entered the village, he had begun to worry over whatever dangers that passage might incur. They passed through, edging their way around pigs and chickens, dogs and horses. Residents watched them with apparent curiosity, but no one shouted insults.

Beyond the village, the long straight roadway was lined on both sides with high poplars. The leaves shimmered in the meager sunshine breaking through the clouds, and a tiny bridge crossed over a gently bubbling brook that extended out into the pasture on both sides. To the right, Laurens spotted an oak tree spreading out to the water.

"Vrouw, look," he said, "a quiet spot invites—a place to sit and nibble on what the soldiers left us of bread and cheese."

They seated themselves on two large rocks, and Adriana rummaged through the bag for their midday meal. "Strange," she began, her voice tinged with a sort of unexpected wonder. "Never have bread and cheese looked so inviting."

Laurens bowed his head and prayed, "Oh, Thou great and powerful

King forever, we, your humble servants, bow and give you thanks—for these sumptuous rations, for a day without rain to travel, for very life itself. The simplest of gifts have grown exceedingly bountiful in our eyes. We see not whence comes our next meal or bed, but we anticipate it from Thy hand. Send ahead of us Thy cloud to guide by day and a pillar of fire to warm by night. In the name of Jesus, Lord and Savior, Amen."

Duisburg

Pieter-Lucas and Blesje arrived at the market square in the center of Duisburg just at dusk. No lamplight shone yet from windows, and people, animals, and horse-drawn carts still trudged about.

"Now, if I can just remember the lines and names scrawled across that map Willem showed me," Pieter-Lucas told his horse. "At least it's not yet stick-dark, and we're still in the city. Besides, I have a lantern."

They'd barely started down the street leading away from the market when a scrawny runt of a dog appeared out of nowhere. He headed straight for Blesje, barking fiercely and snapping at his heels.

"Go away!" Pieter-Lucas ordered.

The dog ignored him until Blesje sent him a short kick and picked up his pace. Then the dog backed off, but only until he was safely out of range of the horse's hooves. He followed on barking, and added to this annoyance, Pieter-Lucas heard a snicker of sharp girlish giggles from somewhere in the same direction. Turning to look, he saw nothing but the churchyard with its scattered outcropping of burial stones. He patted Blesje on the neck and consoled, "Steady now, just keep moving to the end of this street, out through the gate, and across the heather field!"

Little by little, they pulled away from the dog. But both the barking and the laughter continued. Then abruptly the laughter turned into a three-pitched call in a piercing, sirenlike voice, "Pieter-Lu-u-cas! Son of Hendrick!"

"What? Where? Who?" Pieter-Lucas stammered. Not looking back, he urged Blesje faster forward. The last thing he needed was to be singled out for attention by some demented giggling woman. Whoever could know him in this place, anyway? If only Blesje would keep pace with his racing heart.

But on this narrow city street, crowded with people, animals, coaches, and piles of slippery refuse, the best Pieter-Lucas could get from Blesje was a slow trot across the uneven slickened cobblestones. Always the voice followed, never falling behind, continually repeating its unnerving message. And the dog kept barking.

"How much farther will they pursue us?" Pieter-Lucas mumbled. "Come on, Blesje, keep moving."

When they passed through the city gates, both the yapping and the mysterious voice stopped. By the time the street ended in a heather field, the darkness had deepened to the point where the pathway to the farmhouse was almost indiscernible. A lighted window not too far ahead gave evidence of a house nearby.

Relieved of the nagging irritation, they soon approached the low door at the back of the house, opposite the horse stable. The thatch on the roof above the door hung nearly to Pieter-Lucas' eye level, so he had to stoop slightly. Following Willem's instructions, he gave two short swift knocks, followed by a pause, then two more knocks.

The upper half of the divided door opened the tiniest wedge, and a gruff voice demanded, "Who are you and what brings you here?" Lighted by the unsteady flame of a lantern, an eye peered around the corner of the door.

"I'm a messenger in search of *Heidebloem*." Pieter-Lucas whispered the watchword by which Willem had instructed him to identify Dirck Coornhert.

"From whom do you come?"

"From *The Desert Flea*." Again using Willem's watchword name. "I am expected," he added.

"My stableboy will take you to the man you seek and put up your horse," said the voice. The door closed in Pieter-Lucas' face.

Almost instantly a young man appeared at his side and took Blesje's reins from his hand. He led Pieter-Lucas across a courtyard and around to the far side of another building. Here he unlocked a door and ushered him down a short hallway into a plain little apartment.

Dirck Coornhert looked up from where he sat at a tiny cloth-covered table before a low-burning fire. He rose quickly and came toward Pieter-Lucas. "Greetings!" he said, smiling and reaching out his hand. "It's the new bridegroom!"

"Good evening, kind friend," Pieter-Lucas responded, shaking the man's hand and offering his own smile in return. "*Ja*, thanks to you, I'm twice wed. Ludwig's army clergyman put us through one more ceremony."

"And he wrote it in his book?"

"He wrote it in his book. But I come bearing a message from our prince."

He rummaged in his doublet and produced the letter Willem had entrusted to his care. "The wax seal was still warm when he thrust it into my hand this morning."

The man gestured his guest toward a three-legged stool at the table, resumed his place across from him, and began to read the letter eagerly. He leaned back against the wall and sighed. "Great and merciful God, but we do have a real war brewing out there," he said. "It's beginning to burst the iron bands that have kept it shut up until now in its fermenting barrels."

"I know," Pieter-Lucas said. "We saw unthinkable things at Heiligerlee."

"War is always unthinkable."

"So I am learning." Pieter-Lucas hung his head and tried not to remember.

"You have entered Willem's service as a messenger, have you?" Coornhert's blunt question jolted Pieter-Lucas.

"Perhaps," he stammered, wishing not to think about it.

"But you came bearing his message."

Pieter-Lucas fingered the rim of his cap. "One thing led to another, and . . . well, now that my friend Yaap is gone, both Ludwig and Willem expect me to take his place. Ludwig told me as much, and Willem gives me his assignments. And I cannot say them 'nay'. . . ." His mind trailed off with his voice.

"Why not?" The question came too quickly.

"They need me . . . and Yaap would have wanted me to do it." Pieter-Lucas sighed, then looked up at Coornhert and said with more feeling, "But war or no war, there is one thing I have promised myself, my vrouw, her vader—and God."

"What might that be?"

Pieter-Lucas stretched out his hands. "These hands of mine were created to wield an artist's brushes and a carving knife. They shall never tote a sword in battle."

Coornhert raised his eyebrows. "Not even if Count Ludwig or Prince Willem should ask it of you?"

"Never!" Pieter-Lucas felt the blood warming his temples and his hands forming into fists. "I am the son of Kees, the peace-loving artist, not Hendrick, the mad Beggar!" He stared hard at his companion, feeling the anger tighten his whole body.

Coornhert nodded. "I know all about that, *jongen*."

"At the first opportunity, I take my bride and go to Leyden," Pieter-Lucas added, his whole being stirring with a passion. "My opa promised, and someday I will go there to become a master painter."

Coornhert rested his arms on the table and looked straight into Pieter-Lucas' eyes, his small mouth half-smiling. "That will not happen until the war is over, *jongen*. In the meantime, Hans and his ilk will always question your decision to serve Willem, and Willem and Ludwig will never understand your vow of nonviolence."

"And you?" Pieter-Lucas asked. "What think you of my decision and my vow?"

"I?" Coornhert drummed the table with a single pointer finger, never taking his eyes off Pieter-Lucas' face. Then methodically, as if he'd had a year to think it through and devise an answer, he said, "I'll reserve my deepest admiration for you and pray you good fortune in the prudent practice of your decision and your vow, for they are both godly ideals."

He reached for his paper and writing pen. "Now, I must reply to Willem's message while you give your tired body a bit of rest so you can return to Dillenburg first thing in the morning."

He gestured toward a mat and a feather bag rolled up on the floor near the fire, then bent his head over his work, muttering, "It's not ten of the clock yet."

Pieter-Lucas spread out the mat and laid his weary body on it. How hard the floor felt, and how empty his arms! His eyes had barely closed when he heard a familiar piercing siren voice coming from the other side of the wall.

"Pieter-Lu-u-cas! Son of Hendrick!"

He sat up with a start. "Not again!" he sputtered, running his fingers through his curls.

Dirck Coornhert looked up. "You've heard this voice before?"

"Tormented me all the way through the city."

"A friend you brought along?" Coornhert asked.

"Friend? Bah!" Pieter-Lucas spewed out his words. "No friend of mine would call me son of Hendrick! Besides, who would know me in this place?"

"Whoever she is, she's pretty bold." Coornhert chuckled and went back to his work.

"I've no idea who she is or how she found me here! I never did even see her. It was almost dark and she kept to the shadows. A slippery one she is, that's sure!"

The voice persisted even as the men talked. Soon there was a loud pounding on the outside door. When no one responded, all grew silent. Next, there were scratching noises above them, along with the scrambling of feet across the attic floor.

Then, when all had fallen quiet once more, the door burst open and a wiry little woman charged into the room. She had stringy curls hanging halfway to her waist below a headdress that was fastened askew. In one arm she held a squirming dog. In the other, she cradled a large leather-bound book.

Both men jumped to their feet. "Who are you, and why do you enter where you were not invited?" Coornhert demanded.

He grabbed her by the shoulder and tried to turn her around. But she slipped from his grasp, flashed him a missing-tooth grin, and resumed her possessive stance, this time on the other side of the room.

"Pieter-Lucas, here, he's a-knowin' who I be," she said as sweetly as her raspy voice would allow.

Pieter-Lucas gasped. "Indeed, I do know who you are," he said, his head reeling. It couldn't be, and yet . . . "You're Lompen Mieke, the street rat, beggar, and thief from Breda! How did you find me here—and why?"

She smiled an impudent smile, obviously believing she was disarming them with her charm. For an answer, she held out the book and said, "I sell. You buy."

Coornhert moved toward the book. But when he reached out his hand for it, she snatched it back.

"Give me coins, an' then ye can look at it all ye likes." She hugged the book tightly to her chest.

"Where did you get it, Mieke?" Pieter-Lucas demanded.

With practiced coyness, she half pranced, half dragged her lithe little body around the room. "B'longs to a friend what's been in the tower prison fer a dreadful long time. His vrouw done took as good a care o' him as she could. Then, when the bailiff decided to put Pieter van Keulen an' Tante Lysbet to the torch . . ."

"Tante Lysbet to the torch?" Pieter-Lucas grabbed Mieke by both arms and wrestled her into submission. "How dare you tell such monstrous lies?" he snarled at her.

She jerked herself free from his grasp and sprang to the other side of the room. "I not a-lyin' to ye. I seed it with my own eyes."

Pieter-Lucas felt a huge lump rise from the pit of his stomach. Tante Lysbet may have been a stern woman, but she surely never did anything deserving of death at the stake! And in Breda? Vaguely aware that Mieke's shrill voice was rattling on about stakes and torches and decrees of banishment, he held his head in his hands and moaned softly. "Great God, if you've got a drop of mercy left for us all, don't let my vrouw ever hear this story."

He heard Dirck Coornhert challenging Mieke. "What has all this to do with the book you want me to buy?"

She gave Pieter-Lucas a tilt of the head, then cleared her throat. "My friend what expected he'd be consumed on th' stake was taked out o' th' prison an' banished from th' country, along with his vrouw. An' they didn't allow 'em to take a single treasure along from their house. So I lifted out th' book b'fore th' soldiers could come an' help their nasty selfs. I followed my friends from a distance. They got a few scraps o' bread left an' not a coin to their names. I got to take care o' these folks, don't ye see?"

"If all you want is coins for a book, why didn't you search for a book-seller in Duisburg?" Pieter-Lucas asked. "You had not reason to follow me."

"I was a-lookin' fer such a shop when I spotted ye in the market. A face what I seed b'fore. An' I 'membered how ye was always a frequentin' that shop o' books in Breda. I figgered th' God that Betteke an' Lysbet both use to talk 'bout when I was in th' same prison cell with 'em musta sended ye here to buy th' book to feed my friends."

"Who is this friend you talk about?" Pieter-Lucas wanted to know.

"Can't tell!" She turned up her sharp nose and hugged and rocked the dog and the book together as she spoke.

"Anybody I know?" he prodded.

She said nothing but went on hugging her treasures and grinning in triumph.

"Listen to me, you saucy little thief," Pieter-Lucas snapped. "All your pious talk about God won't do a thing to make us trust you. You give us no names for your friends, we give you no coins."

She turned her gaze toward Coornhert.

"You heard it," Coornhert said as calmly as if the woman were completely sensible. "And that's not all. If we can't see the whites of the man's eyes—and his vrouw's as well—how can you expect us to believe you? Until you tell us their names and bring them here, you'll not collect one thin *stuiver* from either of us."

For a long moment she stuck to her ground, feet spread wide apart, chin elevated, mouth hard-set. She stared by turns, first at one, then at the other. Then with an air of wounded haughtiness, she gathered both the book and the dog more tightly to her and rustled her skirts in a broad swirling motion toward the door. "So that's the way ye wants it? That's the way ye gets it."

She reached for the door handle. Coornhert blocked her way. "The name?"

Nose still in the air, she mumbled without looking at them, "Meester Laurens."

Coornhert nodded toward Pieter-Lucas. "You know anyone by that name?"

"A good friend of my vrouw's vader. But why would they banish him?"

He shook his head and tried to bring some order to the wild thoughts swirling through his brain.

Mieke shouted, "I done telled ye what ye asked. Now let me go!"

Coornhert didn't move but held out his hand. "You'll have to leave that book here while you go for them."

Yanking the book as far as her arms would stretch, she looked at him with daggers in her eyes and her lip curled into a pout. "*Nay, nay, nay!* No coins, no book!"

Calmly, Coornhert said, "That is a dangerous book to be toting around the countryside with you. If you value your life, or the book itself, you will leave it here. I can assure you, it will be far safer with me than in your arms."

Pieter-Lucas held his breath. He had no idea what she was up to, but he knew it could not be a good thing. Yet how could he stop her?

Mieke stared at Coornhert for a long time before she relaxed her hold on the book and laid it in his outstretched hands. Still holding on with one hand, she sneered, "An' if'n ye deceives me, God'll burn yer soul in the lake o' fiery torments!"

She lifted her dirt-encrusted fingers, then demanded, "Now, let me go!"

"Just one word of warning," he said, still barring her way. "I have a few unchanging rules in my life, which probably means nothing to you, undisciplined as you obviously are. But I go to sleep at ten of the clock at night and always arise at four in the morning. So if you would see your cause blessed, you will be careful not to bring your friends here between those hours."

Pieter-Lucas took his place next to his cohort, and to the backdrop of a rapid heart-pounding, he added, "And if you come after the clock strikes six times, I shall not be here to attest that Meester Laurens is who you say he is—and you'll get no coins."

They both stepped aside and Coornhert let the girl go free. She darted out into the darkness. When he'd closed the door, Coornhert leaned against it wearily and held out the book. "Did you see what she is trying to sell?"

"*Nay.*" Pieter-Lucas stared at the large volume with thick brown leather covers, carved in intricate pattern. "It's a Bible!"

"*Ja!* Can you imagine what would happen if she took it to a bookshop?"

Pieter-Lucas felt a shiver run the length of his back. Then pointing at the man, he challenged, "And can you imagine what will happen when she brings back her friends, and they turn out to be Spanish soldiers and they arrest you for possession of the first book on King Philip's list of *verboden boecken*? I can't believe you walked into her trap—and with your eyes wide open."

Coornhert fingered the carvings on the cover of the big book. *"Jongen,"* he said, "I cannot always explain the things I feel in my heart. I only know that when I looked into that girl's eyes, I saw goodness bubbling up from the deepest places of her being."

" 'Goodness,' nothing! If you'd ever lived in Breda—if you'd reason as I do to believe she had tried to kill your grandfather—you'd know there's nothing good about Lompen Mieke!" He paused, stunned, and stared at the older man. Coornhert appeared calm as ever. Every hair of his perfectly white beard, mustache, and hair lay unruffled—nothing bespoke anxiety. In Pieter-Lucas' heart, though, everything was churning or pounding or shrieking. "We have to flee this place now while there's time!"

The man shook his white head slowly. "If she's as devious as you say, our doom is already sealed."

"What do you mean, already sealed?"

Coornhert shrugged. "It's simple. The soldiers, if there are any, would never have trusted her enough to let her come this far without following her themselves. They'd be lying out in the pastures awaiting the perfect time to descend. So let me creep out of my safe den, and they'll fall on me before I can take my first breath of countryside air."

Pieter-Lucas listened with his mouth gaping. The old man's reason was irrefutable. "Then you're telling me it's too late to save ourselves?"

"If indeed she is betraying us."

"If? Lompen Mieke never tells the truth!" Either Coornhert was right about Mieke's goodness or he had to be right about the soldiers out in the fields. In either case, Pieter-Lucas had nothing to trust and everything to fear. Yet way down deep inside, he felt the tentacles of fear begin to loosen their grip.

"At least," he said lamely, "we could hide out someplace in this building."

"Hide from this Mieke?" Coornhert laughed. "Now, I've a few minutes left before my bedtime hour, and I must finish my letter to Willem before I retire."

He seated himself at the table and picked up his pen. "If you want to find your way into the attic or cellar, go ahead. Or you may sit in the corner and pile all my blankets on your head. My suggestion is that you lie down on the mat and sleep. Sunrise comes early, and with it, our extraordinary little visitor. 'Twill be much more pleasant if you've had some sleep the night before. Rest well."

Long after Coornhert had finished his letter, blown out the light, and begun to snore, Pieter-Lucas was still tossing on his mat in the corner, listening to each scratch and creak and the whistling of the wind around the corner above his head. "Great God," he prayed at last, "keep us safe and send both devious Mieke and her evil soldiers sprawling on their faces in the mud."

Cleveland Countryside
2nd morning of Summer Month (June), 1568

Meester Laurens and his vrouw found shelter for the night in a deserted animal shed in the middle of a field somewhere between the frontier and Cleve. With decaying straw for a bed and their own capes for covers, they slept fitfully. Laurens' dreams combined a senseless profusion of cramped riverboats, burning stakes, and books being torn from his shelves in Breda. When a pair of hands began shaking him into an untimely wakefulness, he thought he was dreaming still.

"Run fer yer lifes!" The high-pitched words jarred him.

Where was he? Laurens pushed at the haze that shrouded him from his surroundings. What sort of messenger—demonic or angelic—was attacking? He sat up and reached for Adriana, who was also sitting up and staring at their intruder.

Partially lightened by the rays of a half moon, Laurens made out the shadow of a small elfin form standing over them and heard nearby the sharp yapping of a little dog.

"Go away!" he ordered, above the pounding of his heart.

"*Nay, nay, NAY!*" the woman's voice rose in pitch and intensity, and the dog yapped on. "We got to run now!"

"Who is it?" Laurens stammered.

"It's Mieke!" Adriana said.

"Who?"

"Lompen Mieke!"

He stared in disbelief. "From Breda? We're both dreaming!" That crude little street thief was as sly as a demon and just as unpredictable. Yet how in the name of believable reasoning would she end up out here?

"*Nay!* I be Mieke in th' flesh," the shrill voice that had awakened them piped. "An' I tells ye, ye gots to run fer yer lifes!"

"What's this about?" Laurens asked.

Adriana laid a hand on his. "Shh. Leave it to me."

Turning to their visitor, she said with calm firmness, "Mieke, before we move from this place, you will tell us why we're moving, what we're running from, and why this cannot wait until the light of morning."

Finally the young woman fell silent. Against the door-framed splotch of faint moonlight, Meester Laurens watched her gather her dog into her arms and tremble slightly as if hesitating to answer.

"There's two men a-sleepin' in a room in the inn back in that village ye done passed through what're layin' fer ye both."

"How do you know such a thing?" Adriana asked.

"I heared 'em talkin'. They was so full o' beer they had no idea their waggin' tongues was a-reachin' ears what might care what they was up to."

"Mieke, it is very good that you are so eager to watch out for us," Adriana said, "but how did you know where we were?"

"I got two good feet an' a brain what turns with th' wind like th' wheels o' th' farmer's mill."

"But we're so far from Breda," Laurens said.

"Ain't no place too far from home when ye got friends what need ye."

Friends? The thought was too ridiculous even for laughter.

Mieke was offering her hand to tug them to their feet and out the door. She snatched up their cloaks and ordered, "Now, grab yer bags an' follow after me. If'n I don't watch out fer ye two, who's a-goin' to keep ye safe from Alva's nasty long arm?"

"Alva's men can't reach us here," Laurens argued. "We've been banished beyond the spot where he has control."

Mieke grew agitated. "No time to prattle on 'bout it. Ye got to come now. Them evil men's plannin' to rise b'fore sunrise so's they can catch up to ye an' fall on ye nice an' quiet and friendly like while ye walk through the wood. I ain't a-goin' to let ye dally here under the thumb o' deadly trouble."

Laurens stumbled out into the damp predawn air, and Adriana followed. What if, after all, Mieke was speaking truth? Had God perhaps sent her here to rescue them? On the other hand, if they refused to follow her instructions and she turned against them . . . Besides, which was more to be feared—Alva's fury or Lompen Mieke's shiftiness?

"And where are you taking us that we will be safe from danger?" Laurens asked.

"I'se finded a hidin' place with a white-bearded man, friend o' a friend o' yours."

"Friend of a friend of mine?" Laurens stared at her. "In this country?"

"Ye heared me! An' fer right now, there's no time fer talk. Jus' get to movin,' b'cause yer friend's leavin' the place b'fore six bells, an' we gots to catch him first."

A friend out here, leaving at six bells, hiding them from Alva's soldiers? It simply didn't hang together. *Nay*, Alva's men were not following them. This strange creature had something else on her mind. Laurens felt it in his bones. Whether for good or for bad, he had no idea. But what else could they do but go along?

With sure-footed stealth, Mieke led them across the field and onto the trek path that ran along the riverbank. At her heels scampered her little nondescript dog that seemed to be mostly wagging tail. A light mist filled their nostrils and lungs, and a chorus of unknown insects and frogs filled their ears.

Meester Laurens held to his vrouw with one hand and to their bag of possessions with the other. His mind raced with questions—*What if? Where? How? What next?*

He slipped an arm around his vrouw's waist and spoke softly into her ear. "What do you know about this Lompen Mieke to make you trust her so?"

"As soon as they let her out of prison, she began coming to see me every day."

"You?"

Adriana shrugged. "I never knew why. Some days she'd knock on my door and give me wilted flowers. Other times she'd accost me at the market or jump out of the bushes beside me. Often she gave me herbs to take to Betteke."

"How many things did she steal from you?"

"She never stole anything."

"Impossible!" Laurens insisted. "Like my vader always said, 'You can take the pig out of the mud, but you can't take the mud out of the pig.'"

"I know, and I agree. Still, I swear I never missed a thing."

Laurens bristled. "*Ach*, she's a sly one. I suppose you believe her story about Alva's men chasing us out here, too."

Adriana shook her head slowly. "Probably not. But I do believe that in her strange way, she is trying to take care of us."

"Adriana," he moaned. "Think, vrouw. Mieke's sort never takes care of anybody but herself. She's got a trick tied to the end of her string. Mind my word!"

Adriana began slowly, "I know you speak great wisdom. But . . ."

"But what?"

She slipped her arm into his and spoke with quiet persuasiveness. "It's just that the Mieke who went into that prison tower with Betteke and

Tante Lysbet is not altogether the same Mieke that came out."

"Adriana, will you never learn? Evil people don't bait traps with rotten food."

"I know all that," she protested. "I've watched this creature closely for years. Never before have I known her to help anybody—not even when she was getting ready to steal from them. She even asks me questions about right and wrong. I can't explain it, and you can think what you like, but I know something in this woman has changed."

Still shaking his head, Laurens said, "We'll see."

They walked on in silence, their steps growing slower and their sprightly guide running on far ahead. The moon sank in the sky. The mist lifted, and the open fields around them turned to woods, then to open fields again.

Finally the little elfin figure and her dog stood like a silhouette against the lightening sky, beckoning vigorously.

"Think we're almost there?" Adriana asked.

"Only God and Mieke know," he answered. "I see a city up ahead, not far."

"And I think I hear five bells. Sounds like a clock."

"Judging from the sky, I'd say that could be so."

By the time they'd caught up with Mieke, Adriana was leaning heavily on her husband for strength to keep up. They followed their guide onto a narrow weed-fringed lane that led to a farm settlement. Dodging in and out between buildings, they stopped at last before a small one in the far corner. Mieke pounded on the door, demanding entrance.

The man who opened to her did indeed have a white beard and mustache as well as a full head of white hair, presided over by a black wide-brimmed hat.

"I'se returned," Mieke said, grinning, "jus' like I told ye—with my friends."

"I see." The man's eyes were both kind and piercing.

Mieke rattled on. "Now, let us in to see yer young Pieter-Lucas, so he can tell ye fer certain that they're true upright citizens o' Breda what he knows, an' ye kin give 'em coins fer th' book."

Laurens and his vrouw exchanged glances of unbelieving awe. They'd walked all this way to help her sell a book? Who had she stolen it from? What did they have to do with it? And this Pieter-Lucas—van den Garde, was he?

The white-bearded host had not yet invited them in. Rather, he called back over his shoulder, "Your guests have arrived, *jongen*."

Meester Laurens stared in disbelief at the young man moving toward the door, throwing his arms around his shoulders, and crying out, "Meester Laurens! She told me it was you, and I almost didn't believe her. This is our host, Dirck. . . ."

The white-bearded man pulled them quickly across the threshold and shut the door. Pieter-Lucas seated Adriana in his own place at the table, and Mieke planted herself firmly by her side.

Laurens stared at his host's face. "Dirck . . . Coornhert, could it be?" Laurens asked.

The man of the house eyed him for a moment. "What makes you think that?"

"My good friend Barthelemeus de Koopman has spoken of you often. With white beard and dark eyes, I can't imagine there's another. From Haarlem, is that not so?"

Coornhert nodded.

Laurens rattled on. "You've been chased into exile too?"

He shrugged. "When Prince Willem has to go, what more can we expect?"

Laurens shook his head and sighed. "I've lost a lot of friends fleeing for their lives—good friends, my best friends, like Dirck Engelshofen. Not still in Emden, is he?" He looked at Pieter-Lucas.

"He left the same time I did. Sailed to Engeland with Barthelemeus."

Laurens nodded. "None too soon, believe me. It's awful what's happened to our safe city. Just days ago, I stood in the market square of Breda and watched two innocent friends turned into torches."

"Who?" Pieter-Lucas asked.

"The goldsmith, Pieter van Keulen, and his housekeeper, Betteke."

"Whatever for?"

"Image-breaking, they said."

"*Nay!* It couldn't be!" The young man showed an animated indignity that startled Laurens. He was, after all, no longer a boy.

Laurens shook his head. "So said we all. . . ." He let his voice trail off while he swallowed a lump of painful memories. "And they banished Tante Lysbet on false charges!"

"Mieke here told me they executed Tante Lysbet," Pieter-Lucas said, a question mark coloring his voice.

Laurens remembered how he'd prayed God to spare Betteke. "Why did you say it was Tante Lysbet, Mieke?" he asked. He searched her face for a cloud of uneasiness, a flinching expression. Instead she held her head high and answered forthrightly.

"The bailiff told th' whole world 'twas Betteke. But on th' night b'fore th' stakin', I watched 'em take th' body o' Betteke out o' th' prison and dump it in a hole in th' field outside th' Guest House Gate. She died o' th' consumption. All of us in th' prison knowed she had that sorely awful. Ye heared her coughin' day an' night when ye was there." She nodded toward Laurens.

"No question about that." So maybe it was Tante Lysbet, after all.

"I can prove it to ye." Mieke reached inside her bodice and pulled out a long chain with an object dangling from it.

"What's that?" Laurens asked.

"A key what Tante Lysbet always hung round her neck—"

"Where did you get it?" Pieter-Lucas interrupted, frowning.

"Digged it out o' th' ashes of Lysbet's burnin', along with this." She held up a second metal object that Laurens couldn't identify in the dim morning light.

"And that?"

"Th' screw what they fastened to her tongue to keep her from talkin' so nobody'd guess who she really was."

A round of gasps filled the room. Mieke said, "What else ye think they throwed that cloth over her head fer, if'n they didn't want to hide somethin'?"

For a long moment, the only sounds in the room were the scratching of the birds in the thatch above and a muffled sniffle from Mieke.

Then abruptly Mieke edged her way up next to Coornhert. "Now that ye see I been a-tellin' ye th' truth," she said, "be ye ready to buy this man's book what I left b'hind, so's he an' his vrouw kin buy what to eat an' a place to lay their heads?"

Coornhert reached into a cupboard behind the table, pulled out a large leather-bound book, and placed it in Laurens' hands.

"My Bible!" Laurens gasped.

"That's th' one," Mieke shouted.

"Mieke, where did you get this?" he demanded.

She crossed her arms and said saucily, "From yer house where ye leaved it."

"When did you take it?" Laurens cast a swift sidewise glance at his vrouw.

"Th' evenin' o' the burnin'. While they was a-packin' ye both into th' coach, I sneaked in an' lifted it out b'fore they'd have a chance to find an' steal it."

"But why, Mieke?" Adriana asked.

"Couldn't let the soldiers take what could bring ye so much good coins fer eatin'. I knows what it feels like to have a hungry hole in yer belly. Your vrouw's been so kind to me, an' I simply cannot let ye die from hunger." She paused and swallowed before going on. "Ye know, this is th' first time I ever stealed anything fer th' intent to give th' money what it brings to its rightful owner, an' it gives me a warm feelin' down here somewhere." She was rubbing her chest over her heart and smiling.

"Your kindness warms my heart too," Laurens stammered. "But I cannot sell this book."

Mieke stared at him with a puzzled expression. "Why not? It's big an' fancy." Then nodding toward Coornhert, she added, "You'd buy it, wouldn't ye?"

"You don't understand," Laurens said. How could he make it clear to her simple mind? "I must keep this book. I need it."

She held her head to one side and challenged, "But what good's a book a-goin' to do ye when yer stomach's got the growls?"

"The God who delivered us from the stake will also feed us—with His ravens, if need be—but not with coins from this book."

She frowned. "I dunno 'bout ravens, an' I'se not one o' ye schoolish folks what reads books. I only know that when yer belly's empty, ye needs coins."

Laurens nodded slowly. "Some of my books I might sell someday if I was hungry—and if I had them anymore. But this one? Never!"

Mieke looked at Coornhert, then around the room to the others—Pieter-Lucas, Adriana, and back at him. She stared proudly into his eyes, and he stared back, waiting.

"Then where ye goin' to lay yer heads in the night?" She spoke in pleading tones. "Ye can't sleep under the stars and in the mists like I do. One night in that rotten straw was more'n enough fer folks like ye."

Coornhert spoke up. "I have friends in these environs that will give them a home for now. God brought you to the right place."

She looked up, then slowly picked up her dog and held him tightly in her arms.

"You've done me a greater kindness than you could imagine by rescuing my Book," Laurens said. "I shall always be grateful. Nothing of all my possessions will ever be so precious to me as this book."

Mieke squirmed as though she didn't know how to express some thought that troubled her. Then looking at the floor and raising her eyes gradually, she began, "Must be somethin' pretty special!"

"More than all my possessions put together." Laurens held the book close to his breast and curled his fingers around its smooth leather edges. With his lips, he caressed it lightly and let its rich aroma fill his nostrils.

"I figgered it musta been good fer bringin' a lot o' coins, b'cause I found it in th' secret hidin' place in th' wall, where most rich folks hide their bags o' coins."

The young woman was looking up at him with a wistful expression—almost of innocence. Impossible! Yet the look he saw in her eyes pierced through the heavy accumulation of great wisdom with which he faced all of life. It released something he could no more explain than Adriana had been able to do out there on the roadway in the middle of the night.

Suddenly he realized she was no longer talking, but waiting. How could he make her understand?

"Mieke," he said tentatively, "this book is just like the one that Betteke used to read and talk to you about in the prison cell."

"God's Book?" she asked.

He nodded.

"Oh!" she exclaimed, her face alight with an almost holy reverence.

"One thing you need to know about it," Laurens went on, "that could save your life—and ours along with it."

"What's that?"

"You must never try to sell God's Book. Never!"

"Why not? Any book that kin help ye get ready to die like it helped Betteke ought to bring a lot o' coins. Doesn't th' whole world want that sort o' book?"

"What you say should be true, Mieke. But the men that run this world are afraid that if people like us read God's Book, we'll know more about God than they do. So when they see you with one of these books, they'll not only put you back into the prison, they'll probably tie you to a stake and torch you and the book along with you."

A light went on in the dirty face with the stringy curls framing it. "No matter how important a man is, if'n he kin put th' screws to Tante Lysbet's tongue an' th' torch to her body, then he's never read this book. 'Cause Betteke read to me from it 'bout love an' kindness what would never let 'em torch another body."

Maybe it wasn't so complicated after all. Laurens looked at Adriana. She was resting her elbows on the table, cradling her chin in her hands and smiling as if she'd just seen a bright fresh rainbow spread across a bank of angry gray clouds. Maybe that's what they'd all just seen, Laurens decided.

CHAPTER FOURTEEN

Dillenburg

2nd evening of Summer Month (June), 1568

*A*s soon as the evening meal was over and Willem's brother Jan had read from the big Bible, Aletta slipped away to the fragrant stillness of the herb garden. Surrounded by her precious herbs, she was nearly contented as she awaited the return of her Pieter-Lucas. He would be home this night.

But he did not come, and the wait grew endless. When the first stars appeared in the deepening sky and a faint sliver of a moon peeked over the nearby hills, the plants seemed to fold themselves up for the oncoming night. The chill of the breeze that rustled through the lindens, the oaks, and the willows began to seep in through her bones.

Somewhere deep inside, she felt a wave of fear chilling her soul and heard an inaudible voice tormenting, *He's traveling in strange places and in darkness.*

"He has Blesje with him," she protested aloud.

What could a horse do if something went wrong?

"Nothing will go wrong! I've spent my day praying him Godspeed!"

Think you not that Countess Juliana and her whole family prayed Adolph Godspeed when he last set out over this same road, and—

"Stop!" she shrieked out into the wind.

Her dialogue with fear led her out of the herb garden, and soon she was climbing the pathway up toward the road. At the gate tower, where her husband had given her that memorable farewell kiss yesterday morning, she lingered as if rooted. Gazing out over the hill, the village, the River Dill, across the fields and beyond to the hazy layers of purplish mountains, she remembered the words Jan had just read in the eating hall. "Unto the hills, I lift up my eyes . . . but in God . . . I will lay my firm foundation."

A soft sigh drained the tightness from her body. "Great God," she prayed, "keep my Pieter-Lucas wrapped in Thy mighty hand."

Then she smoothed out her skirt and spoke briskly to herself. "Young woman, you cannot stay out here all night."

Straining against the memories that bound her here, she coerced her steps at last back up the hill toward the *kasteel*. She had scarcely entered the courtyard when a curdling scream from the apartment of Willem and Anna pierced the air. A tirade of babbling obscenities followed.

Princess Anna was yelling at her husband again. It was no secret how much the woman hated Dillenburg. She spent her miserable existence making sure everyone knew it. But she was not happy anywhere. When they still lived in Breda, the whole city knew about her frequent fits of anger, her childish pouts, and amorous infidelities. Until she came here, though, Aletta had never actually had to listen to any of it.

The deranged words came clear. "You want to play the field hero and free your precious Lowlanders? I shall not stop you. But while you are gone, I shall free myself from the confines of this chicken coop. I shall go to Cologne and sell my jewels to rent an elegant room and dance and drink and enjoy the life of a princess."

Aletta felt her blood run cold. How could a noblewoman act so self-ishly? All she cared about was merrymaking, reading tawdry love tales, and casting sheep's eyes at every man that came in view.

"Addled by overmuch strong drink," Pieter-Lucas always said.

Shivering with the dampness of nightfall and the terrors of what she'd just heard, Aletta hurried inside her room. She lighted a lamp, then lay across the bed and wept. A shrieking princess, a husband roaming the countryside, rumblings of war—must she and her beloved Pieter-Lucas live this way always?

How long she lay there questioning, struggling, grieving, she had no idea. In her mind, she fancied that all the people and places that had ever been dear to her were passing by in one giant procession. Not a one lingered long enough or drew close enough for her to apprehend or clasp to her breast. Even the herb garden at the foot of the hill greeted her with drooping plants and wilted blossoms, then vanished.

"Great and merciful God," she cried out, grabbing at the corner of the feather bag, "don't let Pieter-Lucas be dragged past me too. Bring him tonight back to my side and let him place his hand again in mine. . . ."

She gasped in midsentence and could say no more. Her tears seemed finally spent. With visions of Pieter-Lucas' smiling face and open arms calling to her through the mists of the drowsy exhaustion those tears had spawned, she drifted into sleep.

The next thing she knew, the arms she had dreamed of were wrapping her up, and Pieter-Lucas' voice was whispering in her ear, "My beloved vrouw, I'm back."

She came awake instantly and entwined her arms around his neck. "Pieter-Lucas, my love, I missed you so."

He caressed her head with his lips and mumbled into her hair, "If I had my way, I would never leave your side again . . . never!"

"I know. I know," she whispered, "someday. . ."

Long after Pieter-Lucas had fallen into a sound sleep, Aletta lay awake hearing Anna's voice. "Dear husband," she whispered over his sleeping body, "I may not be always happy with the lot that falls to me in this ugly war. Every moment when you are gone fills me with loneliness and fear. But as long as I can remember the princess's selfish ranting words, I shall never rail on you or demand my own frivolous pleasures at the cost of whatever noble cause God joins you to."

She covered him with her kisses and prayed, "God, in whom I have fixed my firm foundation, keep me ever true to this promise."

3rd afternoon of Summer Month (June)

Pieter-Lucas stood in the courtyard watching Aletta start off for a visit to her ill friend Petronella. Each fold of her yellow skirt and blue shawl hung in precise order. A large basket swung from her arm, her steps were light and graceful.

He felt a quick jab in the ribs and remembered the servant boy who had just summoned him to a meeting with Counts Willem and Jan. "Come now," the boy bantered, "can a vrouw be that interesting?"

"Just wait till you have one." Pieter-Lucas grinned.

He followed the boy into the main building, up stairs and down hallways and at last through a pair of high arched doors into a large room with windows on one side. Already, several places around the huge table that filled the center of the room were occupied by an assortment of messengers and official-looking personages. The sound of subdued voices rippled over the room.

Pieter-Lucas had scarcely settled into the seat indicated to him when Juliana von Stolberg, Countess of the *Kasteel*, entered the room. Straight of stature, pleasant of face, with movements of grace, she joined her two sons, Willem and Jan. Jan seated her, then himself. Willem, looking as old and burdened as if the weight of a world rested on his shoulders, took his place between them at the head of the table.

How unlike brothers the two Nassaus looked. Wherever Willem was lean, Jan was roundish—eyes, face, chin, and torso. One thing both they and their moeder had in common today was a sober countenance that clouded the entire room.

"We have called you to our chambers this day," Willem began, "to lay out the strategy, which, after much thought, discussion, and prayer, we have decided upon."

He paused and looked around the table, gazing intently into each face. "You have each been chosen to play a specific part in the battle that lies before us."

Resting his hands on the table, he leaned toward them as if pleading for a life-and-death cause. His melancholy urgency reminded Pieter-Lucas of the many times in Breda when he'd watched the prince pacing the length of the *kasteel* gallery, hands behind his back, head down, uttering no words but pounding out each step on the blue and gold tiles with a silent fierceness of energy.

Willem spoke in a low-pitched voice. "In retaliation for his defeat at Heiligerlee, the Duke of Alva has unleashed his vengeful spirit on my noble friends. In the past two days, nineteen of them have lost their heads on the scaffold." He paused, wiping the perspiration from his brow before going on.

"We have received reliable reports that sometime in the next few days he plans to stage a gigantic spectacle in the *Grand Place* of Brussels, at which he will remove the heads of two of my respected brothers in the Order of the Golden Fleece, Counts Egmont and Hoorne. All of this in spite of the well-known fact that both men have steadfastly refused to join our revolt and have maintained their loyalty to the cause of His Majesty King Philip. When this unspeakable deed is completed, Alva will march with his own troops to Friesland, intending to wipe out Ludwig's army in person."

An air of terror gripped the room. No one spoke or sighed or coughed or shuffled a foot beneath the big oak table. What would Willem do? He would not stage an armed resistance in the *Grand Place*—that was not his way, and it would be doomed before it began.

The prince straightened and lifted his chin. "For these next days," he said in a clear strong voice, "you will be the eyes and ears of this revolt. While I attempt to raise more troops and the funds to hold them with me, I shall need you to see and hear what goes on in the *Grand Place*, the apartment and Council Chambers of the duke, the streets of Brussels, and the military encampments where the duke recruits and trains his men."

Spies, hole-peepers, intruders on the back stairs! Pieter-Lucas sat immobile and tried not to think what it meant.

With an almost detached swiftness, Willem addressed each man around the table. "Wouter and Nicolaas," he began, "you are to mingle with the crowds in the *Grand Place* and nearby streets. Change your guises whenever it seems advisable. Listen to the words around you and pay special attention when officials come near. Let nothing miss you."

To the next two men, he said, "Allard and Joost, you will enter every official building possible, witnessing councils, any hidden proceedings, and intimate conversations."

"And you, Pieter-Lucas, son of Kees"—his penetrating gaze and authoritative voice made Pieter-Lucas feel the weight of the revolt on his own shoulders—"you are to play the half-blind street beggar and sit with your bowl before the place where they have confined Egmont and Hoorne. You will sit there until you have learned their fate, either from what you see or from reports that your ears tell you. Be on especial lookout for deeds of importance done with impunity before a blind man. Your fancy will guide you into all the ways you can use this scheme to your advantage."

His fancy indeed! Already he pictured himself looking out at the color and action around him as if through a secret peephole. He also saw himself being kicked, ridiculed, stumbled over, chased away by some beggar with a prior claim to the space he chose, hauled off to the magistrates and left to rot in a prison tower in the heart of Brussels.

But Willem had asked it. What choice did he have? He moistened dry lips and forced out the words, "That shall I do, Your Excellency."

Willem's gaze lingered on him. "You would make your vader very proud."

Pieter-Lucas felt a thrill dart through his body. When Willem said vader, he did not mean Hendrick, the imposter and image-breaker who had sliced Opa's painting and pierced Pieter-Lucas' leg. Hendrick and his fellow Beggars had joined the revolt, but they were violent men who did things their own way and paid little attention to Willem.

Nay, Willem always called him "son of Kees," Willem's former stable-boy and dear friend. Pieter-Lucas had never known this man who actually fathered him, but he knew that Kees would have left his carving and his painting and undertaken this dreaded hole-peeping duty because he loved the prince and the Low Lands more than his own life. Pieter-Lucas must do the same. And when God in heaven allowed him to return and pick up his paintbrushes, he would do it with a clear conscience, for he would be acting like a son of Kees, not of Hendrick!

Willem addressed the whole group. "You will leave today, immediately after the late afternoon meal and spend the night in Keulen's *Proud Stallion Inn*. The instant you have firm news of which there can be no doubt, you are to run to me with it."

"We come back here?" Pieter-Lucas asked.

"*Nay*, I leave tomorrow for Strasbourg and know not where I will be when you have news. You will return to the *Proud Stallion*, where you shall be met by either Gillis or Paulus." He gestured toward the two men at the far end of the table. "They will lead you to me. If you find neither of them, return to Dillenburg and bring your word to Jan."

With both hands on the table, he leaned once more toward them. "This is a secret mission," he said. "Not one word you've heard here today may find its way out into the *kasteel*—not to your vrouw, your friends, your families. Is that clear? Not one word."

Pieter-Lucas nodded, along with the others, and rebuked the wrenching of his new bridegroom's heart with the reminder, *It is your duty, jongen*.

Willem straightened. "And now, my moeder has a word for you."

He helped her to her feet, then stood behind her, his hands clasped before him, his head down. The countess looked out over them, her compassionate face sober.

"The mission my sons are sending you to fulfill is of utmost importance. God only knows how many of your observations may provide the guidance needed to plan the next moves in this revolt. While you are away, I will carry each of you on my heart all day every day, as well as at night whenever I am awakened from sleep. Further, I shall carry each of your names to the chapel and present them to the God whose cause we fight. I will ask that He build a hedge of thorns about you and fill you with wakefulness to danger and understanding of all you see and hear. Most of all, I will ask that He bring each of you back with His perfect safety." She looked down and obviously struggled to remain stoic.

Raising her hands at last, she beckoned them. "Come now, I lead you to the wardrobe room, where you shall be given your disguises."

Pieter-Lucas and the other men rose from their seats and followed her in silence.

———

Aletta stood at the door of the millhouse, staring at the chaff-filled cobwebs that draped themselves around the lintel and posts. She listened to the cumbersome old millstones groaning and shrieking in their relentless grinding process. "Gracious God," she prayed, "don't let Petronella be so crushed by her physical illness today as on my first visit."

When the elderly woman of the house had let her in, Aletta slipped up the stairs and into the room undetected by her patient who was propped up in bed, nursing her baby. The frail young moeder held her baby's pink fist in her hand as if it were a rare jewel and hummed a soft refrain. A stray shaft of light played with her uncapped hair and brushed her cheeks with a faint rosy blush.

Aletta moved with gentle steps toward her friend, loathe to disturb the tranquil scene. So absorbed was Petronella in her son that Aletta was nearly upon her before she stopped humming and acknowledged her presence.

"Ah, Aletta, the countess' new herbal concoction has done wonders."

"Thanks be to God," Aletta whispered. She pulled a chair close and sat down.

The child stared up at her. His eyes widened and he continued suckling out of the side of his mouth. Aletta felt her heart warm under his scrutiny. "Beautiful child!" she mused.

"Like a perpetually fresh sprig of *borage*," Petronella said, smiling, "he cheers my soul, even when my body grows too weary to go on."

He stopped nursing. Petronella lifted him to her shoulder and patted his back.

"He looks robustious enough," Aletta remarked.

"A true miracle, since we had to flee with him so soon . . ."

Aletta leaned forward in her chair and laid a hand on her friend's arm. "Tell me, Petronella, what sort of danger forced you to flee at such a time?"

The young mother lowered the baby from her shoulder and cradled him in her arms. For a long while, she rocked him gently. Both women watched his eyelids flutter shut and his tiny mouth make empty sucking motions.

"Forgive me." Aletta broke the silence. "I should not have been so eager. You need not to give me an answer."

Petronella looked up, a weariness akin to pain in her eyes. "*Nay*, but I want you to know it all—from my lips, not another's."

"Perhaps not today."

The moeder sighed. "Today is what we have. Who knows about tomorrow?"

"Petronella, we are both young." Aletta bade her ruffled heart be still.

A thin smile curved Petronella's lips, then vanished. She gazed at the boy and began. "My labor with this child was long and grueling, and . . . and the midwife had a dreadful struggle to free him from his wombe bed."

"Was it Tante Lysbet?" Aletta felt her heart quicken at the thought of the woman whose instructions had so recently turned her into a midwife.

Petronella hesitated. "It was." She hugged her baby, nodded her head, and wiped her eyes on his blankets.

"You have not to say more," Aletta spoke gently.

"You must know the awful truth." She sniffled. "Forgive me that I stumble. It's just that Tante Lysbet was dear to me as well."

"She *was* dear?" Aletta heard the words burst forth from her own mouth. "What . . . what does this mean? Surely Tante Lysbet is not gone!"

"*Nay* . . . I mean, I know not what has become of her since we left."

"What, then, is the awful truth you do know?" Aletta asked in a manner more demanding than she intended.

Petronella laid the child on her lap. "Once the birthing ordeal was past, the child and I both slept. The next thing I knew, Spanish soldiers burst into my home and took Lysbet away in chains."

"In chains!" Aletta gasped. "Whatever was the accusation against her?"

"I had no idea. I think she knew not either." She paused and swallowed hard. "Later, Maarten told me that they had accused her of possessing books of witchcraft."

"Witchcraft? Tante Lysbet?" Aletta stared in disbelief.

Petronella simply shrugged.

Aletta stammered, "What did they do with her?"

"Maarten told me they dragged her off to the tower prison at the Gevangenpoort. But we could not stay to see what would happen. We knew that our son was in mortal danger in Breda from that moment on."

"*Ach!* Awful indeed!" Ghastly visions burst into Aletta's imagination. Too well she knew what punishment was reserved for witches—and the babies they delivered.

Petronella reached out and grabbed Aletta's hand. "I was so afraid, Aletta, so afraid. Before that day was over, Maarten had gathered together a bag of food and clothes, as much as he could carry. When darkness fell, we left our little home."

Aletta squeezed her friend's hand and shook her head. "You . . . you gave birth to a baby in the middle of one night and the next you were traveling—afoot in the cold?"

She nodded. "Fear makes us do strange things for our children."

Aletta stared at her. "Where did you go?"

"A strange and wonderful thing happened that first night," Petronella said, her voice smooth and filled with wonder. "I was so weak and fearful, and Maarten led us along so gently, always insisting God would take care of us. Even he never dreamed that we would spend the night under the watchful eye of an angel."

"An angel?"

"Of sorts! Or so it seemed."

"How?"

"We were creeping through the woods just outside of Breda and stumbled across an old crumbling building inside a hedge of roses."

"The hidden studio of Pieter-Lucas' opa!" Aletta squealed.

"I had no idea what it was," Petronella said, "but it provided a bit of shelter."

"In its decaying condition, was it not dreadfully cold—with a newborn?"

"That was a part of the miracle. Inside, we found a simple little woman who heated broth for us on her fire and gave us her bed—such as it was. Never could I have imagined that a pile of dirty rags beside an open fire would invite me to rest. But we were warm, and I slept soundly the whole night through."

"And the woman?"

She shrugged. "By morning she was gone. When the baby awakened us just before daylight, I heard loud voices and terrible screams. I hope and pray it was not our angel, but I'll never know. We never saw her again."

Aletta held her head in her hands and sighed. If only she could believe this was a dream. "Did you stay there long?" she asked.

"Only one more night. Then we moved on. For the next weeks, or however long it was I could not tell you, we slept in wooded glens and caves and deserted buildings and behind stacks of hay in open fields. We never knew what sort of shelter we would uncover next. We parceled out our food supply as scantily as possible. Still, in a way I could not explain, no matter how ill I was, I never lacked for milk in my breasts, and Maarten's bag always held food."

Petronella was looking tired once more. She rocked her baby gently as she spoke, but her breath grew shallow. "God brought us this far, and the miller's family and the countesses have welcomed and nursed and provided for us."

"And now you need to sleep again. I have caused you to talk too long. I'm not much of a healer lady to you, friend."

"*Nay*, I chose to talk. You forced me not. I haven't breathed a word to anyone since we arrived. I still know not whom I can trust. I so much want to know all about you. . . ." Below her drooping eyelids, a pleading expression reached out toward Aletta.

"There is enough time for that," Aletta assured her. "Here, let me put the baby in his cradle so his moeder can rest."

She lifted the infant from her and let his heart beat against her own as she hugged him to her breast. Then she put him in his cradle and went to Petronella's bedside.

She leaned over the weary woman, and they exchanged smiles.

"Thank you for telling me your story. One thing you didn't mention."

"What is that?"

"Your son's name?"

Petronella cast an anxious look at her. "*Ach*, Aletta, he's not been christened yet."

Aletta opened her mouth to speak, but her friend laid a hand on hers and went on. "I know it's not good. If she were alive, my moeder would have carried him off to the church to make sure he received the baptism no matter what. May God forgive me, I was too ill to go into the church, and I insisted it could not be done without me."

Aletta offered her a reassuring smile. "God's hand often rests on unbaptized babies," she said. "I've known a few." She sighed, remembering all her Children of God friends who baptized only adult believers. "But surely you have a name for him."

She brightened. "Ah, *ja*, we call him Maarten! There must always be a Maarten de Smid to shoe the horses for the House of Nassau."

"What else?" Aletta said. "Now I must go."

She reached into her basket and brought out a vial of Juliana's elixir. She cradled Petronella's head in the crook of her arm and poured the liquid through her lips.

"I leave some of this with the oma to give to you, and I shall come back tomorrow or the next day." Aletta squeezed her hand and added, "My husband awaits me at the late afternoon meal."

Petronella swallowed the medicine down with a gulp. "Pieter-Lucas?"

"Who else?"

"Oh, I long to hear all about it."

"Later."

Aletta bade her friend a soft *Tot ziens*, planted a kiss on tiny Maarten's forehead, and scurried home with an eager step.

————

At the *kasteel*, Aletta found Pieter-Lucas in the midst of a circle of men just outside the door of the eating hall. All were dressed to travel and had bulging knapsacks at their feet. He bounded toward her.

She grabbed him by the flaps of his doublet. "You're going away again!"

With a gentle arm, he led her around the corner of the building for a spot of solitude. "It is my duty, Little One."

"But you just came home last night, and you said you did not promise Willem—"

He placed a finger across her lips. "Nor can I say him *nay*," he interrupted. "He counts on me, my love, and for the love our vaderland, I must go."

"You go farther and longer this time," she said. "I see by your bulging knapsacks. Where? How dangerous is it?"

He lifted her chin with his forefinger. "I cannot breathe a word of it. I can only promise I will be back at my first opportunity."

Holding her tighter than ever, he nuzzled his nose into the hair hanging loose around her headdress and whispered into her ear, "The only secret I am allowed to tell you is how very much I love you. Nothing under the heavens will ever beckon me like the memory of your beautiful face."

She looked up into his eyes and plied his shoulders with trembling hands. "Every day, I shall keep my ears attuned to the hunting dogs and my eyes fixed on the roadway running up from the village, until I see you riding toward me."

She let him kiss her with as much intensity as if she knew he'd never have another opportunity. After all, in the middle of a war, who could know how many more of these precious moments would be theirs?

CHAPTER FIFTEEN

Brussels

5th morning of Summer Month (June), 1568

*P*ieter-Lucas squinted and hobbled stoop-shouldered into the *Grand Place*. Leaning on a crooked stick, he carried a beggar's bag slung over his shoulder and a beggar's bowl in his mud-smeared hand. He had let his sparse whiskers grow unchecked for three days now, and they were just long enough to itch.

"You are a street beggar," he mumbled into his ragged jacket, squirming beneath the tight-fitting cap that extended to the nape of his neck.

He skirted the fringes of the square, tapping his stick in all directions, pretending to be straining to find his way over the cobblestones. At the edge of his vision, he saw an array of magnificent buildings with intricately carved gold-decorated facades and impressive toppling gables. What an artist's utopia! If only he could wander among them and examine each one.

Instead, he must stare through eyes feigning blindness at hundreds of people milling about the square. A heavy somber cloud hung over the crowd. No one smiled or laughed, many talked in hushed little knots or behind protective hands held to their mouths.

Shops remained closed, even though the sun had arisen long hours ago. Soldiers swarmed everywhere, some waving huge banners of red, green, or white. Their long lances and shiny metal helmets glistened in the daylight. They marched or stood as ominous reminders that all of Brussels belonged to the King of Spain.

In Philip's name, the Duke of Alva had erected a gigantic raised platform in the center of the square. A crude ladder of stairs led up to it, and the pair of high stakes supporting it at two corners were crowned with ominous pointed metal spikes. Draped all over in black cloth, it was furnished with two large black cushions and a table also draped in black.

"A scaffold!" Pieter-Lucas gasped. "The reports were true!"

He stumbled along, raising his head at each building to gawk, blind-man style, in search of the building where Egmont and Hoorne were confined. Every time he stopped, someone shouted, "Move along, despicable beggar."

The crowd jostled him from all sides and a few people spat on him. Finding one building just behind the scaffold more closely guarded than the others, he lingered and watched and listened for further evidence that this was the spot he sought. But the press of people was so heavy here that from his stooped position, the legs and lances of soldiers barred his way like an impenetrable forest.

He had just started around the scaffold, hoping to find another access to the building, when someone shouted orders out in the square. A wide line of soldiers came marching straight toward him. He backed up awkwardly and tripped over a protruding cobblestone, stumbling to the ground at the edge of the scaffold. While he scrambled to get up, he felt the toe of a soldier's boot kick him sharply in the shin of his bad leg, shoving him to the ground under the folds of the scaffold's heavy drapery. His elbows were scraped raw and his face rammed against the rim of his wooden beggar's bowl. He lay still and hoped no other creatures had taken refuge in this same place.

At that instant, from the church on the edge of the square came the mournful tolling of a huge bell, its vibrations pushing against his ears. An uneasy hush fell over the crowd, and the atmosphere seemed charged with the capricious tumult of a thunderstorm. Each stroke of the bell resembled a strike of lightning and sent a fresh shiver through Pieter-Lucas' body.

It feels like Judgment Day! he told himself.

Suddenly the hush gave way to the sound of slow measured steps and voices, moving as if in procession across the square. From the crowd came an occasional wailing cry, and the name Egmont echoed in the distance. In no time, Pieter-Lucas heard footsteps on the stairs, then moving across the platform above his head. As if in rhythm with the steps that shook the whole frame, there came Egmont's loud voice. "Would to God I had been permitted to die, sword in hand, fighting for my vaderland and my sovereign, King Philip."

Pieter-Lucas heard a scuffling of feet, followed by the condemned man's plaintive question. "Tell me there is a shred of hope that my sentence can yet be revoked, for as the whole world knows, I have been a long and loyal vassal of His Majesty."

The response came in a simple muffled grunt. *"Nay!"*

What was this man's crime? Pieter-Lucas' memory painted a picture of Count Egmont, the handsome nobleman who was once a frequent visitor of Prince Willem in Breda. He'd always displayed an arrogant air, especially with the stableboys.

Nor had Egmont been willing to join the revolt, and after the image-breakings, Pieter-Lucas heard he'd taken delight in hanging rebels in his own province of Flanders. He appeared to give to King Philip his unwavering support. Why, then, was he being led to execution by Alva's men?

Pieter-Lucas heard Egmont's voice reciting, "Our Vader who in the Heavens is, Thy name be hallowed, Thy kingdom come. . . ."

His last prayer! An unintelligible jumble of voices was followed finally by a cry so loud it set the frame once more to trembling. "Lord, into Thy hands I commit my spirit."

In a flurry of movement from the far end of the enclosure beneath the platform, the executioner dashed from under the curtain with sword drawn and climbed the stairs swiftly. Pieter-Lucas clapped his hands over his ears to shut out the ominous sounds he knew would follow. But he heard them anyway—the sharp swishing of the sword through the air, a loud crack of blade against bones, and a solid thud on the floor above him. He felt the shuddering silence that gripped the crowd while the bell from the cathedral continued to toll, not missing a beat.

The crowd uttered a long stunned gasp, then broke into a wild cry of horror, as if from a single voice echoing around the square. A mad scramble of feet and clashing weapons signaled the stampede of a host of people, overcome with shocked grief, shoving their way to the scaffold.

"Why do the soldiers not stop them?" Pieter-Lucas mumbled.

The wailing continued, pierced by hysterical screams. The stampede of feet closed in around the platform. Pieter-Lucas stripped off his uncomfortable beggar's disguise and stuffed it into his knapsack. He had heard all he needed to hear. He could watch the rest in his own street clothes, which he wore beneath the disguise.

With heart pounding loudly, he crawled out from under the platform and mixed with the mass of frantic mourners. He joined in their wailing sounds and motions, even reaching out with the others to touch the platform. But when they began dipping handkerchiefs in the blood spilling onto the ground, he made haste to find an escape.

The soldiers were pushing the whole crowd back with shields and lances and brawny arms. Pieter-Lucas found himself suffocating in the hysterical press of sweaty surging bodies. Slowly, steadily, he fought his way back farther and farther away from the platform. At times he struggled just to keep from being shoved to the ground and trampled to death by the mob.

He had reached the far edge of the *Grand Place* when he saw the soldiers parting the crowd to make way for one more procession to the scaffold. The second victim, a straight tall man in a plain black suit with a Milanese cap on his head, followed in his friend's train. Pieter-Lucas remembered Count Hoorne, too, from occasional visits to the *kasteel* in Breda. One more of Willem's one-time friends, separated from him by the revolt.

Pieter-Lucas wrestled with anger and pity as he watched the nobleman ascend the stairs, address the audience, and then kneel on the cushion reserved for his final devotions. He had to force himself to watch the executioner wield the awful weapon, then pick up the severed head and attach it to the spiked pole at the back of the platform opposite the stake where Egmont's head had already been placed.

Pieter-Lucas pushed on through the mob-clogged streets until he could breathe once more and choose his own direction. By now, every church in the city had joined its bell in the mournful tolling chorus. With enormous effort, he finally passed through the gate and left the gloomy crowds behind. The church bells grew fainter, but the awful heaviness of an almost despair still weighted down his soul.

"I must get far, far from this place—as fast as possible," he told himself.

When he could no longer see the city, his pathway emerged from a small stand of oaks and poplars. A welcome shower of rain descended from the heavens. The fleeing hole-peeper lifted his face to the drops and let them splash his eyes. He shook out his curls and gave his ears to the water. Somehow, he fancied that the fresh cool water would wash away the spilling of innocent blood that he had been forced to hear and see and feel in his bones.

Strasbourg
7th day of Summer Month, 1568

From the *Proud Stallion Inn* Pieter-Lucas was whisked into a boat and spent a day and night floating down the Rhine River. When finally he succeeded in falling asleep, he dreamed he was back in the *Grand Place*. The executioner spotted him in his hiding place beneath the scaffold, dragged him up the stairs, forced him to his knees, pointed a sword at his breast, and roared, "Decide, *jongen*, whether you will fulfill Yaap's mission like a man or go back to your paintbrushes and the Anabaptist cowards!"

Pieter-Lucas trembled. The executioner's eyes turned into hot red coals, and he screamed, "Those who cannot choose must die!" Then he grabbed and bound his arms, snatched him by the hair, and pulled his head to the bloody block.

"Have mercy," Pieter-Lucas strained to cry out. But his throat was filled with strange balls of liquid, and his voice warbled like a drowning man's.

The executioner laughed with an evil sound so resounding that it brought him sharply awake. His arms were thrashing and the boatman was shouting, "Sit still, you crazy man! You'll dump us both overboard!"

For the rest of the trip, Pieter-Lucas kept himself awake. He chattered nonsense, moved his legs and arms about, splashed water on his face, and sang loudly. He dared not sleep again.

Paulus met him at the harbor in Strasbourg and led him through the grand old city. Pieter-Lucas stared at the enticing display of painted and sculpted walls, decorative windowpanes, the colorful curved roof tiles. Instinctively his fingers reached to his knapsack for the charcoal and brushes they normally contained.

But he found only a hunk of moldy bread and his beggar costume. This accursed war had stolen his paints and brushes and made him hear and see and touch ugly things instead—soldiers' bullets, gaping battle wounds, severed heads! He shuddered!

Great God, his heart screamed, *tell me I'm not a coward because I hate war! Tell me, God!*

He listened and stumbled on behind his guide. The people and animals and carts that swarmed the streets and plazas and alleyways filled his ears with the sounds he did not want to hear. As always, God remained silent.

Paulus brought him at last to Willem in a large hall with tapestried walls and painted glass windows. The prince looked up from his place at one end of a long bench-rimmed table. An official-looking man in velvet doublet and feathered hat sat beside him.

"What is the news, *jongen*?" Willem asked, his whole body leaning toward him.

"The rumors were true." Pieter-Lucas fought to control the turbulence in his stomach and give a calm witness. But he felt his voice stumbling as he went on. "Yesterday, in the morning, I witnessed the beheading of both Counts Egmont and Hoorne." He could say no more.

He watched Willem grip his own legs and stare at the floor. "His Majesty King Philip would never forgive the counts for being my friends," he mumbled. "And Egmont's vanity deceived him into trusting him implicitly. Hoorne followed blindly in his shadow."

The prince sat a long while, shaking his head and moaning. "*Ach!* Egmont, Egmont! How often I tried to warn you!"

After a pause, he breathed deeply, then raised his head and looked directly at Pieter-Lucas. "And the people? Did they cheer the action or mourn it?"

"The city groaned with soul-numbing despair," Pieter-Lucas said, feeling it again as if he were still in the midst of the dismal crowds. "The only animation I saw was horror and outrage once the deed was done on Egmont." He stopped and wiped dampening hands on his breeches. "Clearly, they loved the count!"

Willem turned to his host and spoke with eager agitation. "The people are finally ready for resistance. Now is the time to strike. Can you not see it?"

The official sat motionless. "That sort of fervor does not last."

"Exactly why we must fan the fire into a raging inferno of rebellion now before the embers have died on the hearth of outrage," Willem pleaded.

"It touches us not here in Strasbourg," the man responded. "Our businessmen have already poured hundreds of thousands of crowns and florins into your fruitless efforts and seen nothing in return. I cannot extract one more *stuiver* from any of them."

Willem spread desperate hands toward him. "There was Heiligerlee! With troops and funds, there will be more!"

"Heiligerlee indeed!" The official laughed. "One tiny regiment of ill-prepared Spaniards caught in treacherous, unfamiliar turf in a lonely corner of Friesland! And look what revenge it has already wrought from the powerful hand of Alva! Have you any idea of Alva's strength?"

"Obviously you have no idea of the power of a populace enraged by Alva's arrogance against one of their own champions. I tell you, now is the time!"

At that moment the door opened and Nicolaas and Allard burst through. They bowed hurriedly before Willem. Nicolaas began his report. "The Duke of Alva has already amassed several thousand troops near Brussels, and they are being daily trained in preparation to go to Friesland and cut Count Ludwig and his men in pieces."

"You have seen his encampment?" Willem asked.

"I have seen it well, Your Excellency. I have watched the men drilling in the fields around the city. Like war horses pawing the ground, pressing for action."

"The duke himself has plans to take full command at the lead of his troops," Allard added. "From our precarious peephole in the city chambers, Joost and I heard him boasting of how easily he would lash out at Ludwig with his little finger and instill a holy terror in his heart never to be forgotten or trifled with again while his back was turned."

"And what mood did you find among the people on the streets?" Willem pressed the question.

"They are terrorized," Nicolaas said.

Allard nodded his head in vigorous agreement. "All they need is a champion to sweep through the streets the instant Alva has marched out, and they'll follow, driven by frenzied revenge."

Willem reached imploringly once more toward his host. "Can you not see how opportune is this moment? We can provide that champion, wage a victorious war of our own, and solidify the support of first Brussels, then Antwerp, and on up the line, while Alva is off up in the far corner of Friesland spending all his choice troops in the petty cause of revenge. But we must have the men and the money to keep them with us."

The official offered one lame concession. "Your strategies sound almost convincing." Then, shaking his head, he began, "But I warn you . . ."

Willem jumped to his feet. "Surely when the merchants of this city have heard what you and I have just heard, they will agree that this is the time."

The official stood, faced Willem, and went on with his speech as if he'd never been interrupted. "I warn you, even if you told them that Gabriel and all his heavenly hosts had come to your aid, they would do nothing more, Count Willem, nothing more. We've given you our last crown."

The room grew suddenly still. The two officials stared at each other. Pieter-Lucas watched, openmouthed as Willem reached out to shake the man's hand and said calmly, "I thank you, wise burgermeister of this fair city, for listening to my pleas. It vexes me more than you can imagine that you refuse to trust us at this most auspicious of times. But know this. We move on and will not fail, for ours is the cause of God Almighty. His are the gold mines of this world and the next. Somewhere, somehow, we shall raise our troops and hold them to the cause. Good day."

Willem strode through the door and the labyrinth of halls and stairways. Pieter-Lucas and the rest followed him out into the midday, up and down cobbled ways in the shadow of majestic old buildings, back to the harbor, and into a waiting boat.

For four long gray days, Pieter-Lucas accompanied Willem to the courts of German noblemen who refused his pleas for support in this "most auspicious of times." With his ears, he heard the prince's arguments and the noblemen's disappointing responses. But his mind, tormented with visions of spears and scaffolds and bloody handkerchiefs, worried two nagging questions, as a dog would worry an old bone. How could he ever tell Willem that nothing could hold him to Yaap's mission? Failing this, how could he ever tell Aletta, who needed him by her side, that he must fulfill Yaap's mission? He had to find a way!

PART THREE

Warning

*T*he righteous shall in eternity not
totter,
but the godless shall not occupy
(inhabit) the land.

Proverbs 10:30 as quoted in Willem's
Warning (September 1, 1568)

*We have always said that it is better to
act with gentleness than with severity,
and we think that it is better and more
reasonable to keep promises than to
break them and to violate oaths.*

—Willem's *Warning*

CHAPTER SIXTEEN

Dillenburg

10th morning of Summer Month (June), 1568

A pre-sunrise mist sprinkled Aletta's nose and sent a host of fresh damp aromas wafting through the air toward her from all sides. They rose from dusty mud balls on the pathway, from the gray grooved wood and mossy stones of the ancient *kasteel* walls, from the profusion of summer greenery that flourished in every corner.

"Nothing smells half so delicious," she told herself as she descended the pathway toward the herb garden and prepared to laugh with the meadowlarks that were singing their antiphonal chorus from the *kasteel* ramparts and the linden trees.

Instead of laughter, though, she felt a wave of loneliness swell up and choke off the joy that had just sent her tripping down the path.

"If only my Pieter-Lucas would return!" she moaned.

This was her favorite time of day, the weather that delighted her, and she was headed for the most exciting spot in Dillenburg. But none of that seemed to matter at all as long as Pieter-Lucas was still away on some dangerous secret mission. Nothing could ever be right without Pieter-Lucas.

By the time she entered the garden, her face ran with tears. She stumbled down the rows toward a small stone seat she called her Pondering Bench. Almost without a thought, she plucked a sprig of borage, the "gladness" herb, from the shrub at her elbow.

She munched on one of the fuzzy prickly leaves and twirled a cluster of its purple star-shaped blossoms between her thumb and forefinger. Gradually her tears subsided and she began to meander through the garden with its profusion of softly colored blossoms, lifting their faces, caressing their leaves.

"Dear God in the Heaven," she prayed. "Thank you for so much delicate loveliness—and healing power."

Then in an eyeblink the sun broke over the horizon in long straight shafts of transparent gold. Just as suddenly, Aletta felt the tears well up and engulf her once more. Longing thoughts of Pieter-Lucas' heart-melting smile and the protective embrace of his warm strong arms gripped her again and set her fleeing back to the bench, where she buried her face in her hands and sobbed.

Overcome with sadness, she forgot even where she was until the pressure of a hand on her shoulder startled her. She looked up into the concerned face of Juliana von Stolberg. "My dear young woman, why such deep distress?"

Aletta lifted her head and sat straight, clasping her hands in her lap. "I am sorry you must find me crying like a child."

Juliana smiled. "Nay, to weep is womanly, not childish."

Aletta daubed at her eyes with the corner of her cape. "I know my Pieter-Lucas shall return soon. It's just that we have not been married long and I miss him so."

The countess shook her head gently. "War is a many-fisted bereaver. When it takes not the lives of our sons and husbands, it at least deprives us of their presence and leaves us with a haunting uncertainty that spawns many deep and tremulous tears."

Still wiping at her eyes, Aletta confessed, "I want to be brave, not petulant or morose. I hope it falls not to my lot to cry the whole way through this war."

"Tears are God's medicine," the countess said. "Every bit as healing as borage or calendula or goldenrod. Some days you will not be plagued by so much weeping and will feel stronger. But when tears do come, flee to this sacred haven and let them flow with freedom."

Aletta forced a smile to her own lips. "You have soothed my spirits greatly."

Juliana walked a few paces down the pathway. Bending over a low-growing clump of bright green plants, she plucked off a stem covered with broad pointed leaves. "Try these," she offered.

Aletta took the leaves, broke one off, and slipped it into her mouth. "Garden mint!" she said. "Ah, but it's wonderfully delicious!"

"Keep a sprig always with you," the Healer Lady of Dillenburg said. "Chew on it when you feel distressed or unsettled in the belly. Use it as a plaister when your head gives you pain. Come and help yourself however often you have need."

The countess smoothed her hands across her apron and picked up her basket. "I go now. The morning sup is served shortly. You will come?"

"I come." Aletta rose and followed the woman through the garden up to the *kasteel*. Walking felt good to her bones, and for now, at least, she had no need to cry more.

———————

At the end of a crashing thunderstorm, just at sunset, the hunting dogs announced the arrival of Willem and his entourage. Soggy and weary, the men trudged up the hill and met their waiting families beneath the gently swirling flag of Nassau. Their somber faces told the whole household that whatever their secret mission, it had not met with success.

In the solitude of their own room, Aletta and her husband sat side by side on the bed. She stroked his tangled curls with her fingers. "I was lonely in this place without you," she said.

Pieter-Lucas looked at her with a sad, tired smile. "And without you, the whole world is a lonely place."

She felt a lump rise in her throat and swallowed it down quickly. "Have you been that far?" She managed a laugh, wishing she could entice them both with playfulness.

He grabbed her in both arms and uttered an almost chuckle into her hair. "At least that far, maybe even farther!"

He held her tight while she made laughing sounds and prayed he'd never guess she was crying instead. Were they tears of joy this time? Surely not sadness in this glorious moment of reunion. Yet a melancholy spirit seemed to hold her in its grip.

When he released her from his embrace, he smoothed her forearm with the strong fingers of one hand. Still looking down, she wiped her eyes on her bodice sleeves and watched the plump cords on the back of his hand. They sent shivers of admiring delight down her back.

"I wish," he mumbled, "I wish I could promise you that I'll never again be gone so long."

She lifted her eyes to his and saw in them the same sadness approaching fear that she felt gripping her own soul. "Say it not, Pieter-Lucas. Promises are not made to be broken. It is enough for me to know that the desire burns in your heart."

"You also need to know," he added, lifting her chin with his forefinger, " 'tis the memory of your waiting arms and radiant smile gives me courage to do the hard things Willem asks of me. And when I return, bone-weary and dejected, the most powerful elixir concocted by the world's finest herbal healers could not restore me like the smile of your lips and the brush of your fingers through my hair."

The two young newly marrieds both put away all thoughts of wars and separations and feasted on the admiration in each other's eyes. He enfolded her in his arms, and for the rest of a long and *unlonely* night, she never shed a tear.

———

15th day of Summer Month (June), 1568

The sky hung heavy, low, and dark on the morning Pieter-Lucas left Dillenburg again. He and Blesje walked with Aletta all the way to the miller's house in the village. She kept her hand snugly fitted into his and longed for a way to break the awkward silence that had hung between them ever since the morning after he returned from his secret mission. He still refused to talk about the mission. Often in the night he thrashed about on the bed and screamed out in nightmarish terror, "Have mercy!"

Perhaps it was all in her mind, but she fancied that he never seemed quite to look straight into her eyes the way he'd always done. Something was troubling her beloved and changing him into a stranger.

Aletta, too, was troubled. The sudden weeping spells went on, grabbing her when least expected. Further, it grew more difficult each morning to awaken and crawl from her bed. She'd taken to carrying sprigs of the garden mint with her everywhere she went. Repeatedly she nibbled, and mostly it soothed her.

On the miller's doorstoop, the two troubled young people faced each other. Pieter-Lucas quickly drew her to him and whispered into her hair, "I go not far. I shall return within a day or two."

Then holding her at arm's length, he looked into her eyes for a brief moment and begged, "Take good care of my precious vrouw, and . . ."

"And what?" She searched his face, but it was awash with confusion, and he would not look into her eyes again.

"And . . . I come home soon," he said.

Hastily he kissed her, then mounted Blesje and was off. She gazed after him, waving and catching the fewer-than-usual kisses he threw her way. All too soon he rounded a bend in the road, and she could see him no longer.

"Great God in the Heaven, heal my Pieter-Lucas in the wounded places where neither my smile nor the brush of my fingers through his curls seems to reach these days."

She closed her eyes, stifling the cry coming up from her heart, then knocked at the old chaff-covered door. Once inside, seated by Petronella and holding tiny Maarten in her arms, she could smile again.

"I'm so glad you've come this morning," Petronella said, her eyes big with a hint of surprise.

"You look as if you're bursting with news." Aletta felt the tug of a little hand wrapped around her finger.

Petronella laughed. "Indeed I am! Now that I'm feeling better, Maarten and I are preparing to take little Maarten to the church at the foot of the *kasteel* for his christening."

"Oh, Petronella!" Aletta caught her breath and spread a smile across her face. "Remember how we used to play with our dolls and pretend we were having them christened?"

"And how we always stood in as godmothers for each other's dolls?"

"Remember the sweets and little cups of pretend wine we begged from our moeders?"

"And how we would spread them on the big old stone in the garden courtyard of my vader's house on a rare sunny day? Oh, Aletta, we had big dreams."

Aletta gulped back an unexpected flood of tears and said, "Indeed we did!"

"But nothing could compare to the wonder of having our own real babies." Petronella was eyeing her with especial keenness. "Are you all right?"

"I'm sure I am," she tried to assure her friend. Why more crying at such a happy moment? Perhaps it was because she had heard the Children of God talk so much about believers' baptism that the whole idea of christening a baby left her more than a little confused. But this was her childhood friend, and they had waited and prepared for this day all their lives. Was the anticipation of those happy hours now to be clouded by some sort of religious shadow?

Petronella's eyes registered concern. "You must be well, dear Aletta. It would never do for the baby's godmother to be ill—or sad—at a christening."

"*Nay*," Aletta said. She looked at the baby sleeping contentedly in her lap, his face resembling a painting of an angel she'd once seen in the Great Church in Breda. Lifting her gaze to her friend, she added, "This godmother shall be neither ill nor sad at Maarten's christening."

"That's a promise?"

"A promise from my heart." Aletta laid her hand on Petronella's, closed her eyes, and waited for the latest wave of sadness and tears to pass.

Duisburg

Pieter-Lucas pursued his path with an unusual combination of eagerness and dread. Well before nightfall, he found Dirck Coornhert in a rented attic room above the cobbler's shop in Duisburg.

"Welcome, *jongen*," the man said, motioning him to a seat at his table. The table was big enough for only two people and completely covered with a clutter of papers, an empty tankard, a crust of bread, and a quill pen in an inkpot.

"A cartoon!" Pieter-Lucas exclaimed. "I didn't know you were an artist."

"Engraver mostly," Coornhert said. "For years I earned my livelihood creating plates for an artist. But you came with a message!" He extended his hand.

"*Ja,*" Pieter-Lucas muttered, straightening quickly and removing the message from his doublet. He handed it to his friend and promptly went back to studying the drawing. "At least sometimes you draw as well as engrave," he said, forgetting that the older man had turned his attention to more pressing matters.

Coornhert grunted, then laid the message on the table. "*Ja,* when there is no one else, it falls to me."

Pieter-Lucas looked up. "That happens to you too?"

"These are not quite the ideal times, you know, when we can have things the way we'd like them."

"Nobody knows that better than I," Pieter-Lucas retorted. Leaning forward, he looked hard at his host and asked, "Tell me, why is it that God puts paint in a man's blood, then separates him from his tools and consumes his life with more important things, like ugly evil wars? What pleasure does He gain from tormenting us so?"

Coornhert spread his hands out on the drawings littering the table. "No honest man can give you real answers to *why* questions about God. I only know that nothing will ever be more important than whatever it is God has set to running in your blood, and I don't believe He finds delight in tormenting us."

"Why, then, does He make us wait?"

Coornhert shrugged and raised his hands, palms upward. "His *whys* for you are not the same as His *whys* for me. When you need to know, He'll tell you."

"*Ach!*" Pieter-Lucas hung his head and strained to hear the silence of the room above the thunderous beating of his heart. Without looking up, he spoke at last in a hushed voice. "Ten days ago I witnessed the beheading of Egmont and Hoorne." He paused and watched Coornhert shake his head ever so slowly and heard a low soft moan come from deep within the man. "Ever since, I have been plagued with nightmares of the executioner dragging me to the scaffold, pointing a sword at my breast, roaring, 'Decide whether you will fulfill Yaap's mission like a man or go back to your paintbrushes and the Anabaptist cowards.'

" 'Twas bad enough to see it one time, but every night . . . I am never free from it. I awaken screaming, and God only knows what my dear vrouw thinks or hears. I can neither tell her where I've been nor what I dream."

"Why not?"

"Already she fears greatly for me to be out roaming around the countryside on dangerous missions. If I told her my dreams, she'd never rest again. Nor can I tell her where I've been, for Willem insisted our mission must be kept secret."

"You told me."

"May my soul be condemned if I did wrong, but I must have a vader's counsel, and I trust you, Dirck Coornhert, above all other men I know. If you betray me, I am betrayed. Better than to go on this way."

"What do you need from me?" Coornhert asked.

"I must know the truth. Am I a coward just because I hate war as the Anabaptists hate war? Or would I be a coward if I refused to fulfill Yaap's mission? Or, worse yet, would it be an act of cowardice to go on in Willem's service simply because I fear to say him *Nay* or because to love one's vaderland means fighting for it?"

The white-haired man leaned back in his chair, stretched a leg out into the room, and looked hard into Pieter-Lucas' eyes. "When you shut your ears to all the voices and search your own heart, what does it say about the matter?"

"I don't know."

"*Ja, jongen.* Deep down inside, you do know exactly what you believe. Else you would be easily led astray by every new suggestion coming along."

"That I am. Hence my great confusion."

"*Nay*, you are not led down side pathways. Rather, you resist them, every one. You are but confused in the hearing and not quite trusting that that which God has put within your heart is right. Now tell me, if you could be free from all the tormenting voices, what course of action would you pursue?"

Pieter-Lucas stared at his own fingers, tapping a dull rhythm on the table.

"Just say it," Coornhert urged.

"I believe," he began hesitantly, "that the cause of Willem and Ludwig, the cause of rightness and goodness and freedom must be God's way—

and 'tis my appointed part to fulfill Yaap's mission. At the same time, God created my hands to wield a paintbrush, and I could never bring myself to allow them to be stained with another man's blood."

Coornhert sighed. "Just as I thought."

"What did you think?"

"You and I are agreed on this matter."

"And we are not cowards?"

Agitation sparkled in Coornhert's uneasy eyes. "*Jongen*, remember this. A pathway is not cowardly simply because it is less trodden. It often demands far greater courage to tread on the lonely trail than the thronged highway."

"Greater courage?"

"To some of us is granted the vision to see beyond the clear horizons of our day. We shall not often find the words to explain that vision. Nor shall we find many who will understand or sympathize. Yet in our hearts we'll know that for us 'tis right, and we can do no other."

Courage indeed! Pieter-Lucas sighed. "And where shall I gain the courage to tell my vrouw that for this moment God has appointed me to fulfill Yaap's mission?"

Coornhert laughed. "Where do you gain courage to perform the mission?"

"I've no idea whence it comes. I only do what must be done each day. But my vrouw must know my intentions. Since I returned from the ghastly beheading, we've scarcely talked to each other at all. I felt such a coward that I could not even look her in the eye. I know this distresses her, for she lives on the verge of weeping these days."

"Go home, *jongen*, and exercise the courage God has planted in your soul to tell your vrouw all she needs to know. And fear not that you have caused her tears. Any man who sets his course by his vrouw's tears will surely end in shipwreck."

Pieter-Lucas ran his fingers through his hair. "You speak wisdom, kind friend."

"Now I must write Willem an answer and send you on your way. While I write, can I ask of you to run a short messenger's errand for me?"

"Gladly. Just tell me what and where."

"Your friends Meester Laurens and his vrouw have settled on the northern edge of the village with a nest of like-minded folk who take in Lowland refugees like themselves. Could you find the schoolmaster and tell him I have a surprise for him?"

"*Ja!* What sort of surprise?"

Coornhert smiled. "Remember that strange woman who wanted me to buy the meester's Bible?"

"Mieke! What's she done now?"

Coornhert gestured toward a stack of books near the fireplace. "I have bought all these from her."

"And she's used every *stuiver* to buy food and shelter for the schoolmaster and his vrouw, ja!" Skepticism colored his voice with sarcasm.

"My friends who give them lodging tell me that she has."

"Are they his books, stolen from his house, like the Bible?"

Coornhert nodded. "I am sure of it. I know he will be overjoyed to be reunited with them. He has been put to work teaching the refugee children. Surely he can use them well. When you find him, make no mention of the books. Simply tell him I wait to talk with him."

Dirck Coornhert gave him quick directions, and Pieter-Lucas hurried out into the early evening still flooded with midsummer daylight. A warm new calmness seeped in around the edges of the musty questions that had nagged at him so long. Was it possible, after all, that he could be certain of the rightness or wrongness of a thing even while the reasons remained a mystery to his own heart? If so, he was ready to go home and tell his vrouw all she needed to hear.

Pieter-Lucas found Meester Laurens in a large low building on the edge of the refugees' farm. Ten to fifteen students, mostly boys in assorted sizes, were seated at an equally varied assortment of small tables. The man looked up from the student he was helping and came quickly to him.

Grabbing him by the hand and squeezing his shoulder, Laurens led him to a secluded corner at the back of the room.

"Heer Coornhert asked me to bring you a message," Pieter-Lucas said.

"How so?"

"He has a surprise for you."

"For me?"

"Believe me, Meester, you will be glad you answered this call. How wonderful that you are teaching again—using the thing that runs in your blood, eh?"

Laurens folded his hands across his chest and rested them on his belly. "Ah, but God has made my most cherished dreams come true!"

"And your vrouw?"

"Vrouw Laurens finds herself happily busy day and night, clothing the destitute, comforting the homesick, and trying the best she can to scrape up herbs to heal the many maladies that follow these refugees across the fields."

"Are there no herbalists in this place?"

"*Bah!* Practitioners of ancient superstitions is what they are. Take it from a schoolmaster, descended from a long line of schoolmasters," he said, thumping Pieter-Lucas on the chest, "there has to be more to healing the body than waving a few sprigs of good luck purslane and hanging button leek on the gate to protect from evil spirits."

"Indeed there is," Pieter-Lucas retorted. "You should see the herbal garden of the Julianas in Dillenburg. Willem's moeder and his sister are teaching my Aletta to tend that garden and mix and dispense healing potions from all the herbs that grow there."

"Would to God we had such women in this place."

"But your vrouw has skills of this sort, has she not?"

"Only what necessity forces her to learn. You won't believe what a helpful assistant God has provided for my vrouw in that most unlikely of all persons, Lompen Mieke."

Pieter-Lucas shook his head. "*Nay*, I can't believe it."

"I admit she is a strange one," Laurens mumbled. "She will still never sleep inside a building nor eat at a table with another soul. No one knows where she stores her belongings or whether she has any. Yet every day, all day long, she lingers at Adriana's elbow, never asking what needs to be done but always doing it."

"Who knows what she is up to?" Pieter-Lucas suggested. "You and I both know the likes of this sly woman does not change for the better."

Meester Laurens gripped Pieter-Lucas' lapel in a thumb and forefinger and drew up close. "I said exactly the same thing to my vrouw when Mieke first began to follow us. But ever since the maiden Betteke wielded God's Sword against her evil heart in the prison, Mieke has changed in ways you and I would never believe possible."

Pieter-Lucas frowned. "What do you mean by God's Sword?"

"The Bible, *jongen*. That Betteke had a way of reading it that made you expect to look up and see God sitting there in the room speaking the words himself."

Pieter-Lucas shook his head. "I still don't believe even that could make a difference in a woman like Mieke."

Laurens raised a hand. "You are just like me. You have to see it for yourself. Well, I see it every day. And she begs my vrouw to keep on reading to her from the Book. It's powerful, *jongen*, powerful!"

Pieter-Lucas shrugged. Often he'd heard Children of God claim that they'd been changed from wicked sinners to godly people by reading the

Bible. But he had always wondered. He hadn't known them before this supposed change took place.

"Mark my word." The meester was wagging his finger at him. "If Alva and Philip, along with every clergyman, nobleman, and man of war in our vaderland would become experts in the knowledge and use of this powerful Sword, the revolt with its bloodshed would end in an eyeblink."

Neither man spoke for a long moment. Suddenly Pieter-Lucas realized the students were growing rowdy on the other side of the room, and their meester was rubbing his hands on his breeches.

"Well, well, I intended not to give you such a lesson. I hear my students need some attention. I go to them now and to Coornhert later. Blessings on your travels—and your bride's herbal studies."

"And my greetings to your vrouw."

No sooner had Pieter-Lucas stepped out into the lingering twilight air than he heard the patter of approaching feet and looked up to see Mieke hurrying toward him.

"So, your vrouw's a healer lady now," she said, walking beside him.

"Who told you?" Pieter-Lucas snapped.

"I heared ye say it yerself."

"How dare you go hole-peeping on conversations where you're not invited?"

"God's put me in the healin' work in this place, an' whatever anybody says that kin help the sick'uns what come to us fer help, I'se goin' to do it. Can ye bring yer vrouw here with ye when ye come again—with a satchel full o' herbs from that wonnerful garden ye was a-talkin' about?"

Bring Aletta here? Never! He ignored Mieke, but she followed and at last grabbed on to his arm and begged, "Please, Pieter-Lucas, if'n ye got even a touch o' the love o' God in yer heart fer the human creatures He's done made, ye'll bring her here—or at least some o' her herbs. Please!"

Without intending to, he looked quickly toward the girl. Her eyes captivated him. They were neither wild nor dull nor seductive—not the eyes of a street thief with dishonest plans to hide. Instead, he saw warmth and compassion.

He jerked his arm free from her grasp and bolted toward the road. "I shall see what I can bring you next time," he shouted as he fled. Never that he could remember had he so blatantly lied to anyone just to get them off his track.

He heard her thin piercing voice call after him, "God'll bless ye fer yer kindness!" The words pounded around his brain in a storm of haunting, vibrating echoes of guilt.

He had to get away from this place—NOW. Mattered not that it was night. Once he'd picked up Coornhert's reply to Willem's message, he'd travel through the darkness and reach Dillenburg by morning. The pounding of Blesje's hooves across the countryside must overpower the memory of Mieke's words and pleading face.

––––––––––

All through the night, Pieter-Lucas drove Blesje as hard as he could go. The sun had scarcely risen when he rode up the hill and through the gate to the music of the hunting dogs. He stabled Blesje and rushed to his room, where he found his vrouw drowsing on the edge of wakefulness.

"Pieter-Lucas, you're back!" she cried, throwing her arms around his neck.

When he'd kissed her fully awake, he stroked the hair back from her face and spoke while his heart beat wildly. "My love, I must tell you something. NOW!"

"Are you well?" she gasped.

"*Ja*, love, my body is well. It's just that ever since my secret mission, I've been trying to find a way to tell you the one thing I know you don't want to hear. I couldn't bear to break your heart, and yet it seemed that my silence kept you constantly in tears." He paused and watched her quiver in his arms.

"Tell me, Pieter-Lucas, tell me," she begged. Something in the adoration of those deep and wonderful eyes gave him the courage he sought.

"I fear," he began, "that until this war is over and Leyden is freed from Alva's iron fist, I must give myself to Yaap's mission."

He felt each word like a dart as he said it and looked for her to wince. Instead, she reached up and caressed his cheek with her hand. "Oh, Pieter-Lucas, my love," she said, unsmiling but without weeping, "I knew you would."

"Did I tell you in one of my nightmares?" he blurted.

"*Nay*, my love. It was just so clear to see. Willem needs you and you're a brave man. If you didn't do it, I'd be disappointed in you."

"Then you're not angry or distressed?"

"Sometimes, *ja*. But out on my Pondering Bench among the Julianas' precious herbs, I have talked long hours with God about it. I've learned that when He knows it's time, He'll let you come back to my side and to your painting. In the meantime, I know He'll protect you whenever He takes you away."

For a long and tremulous moment, he stared at her in amazement. "What a wise and extraordinary vrouw I have! I shall do my best never again to make you weep."

Smiling, still caressing his cheek, she said, "When I weep, my love, be not so quick to think you caused it. To weep is womanly and healing as well. Now, let us talk no more about it but enjoy the precious moments given to us."

Pieter-Lucas took his vrouw in his arms and soon fell into a weary traveler's satisfied slumber.

CHAPTER SEVENTEEN

Dillenburg

25th day of Summer Month (June), 1568

*A*letta spent the day before the christening of Petronella's son help-ing to prepare for the celebration. She joined Oma Maryka in scrubbing the miller's house from attic roof to entryway door until the cobwebs and chaff were gone and all stood in readiness for the feast that would follow the ceremony.

When the big morning dawned, however, Aletta did not awaken until Pieter-Lucas aroused her. She could hardly pry her eyes open and drag herself from bed. The room seemed to heave around her, and it was almost more than she could do to splash a handful of water on her face.

"Great and merciful God," she prayed beneath her breath, "help me. This day, of all the days, I cannot feel like this."

From the bag she would tie round her waist, she pulled out a leaf of garden mint and slipped it into her mouth. Even its fresh taste upset her stomach. Why must she continue to be plagued with these discomforts day after day? Since Pieter-Lucas was with her, she had no reasons to be distressed.

Of late she could never seem to feel awake in the mornings. Often after she returned with Pieter-Lucas from the morning sup and sent him off to work in the stables, she must spend one more hour in bed before she could face her day.

Until today, she'd succeeded in smiling whenever Pieter-Lucas was by her side. This morning, though, nothing worked. At every move, she de-tected her husband watching her. "Dear me," she sighed to herself, "how shall I ever come through this day?" She turned her back to him so she could brush away a tear and slide another mint leaf into her mouth.

Before she could resume her feigned composure, she felt Pieter-Lucas' arms around her waist and his breath on her neck. "What is it that plagues you this morning, my love?" he asked in a tone so gentle that she burst at once into a shower of tears and buried her face in his embrace.

"I must call one of the Julianas," he said.

"*Nay, nay!* I am not ill," she protested.

"What then?"

She sniffled. "It's just . . ." *Ja*, what was it? Was she lonely? That couldn't be. Sad? *Nay!* What, then?

"Just what?" he asked, an edge sharpening his voice.

"I don't know." Then, with enormous effort, she went on. "I only know that Petronella and Maarten are counting on us. We must help them christen their baby."

"And how do you think it will make them feel if you drag yourself through the christening procession into the church, weeping at the least provocation?"

"But I promised Petronella," she insisted, twisting the hem on her shawl into tight little spirals. "Let me lie down while you go to the morning sup."

"And leave you alone in this state?"

"Go on," she pleaded. "Let me rest and I shall feel better. Trust me."

Without waiting for his response, Aletta lay on the bed and pulled her knees up into her tummy. Pieter-Lucas spread a cover over her body. She patted his hand and tried to reassure him. "Fret not, Pieter-Lucas. A short hare's nap will restore me."

The last thing she knew was the warmth of a kiss on her forehead, the shuffling of her husband's feet across the rushes, and the latching of the door. Her head swam gently and she was drifting into a dream world of clouds and soft colors, indistinct images and sounds.

When she came awake again, Pieter-Lucas sat beside her on the bed, holding her hand in his, a worrisome expression wrinkling his brow. "Juliana the Younger sent you a decoction that she claims is good against all crudities of the stomacke," he said.

Aletta sat up, yawning, and smiled easily. The world did not swim as it had earlier. "Is it bitter or sweet?" she asked.

Pieter-Lucas sniffed at the cup of liquid in his hands. He made a face and answered, "You try it. I'm not the one with the sickness."

She put it to her lips and tentatively sipped the lukewarm liquid. Mixed or boiled in honeyed water, it had a slight garlicky fragrance and a bitter bite.

"What is it?" she asked.

Pieter-Lucas shrugged. "What do I know about such things? I only implored the countess to give me something that would restore my vrouw immediately."

How like a man to ask for an instantaneous cure! Aletta had seen many a solicitous husband show his deep concern in ways most impatient. Oma Roza once said, "Men feel strongest when they can protect their vrouws, and when they cannot do it, they fly into a disarray from which they can in no way recover until the illness has gone. Helpless they are, all of them!"

She recalled the laughter with which Oma had punctuated her statement and chuckled. "Could it be brewed pappenkruit mixed with a powder of Garlick Germander in honeyed water?" she asked with studied seriousness.

He shrugged. "I only want to know, does it work?"

She lowered the cup from her mouth. "I think it is helping already."

"So quickly?" He stared, his expression a combination of joy and puzzlement.

"With the help of the hare's nap!" She laughed.

Still eyeing her curiously, he reached into his doublet, saying, "I also brought you something to eat. Surely you will grow hungry before the feast at the miller's house." He handed her two thick pieces of dark bread and a chunk of yellow cheese.

"It looks wonderful!" she said. "Already I feel the hunger growls in my belly."

The swimming in her head had vanished—the heavy drowsiness as well. Rising from the bed, she proceeded to dress and put her hair in order. All the while, she nibbled on the bread and cheese and continued to drink Juliana's herbal cures. Once more she sensed that Pieter-Lucas did not take his attention from her, but now it brought her joy instead of weeping.

"How do I ever get on when you are away?" she remarked as they set out on the long pathway that led to the church on the side of the hill. She tucked her arm snugly into her husband's and added, "I feel like a princess on the arm of my prince!"

"Are you sure you feel well enough for this day?" Pieter-Lucas asked.

"Perfectly well," she answered, wondering herself at the feeling of well-being that possessed her.

He laid his hand on hers and, in a manner so sagacious that it made her smile, said, "I may be no healer of any sort, but this seems to me an exceedingly strange malady—afflicting you from the moment of wakefulness, then going as quickly away as it comes and returning day after day."

Strange indeed! Or was it? Aletta gasped, then clapped a hand over her mouth.

Pieter-Lucas stopped and cast a worried glance at her. "What is it now, Vrouw?"

Aletta's heart was racing. Caught between elation, disbelief, and fear, she stammered, "I . . . I . . . Oh, Pieter-Lucas!"

"Are you ill again?" he demanded.

"*Nay, nay!*" She began to chuckle.

"What, then?"

Her laughter turned to tears—happy tears, accompanied with a smile so big she felt her face would burst. Still, she felt powerless to speak.

"What did Juliana put in that recipe?"

She heard the bafflement in his voice, felt it in his arms holding her tightly, saw it in the lines around his eyes and mouth.

At last she spoke. "I know not what you shall think, Pieter-Lucas, but I think my malady is not only not strange but it may be wonderful!"

"Wonderful? How?"

"I believe this strange malady is telling us something," she said.

"What is it telling us?"

Aletta closed her eyes momentarily before looking up into the face of her most beloved on earth and saying, "Perhaps that we are going to have a child!"

"A child?" His mouth dropped open, his eyes widened, and he did not move.

"Oh, Pieter-Lucas"—she grabbed at his arms—"you are to be a vader."

"Me? A vader?" he stammered. He flashed her a dazed smile, then folded her in his arms. "And you, my beautiful vrouw, a moeder?"

Aletta snuggled into his embrace. "After all the women in a family way that Oma and I have attended with our herbs," she mumbled into his chest, "why did I not suspect this from the very beginning?"

Arms around each other, they floated down the hill as if on a white gold-rimmed cloud. All too quickly they arrived at the entrance of the pathway that led to the church where guests and family were gathering. With a heady delight, they found their place in the christening party and marched with the procession into the church.

Two city elders led the way, each carrying a pair of lighted candles.

"Symbols of good deeds," the minister had told them when he instructed them in their duties as godparents. Whose good deeds or what they had to do with the ceremony he had not made clear. But the candles added a glow, a fragrance, an elegance that kept the tears near the threshold of Aletta's eyelids.

Next, the minister carried the baby, and behind him walked the elderly oma from the miller's house, carrying a blanket, a christening gown, and a small jar of salt. Pieter-Lucas and Aletta came after her, with Petronella and Maarten behind them. Finally came the handful of guests— mostly neighbors and fellow workers from the *kasteel*.

When they'd been seated, the minister put the baby in his moeder's arms. He exorcised any demons that might be at bay from the premises of the church, from the home where the child was being raised, and from the entire village. Then the singers began a mass.

Aletta sat close to her husband. How like the christening masses back in the Great Church in Breda, she thought. Though these folks were followers of Luther rather than the Pope, it had always seemed to Aletta that their services adhered to the old Papist ways more often than not. Probably Hans would not be happy to see them in such a service as godparents for a baby's christening. But Petronella was her friend, and . . .

The minister began his sermon.

"Beloved in the Lord Jesus Christ, we are gathered here to perform the service of Holy Baptism. Though we have all experienced this rite, in our propensity to forgetfulness I fear we do not often remember to what end we were baptized. Through this act, this infant is committed to God and made acceptable to Him, set apart to a life of holiness and service of Almighty God. . . ."

Aletta's eyes began to slip closed and she leaned against Pieter-Lucas, struggling to remain alert. Now and again a cry from the child startled her, but until the sermon had ended and the priest had asked the godparents to take their places before the baptismal font, she continued to struggle with drowsiness.

The elderly oma took the child from his parents, laid a blanket across his body, and sprinkled the blanket with grains of salt. "Symbol of the acceptance of the religious doctrine, while making the unfruitful water effective as a sacrament," the minister explained to the guests as it was being applied.

Next, Oma placed little Maarten into Aletta's arms. He stared wide-eyed up at her, and she felt a new kind of awe sweeping over her. She baptized him with her tears, then handed him to Pieter-Lucas. They exchanged the kind of deep-sprung smiles that none but newly expectant parents can appreciate. Carefully, inexpertly, Pieter-Lucas presented the child to the priest.

The minister prayed over little Maarten, then sprinkled him with water from the font. Finally, Oma removed the blanket, dressed him in his christening gown, and gave him back to the minister. He gave the parents a final word of admonition. "You, entrusted by God with this immortal soul, shall teach him by word of mouth and by example so that he may be born again into eternal life and be useful as God's instrument, for which purpose he was born into the world at this time."

The minister placed baby Maarten in Petronella's arms. With glowing faces, the young parents turned and faced their friends. Then Petronella announced, "You are all invited to the miller's house to join with us in a feast of celebration in gratitude to God for this child."

How thin she still looked, Aletta noted. But the color had returned to her face and the sparkle to her eyes, and she was going to be well enough to bear more children.

———

The summer's late-night darkness had already settled in over the village when Pieter-Lucas and Aletta left the miller's house. They made their way along the River Dill and up the long serpentine pathway to the *kasteel*. A large moon cast its luminous haze across the landscape and turned their steps into starlike silver markers.

Pieter-Lucas held his vrouw tightly to him. Why had she not said a word since they'd left the feast? He sighed. Was there anything so strangely incomprehensible as a woman?

"Are you tired, Little One?" he asked at last.

"Not too tired to walk with you at my side," she said, then added in a dreamy voice, "Will you still call me Little One when our baby is born?"

He chuckled and gave her an extra squeeze. "Always!"

Once more she fell silent. He made several other attempts to engage her in conversation, but she never offered more than a cryptic response.

"What is it, my love?" he asked at last.

"What is what?"

"The thing that keeps you so quiet tonight."

He heard and felt her sigh. It was smooth and deep breathing in, then released in soblike jerks.

"My thoughts," she said shakily.

"What thoughts could distress you so much that you cannot talk all the way home from such a happy celebration?"

She did not answer. Instead, from the body he continued to hold close, he felt and heard a series of sighs and sniffles. He planted a lingering kiss on her forehead and said nothing. She reached up and squeezed his hand, and her whole frame shook with sobs.

He'd never seen her like this before. It must be the carrying of a child in her belly. He remembered his moeder, Kaatje, who had always carried a baby in her belly, never one in her arms. He could scarcely recall a day when Kaatje was not weeping.

They had reached the gateway that led through the *kasteel* walls before Aletta stopped sobbing and spoke. "Pieter-Lucas," she ventured, "when our child sees the light of day, how shall we avoid christening him?"

"Must we avoid it?"

She stopped in the middle of the road and lifted her face to his. Her cheeks glistened in the moonlight. "But . . . I thought we were Children of God."

So that was it! Feeling trapped, he scrambled for an answer. He hesitated.

She went on. "Surely you can't forget what Hans taught us!"

"Forget? 'Baptism is an intelligent act of witness to faith, chosen by the person being baptized, not by his parents.' I could recite it in my dreams."

"Then you know we must never baptize any of our infants." Her voice held a heavy tone of disappointment.

"If we lived still in Emden, I must agree. But sometimes even Children of God must make exceptions. It's a matter of getting along in the community."

"*Nay*, Pieter-Lucas, it's a matter of right and wrong."

"Oh? Your parents were secret Children of God, yet they had you baptized and took you to the Papist church as long as they lived in Breda, a Papist city."

She shook her head. "*Nay*, they did not baptize me."

"What?" His heart seemed for the moment to stop still. "Surely . . ."

"My vader told me himself."

"But that's impossible," he protested. Then taking her head in his hands and holding her so the moon's light could illuminate her face, he went on. "Think you for one moment that Dirck Engelshofen would have been allowed to continue to sell books in Breda if he had not baptized his daughter?"

She reached for his hands. "Hear me well, Pieter-Lucas. As you know, when I was born my moeder was suffering from the madness freshly come upon her that very day, and no one thought it strange when they delayed the ritual. Shortly thereafter, Vader took us all to Antwerp to stay with their families for a time, and when we returned it was assumed the thing had been done while we were away."

For a long while he still held her head in his hands, and they stared hard at each other. Now it was his turn to keep the silence. Were they Children of God? That was her real question.

No doubt Aletta was one in heart. As for himself, he'd tried hard to believe it didn't matter what faith he called his own. Down under his doublet where no one could see, he believed in Jesus Christ, the Son of God, born of a virgin, crucified, buried, and risen again. He tried to trust Him and live the way He did as much as possible. Beyond this, what could be important enough to argue about?

Pieter-Lucas could no longer look into the eyes of his beloved. For once he had to admit that if Aletta would speak no more about it, he would be content to live like Coornhert, refusing to align himself publicly with any one of the many confusing religions. "Someday," the mild-mannered man had told Pieter-Lucas on one of their long visits, "the perfect church shall emerge from all the confusion and bloodshed. Until then, no matter how much I may disagree with the Roman church, neither shall I take up with any of the sprouting little groups along the way."

Pieter-Lucas could never say such things to his vrouw. He felt her eyes probing him, waiting for his answer. It must be the answer she wanted or she would again dissolve into those maddening tears. But how could he know what that answer was?

"Whatever you and I do about our baptism," he ventured at last, "must wait till this war is over."

He heard her gasp and stroked her arm as he went on. "As long as I must fulfill Yaap's mission, I dare not to do anything to offend either the Calvinist Beggars or the Nassau Lutherans."

Aletta stared up at him. "For myself, I can wait, Pieter-Lucas. But we must find a way to keep from christening our child."

"Hans taught that baptizing a baby who knows nothing of what is happening is useless. So what tragedy would occur if we christened our child in order to keep the peace?"

Aletta hesitated. "I don't know all the answers, Pieter-Lucas. I only know that christening a baby says to the whole world that your child belongs to the religion of the church where it is done. Can we declare our child and ourselves Lutherans?"

Pieter-Lucas felt a heat building within. "What is wrong with being Lutherans until this war is over?" he challenged her. "Is Prince Willem's Lutheran family not pious enough? They read the Bible five times a day— they're kind to their servants and charitable to the villagers. Countess Juliana prays for her sons and their messengers. They're not Papists. How, then, can the baptism of their infants be so great an error?"

Between sobs, Aletta continued, leaning into his chest and pouring out her confusion. "I know not all of what is right and what is wrong," she began. "But when I see images in the church here and think about the baptism, I must ask who is right—Hans and my vader, or these God-fearing Lutherans."

"Is it not possible that both could be right?"

"I don't know, Pieter-Lucas. I only know that I fear nothing more than arousing God's displeasure."

"Think you not, then, that Maarten and Petronella have displeased God when they baptized little Maarten? And we, as well, for being the godparents?"

Aletta was quiet for a long while. Finally, pushing herself back from his embrace, she looked up and grabbed both his hands in hers. "*Nay*, that cannot be. Nell and Maarten have never sat at Hans' feet, and they have done what they know best to do."

"Ah, so! Then 'tis not always a clear choice between right and wrong." He reached for her face and smoothed back the dampened curls from her cheek.

"That may be. For me, though, one thing is clear just now. I simply cannot even think of presenting our child for christening."

"Nor can I think how we shall avoid it." Pieter-Lucas fought down a rising inner turmoil. Caught between the demands of Yaap's mission and the relentless faith of his vrouw, how would he ever manage to protect both her and the child she would soon bear?

Aletta had ceased her sobbing. "I see you do not understand," she said. "I must simply trust God to show us both a way." Her voice was once more calm.

Without another word, the two walked hand in hand through the sleeping *kasteel* grounds. Pieter-Lucas struggled with his thoughts all the way and yearned for a way to believe as his vrouw believed—and to be quiet.

That is not the lot of a good and careful husband, he told himself. *For only when I wrestle away the thoughts that threaten her, can she live in peace.*

Having settled this his duty, he felt relieved. Who knew whether indeed God would answer her prayer? Stranger things than that had already happened to them since they had left Breda.

———————

27th day of Summer Month (June), 1568

Every day Aletta went to the herb garden to gather supplies for the Julianas' apothecary cabinet. Nearly always, before she climbed the hill with her basket load of precious plants and flowers, she would take time to walk through the garden or sit on the Pondering Bench and soak up the beauty and healing warmth of the old place.

Today, though, the summer afternoon had grown so warm that Aletta decided not to linger but to return directly with her basketful of clippings. She was just snipping the last of the leaves for the day from the rosemary bush beside the stone wall when she heard the distant barking of the hunting hounds, followed by a rustling in the leaves of a nearby linden tree. Next came a solid thud on the ground. Startled, she looked up to see a slight-framed woman, arms askew, righting herself from her tumble to the ground. The woman brushed at her skirts and smiled at Aletta.

"Looks like as if'n I finded th' right spot," she said with animation. "An' the right person, to be sure."

Aletta straightened and held tightly to the rosemary sprigs in one hand and her cutting knife in the other. "Oh, *ja*?" she asked, puzzled. "Who might that be?"

The woman grinned, stretching her upper lip over a row of dark snaggled teeth. "Aletta, th' healer lady what I'se been telled 'bout."

Aletta shuddered. "And who are you?" she asked, her eyes following the woman's every move and her hand instinctively tightening its grip on the knife. Who indeed? A familiar figure she was, but just who, she couldn't quite recall.

"I come from your old friends th' schoolmeester an' his vrouw. We all been a hassled from our nestin' places in Breda. Guess ye was, too, only ye an' yer family went long b'fore we did, leavin' that bookshop to th' cobwebs an' rats."

Aletta frowned her forehead into a squint and asked, "Lompen Mieke?"

The little woman clapped her hands and chuckled. "Ye knows me. Ye knows me."

"What brought you here?" Aletta asked. Everything she knew about this woman told her to run, to chase her away, to call the *kasteel* guards. But inside, where she knew things but couldn't explain them, she sensed a calmness bidding her, instead, to trust.

"I come fer a basketful o' herbs what the meester's vrouw can use to heal th' people what keeps a-runnin' to us fer help. Lots o' sick'uns, there is, an' she never done learnt how to heal 'em."

"How did you know where to find me?"

"I kin find anybody, if'n ye jus' tells me the name o' the village where they be. I heared your husban' a-tellin' the meester that ye was here in Dillenburg. Besides, he talked 'bout a healin' garden. Jus' made sense to look over th' wall, seein' how that's where most noble ladies keeps their gardens."

Aletta dropped the last of her rosemary snippings into the basket, along with the knife. She held the basket tightly and asked, "My husband told you about the garden, too, and the herbs?"

Mieke gestured wildly at the same speed that the words burst forth from her lips. "He promised me that he'd bring ye to us soon, with th' herbs what we needed. But he hasn't come an' folks is a-dyin'. We couldn't wait no longer, so I tells th' good vrouw I'se comin' to get ye with yer herbs now, b'fore any more folks dies off."

Aletta stared, her mouth open. Why had Pieter-Lucas never mentioned this to her? "Tell me, Mieke," she ventured, never taking her eyes off her visitor for an eyeblink. "What sort of herbs does the meester's vrouw need?"

"She doesn't know—only that some o' th' people's a-dyin' fer lack o' somethin'. Me thought sure ye would know what sort o' healin' powders to send."

Aletta sighed. What could she say to this vague request, coming from a mind so devoid of understanding?

"Mieke," she began, "the herbs in this garden are not mine to give to you. 'Tis the countesses of the *kasteel* that own them."

"If they's healin' ladies, then it seems to me as how that's what th' plants are fer, an' there's no chance they can say ye *nay*."

"I still must ask."

Mieke stamped her foot in the dirt and made little shooing motions with her hand. "Then what ye waitin' fer? Be gone an' at it," she urged.

Aletta stifled an impulse to laugh outright at the audacity of this crude little person challenging her. "First of all, I need to know, are the people mostly ill with coughs and *heatte* and rawness in their heads?"

Mieke pursed her lips and nodded her head while a look of assumed importance knit her brow. "Coughs indeed an' runnin' sores, but most o' all, lotsa women birthin' screamin' babies. Ooei! Some days an' nights, it's enough to make ye stuff yer ears with rags."

Aletta's mind raced with a quickly growing list of things she could send. "But," she said suddenly, "how will the meester's vrouw know what to do with them?"

Mieke pranced excitedly, pushing up closer to Aletta. "That's why I begged yer husban' to bring ye along with th' herbs, so ye can teach her how to use 'em."

"That I cannot promise," Aletta retorted.

"An' what's to stop ye?"

"Mieke, I am married to my husband, and I must have his permission to take myself along."

Mieke stared at her, her eyes growing wild. "Then don't stand here any longer. Get ye at it. I'll be a-waitin' here when ye comes back, b'fore the clock sings out again."

"*Nay*, Mieke, you may not wait here, nor can I have it all assembled before the clock strikes one more time."

Mieke stamped her foot again. "I knows yer tricks. Ye fancy people always works th' same. Ye thinks if'n ye sends me away, I'll not come back to hound ye more. But ye're wrong! Pay yer mind to me, Healer Lady. I ain't a-goin' to be chased off without what I comed fer."

"I will come back to you, Mieke. You can trust my word. But you cannot wait inside the *kasteel* grounds." Aletta was firm. "You climb back over the wall and do not return until the sun lies low in that sky." She pointed in the westward direction. "I shall meet you here with an answer of some sort. If you come snooping around before then, I cannot promise you'll not be chased off by *kasteel* guards or hunting hounds."

Mieke stood, hands on hips, glaring at her defiantly.

"Do you hear me?" Aletta asked.

"I hears, but I move not from this place," she said.

"Then I shall have to call both the guards and the hounds, and they shall remove you forcibly. You were not invited here, and you do not belong in this place. Now, go, Mieke, go, and I shall do all I can to help you with your request."

With a saucy look in Aletta's direction, Mieke turned and clambered over the wall as quickly as she had come. Aletta heard the woman's raspy voice whistling a tune along the outside of the wall. Then she fled, basket tucked over her arms, toward the *kasteel* stable where Pieter-Lucas curried the horses this afternoon.

If Mieke spoke the truth, why had Pieter-Lucas not mentioned her request? The question resounded in her brain with each step pounding on the pathway. She must find an answer quickly before Mieke came bursting back across the wall. Something told Aletta that no army of guards or hunting hounds would ever stop this slippery little woman once she had determined to get a thing.

She shoved open the stable door and stepped gingerly across the threshold. The strong odors of horse dung and urine assaulted her sensitive stomach and sent it into the kinds of upheaval that early morning brought to her each day. So overpowering came the urge to wretch that she fled at once behind the stable and vomited into the sour rotting straw.

Leaning against the side of the building, gasping for breath, wishing for a clean-smelling spot to sit and ease the pounding and swimming of her head, she heard Pieter-Lucas' voice.

"Aletta! What do you here, retching in the straw with your face as pale as an apparition?" He draped her arm around his shoulder and helped her to a low stone fence on the edge of the barnyard, where he sat beside her.

Aletta smiled at him, grateful for the shade of a spreading willow, and said simply, "Will our child always have such surprises for us?"

Pieter-Lucas shook his head. "Not like this, I hope. Are you feeling better?"

She nodded. "Not having to smell the horses helps. The heat hinders, but it will pass. Whatever else, I must ask you some questions."

"Questions? About what?"

"Lompen Mieke!"

He started. "What about Lompen Mieke?"

"She just climbed over the fence in the garden—"

"In the Julianas' garden?"

The look of incredulity on his face made her laugh. "I never would have thought it, either, but it's true," she assured him.

"However did she find you?"

"Said you'd mentioned Dillenburg and the garden, and that if she knows the name of the village, there's nothing she can't find."

Pieter-Lucas shook his head. "That woman! What did she want?"

"If her story is true, you already know what she wants." Her eyes sent him question marks.

"If Mieke tells a true story? What do you mean?" he stammered.

"She says you made her a promise that you have never mentioned to me."

"Just what did I promise her?"

"That you'd bring your vrouw with a basketful of herbs to Duisburg to help Vrouw Laurens with the refugees." She watched him carefully as she spoke.

Pieter-Lucas grew agitated and gestured with a pointed finger. "What I finally told her when she would not leave me till I said what she wanted to hear was that I would see what I could do about taking some herbs on my next trip. But I flatly refused to take you there, and she heard me well!"

"Did Vrouw Laurens ask you for my help?"

"I only talked to Meester Laurens. He told me they had no reliable healers in Duisburg and that his vrouw was struggling to do the best she could, learning as she went. I simply told him you were learning from the Julianas in their garden here. That little hole-peeper, Mieke, was listening from who knows where and accosted me on my way out of the yard."

"Why did you not tell me?" Aletta puzzled over her husband's uneasy manner.

He shrugged and worried a pebble with his toe, not looking at her as he spoke. "I won't take you there."

"Why not?"

"It's no place for you. Especially now, with your tired mornings and heavy stomach. You need to stay here where the Julianas can take care of you."

She laid a hand on his arm and tried to coax him to look at her. "But, Pieter-Lucas, people have been chased from their homes, and they're ill and dying for lack of some healing gift I can give to them. It sounds to me as if I have no more choice about this than you had a choice about Yaap's mission."

"*Nay*. You are not going!" He snapped.

"Why am I not going?"

"I told you. It's not safe."

"You run off all the time to places we both know are not safe, and never yet have you once paid a mind to me when I begged you to avoid some dangerous assignment. I stay behind and pray Godspeed on each mission. Now, why can we not both pray Godspeed on this mission of mercy?"

When he looked at her, a frightening fire smoldered in his eyes—along with dismay such as she'd never seen there before. He grabbed her by both arms and ordered, "Aletta, I am your husband, and you will do as I say! Do you hear me? You will not go with Mieke!"

From behind them came a familiar piping voice. "I brung ye somethin'!"

Aletta turned to the uninvited guest and gasped. "Mieke! I told you to wait outside the *kasteel* walls. I will come to you later in the garden, as I said."

Mieke stood firmly, her feet wide, one hand on her hip. In the other, she held a bulging bag. "Ye both needs to see this thing an' hear its story b'fore ye come to help th' vrouw."

She stared at Pieter-Lucas, who persisted in sitting with his back to her. He hung his head and held it in big hands, elbows resting on his knees.

"Why doesn't ye face me like a man?" Mieke challenged.

When he didn't move, she scrambled over the stone fence and planted her feet squarely in front of him. "In this here bag, I'se got a treasure box fer th' bookseller's daughter."

Pieter-Lucas lifted his head slightly and asked, "Where did you steal this one?"

"From the bookshop," she said. "But I had to do it. It b'longed to Tante Lysbet."

"Tante Lysbet?" Aletta started. "Did they chase her from Breda as well?"

Pieter-Lucas spoke up now. "I forbid you to be pouring frightening stories into my vrouw's ears. Now, Mieke, take your bag and be gone!"

Mieke did not move, but when she spoke, all the defiance was gone. In a tone softer than Aletta could imagine, the woman began. "I gots to tell ye 'bout the two Lysbets an' how they done chased the thief out o' Mieke an' poured in th' love o' God instead."

Had she heard right? Aletta felt her heart moving toward the strange visitor. She laid a restraining hand on Pieter-Lucas and urged her on. "Tell me, Mieke."

"Jus' b'fore Vrouw de Smid birthed her baby, I was in big trouble with th' soldiers o' Breda. They was 'bout to throw me into the tower, an' I had no mind to let 'em. So I was ready to do most whatever they wanted, if'n they'd jus' let me go free. They sended me to steal Tante Lysbet's treasure box out o' her room where she was a stayin' with th' Vrouw de Smid. I got it all right, but then I picked th' lock an' took ever'thin' out o' it fer myself. Figured at least I could sell that much an' use it to fill my belly fer a day or two."

Pieter-Lucas was watching the woman now, and Aletta held his arm fast with both hands.

"They was mighty happy to get th' box, but madder'n a bunch o' crazed demons b'cause of it bein' empty, an' never did b'lieve me when I told 'em I finded it that way. B'fore I could sell a thing, they throwed me into th' tower. Two days later, they throwed Tante Lysbet in, as well, an' next mornin', they dumped Betteke de Vriend in with us. I treated 'em both downright ugly, I have to say it."

Pieter-Lucas mumbled to Aletta, "Not hard to imagine."

Mieke picked up his words. "*Nay*, I cannot blame ye fer such thinkin'. Ye all knowed me as th' rotten thief o' Breda, an' ye was right, b'cause that's what I was. An' if'n Betteke de Vriend hadn't been so kind to me, even when I treated her so awful, an' if'n she hadn't kept on a-readin' to us day after day from those pages what she'd tored out o' that book o' God, I'd still be out on th' streets o' Breda, pickin' pockets."

Pieter-Lucas stirred beside Aletta, then interrupted Mieke's narrative at this point. "But you went on stealing, Mieke. You stole the meester's books, and you must have stolen Tante Lysbet's box back from the soldiers—if you really have it as you claim. How do we know you won't steal anything from us or from the prince's family?"

"Ye doesn't understand. I stealed the books not from the meester, but from the Spaniards what was a-gettin' ready to steal 'em from the meester. An' I gived 'em back to him. An' as fer Tante Lysbet's box, I couldn't let those wicked men keep it after they done burnt her at th' stake. Jus' lucky they didn't burn it with her body!"

Aletta gasped. "*Nay!* Not Tante Lysbet! They wouldn't burn her."

She sat rigid, staring at Mieke, but seeing a picture in the eye of her memoried imagination. Tante Lysbet was standing in her room in the attic of *The Crane's Nest*, pulling from her treasure box her mother's little herbal book and handing it to her. Aletta had carried it in her bodice ever since. It was there this minute, rising and falling with the heavy heavings of her heart.

Pieter-Lucas stood to his feet, stretched out his hand, and pointed a finger directly at Mieke. "I told you not to tell such stories. See how you upset my vrouw?"

Mieke stared at him, her sharp chin held high and fire in her eyes. "I didn't intend to upset your vrouw. I was only tellin' it like it done happened."

"Like you want us to think it happened," Pieter-Lucas retorted. "Meester Laurens told me Tante Lysbet was banished, not burned—and he was there."

"But the meester never seed her face b'cause it was covered, an' like I telled ye b'fore, I watched 'em carry Betteke's body out the night b'fore—"

"Enough!" Pieter-Lucas interrupted. "Mieke, I want you to go now!"

Mieke didn't budge. She was rummaging through her bag and talking all at the same time. "First, ye gots to let me give yer vrouw th' box."

Pieter-Lucas raised a hand to stop her, but Aletta pulled it down. Quietly, they watched the little street woman take out the box and place it almost reverently into Aletta's hands.

"'Tis the very one," Aletta said softly. "No other box has these painted flowers and golden lock."

Mieke reached into her own bodice and pulled out a long blackened metal chain over her head. Dangling from the chain was a key.

"Where did you find that?" Aletta asked.

"In th' ashes at th' foot o' th' stake," Mieke said. She inserted the key into the treasure box lock and turned it, adding, "On th' mornin' after th' burnin'."

The lock snapped open, and Aletta lifted the lid. Inside lay a prayer book, a lock of baby-fine hair, a wooden crucifix, and a small paper-covered pamphlet. "Too sacred to touch," Aletta whispered. The tears flowing slowly across her cheeks warmed her heart.

"Mieke," Pieter-Lucas spoke up again, "if you hadn't stolen this box as the soldiers asked you to, they wouldn't have had any evidence against Tante Lysbet, and she might never have been banished—or burned—or whatever."

He stared at her for a long spell. Aletta drew a sharp deep breath and watched cocky confidence give way to trembling on the dirty little face. Mieke shifted her weight from foot to foot and stammered, "I . . . I didn't hurt anybody."

Before Pieter-Lucas could respond, Aletta blurted out, "Mieke, do you know what you did was wrong?"

After a long silence, Mieke said in a broken voice, "*Ja*, I knows it now." She stood twisting the frayed hem of her shawl in her gnarly fingers. "An' I also knows I could never do it again."

"How do we know you wouldn't do it again?" Pieter-Lucas challenged.

"God's Book done teached me that stealin's wrong, except like stealin' th' meester's books from the men what was fixin' to steal 'em from him— an' sellin' 'em to buy food fer the meester."

Pieter-Lucas moved uneasily beside Aletta and questioned the woman once more. "So now that you know it was wrong, what are you going to do about it?"

She stared up at him openmouthed. "Do? What can I do? I'se already begged Betteke's Vader in th' Heaven to forgive. Tante Lysbet's gone." She hung her head.

Aletta dampened dried lips with her tongue. "I remember reading how Jesus forgave a woman for a great sin and then said, 'Go and sin no more.' I think that's what He would say to you, Mieke."

Aletta reached out and hugged the trembling figure before her. "What God has forgiven, I am certain Tante Lysbet would forgive," she murmured. "And so do I!"

With a start, Mieke pulled free from Aletta's embrace. Her eyes filled with wonder. She wiped her hands clumsily on her skirts and stammered, "N-nobody ever gived me a hug b'fore."

She turned then and ran away toward the gate. Aletta called after her. "Meet me in the garden before sundown."

Pieter-Lucas drew Aletta close with his big embracing arms and smoothed her hair with his hand while she stood silent, exhausted. At length, she whispered, "When can you take me to Duisburg, my love?"

She felt a sighing in his chest and a tightening of his arms around her. "When God wills it," he said at last.

Aletta snuggled into his embrace. She could ask no more.

CHAPTER EIGHTEEN

Duisburg

11th day of Hay Month (July), 1568

All the way to Duisburg, Aletta had to remind herself that she was on a mission. A perpetual wind under a canopy of gray clouds chilled her, the jostling gait of her horse unsettled her stomach, and she fought sleep the whole time. At least it gave her a few more hours with her husband.

"If it weren't for the duties that call us and the war that threatens us," she called out to him, "we could both go all the way to Friesland."

"Or better yet," Pieter-Lucas answered, the wind blowing his words away from her, "we could have stayed in Dillenburg." He grew sober and shook his head in shuddering movements. "*Nay,* Opa's brushes and paint-pots are calling from my attic nest at *Abrams en Zonen.*"

A long way to go for a handful of paintbrushes, Aletta thought. Yet she knew that for some reason, they were almost the life and breath of his passion to paint.

Traveling at a pace slower than Pieter-Lucas kept when alone, they spent a night in the *Proud Stallion Inn* in Keulen. As the morning of the second day wore on, Pieter-Lucas grew increasingly silent and somber. Trying to draw him out from his aloof distance, Aletta asked, "What shall we name your son?"

He showed a hint of a smile. "Son? Why, Lucas, of course. What else?"

She chuckled. "I thought so."

"But what if it is a daughter?" His words reached her ears wrapped in wind.

"Kaatje, for her oma! The girl your moeder yearned for and never had."

"She would have been pleased," he said, then stared ahead and said no more.

The sun had reached its highest peak in the sky when they passed through the crooked streets of Duisburg, lined with rows of brown look-alike shops and houses. Beyond, they rode across a series of large flat fields, broken only by a settlement of buildings just ahead. The hooves of Aletta's horse were clopping out a rhythm that seemed to say over and over, "He's going to war and you're staying behind. . . . He's going to war and . . ." She shivered and drew her cloak closer to her trembling body.

At the spot where a narrow pathway led off from the main road to the refugee's farm, Pieter-Lucas brought both horses to a halt side by side. A long ray of sunlight had broken through the clouds and rested on his hands where they held Blesje's reins. He looked down at the reins, then up at Aletta with a flat unreadable expression.

"Two things I must say before I leave you here," he said.

Aletta's heart pounded, eager to hear his voice, dreading his words.

"It still unsettles me to leave you without an experienced healer to watch over you," he began.

She reached toward him. "But, Pieter-Lucas—"

He laid a finger on his lips and shook his head. "Shh. Hear the rest. I now realize you had to come here just as much as I had to take Yaap's place. It's just that I still cannot quite trust Mieke."

"Not even after her confession?" A part of her agreed with him, but something had happened in her own heart that day when she hugged the thief and offered her God's forgiveness, something she could not expect Pieter-Lucas to feel.

"I leave you in Vrouw Laurens' care, otherwise I would not do it," he said.

Aletta waited. "You said there were two things. What more?"

He squirmed in his saddle and Blesje lifted his hooves and snorted lightly beneath him. Aletta watched the cords tighten in Pieter-Lucas' neck and the muscles around his mouth twitch. Whatever could be the great struggle tearing him apart?

"If anything happens to me on this trip to Friesland—"

"*Nay*, Pieter-Lucas," she interrupted, "you said the message you bear commands Ludwig not to engage in battle for now. If there is no battle, what do you have to fear?"

He shook his head. " 'Tis not so simple, Little One. True, my message urges Ludwig to wait, but when it comes to battles, Ludwig is a racehorse, always eager for the contest. Besides, Alva himself is on his way to Friesland—may already be there. Even if Ludwig should follow Willem's orders, Alva would probably root him out of his hiding place and create a battle."

"Oh, Pieter-Lucas, he may still heed the warning." She had to believe the best, even while her heart beat out of control.

For a long moment he smiled at her, his eyes heavy with admiration. Then he added, "Whatever may be—with me or without—you must promise to return to Dillenburg to the care of the Julianas before our child greets the day of birth."

"Pieter-Lucas, you talk as if you were a foot soldier headed into the thick of a battle. Messengers don't fight. They return home with news of the battles."

"Have you forgotten how I became a messenger in the first place?" he retorted.

She stretched her hand out and laid it on his knee. "Nay, I have not forgotten." She swallowed hard to keep the tears from spilling. Forcing a smile, she finished, "I only know you will return long before the birth of our child. It's still many months away, you know," she added, patting her not-yet-bulging tummy.

He returned the smile. "I hope you are right. In the meantime, may God's smile light your every day there." He nodded toward the cluster of roof lines rising out of the pasture.

"The Julianas have stocked my apothecary till it groans," Aletta assured him. "I even have my own precious garden mint plant to grow as much as I need. And the promise of more of everything with any messenger coming this way. Just pray me Godspeed, as I pray the same for you."

"That shall I do." He looked at her for a long time, then jostled Blesje's reins and urged him, "Get moving, old boy."

Together they rode on to the farm, still speaking little. But the gloom had lifted, the sun warmed their way, and Aletta's stomach ceased its churning.

———

Countryside from Duisburg to Groningen

Never had Pieter-Lucas approached a trip with so much apprehension. What if he should encounter an unfriendly Alva or his soldiers? What if he could not find his paintbrushes? Both thoughts sent terror running up and down his spine.

On his first night in the stable of a wayside inn, he dismounted Blesje and gave the reins to a stableboy. Out of the corner of his eye, something caught his attention. Through a gaping hole window, a stubbly face stared at him. A faint flickering lamplight revealed simply that the man wore a peasant cap fitted tightly around his ears.

An inexplicable uneasiness gripped Pieter-Lucas. "He's only a stranger, with no reason to pursue you," he told himself. But the uneasiness grew into a sense of impending disaster. He checked carefully to make sure he had all his belongings in hand as he scurried into the inn, pulling the door shut with an extra tug.

All through the evening meal, he searched the perimeters of the room but did not see the stranger again. When he was shown to his room, he latched the door, then tied it shut with his rope belt. He crawled into bed fully clothed, even down to his shoes. On this trip, that was the place where he kept Willem's message to Ludwig, neatly folded and padding the top of his foot.

Sleep eluded him for most of the night. Thoughts of Aletta's weakness, Mieke's shiftiness, Alva's madness, and images of the stranger's eyes darted in and out of his brain in rapid circular succession. Every time an old timber beam of the inn creaked or the wind set tree branches scratching at the windowpanes, or a cat prowled across the thatch above his head, he was certain the stranger was about to descend upon him.

The tormenting thoughts tossed him from side to side until the light of morning broke and he could mount his horse and move on his way. All day long his mind alerted his eyes for that sly stranger. Every time he passed through a town or a wood, he fancied the man lying in wait for him around each blind corner.

However, the face did not appear. By evening, when he turned into another wayside inn, he had convinced himself that either the appearance was an illusion, or his uncontrolled imagination had made far too much of it.

When he left Blesje in the stable, he mumbled into his ear, "Tonight it will take more than wild fantasies to keep this weary body awake."

He had barely seated himself at a table in the inn when he spotted a circle of lamplight in the far corner of the common room. Again, something drew his eyes in that direction. One man sat alone at a tiny table. He wore a familiar tight-fitting cap and stared straight at him.

Terrified, Pieter-Lucas rushed off to bed without so much as a crust of bread. Once more he crawled in fully dressed and pulled the covers over his head. This time he slept but dreamed all night of Spanish soldiers chasing him with long curved swords. Their faces lighted by lamps, they looked like the haunting stranger.

The third day he drove Blesje as hard as he dared. Maybe he could outrun the man. That night the stranger did not appear either in the stable or in the common room. Pieter-Lucas hurried through his supper, resisting attempts on the part of a table mate to engage him in conversation. Then he climbed the stairs to his assigned room. With a good sleep tonight he would surely reach his destination tomorrow.

When he opened the door to his room, he heard footsteps coming up the hallway behind him. He dismissed them as of no consequence, but the light carried by his fellow traveler caught his eye. When he cast a hasty glance back over his shoulder, there was that face once more—with the close-fitting cap. Pieter-Lucas burst into his room and again crawled into bed fully clothed.

"Where are Aletta's prayers and the Godspeed I need just to keep me alive?" he said barely aloud. "God, deliver me from this stranger. Bring me to Ludwig tomorrow and take me back to my vrouw. Please!"

Prayer was of no use! Never had God seemed so far away.

All night he lay in one position—as if frozen into a pond—and never slept an eyeblink. If only Yaap had lived, he, Pieter-Lucas, could be in Dillenburg this minute. Or maybe in Duisburg with Aletta, using his paintbrushes and charcoals to help Dirck Coornhert make illustrations for Willem's pamphlets. That would be serving the revolt without having to limp onto battlefields and take a chance on turning his vrouw into an early widow.

But Yaap had not lived. . . .

At the first hint of daylight, Pieter-Lucas mounted Blesje. Today he was riding along the narrow wooded causeway where he and Aletta had brought herbs to the wounded men of the battle of Heiligerlee, past the pathway that led off to his old sod house hiding place and the spot where he'd seen Yaap gunned down.

As the memories grew stronger and his goal came steadily closer, his fears of the persistent stranger subsided. No more inns to stop at and discover him still following. Pieter-Lucas looked frequently back over his shoulder, then straight ahead toward the long-awaited outline of Groningen against a gray cloudy sky.

"I will forget the trip behind me," he said to Blesje, patting his mane, "along with the unbearded stranger. Groningen lies within reach, and Ludwig is nearby. I'll deliver my message, retrieve my paintbrushes, and . . . return to Aletta."

Groningen
14th day of Hay Month (July), 1568

Delicious smells of savory stew floated over the sultry late-afternoon air from Ludwig's encampment half a cannon-shot distance from the high-walled city of Groningen. Cannons glared at Pieter-Lucas, forming a wall inside the deep trenches around the perimeter of the village of army tents. Heavily armed soldiers rolled their eyes and lowered their spears toward him as he approached.

"Halt!" three soldiers shouted at once.

"I've come with a message for Count Ludwig," Pieter-Lucas said.

"Know you the word?" demanded one soldier.

"I do."

"Then put it here," the guard pointed to his ear and let Pieter-Lucas approach and whisper the watchword that would open the gates to Ludwig's camp.

"Where will I find him?" Pieter-Lucas asked, still whispering into the man's ear.

"His tent is the tall one there with the coat of arms of the House of Nassau just below the peak." He gestured in the direction of the heart of the camp, then let Pieter-Lucas pass over the drawbridge that spanned the defensive trench.

At that instant Pieter-Lucas heard a flurry of scuffling movements by the guards. He turned to see three of them surrounding a now familiar peasant man with a tight-fitting cap. His heart started and he gestured excitedly toward the culprit.

"Seize that man!" he shouted. "He's followed me for three days. Look at those dark shifty eyes—a Spaniard, a spy, a demon. Search him well and keep him in chains!"

Pieter-Lucas watched in amazement as the man submitted willingly to the chains and let the guard lead him, unprotesting, from the camp. "Why did we never see him all day long?" he asked Blesje. "Must be a spirit!"

His legs continued to tremble as he hurried on past rows of tents, cooking fires, and knots of men sharpening swords, cleaning guns, carrying large pots of water or armloads of wood. Already he could see the tall pointed pitch of the tent he sought, with its coat of arms glistening in the waning daylight. But before he could reach it, his way was abruptly blocked by a mob of soldiers surging toward the commander's tent.

From his place on Blesje's back, Pieter-Lucas could see over the mass of waving arms and spears, halberds and firearms, to the Nassau tent, where Ludwig was emerging and raising a hand toward the crowd. The loud angry voices unnerved Blesje and set his hooves to prancing.

"Quiet, old boy, quiet," Pieter-Lucas urged, patting his horse reassuringly on the neck and backing away slightly. Slowly he skirted the crowd, ever circling toward the tent, hoping to see all without being seen.

Pieter-Lucas surveyed the motley army from his vantage point. No neat uniforms and heavy coats of mail here. Instead, the assortment of Lowland patriots wore an equally assorted array of unofficial-looking garb. Easily he picked out the Beggars, dressed in the ashen gray balloon britches, doublets, and hats, with those ludicrous beggar's bowls and bags dangling from their necks and waists. But the shouts and protests came from a group of Germans. "Mercenaries!" he told Blesje.

"Ludwig, Ludwig" came the shouts.

"Come and face us, you thief!"

"We want our money!"

Ludwig raised his arms and shouted, "Be still, all of you! Be still!"

The rumbling gradually slowed to a near silence, and Ludwig spoke again. "Let your leader speak for you!"

One man's voice rose above the uneasy calm. "We must be paid if we are to stay and fight your battles!"

From all around the calls sounded. "Gold, gold! We want gold!"

"You shall be paid all the gold coming to you," Ludwig shouted.

"When?" came the leader's sarcastic challenge.

"Soon," Ludwig answered.

"*Nay!* Give it to us now!"

A barrage of shouts echoed around the camp. "Now! Now! Gold now!"

"We prepare for war now!" Ludwig shouted. "With fortifications to build and swords to sharpen, how dare you speak of pay? We lie in the path of thousands of Alva's well-aimed pistols and halberds. When he finds us grumbling, unprepared, and forces us to surrender, think you for a moment that he will allow you the luxury of keeping a bag of gold tied around your waist?"

A loud hissing arose from the troops, followed by more shouts. "Gold now! Gold now!"

Ludwig waved his arms for attention. "When you have captured Alva and taken his booty, we shall have spoils in abundance!"

The leader retorted, his voice fierce and fiery, "If we are to fight, we must be paid NOW!"

Ludwig thrust his face toward the leader. "My paymaster has no money to pay you now!"

The crowd surged like one angry sea of weapons and fists and erupted into a shower of guffaws, jeers, curses. The leader of the mob raised a fist to Ludwig's face and challenged, "You bring us gold from the paymaster by morning, or we shall force his hoarded stores from him and be gone."

"Where will you go?" Ludwig asked.

"We shall find a commander who will fairly distribute the booty of battle and pay his troops the value of their services." The man's words came out in angry spurts.

Pieter-Lucas had drawn up nearly to the tent now. He slipped off his horse and waited in the shadow of the tent next to Ludwig's.

Suddenly one of the mercenaries darted in front of Pieter-Lucas, pistol raised, and pointed it directly at Ludwig. Almost before Pieter-Lucas had seen what was happening, he heard a gruff shout and a scuffling of feet from behind him. A Beggar soldier tackled the would-be assassin, knocking first the pistol, then the man to the ground. The two men rolled in the dirt until the Beggar was kneeling with one knee pinning down his opponent. In his other hand, he fired the pistol toward the heavens.

Then he turned it toward the man who had first aimed it at Ludwig and began haranguing, "You mercenary little fox! It isn't your vaderland that's being trampled by some arrogant foreign friend. All you care about is gold for your bag. It matters not a clog to you whether *we* win or lose, live or die."

He fixed a burly hand around the throat of the German soldier and snorted, "You fool, if I hadn't stopped you, you would have put an end to our leader and started an uproar that would have destroyed you and your greedy countrymen. Lest you think we are weaklings in this army, let me warn you that we would have blown you to bits and scattered your parts to the wild beasts of the fields. Then what would you need of gold?"

He spat at the man. He spat again and again and again!

By now, a regiment of guards had arrived and were shackling the attempted assassin with chains. The whole horde of mutineering rebels had dispersed and vanished.

Ludwig said to the Beggar, "A job well done."

He was preparing to enter his tent when Pieter-Lucas stopped him. "Your Excellency, a message from Count Willem."

Ludwig gave him a quick glance. "Another one?"

"*Ja*, Your Excellency," Pieter-Lucas said, handing the letter to him.

Ludwig muttered, "Come in," and led the way.

Pieter-Lucas tethered Blesje to a tent peg and followed the count inside the tent, where the distraught commander seated himself at a low table. Nicolaas, one of the messengers Pieter-Lucas had gone to Brussels with, stood in silence behind the table. The two messengers nodded their greetings.

"Not still insisting that I retreat to Delfzijl and refuse to fight with Alva, I hope," Ludwig groused as he broke the seal and ripped the letter open. Hurriedly he read it, all the time mumbling to himself as if he had forgotten that anyone was listening, "*Ach*, Willem, Willem." He slapped the letter on the table and exploded, "Will he never understand? Alva is an iron man and must be handled with iron. He knows no other language! And Willem thinks I'll sit in Delfzijl and wait till he's ready to fight in the south? He would keep us here for an eternity. He'll never move until a bag of gunpowder is ignited beneath his stool! Too late! Too late!" He pounded a fist on the table, then grabbed his pen and, after dipping it in the inkwell, began scribbling across the page.

Pieter-Lucas and Nicolaas exchanged arched-eyebrow expressions. As they all knew, the Nassau brothers were as different as the turtle and the hare. Willem preferred a battle well timed and organized as a part of a total campaign rather than a repeat performance of the hasty and risky adventure of Heiligerlee. They all knew that with Alva at the head of his own troops another such risk could only fail.

Ludwig sputtered over his work, then folded and affixed a wax seal to it. Before he'd finished the job or looked up, he said, "Nicolaas, prepare to carry this to Willem immediately. I need whatever money and troops he can spare and certainly no more letters begging me to sit in Delfzijl." His voice rose to a frenzied pitch.

He handed the message to Nicolaas with a hasty, "Dally not along the way."

Turning to Pieter-Lucas, Ludwig said, "And as for you, *jongen* . . ." He paused, tapping his finger on the table. His head was bowed, and he did not smile.

"*Ja*, Excellency," Pieter-Lucas answered, "at your service."

"There's a fleet of sea Beggars nearby, in readiness should I need their assistance from the water." Grabbing his pen and another sheet of paper, he began scribbling once more. "Here, take this note to Emden."

Pieter-Lucas took the note and fingered the still-soft sealing wax. How might he find a way to go on to *Abrams en Zonen*? Perhaps later! He started toward the tent door.

"Wait!" Ludwig thundered. "If you can wait until evening, I shall give you more messages. There is a handful of men in Emden who might yet be persuaded to contribute to our cause. God only knows we could use it!"

"I shall be glad to wait," Pieter-Lucas said. He left the tent in search of a pot of stew for his belly. Tonight he would do his duty and tomorrow be reunited with his most precious of earthly possessions.

———

Before the sun set, Ludwig sent Pieter-Lucas off with enough letters to his friends in East Friesland to keep him running for several days. Pieter-Lucas stopped at the guard post on the edge of the camp and inquired about the peasant with the piercing eyes.

"Just want to be certain he's not going to follow me from here," he explained.

"Worry not," the guard assured him, "he'll not follow you."

"You locked him up, then?"

"*Nay*, we put a sword in his hand and assigned him to a regiment."

"What? What kind of feeble story did he give you?"

"Our commanders interrogated him well. He's a defector from Alva's troops. He came all the way from the Low Lands on his own in search of Ludwig's army."

"I know how far he came," Pieter-Lucas spat the words, "in my shadow. Just be sure you don't let him out of these gates."

"Merciful God," he mumbled to himself. He slapped Blesje's reins and set off fuming into the horse's ears, "Warfare turns men's minds soft!"

Pieter-Lucas shivered in the foggy-damp morning air and slipped across the protective moat. First a messenger, now a collector of war monies! And retriever of paintbrushes?

Emden
15th day of Hay Month (July), 1568

The morning after Pieter-Lucas delivered Ludwig's message to the scruffy little fleet of Beggar troops, he made his way quickly into Emden. Each clopping step released a host of memories—some pleasant, some maddening, but all as vivid as if he'd left here yesterday.

Almost a year had passed since he first came this way in search of the girl of his childhood dreams who had become the passion of his manhood. Today he searched for his other consuming passion—brushes, canvases, and paintpots.

"Almost as much hangs on finding my paints as once hung on finding my Aletta," he told himself as he passed through the city gate and headed toward *Abrams en Zonen*. In a world where the sword continually threatened to separate him from everything that he held dear, he had to be reunited with his brushes.

"It's all I have left to remind me of Opa's anointing," he muttered, "whatever good that may do me when this war is over."

When at last he stood before the old printery building, Blesje's reins in hand, his heart beat thunderously. Wiping the moisture from his hands, he knocked loudly on the door of the section where Aletta and her family had lived. No answer came. He peered in the windows. No curtains hung there; no signs of life greeted him.

Running next door to the section of the building where Johannes lived, he tried again, but with the same silent response. Surely Johannes had not fled as well! Pieter-Lucas returned to the street. He stared up at the floors above but saw nothing more than windows reflecting afternoon light and softly stirring branches of the spindly ash tree that stood between the house and the street.

With Blesje in tow, he dashed around the row of houses and down the back alley until he reached the hidden stairway he'd used so often. As always, the way was enclosed with dark walls, but today dangling cobwebs attempted to block his passage.

"You wait here," he told Blesje, tying the horse's reins to a post and dashing up the stairwell. At the top he found the secret door tethered with a long chain. Scarred, splintered, and without a handle, it stood ajar! By stretching thin and tall and pressing hard against both door and frame, Pieter-Lucas managed to shove his body through.

One cursory glance around the empty rooms confirmed his fears—*Abrams en Zonen* was gone! He scrambled up the stairs into the attic room. Worktables, cabinets, straw bedroll—nothing remained but a few straws mixed with balls of dust and here and there a trail of mouse leavings across the floor. He rushed to the corner next to the window where he'd stored his brushes, pots, and canvases. The empty walls and steeply sloping roof screamed at him!

"*Nay!*" he screamed back. "There has to be something left. Johannes, where did you go? What did you do to my brushes, my paints, my wedding canvas?"

For a long stunned moment he stared at the nothingness, trying to take it in. He dashed down the stairs and searched all the rooms—every shelf and counter—and the living quarters on the ground floor where nothing remained but the cupboard beds. On one stairstep near the street door, he found a small stick of wood.

"A paintbrush!" he gasped and snatched it up. He rolled it around in his fingers and felt its familiar smoothness.

"It's been chewed ragged at both ends," he said and felt a rage building inside.

He stooped and sifted through the dust and mouse leavings until he'd gathered up five pieces of bristle. He held the pitiful scraps in one hand and said with bitterness, "This was more than a paintbrush." Then lifting them skyward, he screamed out, "God, is this all that's left of my anointing? Then you can have it!"

Hurling every scrap to the floor, he fled down the alley stairs and did not look back. Fury numbed his brain. He mounted Blesje and urged him through the streets. He had no idea where he was going or why. When at last he came to his senses, he was knocking on the door of Hans' house.

"What am I doing here?" he said aloud. "Hans has fled to who knows where."

He'd not yet remounted Blesje when he heard Hans' voice. "Pieter-Lucas!"

Pieter-Lucas stared at him. "I thought you were gone. Not sure why I came here . . . wasn't thinking. . . ."

"Pay it no mind," Hans said, grabbing out and pulling him inside. "God brought us back, and now here you are. Come in and rest your bones."

Like a dumb farmer's ox in tow, Pieter-Lucas followed. Once inside, he grabbed at Hans' arm and shouted, "Where's Johannes and *Abrams en Zonen?*"

"They all fled to Engeland."

"Did they take everything with them?"

"Why, I . . . I don't know," Hans stammered, a look of alarm spreading over his face. "Here now, come have a seat and let me give you a bowl of soup."

"What good is soup when your anointing is stolen, turned into rubble, mouse-eaten?" He let go of Hans' arm and stood staring beyond the man into the room where he'd fought so many battles just to gain his vrouw.

"At least sit down, Pieter-Lucas," Hans begged, nudging him at the elbow, "and tell me what this is all about."

Still in a daze, Pieter-Lucas followed until he was seated on a bench at the long table. He spread one hand on the surface of the table and felt each familiar grain and unevenness. While he smoothed the timeworn wood, he began to talk. "Remember the night I came to you begging for a wedding date and you sent me home with a promise of an answer in one more week?"

"Ah, how much I wanted to give what you asked, then and there."

"I went home that night and began to paint a picture for Aletta. It was my wedding gift to her, filled with all our dreams for each other. I worked on it every night for all the months until I left with Willem's pamphlets. The night before I went, I put the final touches on my masterpiece, and the next morning hurried off to do the thing I knew in my bones I had to do. I expected to come back that night, and we were to be married five days later."

Hans sighed. "That was the night the world turned bottom side up."

Smoothing the table now with both hands, Pieter-Lucas went on with his story, not looking at his host. "The weeks since then have been filled with the joys of marriage and the pains of separation from my bride in the mission thrust upon me. But always I've cherished one hope that when I came back to Emden, I would retrieve my opa's paintpots and brushes and Aletta's wedding canvas, and that someday God would let me paint again. Today I returned through a broken lock into the printshop building and found nothing but a mouse-eaten handle and a handful of stray bristles mixed with dust balls and mouse leavings."

Pieter-Lucas grew silent. His whole body quavered. He tapped the table with the fingers of his right hand one at a time, as if counting off days or weeks or battles, or . . .

Hans cleared his throat. "What will you do now, Pieter-Lucas?"

"I've missions to run for Ludwig, and when his battle with Alva is over, I return to Duisburg, where I left my vrouw administering herbal cures to refugees. I take her back to Dillenburg where the Julianas can care for her until the birth of our child. As long as the war goes on, I am a messenger for the House of Nassau, filling the bloody cap of my friend Yaap, who was gunned down by a Spaniard before my eyes. Beyond that. . . ?"

Pieter-Lucas felt a gut-wrenching passion to hear his former teacher say, "Blessings on you!" Instead, he heard Hans let out a long slow breath and ask, "So you are a part of the revolt now?"

Pieter-Lucas cringed. "I only run messages," he said, " and try to save lives."

"Patriots' lives, ja. What of the Spaniards? War is destructive, jongen—and wrong."

Pieter-Lucas squirmed. When he and Dirck Coornhert talked about it, it seemed so clear. Now sitting across the table from this man committed to nonresistance in all its forms, he had no more answers. Clasping his hands on the table before him, he said at last, "I know war is wrong. I also know the only way it can be avoided in the Low Lands is if all citizens will bend the neck to Philip and the popish Church."

Hans raised a hand and shook his head. "Or if all who follow Scripture instead of men's traditions will continue to meet in secret and love not their lives more than the Lord Jesus Christ, their Savior."

"That's martyrdom!" Pieter-Lucas jumped up and leaned both hands on the edge of the table.

"Oftentimes it is just that."

"And if all believers are martyred, think how short will be the life of the church."

Hans nodded. "So it would seem." He ran his fingers through his beard and went on. "But God has some secrets not readily understood or imagined by the mind of man. Jesus himself said, 'I will build my church and the gates of hell will not overpower it.' Nothing—*nay*, not even King Philip and his duke—can ever wipe out the true church of our Lord Jesus Christ."

Pieter-Lucas paced the floor behind the bench on which he had sat. "And think you that God never uses the arms and revolts of men who call themselves by His name and read His Book to their households?"

"I've asked that question long myself and can't yet quite see how it can be."

"Why not? Especially when Alva points a determined sword at all forms of religion but his own? What do we do? Lie in his pathway and let him lop our heads?"

Hans nodded. "I know what you say. I've thought about that too. It's just that in the Book, Jesus said it so clearly. 'Blessed are the peaceable'—not the makers of war—'for they shall be called the Children of God.' "

Pieter-Lucas continued pacing. At last he stopped and leaned both hands once more on the table. Looking Hans squarely in the face, he said, "I've not learned the Book as you have, and I suppose that someday I must read it for myself to find all the words that God has said about this. For now, I cannot but believe there is some justice in Prince Willem's cause. His Bible-reading moeder claims it's smiled upon by God."

Hans stood and faced Pieter-Lucas. "One day, perhaps you'll see it more clearly. Until then, Pieter-Lucas, you will not yourself carry a sword, will you?"

He sighed. "*Nay*, I shall not wield a sword." He paused and watched relief spread over his companion's face. "I promised Dirck Engelshofen, and I cannot go back on my word. But more than that"—he shook his head—"to take a life would make of me a son of the despicable, violent Hendrick van den Garde."

Hans laid an arm across Pieter-Lucas' shoulders. "None is so courageous as the man who refuses to kill when all around him are trusting the sword to bring about the things God designs to do through peaceful means—prayers, healing acts, paintbrushes!"

Pieter-Lucas started. "I've heard those words before. I'm not yet sure what they mean. While I search for answers, though, I must go on delivering messages, collecting money, helping send Alva running home to his king with tail between his legs and licking his wounds."

Both men headed for the door.

"Have a care, young friend," Hans said. "As you pass through the midst of the melee of a battlefield, you may find it difficult to keep from falling into the pitfalls of war. They have a way of miring your feet and turning you into the soldier you vowed never to become."

Pieter-Lucas hurried out into the late-afternoon air. "I could never kill a man . . . never," he muttered to Blesje as he went. "I am a messenger and nothing more!"

CHAPTER NINETEEN

Groningen

20th day of Hay Month (July), 1568

A warm steamy sun beat down on Pieter-Lucas' head as he approached what had been the camp of Ludwig when he left it. But all had changed. Where just days ago stew pots had bubbled and angry men had demanded gold, today all was desolate, ominous, bleak. Gone were the tents that had lifted their poles on the horizon. Gone were the cannons, guards, and bridges. A strange mixture of oppressive odors that wafted along the riverbank and across the swampy countryside set Pieter-Lucas' nostrils and innards to quivering.

He sniffed. "Burnt wood?"

He sniffed again. "Rotting bodies! War has been here!"

Pieter-Lucas clutched at the sack of supposed onions draped around his shoulders, grateful for the cover his peasant costume provided both for him and for the coins he had collected from Ludwig's friends. Not that there were enough to pay all the troops, but it was something. Unless their number had been . . . *nay*, he refused to think that way. Ludwig must still be out there somewhere with an army. He stood beside the burnt timbers and looked in all directions. "Which way did he go?" he said into the breeze that slapped gently at his cheeks. "And his pursuers?"

The ruin and stench around him told him that whatever the battle amounted to, Ludwig had lost it. Alva could be on his way home by now. How far away depended on how many days had passed since the battle and how fast they moved. And who but Alva could know? How many of his men might still be lurking about, eager to find a wandering messenger of the patriots?

Ja, it was good to be a peasant farmer once more—good that Blesje lay safely in Emden. Pieter-Lucas looked at the city of Groningen with its high thick walls, ornate church towers, and sharp spires reaching up out

of the streets as if in search of new air. All was too quiet—like the countryside he'd passed through to get here. The roadway leading up to the
tower gate that guarded the moat was deserted. The gate itself was tightly
shut, and no one either came or went through it.

He searched the other horizons, away from Groningen, and finally set
off walking in the direction of Den Dullart. He hadn't gone far when he
noticed a black heap of charred rubble set back off the roadway. It must
be a farmhouse, but it was burnt past recognition! Not far down the road,
there was another, then another. . . .

Shivers ran up and down Pieter-Lucas' back. With tentative steps, he
followed the line of burnt houses until, in a grove of blackened willows,
he spotted a small group of people sifting through the rubble. Leaving the
roadway, he picked his way through the trees and around the no longer
smoldering ashes. Not until he stood directly behind the people did they
seem to realize he was there. A woman and two young children!

"*Ach!* God Almighty! Have mercy," the woman cried out.

Frantically she gathered her children into the safety of her skirts and
eyed Pieter-Lucas wildly. Her face was young and pretty, but along with
her clothes, it was smudged with ashes. Her hair hung in unkempt strings
from beneath a once white cap of the Frisian style.

"I'm sorry I frightened you," Pieter-Lucas said.

"What do you want?" she challenged.

One look at her plight, and his search for Ludwig seemed suddenly
unimportant. What if this were Aletta and the child she would soon bear
him? What would he want a traveling messenger man to do for her?

"Why . . . is there something that can I do to alleviate your suffering?"

"*Nay*, just go away," she said.

"But the torch has left you with nothing. Here, let me give you some
bread for you and your little ones." He lowered the bag from his shoulders
and began to open it. Two sets of eyes peered out at him from the mother's
skirts. The sight filled him with an overwhelming compassion.

"That's kind of you, young man," the mother said, "but I must not
take it."

"I offer it freely," he said, holding two small hunks of bread out to her.
"They are not fresh, but at least they have not been burned to cinders."

She eyed him for a long while and appeared almost ready to accept.
Then she shook her head with shuddering motions and said, "*Nay*, I
cannot. My . . . husband has gone looking for food. He'll return soon. Just
leave us alone."

Pieter-Lucas dropped his hands with the bread. The children's eyes
were fixed on the food. Ravenous, they were. Inwardly he knew there was

no husband out foraging for food. What could he do?

"I leave you, then," he said. "But first, can you tell me, did you see the armies that torched your house and all the others along the roadway?"

Eyeing him tentatively, she offered, "We saw the smoke of others, then fled into the woods and hid until they'd passed."

"Were they soldiers who did this awful deed?"

She stared hard at him. "If you are a peasant farmer, why do you ask about soldiers? What is your real reason to prowl around amid our misery?"

How much dared he say? This was a woman of thinking mind, not some simpleton. How could he be certain she was not also covering up her real person, perhaps searching the rubble for booty? She did not look like a masquerading thief, but then the dangerous ones never did. *Ach!* Could one never trust a stranger—not even an innocent woman protecting her pure-eyed children?

Calmly—so calmly that he startled himself—he replied, "I am no soldier." Turning all round, he went on. "You can see for yourself I carry no weapons. You must believe me, young woman, I'm on an errand of mercy for my master."

He watched her face, looking for a light that never went on. She stared at him as blankly as before, but something in her bearing would not be ignored. "Who is your master?" she demanded.

Feeling almost powerless to do otherwise, he told her the truth. "I come from Prince Willem van Oranje."

"Then I suppose you are searching for Count Ludwig and his men?" she asked, still betraying no feelings.

"Has he passed this way?"

Tears formed in her eyes. "The count has roamed these fields and bogs and woods for months now. Often he and his men pounded on our doors and begged for a crust of bread or a contribution of gold coins. I've heard said that he nailed notices on some people's doorposts threatening to burn them about the ears if they did not give him the gold coins he needed to hire his troops and fight off the terrible Alva. No such notice ever appeared on my door, however."

"Did Ludwig's men ever burn a house?" Pieter-Lucas stood trembling inside.

"Not that I know about. We all wanted him to win, if indeed he could get rid of Alva and restore our peace and quiet. But the tales we heard of the Spaniards made us despair. Then we heard there was a bloody skirmish in Groningen, and after that . . ." She stopped and eyed him once more.

"You need fear no reprisals from me. In fact, if you can enlighten my way, I have the possibility to strengthen Ludwig's cause, when I can find him."

"I . . . I do not know where he is," she stammered. "I only know his men came fleeing through here with torn clothes, bleeding wounds, and tattered bags. Two of the soldiers came prowling around our little house and sneaking out through the woods. I overheard one of them saying he would never go to Jemmingen."

"Deserters from the army, were they?"

She shrugged. "Who knows? I was so fearful, I clutched these babies in bed with me, and my husband took the big sword from its place above the mantel and lay wait in the animal shelter—it used to stand there," she interrupted, pointing toward a pile of burned rubble.

"Did they burn your house?" Pieter-Lucas asked.

She shook her head. " 'Twas Alva came later and did that. We always knew if he won a victory over Ludwig, he'd punish us all. And if we hadn't hidden in the woods, he would have ravaged and burnt us along with the buildings."

She stopped, then pulled her lips inward and said with obvious agitation, "Now I've told you what you wanted to hear, what savage thing do you plan to do to me?"

What savage thing? Pieter-Lucas stood breathless and tried to disbelieve what he had just heard. "Woman, I plan only to promise you the good hand of our God in payment for your kindness. Do I look to be a savage man?"

"Looks mean not a thing in war," she said and suddenly burst into tears. Grabbing her children, she turned them around with her and fled into the woods.

"Halt!" he shouted after her. "I mean you no harm."

But she did not stop, and he dared not follow after her. He reached into his bag and pulled out two gold coins. Tearing a large square of cloth from his peasant shirt, he wrapped the coins with the two hunks of bread and left them at the spot where he had found her. Her children's empty bellies would draw her back when he was gone.

"Great God," he mumbled to himself as he walked back to the road, "do all the faces of war have nasty fangs that gouge the soul?"

Jemmingen
21st day of Hay Month (July), 1568

Pieter-Lucas climbed up over the earthen dike that sealed off the Ems

River Valley from the tidal waters of Den Dullart. He searched the eastern horizon just as the brilliant rays of the sun broke through a long slender hole in the cloud cover and set off sparks of golden reflection up and down the Ems River on the edge of the world. It lit up the distant meager skyline of Jemmingen—a single church spire and the blades of a windmill rising from a cluster of lower roofs crouched down in the boggy pasture-land.

In the still morning air, Pieter-Lucas could hear a rumble of shouts. Pouring out of the village, a stream of men appearing like mice flowed across the field.

What sort of battle maneuver was this? And which army? He strained his eyes to make out the colors of the banners flying above the encampment of tents on the far side of the village. He was too far away to be certain, but it looked like the orange-white-and-blue of Ludwig's troops. As the men drew closer, he recognized beggar uniforms among them.

In no time they were upon him, Ludwig leading the parade. Each man carried a spade, a halberd, or some other sharp implement.

"Dig till the dikes are useless!" Ludwig barked.

Even Pieter-Lucas knew that Alva and his men were not sailors. Partly because of the heavy coats of armor they wore, they would not swim or attempt to cross water that was too deep for wading. With the dikes destroyed, the approaching high tide could turn these fields into a wave-lapping grave for Alva and his water-fearing soldiers!

Ludwig's was the first spade to tear into the earthen dike, and the whole retinue followed his lead. Startled, Pieter-Lucas realized the count was thrusting a halberd into his hand as well. He attacked the wall with all his strength, swinging again and again, tearing huge chunks of the musty-smelling earth and dragging at the fill of rocks.

Soon the water of the sea began trickling, then running in rivulets toward his feet. It made him ravenous to see more. He hacked away again and again. A most unexpected euphoria possessed him. Just when he'd decided he could stay at it for hours, Ludwig grabbed him by the arm.

"Come with me, *jongen*," the count said.

Pieter-Lucas looked up, startled. "But . . ." he began, then remembered the bag of gold coins and stopped digging.

Ludwig was shouting to his men all along the dikes, "Keep at it, men. Send the Spaniards floundering in the rushing sea."

Pieter-Lucas ran after the count across the field, not stopping till they reached the single narrow roadway that led into the little village where the troops were holed up. They stood before five imposing cannons pointed directly at them, and Pieter-Lucas listened to Ludwig's instructions.

"We are doing all we can to turn Jemmingen into an island so Alva can't touch us. I'd hoped we might be able to keep him at bay until our position was a bit more secure. But if he is as near as I fear"—he gestured helplessness—"we need to be prepared. Go back to the beggars' ship in Emden, *jongen*, and tell them to bring the fleet closer, for Alva approaches. We may need fortification from the sea."

He was already beginning to walk toward the cannonaded entry to his encampment. Pieter-Lucas stopped him. "Your Excellency, what shall I do with this bag of gold pieces I have collected from your friends in Friesland?"

Ludwig gasped and drew up close. "Say not the word," he whispered. "I've finally turned the men's minds toward their mission. A bag of gold coins flashing before them now will only inflame them, and all will be certainly lost. Take it with you back to Emden for safekeeping until I call for it. Blessed be the men who emptied their pockets and you who prompted them to do so."

The men parted, and Pieter-Lucas heard Ludwig yelling back over his shoulder, "Come directly back with your horse, ready to carry news of our victory to Willem!"

Pieter-Lucas nodded, waving as he hurried off northward toward the sea Beggars.

"Victory!" Ludwig had said. He wished he could feel Ludwig's confidence. "And if things go not as planned?" He threw his apprehensions to the winds and pushed on.

———

Pieter-Lucas delivered his message to the sea Beggars and headed quickly back to Emden. By the time he'd delivered the gold to the safekeeping place Ludwig indicated and had retrieved Blesje from the stable at *The Black Swan Inn*, the sun stood nearly overhead.

The last place he wanted to go was Jemmingen. Unlike Ludwig, who seemed only to envision the village with the orange-white-and-blue banners of the revolt flying in the breeze, Pieter-Lucas imagined it as a gigantic hornets nest of armed Spaniards.

But he must follow orders! Together, he and Blesje pushed on through the streets of Emden toward the east gate. At his first glimpse of the water, he saw something that turned his blood cold. A flotilla of hats, horse bridles, armor, and body parts bobbed in the choppy waves of the harbor.

The tide whose rise he himself had so eagerly welcomed early in the morning had turned into a swift ebb tide, sweeping the evidences of a bloody battle down the river and into Den Dullart. The helmets and hats were those worn by Beggars and patriots, and the bodies did not belong to Spaniards.

"The quick and terrible sword of the iron man!" Pieter-Lucas exclaimed. "I knew it would happen, but so soon?" He closed his eyes and gave way to shuddering movements that convulsed his body, unbidden.

He passed through Emden's east gate and headed south along the Ems River. The closer he drew to Jemmingen, the more bodies floated past him. In places, blood ran through the water in ribbons of red.

By the time Pieter-Lucas came even with the battle site, the long twilight had begun. He found a clump of willow trees, where he tethered Blesje and pulled the last hunk of bread from his bag, pondering his next move. But the sounds and smells and sights of gunfire, the moans of the dying and the jubilant shouts of the bloodthirsty conquerors, killed his stomach for food.

All through the nearly moonless night that followed, a flood of escaping soldiers swam ashore in search of safety. Pieter-Lucas spent the night pulling wearied and wounded men from the water, doing all he could to make them comfortable. If only he had Aletta's herbal apothecary cabinet! Midst the profusion of grasses and swamp weeds growing along the riverbank, there must be plants that could heal. If only he knew!

Of each person who would talk, he asked one important question. Had they seen Ludwig? Some sneered, others shrugged, a few stared at him expressionless.

"He'll come swimmin' out when it's all over," offered one crusty old Beggar.

"Will the battle go on tomorrow?" Pieter-Lucas asked.

"Battle?" the rough man exploded. "It's been over for hours!"

"There's still gunfire!"

"Ludwig's men are scattered across the fields from Den Dullart to who knows where. The ones that escaped are hiding out in whatever holes, swamps, or thickets they can find."

"Are they safe?"

"Humph!" he grunted. "The Spaniards not goin' to quit till they've ferreted out the last one—and killed or wounded them all."

"Then there's no hope?" Pieter-Lucas felt as if someone had jabbed him in the stomach with a dagger.

"Only for the ones that swim the river. Spaniards won't follow us here!"

The old Beggar wandered off, shivering in his wet balloon britches, still wearing the beggar's bowl around his neck and holding tightly to his sword.

Cold, tough, courageous—like Hendrick van den Garde! Pieter-Lucas shivered.

With daybreak the escapes increased, and the soldiers talked freely about their ordeal. "No battle," groused one. "That was a massacre!"

"A Spanish hunting party!" shouted another.

"May Alva's soul be tormented in Hades," cursed a third.

One soldier sat in the tall riverside grasses and wailed, "We left Ludwig to fire the cannons all alone. We failed him . . . we failed him. . . ."

All through the day, Pieter-Lucas watched in helpless horror as the Spanish soldiers wandered over the battlefield on the other side of the river, routing men out of their hiding places. They set fire to buildings and thickets and bound men's hands and feet, then tossed them into the river to drown. The air rang with gunshots and screams and those ever present shouts of "Long live Philip! Victory to Alva!"

By late afternoon the tide had gone out again. Pieter-Lucas stood stroking Blesje's mane, looking out across the water. "God, don't let the Spaniards wade across while the tide's out," he mumbled.

"They won't get far."

Pieter-Lucas jumped at the sound of a strong deep voice behind him. Turning, he stared into the one face he had hoped never to see again. Instead of the peasant cap, it was framed by matted strings of dark hair. The hair on his chin had grown to a long stubble. But the eyes? He'd know them anywhere.

"What are you doing here?" Pieter-Lucas snapped.

"I swam to safety," he said with a strong Spanish accent.

"Who are you? Why do you never cease pursuing me?" Pieter-Lucas suddenly realized he was clutching Blesje's reins and leaning hard against the animal's flank.

The man smiled. If he didn't know better, Pieter-Lucas would have thought the smile genuine. But how could it be? He had to be a spy whose mission was to destroy Ludwig's army.

"I am Alfonso. I'm sorry my actions frightened you."

Pieter-Lucas stared at him. He was still clad in his peasant clothes, a sword swinging from the hilt in his belt. "What do you want from me?" Pieter-Lucas demanded.

"I only want to serve the revolt. I followed you from Duisburg because I heard you were on your way to Count Ludwig's camp."

Pieter-Lucas' heart raced so hard it was almost deafening. "Who told you that?"

"It was the truth, no, señor?" he asked. Nodding an enthusiastic answer to his own question, he rattled on without waiting for a word from Pieter-Lucas. "Sí, sí, you brought me right into the camp of my new master, and I found great peace at last in fighting with the men who love the Book."

Pieter-Lucas stood immobile and stared at the mysterious Spaniard. "So did you run to Alva with Ludwig's secrets? No wonder you had such delight in fighting in this ghastly battle where all the men of the Book have been butchered."

"No, no, no, señor," he protested. "I did all I could to confuse and mislead the enemies of Ludwig and assist your men in escaping. I know how Alva's men think and fight. I saved many of your men last night. Look!" He pointed toward the north.

Pieter-Lucas looked all around him and clutched his possessions to his body. He would not let this man catch him by distraction. When he did look, he saw that near the mouth of the river, a flurry of activity had erupted on an island. The Spaniards were wading through the receded waters and spreading over the entire island. With guns and swords and torches, they were routing Ludwig's men out of their hiding places.

"Come with me, señor," the Spaniard urged him. "We must help the few who will escape and swim to our shore."

No longer hesitating, Pieter-Lucas followed. They arrived just in time to help the first who swam through the rain of Spanish bullets and hurling spears. From this new vantage point, Pieter-Lucas could see on the far side of the island a small skiff from the sea beggars' ship pulling someone from Den Dullart.

Not too many managed to escape from the island, but all through the late afternoon and into early evening, Pieter-Lucas and Alfonso scurried up and down the bank, dragging the men onto the shore, drying them off, cleansing their wounds. At first Pieter-Lucas felt a nagging fear of betrayal by his helper. But clearly the man was in control of the situation and did nothing treacherous. Then, oddly, he recited a psalm to each person he rescued.

"It's from the Book," he insisted, "and will give you peace.

"The Lord is my Shepherd, nothing fails me.
He leads me to restful waters. . . .
Even though I walk through a valley of deep darkness,
I fear no ill, for Thou art with me."

After the first reciting, Pieter-Lucas asked, "Where did you learn those words?"

The Spaniard hesitated. "I learned them from a prisoner."

"A prisoner?"

He nodded. "A simple servant maiden. I interrogated her when she was first arrested but left her cell feeling as if she had interrogated me. I later went back and begged from her a sheet of the Book that she had quoted to us."

Pieter-Lucas watched the man worrying a clump of grass with the toe of his boot. "I'm now greatly ashamed to say it, but I gave that little page to the bailiff, and he used it as evidence against her. It helped to condemn her to the stake. Mercifully, she died of a grievous illness before they could torch her, but her friend in the prison, no doubt as innocent as herself, died in her place."

Pieter-Lucas gulped and involuntarily backed a bit away from the man. How like the story of Betteke de Vriend and Tante Lysbet! He pointed a finger at the man and asked, "How came you, then, to be such a lover of the Book? Did you get it back from the bailiff?"

Alfonso shook his head. "How I wish it had been so! Instead, the words ran around in my mind. I knew there were more, but these few haunted me every day, no matter how hard I tried to rid myself of them. Finally, one day I knew they were from God. In fear and trembling, I cried out to the Shepherd for His forgiveness as the maiden had told me to do, and He gave me peace."

Pieter-Lucas stared with open mouth. Before he could find words to speak again, Alfonso went on. "The first thing I did was to defect to the army of the revolt. I saw what a dreadful thing my countrymen were doing—trying to keep this Book from the people. I think they know it is more powerful than any sword they carry in their hands."

Stunned, Pieter-Lucas nodded his head and heard himself mumbling, "Ja." Was there something to Meester Laurens' claim for the transforming power of this "maiden's sword"?

Alfonso nudged Pieter-Lucas with his elbow. His face aglow, he said, "This one little poem—and only a part of it, at that—has changed my whole life. Think what will happen when I find the whole Book!"

Each time Alfonso recited the words, the rescued men grew calm in spirit, no matter how agitated they had been in the beginning. Pieter-Lucas had to admit that he felt his own fears slipping away as well.

The sky was taking on a golden rosy glow when a loud struggle broke out on the edge of the island. Gunshots and boisterous shouts echoed across the water.

Then suddenly a Beggar broke free and began wading out toward the deeper river channel. A Spanish soldier stripped off his corslet and waded out close behind him. As the water deepened, the Spaniard lifted his arm, brandishing a sword.

"Will he swim it?" Pieter-Lucas asked his companion.

"He may try," Alfonso said, "though it is against orders."

Pieter-Lucas looked at him askance. "Then why would he do it?"

"If the Beggars have made him angry enough, or he thinks the water is as shallow on this side of the island as on the other, or if he's a madcap—who knows?"

"Will he make it across?"

"Not as long as he holds his sword overhead and wears that heavy helmet."

The Beggar was swimming now, his arms a blur of long deep strokes. The Spaniard, too, had sheathed his sword and committed himself to the water. Pieter-Lucas watched breathless as the deadly race went on. When the Beggar reached the bank, Alfonso reached out a hand to pull him up. One look in the Beggar's face and Pieter-Lucas felt his legs turn to water beneath him. "Hendrick van den Garde!" he cried out.

But he had no time to think about Hendrick. The Spanish soldier had nearly reached the riverbank. Pieter-Lucas looked down the steep slope between him and the water and held his breath.

"Alfonso!" he shouted to his companion—the soldier with the sword. But Alfonso was struggling to keep his balance and drag Hendrick to shore.

Pieter-Lucas looked back and saw two hands creeping up over the edge of the bank, grasping at the long grasses. The Spaniard was pulling himself up and would soon be on top of them all. *Nay*, he could not let it happen!

Then as a shiny helmet rose out of the water and two dark eyes peered up at him, Pieter-Lucas felt a strong wave of strength surge through his whole body. He grabbed at the long hanging branches of a willow tree, then with one foot stomped on the Spaniard's hands, pressing them into the mud. With the other foot, he landed a swift kick under his chin.

The man swore a defiant oath, jerked his hand out from under Pieter-Lucas' foot, then plummeted backward into the surging water.

Pieter-Lucas stood watching, not breathing. The man was flailing bloodied hands in the air, then under the water. For a long moment the struggle continued. Then it was as if some giant from beneath the water gripped the soldier by the legs, spun him around, and sucked him down into the angry vortex of a powerful whirlpool. The body went around, then down, and Pieter-Lucas heard a frantic cry for help muffled by the heavy helmet as it sank into the water. He stared, his mouth open, his legs ready to give way.

Hanging on to a tree for support, he heard his name.

"Pieter-Lucas van den Garde!" Hendrick was shouting at him.

Without saying a word, Pieter-Lucas turned and looked at the man in dripping woolen beggar's clothes.

"You killed a man!" Hendrick said, a leering smile revealing an incomplete line of dingy teeth. Pieter-Lucas' stomach tightened into a hundred angry little knots.

"*Nay!*" he gasped. He was trembling so hard that all he could do was hold his mouth with both hands and lean against the willow trunk.

"I didn't think you could do it!" Hendrick said, his voice a half jeer.

"I couldn't let him kill you." The sweat was pouring down his face, his arms, his legs, and he wanted to crawl off in a lonely corner and be sick. But Hendrick was staring at him, a familiar sneer playing at the corners of the mouth that had so often lashed out at Pieter-Lucas.

He took two steps toward Pieter-Lucas and clapped him on the shoulder. "A few more such acts and you might be something more than a coward someday."

The words could not have stung more deeply if Hendrick had been his real vader.

Faintly Pieter-Lucas heard Alfonso scolding Hendrick. "This young man risked his life to save yours! And you call him a coward?"

In a fog, Pieter-Lucas drew back and swallowed down a throatful of lumps and pain. Why did he still feel so betrayed by this man? Calling on all the strength he could marshal, Pieter-Lucas looked straight into the eyes that had so often intimidated him. "There is no greater coward than a murderer," he said, his voice even, his heart filled with the headiness of control.

He watched the leathery old Beggar begin to draw back. Moving across the murderous meanness and cold bravado in the familiar dark eyes, Pieter-Lucas detected shadows of a trembling fear. Hendrick first looked down, then made as if he would bolt free and run. But Pieter-Lucas grabbed him by the arm.

"*Nay*, Hendrick van den Garde, you who murdered my real vader and tried to murder me in the Great Church, this time you will listen to me."

"Let me go. Let me go," he begged, tugging against Pieter-Lucas' grasp, fear now edging his voice. But Pieter-Lucas held him firmly.

"I've learned a few things since last we met," he began.

"*Nay, nay.* Let me go!" Hendrick insisted.

Pieter-Lucas ignored his pleas. "The man who must rely upon the swinging of a sword to prove his courage will never know its meaning."

Hendrick's head was hanging low, and he cast a furtive sidewise glance toward him. "What do you know about sword swinging, you abominable painter?" He spat at Pieter-Lucas' foot.

Pieter-Lucas ignored his interruption and went on. "The greatest courage comes to those who resist the lure of the sword and search for ways to save life, not destroy it. I leave the battlefield to you and your kind and pray that not all the men who fight Alva are as small-minded and ungrateful as Hendrick van den Garde."

Pieter-Lucas loosened his grip. Without so much as a parting glance, Hendrick wrenched free and scuttled off down the roadway toward Emden.

Pieter-Lucas stared at his foot. "Great God, how can I get rid of this slime? I killed a man—and to spare the life of that most despicable of all cowards on earth?" A gigantic shudder shook his jowls, his shoulders, his whole being!

From over his left shoulder, he heard Alfonso's accented voice. "You never been in a war before, have you, señor?"

"If I have my way, I'll never be in one again!" Pieter-Lucas stumbled along the riverbank until he reached Blesje. He leaned against the trunk of the willow tree that held the reins, then bent over and vomited into the grass.

CHAPTER TWENTY

Duisburg

24th day of Hay Month (July), 1568

*I*n the warmth of a sultry summer afternoon, Aletta and Vrouw Laurens bent over their herbal pot at the open hearth of the aging farmhouse where the refugees gathered. Aletta drew the large wooden spoon to her lips, blew ripples across the healing brew, then sipped gently. Her mouth puckered involuntarily at the bitter flavor that lingered on her tongue and filled her mouth with the hot dry humors. Once more she dipped in the spoon, drew it out, and handed it to the older woman by her side.

" 'Tis ready, I believe," Aletta announced.

Vrouw Laurens sipped and grimaced. "I fear we have several ague patients sufficiently ill to welcome this bitter stuff," she said.

The two women set to ladling the hot liquid into crocks. "In Dillenburg I would have chosen marsh parsley, masterwoort, or hops for this potion," Aletta explained as they worked. "Tante Lysbet used chamomile for chills and shiverings of many kinds. 'Twas Oma Roza taught me that when all else fails, there's always dodder—devil's sewing-thread, she called it. It grows nearly everywhere on common bramble bushes."

"Then praise be to God for dodder," Vrouw Laurens enjoined.

"And wormwood," Aletta added. "Remember, you always mix the two."

By now they had filled the pots and wedged them in between the bottles and boxes of cures in their apothecary chests. They slipped into their street shoes at the door and headed for the cluster of animal sheds on the far edge of the farm, where newcoming refugees spent their first few nights before moving on.

Aletta had just reached the door of the first smelly shelter when Mieke darted up. "Come quickly," she ordered.

"Why?" Aletta asked. "Is there a baby birthing or someone dying?"

"There's a Beggar from th' war what jus' comed to th' house o' th' white-bearded man, with a message fer th' prince."

Aletta started. "Was my Pieter-Lucas with him?"

She shook her head. "All alone, he is."

"How do you know where he comes from and what he wants?"

"Ye thinks I doesn't know a Beggar what's come fresh from battle when I sees him?" she asked in an exasperated tone. "Besides, I heared him myself a-sayin' that th' war's lost, a miserable butchering 'twas. Seems to me yer man should've been here by now—if'n he done keeped hisself from gettin' killed."

Aletta shook her head. Was there nothing Mieke couldn't figure out?

"But he didn't come for me," Aletta explained and prayed it was so. For if Pieter-Lucas had a message for her, he would bring it himself, not entrust it to a Beggar, of all people! And if he could not come himself. . . ? But he would!

As she pushed at the low door and stooped to enter, Mieke tugged at her arm from behind. " If'n ye wants to know where yer husban' is, then leave that chest an' come on. Let's go catch th' Beggar b'fore he gets away."

Aletta hesitated, then protested. "*Nay,* our patients must be cared for first."

Mieke pulled harder. "They can wait."

Aletta broke free from her grip. "Mieke, a healer lady is always a healer lady first."

"There's no good reason why I can't go in there and give some bitter medicine to the ague patients," Vrouw Laurens broke in. "I've given herbal drinks and bathed *heatted* brows before you ever came here, you know. Go see about your husband."

Mieke began prancing up and down between them. "*Ja, ja!* C'mon."

Already she was grabbing Aletta and dragging her off to the village. When they reached the back door of the cobbler's shop, Mieke knocked loudly, then stepped quickly aside and disappeared around the corner. Almost before Aletta realized what had happened, the door opened and she faced an unsmiling woman with a white starched cap.

"Is there a Beggar messenger here," Aletta began, "from the war in Friesland?"

"What is your concern with such a man?" the woman asked, frowning.

"I await my husband's return from the war. He's a messenger for Prince Willem—"

"What makes you think a Beggar has arrived here with news of your husband?" Nothing in the woman's manner bespoke warmth or trust.

"My . . . my friend saw such a man, and . . . oh, it is so hard to have my husband gone for so long. We usually live in Prince Willem's *kasteel* in Dillenburg, but I came here with herbs to help Vrouw Laurens and the refugees while my husband went on an errand for the prince. Please, let me talk with the Beggar!" Her knees were trembling now, and trickles of sweat ran down the back of her neck and legs and turned her hands sticky.

"What is your name?" the woman asked.

Aletta eyed her for a moment before answering. "Aletta, vrouw of Pieter-Lucas van den Garde."

"Wait here!" the woman ordered, then closed the door.

No sooner had she gone than Mieke was at Aletta's elbow again. "She goin' to let ye in? Or do I have to find a way?"

"Just wait, Mieke." So easy to say and so hard to do. Yet somehow, trying to keep Mieke from doing something foolish made her own waiting less painful.

Mieke began pacing back and forth before the house, her stride rapid in a way that matched the wiriness of her body, the sharpness of her nose, the pitch of her voice. The instant the door opened a crack, she skittered once more around the corner.

This time the housekeeper greeted Aletta warmly. "Come with me," she invited and led her up a narrow winding stairway and into an attic room with low beams and the familiar smell of books. From a table by the chimney, Dirck Coornhert, Prince Willem, and the Beggar all looked intently at her.

"A hearty welcome," the white-bearded man said.

"I come to inquire of the messenger here about my husband," she said.

"Pieter-Lucas van den Garde?" Willem asked.

"*Ja*, Your Excellency."

Willem's mouth showed a half smile. "He is one of my most dependable messengers." Nodding toward the small dark-complected Beggar with a scruffy sparse beard, he asked, "What can you tell her, *jongen*?"

He was hardly more than a boy, Aletta noted. Eagerly she watched him spread his hands and shrug his shoulders. "I do not know the messenger you speak of, so have no report to give," he said. "I was told that one messenger was seen with the men that cut the dikes in hopes of holding off Alva's men. If he stayed with them, there was little hope. For hardly had they freed a trickle of water from Den Dullart than the advancing Spaniards struck them down, stopped up the breaches in the dike, and advanced on the city of Jemmingen."

Aletta fought back hot stinging tears. "And if he was not with them?" she asked, hoping her voice did not shake as badly as her legs.

The Beggar raised his eyebrows and cocked his head to one side. "God only knows. The slaughter was swift and bloody. If he stayed close to Ludwig . . . Again, who knows?"

She gasped. Surely Ludwig had not died in the battle. She glanced at Willem, afraid to look too closely, for she was only the vrouw of a messenger. She clasped clammy hands together in front of her and stammered, "Forgive me my eagerness to know more. A messenger's vrouw must learn not to grow weary or impatient. I haven't been at it so long. I shall do better."

She began to back away toward the door. The prince looked at her with sad eyes. "You need never apologize for asking about your husband, young woman. If every man had such a woman to care about him when he tarries long at war . . ." His words trailed off into a heavy sigh.

Aletta remembered Princess Anna's selfish railings and felt as if her heart would break. If ever there was a man who needed a faithful vrouw to watch for him at the castle gate, this was the one.

She rushed for the door. Her prince must not see her tears. As she went, she heard him call after her.

"When news comes, I shall see that you are not overlooked."

At the door she paused. "Thank you, Your Grace," she said, then hurried down the stifling stairwell and out into the summer's rare heat, wishing for two impossible things—that Mieke would leave her to her own quiet grief and that she could look up and see Pieter-Lucas and Blesje riding into the barnyard.

Instead, Mieke plied her with questions all the way to Vrouw Laurens', and Pieter-Lucas did not come home that day.

That night Aletta crawled early into the bed her hosts had given her in a small corner cubicle of the attic in the big farmhouse, but sleep would not come. Rather, her mind served up a perpetual spread of images of her husband, either wounded on a battlefield or bleeding alone in some wood where he'd been ambushed along his journey. In desperation she prayed, "Dear God in the Heaven, put your arms around my Pieter-Lucas and bring him quickly home. Take away all the ugly visions in my head and give me sleep."

Calmed, she cradled her not yet rounding belly in her arms and whispered to her unborn child, "Whatever else you learn in life, dear little one, I want you always to know your vader *is* a courageous man! He will be back, you know, he will be back. . . ."

Twenty-fifth day of Hay Month (July), 1568

By the time Pieter-Lucas found Ludwig in Emden and got his message for Willem, the urgency to put this whole nightmarish experience forever behind him spurred him on like a man at the cracking end of a whip. For two full days and nights, he pushed on across the countryside, along the riverbanks, and through the woods from Emden to Duisburg. Forgetting food and sleep, he did not stop until Blesje could go no farther. Then he left him at an inn and went on afoot.

His mind tormented him all the way.

How could he ever tell Willem how Ludwig had disregarded his warning and had suffered the shameful massacre of thousands of troops? How Ludwig's terror-stricken men deserted him, forcing him to fire all five of the cannons with his own hands, and finally to strip off his uniform, jump naked into the Ems, and swim for his life?

What could he tell his Aletta?

That his paints and brushes and wedding painting were gone? His anointing shattered and mouse-eaten? That Hans had told him he was wrong for taking Yaap's place? That he had killed a man in defense of Hendrick—and himself? He should have found another way—a courageous way! His head throbbed with the pain of remorse.

Worst of all, how could he ever still the grating sound of Hendrick's voice shouting in his brain, *You killed a man, Pieter-Lucas?*

"Not with a sword," he retorted aloud.

You killed a man, Pieter-Lucas! the voice persisted.

With anger mounting, he shouted out into the swirling wind, "I only intended to send him back across the river. 'Twas the water drew him down and sucked the life from his body."

You killed a man, Pieter-Lucas!

"And if I hadn't shoved him into the river, he would have killed me, and Hendrick, and Alfonso, and who knows how many others. And maybe other Spaniards would have followed, and—"

You killed a man, Pieter-Lucas!

"So, what do I do about it now?"

You killed a man. . . . You killed . . .

The maddening accusation pounded through his mind, hour after hour, league upon league. When at length he staggered through the streets of Duisburg and into the refugees' encampment in the late-afternoon heat, his heart was pounding, his head throbbing, his eyes burning.

"Where's my vrouw?" he demanded of the first person he met. The elderly woman pulled away from him, grabbing her shawl tightly around her.

"Who is she?" she asked.

"The healer lady!" he snapped as if she should know without being told.

"That way," the woman said, pointing quickly toward the big house, then hurrying out of his way.

He spun around in circles looking for the house. All the world heaved and blurred, and he felt himself crumple to the ground. The next thing he knew, he was opening his eyes in a dark quiet room and was looking up at his beloved vrouw. She was wiping his forehead with a cool damp cloth and mumbling softly over him.

"You're back," she said, "and alive!"

He forced his eyes to stay open as he reached for her hand and tried to smile. "I love you," he whispered.

The accusing voice that had followed him all the way home jabbed once more, *What would she say if she knew what you did?*

Ignoring the voice, he watched her bend over him, felt her lips press into his forehead. A rush of energy seemed to surge through him. But when he pushed himself up on his elbow, the world swam again and he lay back down quickly.

"Easy, easy," Aletta said. "How long have you had this *heatte* in your body?"

"What *heatte*?"

"Your body is burning up with an ague. Surely you must feel it."

"I . . . I don't know, my love," he stammered. "I just rode and walked without stopping from Emden. There was no time to stop or think or feel."

Tell her the truth, the voice prodded.

He fought desperately to squelch the voice and do what had to be done. "Are you ready to go to Dillenburg?" he asked.

"Dillenburg? In your condition? Are you mad?"

"I may be, but I carry Willem's message. It must get through!" Something inside his confused brain told him that when he couldn't even sit up without feeling like the world was spinning out of control, he'd never make it to Dillenburg. But who knew how much of the success of the revolt hung on the message he carried in his doublet?

"There's no need to go to Dillenburg," she said, quieter now, running her fingers through his curls, pushing them back from his forehead. "Willem is here in Duisburg."

"Have you seen him?"

"Yesterday. I've already sent for him to come here to you."

"Wherever *here* is. I don't even know how I got here or how long ago. . . ."

Looking around, it appeared that he lay in a bed cupboard with curtains. Beyond, he could barely see a large room with a table and hearth. Oh, why did it make his head swim so, just looking?

"Not now," Aletta said, cradling his head in her arm. "Never mind all that. Here, drink this potion. It will take away the *heatte* of your body."

The liquid felt cool on his tongue. How long had he gone with nothing to eat or drink? He drank it eagerly, even though the taste it left in his mouth was bitter. Just as he prepared to swallow the last mouthful, he heard the scampering of feet across the rushes on the floor and a piping voice.

"Vrouw 'Letta, I done called your prince, an' he comes direct."

Not Mieke! He slinked down under the feather bag and pulled it over his head.

"Thank you kindly," Aletta was saying, then added in a whisper, "now just go on. Pieter-Lucas needs some quietness."

"I goes," Mieke said. "Be sure to ask him if'n the Spanish soldier followed him to Ludwig's camp like I told him to."

What had he just heard? A spurt of anger possessed Pieter-Lucas, and he called out, "Mieke, come here!"

"Nay!" Aletta protested. "Later."

"I must talk to her now!" Pieter-Lucas insisted.

Mieke elbowed past Aletta until she leaned up against the bed and stood staring at him with a half grin. "I'se here!"

"Why did you do that?" he asked, wishing his voice could command more strength.

"B'cause ye was a-goin' to th' place he was a-wantin' to go."

"How did you know?"

She shrugged. "Ye never will learn it, will ye, that Mieke hears ever-'thin'?"

Pieter-Lucas sighed. He had no strength to talk, yet somehow he had to set this creature straight or get her out of the way or . . .

Aletta lifted a hand and scolded, "Not everything is meant for you to hear, Mieke."

"Why'd God give me ears?" Her eyes sparkled with a confidence that made Pieter-Lucas furious.

"For listening to instructions," Aletta countered. "Not for hole-peeping,"

Mieke put her hands on her hips, raised her nose, and challenged, "It's not hole-peepin' when ye does it to help yer friends. An' that soldier's my friend!"

Mieke and Alfonso were friends? Who knew what trap they had laid together or how close they were to springing it? Great God, what next?

"Mieke," he said with so little strength it frightened him, "how can you call the soldier your friend?"

She shrugged, lowering her nose ever so slightly, and said, "I was in th' prison tower when he comed an' talked pretty to Betteke. When I got out o' there, I learned how he'd given the bailiff her pages from th' Book, an' I was fixin' to make him good an' sorry." She shifted her weight from foot to foot, then went on, lifting her chin with an air of importance. "I never seed him again till th' night b'fore th' burnin'. I finded him a-sobbin' over Betteke's grave an' made him tell me why. Said he was a-grievin' fer her dyin' an' wishin' he could go back an' undo what he'd done to her. Next day, after th' burnin' was over, an' I'd gathered up th' books from the meester's house, th' soldier put me on his horse an' helped me to find th' meester an' his vrouw an' follow 'em all th' way into exile."

"How could you trust him?" Pieter-Lucas asked.

"Why not?" She frowned at him.

"He might have been laying a trap for you."

"Ye doesn't think I knows anythin', that's sure. But I can tell ye that when a man's repentin', I kin feel it in my bones, b'cause I'se done changed, too, ye know."

"So I've heard you say," Pieter-Lucas murmured.

"But ye still doesn't b'lieve me! I kin tell that too!"

Pieter-Lucas clenched his teeth, closed his eyes, and turned his body toward the wall. Suddenly the girl began stomping her foot so hard Pieter-Lucas thought surely he felt the bed quiver.

"Listen to Mieke!" she shrieked. "I'm no more a thief! I left all o' that b'hind me in the streets o' Breda. This Mieke, she's a new Mieke. Do ye hear?"

He heard Aletta saying, "Mieke, you must go."

A scuffling of feet followed, then the creaking of a door, and silence.

Pieter-Lucas took a deep breath and fought back the dizziness. In his mind flashed a series of pictures of Alfonso pulling soldiers—and Hendrick—out of the Ems River. He heard the voice in Spanish accent, *The Lord is my Shepherd. . . .*"

"Stop!" he cried out. He could not look at the next picture. He forced open his eyes and saw Prince Willem staring down on him, his forehead wrinkled.

"*Ach!* Your Grace," Pieter-Lucas stammered. "I . . . I came as quickly as I could."

"I see," Willem said.

"The Battle of Jemmingen was a complete and dreadful loss, but your brother, Count Ludwig, is well." Pieter-Lucas reached inside his doublet and searched with his fingers till they touched the folded paper with the round hard blob of wax holding the edges together. "So many men lost their lives in the battle. I think your brother had an angel with him all the way. He had to strip off his uniform and swim naked for his life."

"Thanks be to God, he lives," Willem said, taking the letter.

"I did reach him at first in Groningen with your letter, but . . ."

Willem raised a hand and shook his head slowly. "Since it has thus pleased God to bring us to defeat, it is necessary to have patience and to lose not courage. We must conform ourselves to the Divine Will, no matter how strange it seems. As for my part, I have determined to proceed onward in this sacred work with His Almighty aid."

"How soon will you need me to take a letter back to Emden?" Pieter-Lucas asked.

The prince shook his head. "I send word by another. You take care of this messenger. Follow the instructions of your healer lady and regain your robustious health before you run off on another journey." With a nod and a warm farewell, Prince Willem walked across the room and out the door.

Pieter-Lucas stared into Aletta's blue, blue eyes. "Very well, Vrouw Healer Lady, what are my instructions?"

"Drink the potion and sleep," she said with pretended severity. A smile softened the lines around her rosy mouth and laughing eyes.

"That should not be difficult," he said, "but first I must know how it goes with you and our child."

She smiled the smile of a moeder. "God gives us new strength each day." She patted her tummy. "And I never tire of telling the child what a courageous vader he has."

If she knew the truth! Without another word, he turned away and pulled the feather bag over his head, pummeling the bed with his fists. He felt her arms tugging at him and her tender voice pleading, "What is it, my love?"

She was sitting beside him in the bed now, holding him in both her arms. How could he resist her longer? Yet how could he tell her? She would despise him forever if she knew. And if he didn't tell her? He could never look her in the eye again. Courageous indeed!

He lay quietly. Yet deep down inside, where no man could see the secret torment of his conscience, he shook like an oak leaf in a windstorm. Aletta, too, lay quietly, her head against his. Suddenly, he felt something trickling across his face. Her tears!

It was too much! He turned and reached for her. His head still throbbing, he cried out, "God help us, my love. You've no idea what a great coward you've married. I killed a man!"

Aletta continued to sob in his arms. "*Nay!*" she cried out. "On the battlefield?"

"Almost. A Spanish soldier swam across the river in pursuit of . . . Hendrick. I shoved him back into the river and the waters swept him away." He felt his strength ebbing with his voice.

"Oh, Pieter-Lucas, my Pieter-Lucas, my love!" She pressed her head into his chest. "Once more you saved the life of Hendrick van den Garde!"

"But I killed a man! Your vader will come and take you away."

"*Nay, nay!* The water took his life. Had you not stopped him, he would have killed you and Hendrick, and others too."

"But I killed him! No Child of God will ever give me the baptism now. They'll take you away. What can I do?"

Aletta reached up and smoothed back the tangled mess of curls around his forehead. Then she covered his head and face with her tears and her kisses. At last she looked into his eyes and said, "Tell God and ask Him to forgive."

"But—" he began to protest.

She pressed her finger against his lips and went on. "Then lay down your head and sleep. We still have a *heatte* to cure. I can give you potions by the barrel, but if you do not accept forgiveness for your soul and give sleep to your body, you'll never be free from the ague again."

How could she understand? She did not know that Hans had warned him not to get so close to the war, and he had been so sure of himself. *Never! A messenger and nothing more.* He had said it with such confidence in his own ability to remain detached from the soldier's mission. What kind of God—or church—would forgive such arrogance?

Aletta was pulling herself away from him, and he lacked the strength to hold her—or the will. Blurred though she may appear through the *heatte* that seared his eyes, he had to feast them on this remarkable woman who was his vrouw—the most beautiful picture of courage on earth. When it was that he slipped from looking and into his dreams where she continued to hover over him, he did not know.

9th day of Harvest Month (August), 1568

For several days Pieter-Lucas lay abed, battling with the ague. Some days he slipped in and out of awareness so many times that Aletta began to fear he might not come back to stay. Always he sipped the herbal potions she gave him, sometimes he nibbled at the food. Walking came hard at first, and even when the dizziness had passed, his legs still wobbled. He grew thin, a ghost of the Pieter-Lucas she had always known.

Worse yet, he rarely smiled. He seemed to live under a low heavy cloud that neither spent itself in showers, nor was it wafted away on a stiff breeze. She begged him to tell her news of Emden, but he would only say that Hans' family were back in their house and all were well. When she asked about Opa's paintbrushes, the thunder and lightning her questions aroused were so violent she feared she would never see him smile again.

Eventually, he began to grow stronger in body, until one sun-filled morning, she succeeded in coaxing him into the field beyond the refugees' encampment.

"What's that I see?" he asked, pointing westward. "Tents and banners! Surely not a battlefield in Duisburg?"

"Tents and banners they are," she said, "but not a battlefield. Troops are assembling in preparation for Willem's campaign down in Brabant."

"When?"

She heard the tightness in his voice, felt it in the arm she held. "Who knows? The troops have only begun arriving here the past few days."

"Is Willem here?"

"Not that I know of."

"Ludwig?"

"*Nay!*"

"Then I must soon go to Dillenburg. They will have work for me."

Aletta's heart fluttered and she grabbed a tighter hold on his arm. "Your healer lady says you're not robustious yet, and until then you go nowhere."

"War waits not for robustious men." He sighed, then fell silent.

What could she say to bring her cheerful Pieter-Lucas back? One subject had never failed to bring a smile, for it was dearest to his heart. She snuggled up to him and gazed at his face with all the adoration of her heart. "Pieter-Lucas, my love," she said, "when Willem wins this next battle and no longer needs you for a messenger, will we be free to take our newborn son and go to Leyden?"

She felt his whole body tighten and watched him stare at the path beneath his feet. Then astounded, she heard a torrent of bitter words come pouring up from somewhere deep inside her husband. "Leyden was a lovely dream," he began, "for two children who did not know how evil the world can be. Aletta, the anointing in the Great Church has been shattered! We must put Leyden forever behind us!"

Aletta gasped and soon realized she'd released an avalanche.

"*Abrams en Zonen* is no more, and neither are Opa's paintpots and brushes and canvases. I searched the old empty building from top to bottom, and all it yielded was the mouse-eaten stub of one of the sacred brushes, five forlorn bristles wrapped in dust balls, and a multitude of suffocating memories."

"Oh, Pieter-Lucas!" Aletta cried, then gave her own grief a moment's silence. At last she ventured, "Paintbrushes, pots, and canvases—Opa's treasures, all. But you will replace them, and you will paint. For nothing can take the paint out of your blood! Nothing!"

Pieter-Lucas grabbed and held her in both arms. "Oh, Aletta, my Aletta, if only your beautiful words could be true."

"They are, my love, they are!" How could she make him see it?

She let him hold her tight while neither of them spoke for a long while. Then she felt his head nuzzling hers and heard him murmuring, "Can't you see what's been happening? Fate, or God, or whatever it may be, is telling me something neither of us wants to hear. First Yaap died and I had to take his place. I had no choice. And now that I've gone back for my paints, they're gone. Besides, who knows how long this war goes on or where it takes us or. . . ?"

"I do see, Pieter-Lucas, but—" she began.

"*Nay*, Aletta," he interrupted, "no matter how fine and beautiful your dreams and words, without Opa's paints and brushes, I shall never again be allowed to paint."

Lifting her face to look into his and pounding with little fists on his chest, she said, "Pieter-Lucas, Opa never intended you to live and paint in his shadow. He anointed you to soar above him and become the Master Painter of some glorious city. One day you will, believe me, you will! And you'll not need Opa's brushes to do it!"

He lifted her chin with his finger, and for the first time in days, she saw a glimmer of light in those wonderful blue eyes.

He shook his head and stared at her with all the awe of the old Pieter-Lucas. "Was ever a man gifted with so wise and gentle a vrouw?"

For one long and heady moment, the heaviness seemed to lift, the war had slipped over the horizon. Once more she felt as if they were children playing out their dreams as they used to do so long ago in the Valkenberg park across the moat from the old *kasteel* in Breda. If only this could go on forever!

She knew it was over when Pieter-Lucas frowned and said, "We have visitors."

Pulling back, she looked around and saw two men walking directly toward them.

"*Hei* there!" one called out.

"Pieter-Lucas van den Garde?" called the other. It sounded like Hans!

Aletta gasped and clapped a hand over her mouth. One of the two men broke into a huge smile, opened his arms wide, and shouted, "Aletta, my Aletta!"

"Vader! Hans! What are you doing here?" She rushed into her vader's arms.

"They told us we would find you here!" He was hugging her so hard she thought he would squeeze the breath out of her.

Then he took her by the shoulders and pushed her out to an arm's length. "How wonderful you look!"

"Moeder and Robbin are well?" Aletta had to know.

"Very well, if a bit homesick and missing you greatly."

"What brought you back across the water?" Pieter-Lucas asked, his words a bit wooden.

Vader Dirck cleared his throat. "It was as great a surprise to me as it could ever be to you," he said. "The fellowship of the Children of God where we have made our home consists entirely of Lowlanders. We had received reports through our merchants who travel this way about Willem's campaigns against Alva, and someone brought us a copy of Prince Willem's pamphlet."

"*The Justification?*" Pieter-Lucas asked.

Vader nodded, smiling. "I recognized it at once. We all read it."

"Even Johannes?"

"Even Johannes. As we read, we began to pray that Willem might succeed in chasing the Spaniards from our vaderland so we could go home again. Then it occurred to us that there must be something more we could do."

Aletta felt Pieter-Lucas tighten his grip on her arm. "The Children of God praying for the success of a cause so evil as war?" he asked.

"We all concurred that war is evil. But we have decided that the cause for which the Lowlanders are forced by Alva to fight is allowed, though not ordained, by heaven."

"Exactly what Juliana von Stolberg tells me," Aletta said, her mind spinning in circles. "But I never thought I'd hear you say it." Crossing the water must make one think differently.

"To most of us this is a new idea," Vader went on. "We have spent many hours talking, reading the Book, praying over it. As we did, we recognized that not one among us has a whole family gathered in one place. Whatever else may be true, we cannot believe it is God's design that some powerful men of Papist persuasion should wrench our families apart."

"So what did you decide to do that would send you to us?" Aletta asked.

"We collected an offering of money to help Willem's cause."

"Gold from the Children of God for the revolt?" Pieter-Lucas stared, openmouthed.

"It's not a great deal. In Engeland, we will always be strangers and poor laborers. Yet our people gave most generously."

Aletta noted that Hans was shifting from one foot to the other, saying nothing. "And how is your flock in Emden, Hans?" she asked him.

He looked first at Aletta, then at Pieter-Lucas and spoke guardedly, his small mouth causing his great long beard to bob in the breeze. "My people and I, too, have prayed and searched the Scriptures, especially since Jemmingen. We have also listened to Dirck and to my moeder— two people in whom resides a spirit of great wisdom. As the result, we, too, collected an offering, and I brought it along to present to Prince Willem."

Pieter-Lucas frowned at the weaver-preacher. "But when I visited you—"

"I was in error," Hans interrupted.

Pieter-Lucas cast him a puzzled look, then shook his head. "You erred not when you said a battlefield is filled with pitfalls."

"You saw that up close at Jemmingen?" Hans asked.

Pieter-Lucas grabbed Aletta's hand. He hesitated for a time, then looking off toward Willem's encampment, he said in a detached sort of voice, "There's no torture like standing across the river and watching the massive slaughter of the army you run messages for, rescuing the few that swim to safety, and hearing their ugly stories and wishing for herbs to cure their gaping wounds."

Aletta sensed the convulsion of his innards and drew closer to him as they walked. *Be still, still, still,* her heart cried out. *Say no more, think no more about it.*

"This terrible strife must end soon," Dirck Engelshofen said.

"Perhaps after the next campaign," Hans offered. "But for the moment," he addressed his companion, "I think you brought a gift for Pieter-Lucas, did you not?"

"How could I forget it so long?"

Dirck Engelshofen rummaged through his knapsack and handed Pieter-Lucas a lumpy fabric-wrapped package.

"For me?" Pieter-Lucas asked.

"For no one else," Vader said, anticipation sparkling in his eyes. Aletta watched Pieter-Lucas untie the strings that held the wrap, then unwind the layers of rough brown serge. When he'd pulled back the final layer, he started, opened his eyes wide, and gasped, "My paintbrushes!"

"And pots of colors," Aletta cried.

"Where did you find these?" Pieter-Lucas stammered.

"I rescued them the night we prepared for flight," Dirck said. "Not until I'd reached Engeland did I realize I had brought them along. It grieved me to know you were separated from them for so long. But I would not risk sending them back with anyone else. I must carry them myself."

Slowly Pieter-Lucas picked up one brush and fit it into his hand. "I never hoped to see these treasures again."

Aletta caught a disturbing tone in his voice, detected a dark shadow in his eye. Like a cloud, it spread over his face, and he mumbled, "*Ach, nay!* How can I use these sacred brushes again?"

What was he saying? "The same as you ever did," Aletta said.

"But that was before . . ." He stared at the brushes.

"Before what?" Dirck asked.

"Before I killed the Spaniard!"

Aletta looked from Vader to Hans. Both men wore expressions of dumb shock. She looked back at Pieter-Lucas and tugged at his arm. "You only shoved him into the water, Pieter-Lucas," she pleaded, "to save the life of another. You did not kill him. The water took him."

Pieter-Lucas shook his head and looked straight at Dirck Engelshofen. "I had promised you as a condition for the hand of your daughter in marriage never to bear the sword. I failed to keep the trust you placed in me."

Dirck Engelshofen moved to Pieter-Lucas' side and laid a hand on his shoulder. "You killed him with a sword?"

"*Nay!*"

"In battle?"

"I was across the river from the battlefield, trying to rescue survivors."

"And you did not intend to do it?"

"*Nay!*" Pieter-Lucas ran his fingers in circles around his head, tousling the curls in every direction. "But if I had not shoved him into the water, he would still live. I fear God can never forgive me."

"If you honestly believe that," Dirck said, "then you do not worship the same God we do."

"But Hans had warned me, and I was not careful to stay out of the way of temptation. I really didn't think I could do such a thing. It happened so suddenly. He came at us, and I saw no other way. I honestly thought I would only force him back across the river."

"There is a verse in the Book for you," Hans said. "Among the proverbs of Solomon lies this word of great wisdom and comfort. 'Whoever covers up his transgression shall not prosper.' That includes those transgressions we have no intention of committing. 'But whoever confesses and forsakes it, he finds compassion.' You have only to confess and ask forgiveness, and God forgets it forever, just as if it had never happened."

They all stood silent for a long breath-holding moment. Aletta gripped her husband's arm as tightly as if her life depended on it. Pieter-Lucas turned the paintbrush over and over in his hand. Hans bowed his head and closed his eyes, and Vader Dirck continued to look at Pieter-Lucas with compassion.

Finally Pieter-Lucas looked up at the two visitors and asked, "Will the Children of God be as generous with their compassion as you say God is?"

Hans nodded slowly. "If they're not, they need to go back and read the Book!"

Aletta watched the man of her lifelong dreams hold the brush in his fingers and felt the intense struggle that was tearing at his heart. When she could endure the tension no longer, she folded her hand around his and held it close over the worn paint-spattered handle.

"God's anointing is no more dead than the flow of paint in your blood," she said, her whole body trembling. "Promise me you'll never lay it down, Pieter-Lucas."

She felt the struggle go out of him. He hugged her arm and nodded, a true Pieter-Lucas smile lighting up his whole face.

Lost in the soul-stirring power of the moment, she was startled at the sound of Dirck Engelshofen's voice. "I found these, too, in your painting corner."

He was reaching into his knapsack again and handing Pieter-Lucas two more familiar objects—an old wooden palette covered with multi-colored layers of paint and a long rolled canvas.

"Oh!" Pieter-Lucas exclaimed. "Bless you, bless you, bless you!" A smile lit up his whole face, and a pair of tears rolled down his cheeks. For a brief instant, he looked at the latest treasures with fond reverence, then laid the canvas gently in Aletta's hands. A bright sparkle danced in his eyes, and he said, "Later, my love, we shall unroll this, you and I. I've something precious to show you."

Nearly forgetting that they were not alone on the edge of the wind-swept field, Pieter-Lucas and Aletta held each other by the hand. They exchanged deep smiles of the kind that stir up the heart and draw a curtain against the rest of the world.

"*Ja*, later," Aletta whispered.

EPILOGUE

Duisburg

25th day of Dry Stick Month (February), 1569

*F*rom his seat atop Blesje, Pieter-Lucas lowered his head against an afternoon assault of sleet blowing toward him. Each breath sent a knife's thrust through his nostrils and down into his throat.

"Not much farther now, old boy," he said, prodding Blesje onward. "Here's hoping this is our last trip to Dillenburg for herbs before spring. We've had a cold winter."

Not only cold, but for a messenger of the Nassaus, disheartening!

Pieter-Lucas had spent the autumn months crisscrossing the countryside, running messages for a war that Alva refused to fight to any sort of finish. All through Oat Month (October) and halfway into Tallow Month (November), Alva lurked ever in Willem's shadow, provoking him from the sidelines until the prince ran out of money and his mercenary troops forsook him.

The campaign lost, the prince of Oranje took Pieter-Lucas with him on several fruitless trips around France and Germany. Beaten but always with an ember of optimism still smoldering in his heart, he went on selling or pawning what remained of his personal and family belongings and begging his friends to once more come to his aid. Nearly without exception, they sent him home as empty as when he'd come to their doorsteps.

Not only did the cause of the revolt appear to be all but dead, Willem's hopes of regaining his vrouw's allegiance also ended that awful winter. Following through on her mad threats, once Willem left for the Brabant campaign, Princess Anna had removed herself to Cologne to live what she insisted was the rightful pleasure-mad life of a princess. On one occasion, Willem sent Pieter-Lucas with a letter begging her to return. He'd found her, large with Willem's unborn child, carousing with her wild friends.

She read the letter, shredded it to pieces, tromped on it, and shouted her answer at Pieter-Lucas.

"I might bury him with my own hands, but return to his arms? Never!"

That night he'd returned to Aletta in the little corner of a farmhouse in Duisburg, trembling and more grateful than ever for his warm, wonderful vrouw. As hard as he'd fought the idea of wintering in Duisburg, it only took one visit to Anna to show him that anywhere on earth was acceptable, since he had a vrouw like Aletta.

The stream of refugees continued to grow, even in the midst of the coldest weather. People were fleeing now, not just for reasons of religion. The Duke of Alva's many military battles had brought Spain into deep debt. So he imposed exorbitant taxes on the Lowlanders to pay for the war that had been waged to take away their freedoms. The time had come for Protestants and Catholics alike to seek refuge from the unreasonable demands of a foreign sovereign.

The services of Aletta and a growing sisterhood of healer ladies were constantly in demand. From the rising of each new day's sun to the setting of the same, they administered herbs, distributed food, and delivered babies. Pieter-Lucas watched her unceasing smile. And as her belly swelled, he saw her steps drag a trifle more slowly at the end of each succeeding day.

At night when she crawled into bed beside him, his merciful vrouw would rub her tummy and say in a smooth and delighted voice, "Our little Lucas grows, 'Vader.' "

"What makes you so sure it's not Kaatje?" he would question.

She'd shrug and toss a "You will see" at him.

Then they'd laugh and embrace, and she'd add, "Whoever it is, 'tis a great enough miracle to fill each day with golden sunshine!"

She would fall asleep instantly, leaving Pieter-Lucas to lie awake wondering. Would she be all right? Would the baby live? Babies were born every day, and Duisburg had a real midwife now. It was the only way he would ever consent to keep her here instead of taking her back to Dillenburg. Besides, he had never seen her more robustious or happy! Yet in the middle of the night he could not forget that his own moeder had died in the childbirth bed.

But that was Moeder Kaatje, and she was old and had lost many other babies, he told himself. *Aletta is young!*

Still, the deep unsettledness never seemed to go away until daylight. Then all day he would watch with the fascination of an awestruck child the increasing roundness of her beautiful body, the blush of her cheeks, and the smile of contentment on her face. He felt gratitude well up inside—and pride. He shook his head and asked, "This is my vrouw?"

"In only a few more days I am going to be a vader," he said to Blesje as they passed the first house on the edge of the village. "Can you believe it?"

Pieter-Lucas' heart was racing now in spite of the sleet and the wind. Each clop of the horse's hooves brought him closer to his love on this cold-to-the-bone afternoon.

He entered the little house on the edge of a farm, halfway expecting to find it empty. Aletta would probably be out attending to her patients unless the midwife had decided it was her time to stay abed and await the birth. But neither of these happened. Instead, Mieke greeted him at the door—with fingers pressed against her lips. For once she was quiet and seemed intent on keeping him that way as well.

He winced, feeling everything tighten inside him. "What are you doing here? Is my Aletta ill?" he whispered.

Mieke shook her head and motioned him toward the bed cupboard. Here he drew back the curtain and caught his breath. Propped up ever so slightly by pillows, Aletta lay in her place, a wide smile lighting up her face. At her breast she nursed the tiniest human being Pieter-Lucas had ever seen.

"*Ah!*" he gasped.

He stared at his vrouw and she at him. She looked weary but happy.

"Are you all right?" he asked.

She nodded and reached up a hand to his outstretched one. A newly breathing little life bound them together in awed silence. Pieter-Lucas climbed into the bed and kissed Aletta. Then looking down at the child, he whispered softly, "Welcome, Little One."

"It's Lucas!" Aletta whispered back.

"Are you sure?"

Aletta laughed.

"So wrinkled, so small, and yet so perfect. Can it be my son?" Pride and uncertainty fought for possession of him.

The little mouth no longer nursed but puckered into rosebud-shaped sucking motions. Pieter-Lucas stared at the child—his child—in wonder, fearing to touch the matted fuzziness on his round head. He'd never touched a baby before, never been a vader before. . . .

Feeling his voice tremble, he said, "But he came so soon!"

Aletta smiled. "This morning."

"And you, are you well?" Her obvious weakness frightened him. What if she never grew strong again?

She nodded again.

"Who helped you?"

"Mieke!"

Pieter-Lucas gulped. "But . . . how?" he stammered.

Aletta laid a hand on his. Her eyelids fluttered open and closed as she spoke. "She followed my instructions, the ones from Tante Lysbet's herbal. I could have asked for no better help."

Her eyelids closed and she drifted into sleep. Instantly, Mieke was at the bedside, barging past Pieter-Lucas with the officious air of a midwife in charge. He knew well his expected place as vader of a newborn. He must submit to the whims of the women, by whom all matters related to the birthing process were jealously guarded.

But Mieke? She was no midwife!

He raised a hand as if to stop her, but she rebuked him with a sharp glance that he felt powerless to resist. Then picking up the baby and wrapping him tightly in his infant cloths, she moved toward the cradle stationed between the bed and the hearth, where a kettle of water was bubbling and spitting away.

With a nod of her head, she motioned Pieter-Lucas to follow. When she reached the cradle, she looked down at the baby in her arms and shifted uneasily from foot to foot. Finally she looked up at Pieter-Lucas and said in a tone softer than he thought she was capable of, "There's somethin' what I got to tell ye."

His heart stopped beating! Everything had gone too smoothly, and as he feared, it would all end quickly. "The baby . . . my vrouw . . . they will be all right, won't they? Tell me not that they're going to die, or . . ."

Mieke was shaking her head rapidly. "*Nay!* Nothin's amiss with either of 'em."

"What, then?" All the suspicions he'd ever felt about this mysterious street woman seemed rolled into a ball at the pit of his stomach. He had to stifle an urge to grab his son, to protect him from this thief.

"Ye needs to know from th' beginnin' that I doesn't do this here sorta thing right goodly. Truth tellin' is, I'se never in my life done said nothin' th' likes o' what I gots to say now." She stopped and took a deep breath. "B'lieve me, th' old Mieke what ye knowed in Breda, she never would've told ye this, but jus' know, this is th' new Mieke a-speakin' to ye."

New Mieke indeed! What sort of tricks was she hiding behind that name this time? The longer she held the baby, the more uneasy Pieter-Lucas grew.

"Put the baby in his cradle," he ordered, his palms sticky. "Then you can talk, if you must."

She shook her head and edged away. "*Nay!* But I gots to hold him till

I finishes. An' here I goes, jus' goin' to tell it like it is. Long years 'go, back in Breda, when yer opa, the painter, was still a-livin,' I did him wrong."

Pieter-Lucas gasped and pointed a finger at her. "You! You were the one. . . ."

"Which one?" she shot back.

"The one that robbed Opa and left him lamed and bleeding in the alley! I always thought it was you." Heat was rising to his forehead, his fists were forming.

"Ye didn't see me do a thin'," she said.

"I didn't have to see you, Mieke. Who else in Breda would have done it? We all knew you as the thief that roamed our streets and helped yourself to everybody's belongings."

Mieke cleared her throat, and the baby started in her arms, then settled once more, his mouth and nose making soft puffing sounds.

"All ye say is true, but I swear to God in the heaven, I didn't touch yer opa to do him harm," Mieke said.

"Who did it, then?"

" 'Twas one o' my friends what sticked him with a sword. I was th' one what laid wait fer th' ol' man an' gived my friend the signal. He was s'pose to knock him down so I could rush in and steal his bag o' gold pieces."

"Gold pieces?" Pieter-Lucas gasped. "Opa never carried but one gold piece in his bag."

"So my friend discovered once he had it in his hand. Sended him into such a fit o' anger that he pulled the sword out o' yer opa's sheath an' sticked him with it b'fore he done runned away. I never seed him again." She stopped and smoothed the hair back from the baby's forehead.

Pieter-Lucas watched her for a long moment. Almost he had to believe her words were true. Almost! At last he posed the one more question that might cause her to reverse her story, if indeed it was false. "Mieke, why did you hunt me down to let me know Opa had been hurt and tell me where to find him?"

The mysterious little woman looked him straight in the eye and without a shifting or batting motion said, "No matter what ye an' th' rest o' Breda thinks about me, I wasn't ever all evil. Ever' time what I done brung hurt to a body, there was always a deep-down sort o' pity in my innards, what afflicted me somethin' fearful."

Was that why he couldn't bring himself to try to stop this thief from holding his baby boy? It should have been so easy just to snatch the baby from her arms.

"Fer a lot o' days I been a-thinkin' about what I'se done to yer opa an' a-knowin' that I has to make it right. Somewhere in the Book, Vrouw

Adriana's read it to me time an' again, somethin' about restorin' what we stealed. But I hasn't got no gold to pay ye back, an' I cannot go back an' do somethin' fer your opa. I'se been a-askin' Betteke's Shepherd, th' one she called Vader, to show me how to do what's right by ye."

Pieter-Lucas stood stunned, still unable to touch either Mieke or the baby. Thieves still trying to trick you didn't confess that kind of crimes and stand so still before you while looking for ways to make them right.

Finally she held the baby up to him. "Here, this is all I got to give ye."

"But he's not yours to give," Pieter-Lucas protested.

"This mornin' when yer vrouw was a-birthin' th' child, I begged her to let me be th' midwife fer her, but mostly fer ye! It was all I could do. Doesn't ye understand?"

"I . . . I don't know. . . ." He was probing his mind for something to make it make sense. One thing came suddenly clear. He had to accept his baby as she offered him.

He reached out both arms and let Mieke lay the child there. "I . . . I've never held a tiny baby like this before," he muttered. The baby sneezed and opened his eyes a crack. Pieter-Lucas' heart was fluttering so hard he hardly knew what to do.

Mieke was talking again. "I be a-goin' now, but first, I'se got to ask o' ye th' one thing most awful difficult in all th' world." She stopped and stared down at her shifting feet, then wiped her hands on her frayed skirt. Finally she looked up into Pieter-Lucas' eyes and asked, "Can ye forgive me? Please!"

Why did the simple pleading tone of the sharp little voice make him so uncomfortable?

"Forgive you?" he asked, not sure what he was saying. "Why, I . . ."

"I'se been a-knowin' that ye cannot seem to b'lieve that what yer eyes be seein' is a new Mieke. An' ye keeps on a-mistrustin' ever'thin' I says. But that doesn't change anythin'. Betteke's Vader done forgived me. An' if'n ye say *Nay*, that ugly word'll jus' stick in my heart worser than any sword. I know, b'cause ye done sticked me with yer words many, many times b'fore, till I'se bleedin' all over."

"What words?" he demanded.

"Ever' time ye insists on callin' me a thief or ye accuses me o' some sorta misdeed, I feels th' sword again. It's in your eyes as well. God have mercy on ye, is all I kin say. Now, tell me you're a-goin' to change all that an' forgive me now b'cause ye finally b'lieves this is a new Mieke!"

His words were like swords? Stunned, he moistened his lips and, without looking directly at her, said, "I guess if God's forgiven you, that doesn't leave much place for me to say *Nay*, does it?"

"Then ye're forgivin' me? Can it be?"

Pieter-Lucas coaxed his eyes to look at her. The light in her upturned face was clear and pure. A smile played at the crinkly corners of her mouth. The ugly street thief was gone. The mouth and chin and nose were no longer sharp, gnomelike. Instead, he saw a warm soft glow about her. The new Mieke. Could it be? As if in a dream, he heard his own lips stammering, "Ja, Mieke, I'll . . . I'll forgive you."

A smile engulfed the girl's face. She clasped her hands and raised them heavenward. "Thanks be to ye, Pieter-Lucas, son o' Hendrick! An' thanks be to Betteke's Vader in the Heaven! Ye'll never know what a big ol' lump of stones ye jus' now lifted off my back."

Mieke started to scamper from the room, but Pieter-Lucas stopped her. "Wait! I . . . I need to know that you'll forgive me too," he said, suddenly realizing that with this wild woman he'd been acting just like a son of Hendrick.

She cocked her head to one side. Her eyes snapped. "Ye means ye're ready to break that nasty sword o' words into a hundred li'l pieces an' bury it forever an ever an' never call me a thief again?"

Pieter-Lucas swallowed hard, then nodded. "Never again! I do believe in the new Mieke."

She clasped her hands together, twirled around three times, then said slowly, "I'se never b'fore forgived anybody b'cause I'se never b'fore been asked to. Not sure how to do it, so I'll jus' say, ye's forgived!" An enormous smile set her leathery face aglowing.

Then, in an eyeblink, she barged off, leaving Pieter-Lucas alone with a sleeping vrouw, a newborn infant, and a host of perplexing thoughts swirling dizzily through his head. A faint whimper escaped from the baby's lips, startling the dazed new vader. He looked down into the miniature face, watched the eyelids flutter, and began to talk to his child.

"Son, it's a big mysterious world you just got birthed into. Some things you can't expect ever to make sense of. One of those is women, especially the likes of Mieke. Wild, strong-mouthed, always outsmarting everybody, I never guessed anything I said or thought ever mattered one clog to her. Now, here she comes telling me my words stuck her like a sword. And once she tells me that she robbed my opa, her very face changes before my eyes—from thief to saint—what is a man to think?"

He paused and let the stillness hold his thoughts momentarily from moving forward. Then, as if he'd never stopped, he went on. "Speaking of swords, that's one more big mystery. There was a time, son, when I thought I had it all figured out. Like that day in Hans' hidden church in Emden. I can still see the circle of elders sitting there staring at me, waiting for my answer to the question, 'When God gives you a son, what will you teach him about nonresistance?'

"At the moment the answer seemed so simple. 'My son will never carry a sword—only a paintbrush.'

"But that was before Yaap's death and Heiligerlee and Egmont's execution and Jemmingen. . . . I didn't mean to, but I killed a man, son, and ever since, I've struggled to free my conscience. I've come close a time or two, but the heavy guilt never quite went away."

With heart beating a rapid cadence in his breast, he cradled the child in one arm. He reached out a trembling finger and touched one pink little hand that protruded from the swaddling blanket. He smoothed its creamy softness with a gentle caress, then slipped his pointer finger between the child's curled thumb and fingers. Instantly the tiny hand gripped it— warm, firm, trusting. . . . Pieter-Lucas' eyes felt moist.

"Then today that heaviness all went away. As soon as I told Mieke she was forgiven, I knew I, too, was free from the last hint of guilt."

He stopped and stared at the amazing little creature in his arms, saying nothing for a long while before he went on. "I know you don't understand anything I'm saying, but I simply have to tell you all. There is one thing more that if you can truly believe it might keep you from the trouble I've had to live with. I will tell you now, and I'll repeat it every day of your life until you know it by heart and feel it all the way into the center of your bones."

He paused and watched the angelic face and the rhythmic rise and fall of the tiny breathing chest. "It's this way, son. You come from a long line of men with paint in our blood. It's an honor, can you hear me? A calling for a truly courageous man! Let no one—nay, no one—ever, ever, ever steal the paintbrush from these fingers. And mostly, never let them replace it with a sword. These hands," he said, giving the entwined fingers a gentle squeeze, "they're meant for healing, not for killing. And that's no act of cowardice!"

For a long while he stared at the sleeping boy, then lifted him to his lips and kissed both soft pearly pink cheeks. Gently, careful lest he drop him, he lay the baby in his cradle, covered him with the blanket, and stood still staring. After a long pensive moment, he stepped lightly across the floor to the bed where his vrouw rested. Sitting by her side, he spoke softly. "Aletta, my love."

She opened her eyes and smiled.

Pieter-Lucas laid a hand on her arm and said, "What a wonderful child you gave to me!"

She shook her head. "He is a gift from God!"

"And is his moeder, so wise and kindly wonderful, also a gift from God?"

She chuckled. "No more so than his vader, so strong and full of love."

"And forgiven," he added.

When he leaned over and kissed her lips, his nose nestled into a tear-moistened cheek.

ACKNOWLEDGMENTS

Acknowledging the multitude of family, friends, and professionals who have inspired, helped, and coached this series of books into existence is a little like gathering up the blocks my grandson and I have spilled out onto the carpet for an hour of shared pleasure. One or two are bound to get away and show up later when we're not looking for them, wedged under the rockers of Grandpa's chair.

The list at the end of *The Dove and the Rose* filled two pages, and I have no intention of repeating it. But at least one important block got away. Renowned historian of the Belgian Reformation, Dr. A.L.E. Verheyden, welcomed my husband, Walt, and me into his cozy row house on the outskirts of Brussels. We followed him up his narrow carpeted stairwell to a room filled with old books, the smell of pipe tobacco, and a tray of "koffie" and cookies. We will never forget the tales he told nor that huge book in which he had listed all the names of the Anabaptist martyrs executed under the command of the Duke of Alva during his seven-year governorship of the Netherlands—over 12,200 of them. Dr. Verheyden was a pioneer in Anabaptist research. I still thrill to the memory of his going through his bookshelves, pulling out thin yellowed pamphlets and handing them to me with the incredible explanation, "Here, take this. I have another copy." Mostly martyr studies, they date as far back as 1945 and still bear the aroma of that incredible office.

Special recognition is in order, as well, to

The members of The Parts of Speech critique group for their expertise, encouragement, and prayers over the long haul.

Willeke Huijsing for reading the entire manuscript (mostly in a lawn chair in my backyard) and pointing out all the Dutch flaws.

Martha Doolittle, my daughter, dramaturge, script critic, and actress, who gave the entire manuscript its first detailed, whole-book critique.

Husband, Walt, for hanging in there through one more book and listening to it from beginning to end while on vacation, then for helping me handle a couple of getaways specifically designed to finish the job.

Dr. Arthur Brown, retired gynecologist, for the loan of the fascinating old book, *The London Practice of Midwifery*, from his library; and Karen Cushman for her delightful little book, *The Midwife's Apprentice*.

Enough pleased readers of book one, *The Dove and the Rose*, to fill a file folder to the bursting point with letters.

Les Stobbe, faithful agent; and Sharon Asmus, delightful editor, unflagging in encouragement and insistent on quality.

The continuing group of supportive praying friends who keep asking, "How is Pieter-Lucas doing?"

God himself, Vader in the Heaven, who continues to drop just the right resource or word of inspiration or guidance into my hands and heart at the right time, and who gives me enough energy of mind and body and vision of spirit to keep going.